MOLOTOV OBSESSION

THE COMPLETE DUET

ANNA ZAIRES

♠ MOZAIKA PUBLICATIONS ♠

This is a work of fiction. Names, characters, places, and incidents are either the product of the author's imagination or are used fictitiously, and any resemblance to actual persons, living or dead, business establishments, events, or locales is purely coincidental.

Published by Mozaika Publications, an imprint of Mozaika LLC.
www.mozaikallc.com

Cover by Coverluv Book Designs
www.coverluv.com

e-ISBN: 978-1-63142-762-6
ISBN: 978-1-63142-763-3

DEVIL'S LAIR

BOOK 1

1

CHLOE

A CAR BACKFIRES AND THE STOREFRONT WINDOW TO MY left explodes, blasting shards of glass in a wide radius.

I freeze, so stunned I barely feel the glass biting into my bare arm. Then the screams reach me.

"Shots fired! Call 911," someone on the street is yelling, and adrenaline floods my veins as my brain makes the connection between the sound and the glass explosion.

Someone is shooting.

At me.

They found me.

My feet react before the rest of me, propelling me into a jump just as another sharp *pop!* reaches my ears, and the register inside the store explodes into splinters.

The same register I was blocking with my body a second ago.

I taste terror. It's coppery, like blood. Maybe it *is* blood. Maybe I was shot, and I'm dying. But no, I'm running. My heartbeat is roaring in my ears, my lungs pumping for all they're worth as I sprint down the block. I can feel the burn in my legs, so I'm alive.

For now.

Because they found me. Again.

I make a sharp right, sprinting down a narrow side street, and over my shoulder, I catch a glimpse of two men half a block behind me, running after me at full speed.

My lungs are already screaming for air, my legs threatening to give out, but I put on a desperate burst of speed and dash into an alley before they round the corner. A five-foot-tall chain-link fence cuts the alley in half, but I climb up and over it in seconds, adrenaline lending me an athlete's agility and strength.

The back of the alley connects to another street, and a sob of relief bursts from my throat as I realize it's the one where I parked my car before the interview.

Run, Chloe. You can do it.

Desperately sucking in air, I sprint down the street, scanning the curb for a beat-up Toyota Corolla.

Where is it?

Where did I leave the damn car?

Was it behind the blue pickup truck or the white one?

Please let it be there. Please let it be there.

Finally, I spot it, half-hidden behind a white van. Fumbling in my pocket, I extract the keys, and with violently shaking hands, I press the button to unlock the car.

I'm already inside and jamming the key into the ignition when I see my pursuers emerging from the alley a block behind me, each with a gun in his hand.

I'm still shaking five hours later as I pull into a gas station, the first one I've seen on this winding mountain road.

That had been close, much too close.

They're getting bolder, more desperate.

They shot at me on the fucking street.

My legs feel like rubber as I step out of the car, clutching my empty water bottle. I need a bathroom, water, food, and gas, in that order—and ideally a new vehicle, as they might've gotten my Toyota's license plate. That is, assuming they didn't already have it.

I have no idea how they found me in Boise, Idaho, but it might've been through my car.

The problem is, what little I know about evading criminals hellbent on murder comes from books and movies, and I have no idea what my pursuers actually *can* track. Just to be safe, though, I'm not using any of my credit cards, and I ditched my phone the very first day.

Another problem is I have exactly thirty-two dollars and twenty-four cents in my wallet. The waitressing position I interviewed for this morning in Boise would've been a lifesaver, as the café owner was open to paying me cash under the table, but they found me before I could do a single shift.

A few inches to the right, and the bullet would've gone through my head instead of that storefront window.

Blood pooling on the kitchen floor... Pink robe on white tile... Glazed, unseeing stare...

My heart rate spikes and my shaking intensifies, my knees threatening to buckle underneath me. Leaning on the hood of my car, I drag in a shuddering breath, trying to get the mad drumming of my pulse to slow as I shove the memories deep down, where they can't squeeze my throat in a vise.

I can't think about what happened. If I do, I'll fall apart and they'll win.

They might win anyway because I have no money and no clue what I'm doing.

One thing at a time, Chloe. One foot in front of the other.

Mom's voice comes to me, calm and steady, and I force myself to straighten away from the car. So what if my situation has gone from desperate to critical?

I'm still alive, and I intend to stay that way.

I extracted all the glass shards from my arm a couple of hours ago, but the T-shirt I wrapped around it to stop the bleeding looks strange, so I grab my hoodie from the trunk and put the hood up to hide my face from any security cameras that might be inside the gas station. I don't know if the people after me would be able to get access to that footage, but it's better not to risk it.

Again, assuming they're not already tracking my car.

Focus, Chloe. One step at a time.

Taking a steadying breath, I walk into the small convenience store attached to the gas station and, with a small wave at the elderly woman behind the register, go directly to the bathroom in the back. Once my most pressing needs are taken care of, I wash my hands and face, fill up my water bottle from the faucet, and pull out my wallet to count the bills, just in case.

Nope, I didn't miscalculate or miss a stray twenty. Thirty-two dollars and twenty-four cents is all the cash I have left.

The face in the bathroom mirror is that of a stranger, all strained and hollow-cheeked, with dark circles under overly large brown eyes. I've neither eaten nor slept normally since I've been on the run, and it shows. I look older than my twenty-three years, the past month having aged me by a decade.

Suppressing the useless bout of self-pity, I focus on the practical. Step one: decide how to allocate the funds I do have.

The biggest priority is gas for the car. It's got less than a quarter tank, and there's no telling when I'll find another gas station in this area. Filling up all the way will set me back at least thirty dollars, leaving me only a couple of dollars for food to quench the gnawing emptiness in my stomach.

More importantly, the next time I run out of gas, I'm screwed.

Exiting the bathroom, I head to the register and tell the elderly cashier to give me twenty bucks worth of gas. I also grab a hot dog and a banana, and devour the hot dog while she slowly counts out the change. The banana I stash in my hoodie's front pocket for tomorrow's breakfast.

"Here you go, dearie," the cashier says in a croaky voice, handing me the change along with a receipt. With a warm smile, she adds, "You have a nice day now, hear?"

To my shock, my throat constricts, and tears prickle at the back of my eyes, the simple kindness undoing me completely. "Thank you. You too," I say in a choked voice, and stuffing the change into my wallet, I hurry toward the exit before I can alarm the woman by bursting into tears.

I'm almost out the door when a local newspaper catches my eye. It's in a bin labeled "FREE," so I grab it before continuing on to my car.

While the tank is filling up, I get my unruly emotions under control and unfold the newspaper, going straight for the classified section in the back. It's a long shot, but maybe someone around here is hiring for some kind of gig, like washing windows or trimming hedges.

Even fifty bucks could up my chances of survival.

At first, I don't see anything along the lines of what I'm looking for, and I'm about to fold the paper in disappointment when a listing at the bottom of the page catches my attention:

Live-in tutor wanted for four-year-old. Must be well-educated, good with children, and willing to relocate to a remote mountain estate. $3K/week cash. To apply, email resume to tutorcandidates459@gmail.com.

Three grand a week in cash? What the fuck?

Unable to believe my eyes, I reread the ad.

Nope, all the words are still the same, which is insane. Three grand a week for a tutor? In cash?

It's a hoax, it's got to be.

Heart pounding, I finish filling up the tank and get into the car. My mind is racing. I'm the perfect candidate for this position. Not only have I just graduated with an Education Studies major, but I've babysat and tutored kids all through high school and college. And relocation to a remote mountain estate? Sign me up! The more remote, the better.

It's as if the ad was crafted just for me.

Wait a minute. Could this be a trap?

No, that's truly paranoid thinking. Ever since this morning's close call, I've been driving aimlessly with the sole goal of putting as much distance between myself and Boise as possible while staying off the major roads and highways to avoid traffic cameras. My pursuers would've had to have a crystal ball to guess that I'd end up in this remote area, much less pick up this local paper. The only way this could be a trap is if they'd placed similar ads in all the newspapers across the country, as well as on all the major job sites, and even then, it feels like a stretch.

No, this is unlikely to be a trap set specifically for me, but it could be something equally sinister.

I hesitate for a moment, then get out of the car and go back into the store.

"Excuse me, ma'am," I say, approaching the elderly cashier. "Do you live in this area?"

"Why, yes, dearie." A smile brightens her wrinkled face. "Elkwood Creek born and bred."

"Great. In that case"—I unfold the newspaper and place it on the counter—"do you know anything about this?" I point at the ad.

She pulls out a pair of reading glasses and squints at the small text. "Huh. Three grand a week for a tutor—must be even richer than they say."

My pulse jumps in excitement. "You know who placed this ad?"

She looks up, rheumy eyes blinking behind the thick lenses of her glasses. "Well, I can't be certain, dearie, but rumor has it, some wealthy Russian bought out the old Jamieson property, way up in the mountains, and built a brand-new place there. Has been hiring local boys for some random jobs here and there, always paying cash. No one's said anything about a kid, though, so it might not be him—but I can't think of anyone else around these parts with that kind of money, much less anything close to an estate."

Holy shit. This may actually be for real. A rich foreigner—that would explain both the too-high salary and its cash nature. The man—or more likely the couple, since there's a child involved—may not know the going rate for tutors around here, or may not care. When you're wealthy enough, a few grand may be no more meaningful than a few pennies. For me, though, a single week's paycheck could mean the difference between life and death, and if I were to earn that kind of money for a month, I'd be able to buy another used car—and maybe even some fake papers, so I could get out of the country and disappear for good.

Best of all, if the estate is remote enough, it may take a while before my pursuers find me there—if they ever do. With a cash salary, there would be no paper trail, nothing to connect me to the Russian couple.

This job could be the answer to all my prayers… if I get it, that is.

"Is there a public library anywhere around here?" I ask, trying to temper my excitement. I don't want to get my hopes up. Even if my resume is the best they get, the hiring process could take weeks or months, and it's not safe to stick around here that long.

If they found me in Boise, they'll find me here too.

It's only a matter of time.

The cashier beams at me. "Why, yes, dearie. Just drive north about ten miles, and when you see the first buildings, take a left, drive past two intersections, and it'll be on your left, right next to the sheriff's office."

"Wonderful, thank you. Do you have a pen?" When she hands it to me, I jot down the directions on the front of the newspaper.

Not having a smartphone with GPS sucks.

"Have a nice day," I tell the elderly lady, and when I head out this time, there's a definite bounce in my step.

The tiny library closes at five p.m., so I hurriedly put together my resume and cover letter on one of the public computers, then email both to the address indicated in the ad. Instead of a phone number and email address, I put only my email on the resume; hopefully, that will suffice.

By the time I'm done, the library is closing, so I get back into my car and drive out of the small town, randomly turning onto narrow, winding roads until I find what I'm looking for.

A clearing in the woods where I can park my Toyota behind the trees, out of sight of anyone driving by.

With the car safely situated, I open the trunk and take out another sweater from the suitcase I was lucky enough to have with me when my life went to pieces. Rolling up the sweater, I stretch out on the backseat, place the makeshift pillow under my head, and close my eyes.

My last thought before sleep drags me under is the hope that I stay alive long enough to hear back about the job.

2

NIKOLAI

A KNOCK ON THE DOOR DISTRACTS ME FROM THE EMAIL I'm reading, and I look up from my laptop as Alina opens the door and gracefully steps into my office.

"We got a promising application tonight," she says, approaching my desk. "Here, take a look." She hands me a thick folder.

I open it. A driver's license photo of a striking young woman stares at me from the front page. Her brown eyes are so big they dominate her small, diamond-shaped face, and even on the grainy printout, her bronzed skin seems to glow, as if lit from within by an invisible candle. But it's her mouth that catches my attention. Small yet perfectly plump, it's a mix between a doll's Cupid-bow pout and something one might find on a porn star.

She's not smiling in this picture; her expression is solemn, her hair pulled back in either a tight ponytail or a bun. The next page, however, has a picture of her laughing, her head thrown back and her face framed by golden-brown waves that disappear below her slender shoulders. She's beautiful in this photo, and so radiant that I feel something inside me go dangerously still and quiet even as my pulse quickens with a primal male response.

Suppressing the bizarre reaction, I flip the page back and read the info on the driver's license.

Chloe Emmons is twenty-three years old, five-foot-four, and resides in Boston, Massachusetts—which means she's a long way from home.

"How did she hear about this position?" I ask, glancing up at Alina. "I thought we only placed the ad in the local papers."

She moves the printouts with the photos aside and taps a glossy red nail on the page underneath. "Read the cover letter."

I turn my attention to the page. It appears Chloe Emmons is on a post-graduation road trip and just happened to be passing through Elkwood Creek when she saw our ad and decided to apply for the position. The cover letter is well written and neatly formatted, as is the resume that follows. I can see why Alina thought it promising. Though the girl has just received her Bachelor's in Education Studies from Middlebury College, she's had more teaching internships and babysitting jobs than the previous three candidates combined.

Konstantin's report on her is next. As usual, he's had his team do a deep dive on her social media, criminal and DMV records, financial statements, school transcripts, medical records, and everything else about her life that had been computerized at any point. It's a longer read, so I look up at Alina. "Any red flags?"

She hesitates. "Maybe. Her mother passed away a month ago—apparent suicide. Since then, Chloe has basically been off the grid: no social media posts, no credit card transactions, no calls on her cell."

"So she's either having trouble coping, or something else is going on."

Alina nods. "My bet is on the first; her mother was the only family she had."

I shut the folder and push it away. "That doesn't explain the lack of credit card transactions. Something's off here. But even if it's what you think, an emotionally disturbed woman is the last thing we need."

A humorless smile touches Alina's jade-green eyes. "Are you sure about that, Kolya? Because I feel like she might fit right in."

And before I can reply, my sister turns around and walks out.

I don't know what makes me pick up the folder again an hour later—morbid curiosity, most likely. Flipping through the thick stack of papers, I find the police report on the mother's suicide. Apparently, Marianna Emmons, waitress, age forty, was found on her kitchen floor, her wrists slit. It was a neighbor who called it in; the daughter, Chloe, was nowhere to be found—and she never showed up to identify or bury the body.

Interesting. Could pretty little Chloe have offed her mom? Is that why she's on her off-the-grid "road trip?"

According to the police report, there was no suspicion of foul play. Marianna had a history of depression, and she'd tried to commit suicide once before, when she was sixteen. But I know how easy it is to stage a murder scene if you know what you're doing.

All it takes is a little foresight and skill.

It's a leap, of course, but I haven't gotten where I am by assuming the best about people. Even if Chloe Emmons isn't guilty of matricide, she's guilty of something. My instincts are telling me there's more to her story, and my instincts are rarely wrong.

The girl is trouble. I know it beyond a shadow of a doubt.

Still, something keeps me from closing the folder. I read through Konstantin's report in its entirety, then go through the screenshots of her social media. Surprisingly, it's not a lot of selfies; for a girl that pretty, Chloe doesn't seem overly focused on her looks. Instead, the majority of her posts consist of videos of baby animals and photos of scenic spots, along with links to blog posts and articles about childhood development and optimal teaching methods.

If not for that police report and her month-long disappearance from the grid, Chloe Emmons would appear to be exactly what she claims: a brand-new college grad with a passion for teaching.

Flipping back to the beginning of the folder, I study the photo of her laughing, trying to understand what it is about the girl that intrigues me. Her pretty face, for sure, but that's only part of it. I've seen—and fucked—women far more classically beautiful than she. Even that porn-doll mouth is nothing special in the grand scheme of things, though no man in his right mind would pass up the chance to feel those plump, soft lips wrapped around his cock.

No, it's something else that exerts that magnetic pull on me, something to do with the radiance of her smile. It's like spotting a ray of sunlight breaking through the clouds on a winter day. I want to touch it, feel its warmth... capture it, so I can have it for my own.

My body hardens at the thought, dark, X-rated images sliding through my mind. A better man—a better father—would shut that folder right away, if only because of the temptation it presents, but I'm not that man.

I'm a Molotov, and we've never done something as prosaic as the right thing.

Drumming my fingers on my desk, I come to a decision.

Chloe Emmons might be too troubled to allow near my son, but I still want to meet her.

I want to feel that ray of sunlight on my skin.

3

CHLOE

THE TWELVE-FOOT-TALL METAL GATE SLIDES APART AS I drive up, my Toyota's motor whining at the steep incline of the unpaved road leading up the mountain to the estate. Gripping the wheel tightly, I drive through the open gate, my nervousness intensifying with each second.

I still can't believe I'm here. I was almost certain I would have nothing in my inbox when I went to the library this morning. It was way too soon to expect a response. Just in case, though, I wanted to check my email and then spend a few hours looking online for other gigs within a half-tank's driving distance. But the email was already there when I logged in; it had arrived at ten p.m. yesterday.

They want to interview me.

At noon today.

My palms are slippery with sweat, so I wipe first

one hand, then the other on my jeans. I have nothing resembling an interview-appropriate outfit, so I'm wearing my only pair of clean jeans and a plain long-sleeved T-shirt—I need the sleeves to cover the scratches and scabs the glass shards left on my arm. Hopefully, my potential employers won't hold the casual attire against me; after all, I'm interviewing for a tutor position in the middle of nowhere.

Please let me get the job. Please let me get it.

The sleek metal gate I just drove through is part of a metal wall of the same height that extends into the rugged mountain forest on each side of the road. I wonder if that means the wall loops around the entire estate. It's hard to imagine—according to the librarian who gave me directions, the property consists of over a thousand acres of wild mountainous terrain—but I couldn't see where the wall ended, so it's possible. And since the gate opened on its own at my approach, there must be cameras in place as well—which, while somewhat alarming, is also reassuring.

I have no idea why these people need so much security, but if I get this job, I'll be safe inside their compound as well.

The winding dirt road I'm on seems to go on forever, but finally, after about a mile, the forest on the sides begins to thin and the terrain flattens out. I must be approaching the peak of the mountain.

Sure enough, as I round the next bend, the sleek two-story mansion comes into view.

An ultra-modern marvel of glass and steel, it should stand out like a sore thumb among all this untamed nature, but instead, it's skillfully integrated into its surroundings, with a portion of the house built into a rocky outcropping. As I pull up in front of it, I see an all-glass terrace wrapping around the back and realize that the house is perched on a cliff overlooking a deep ravine.

The views inside must be to kill for.

Deep breath, Chloe. You can do it.

Turning off the car, I smooth my sweaty palms over my jeans, straighten my shirt, make sure my hair is still in a neat bun, and grab the resume I printed out at the library. I usually interview well, but I've never had so much at stake before. Every nerve in my body is on edge, my heart pounding so fast I feel dizzy. Of course, I could also be dizzy because all I've had to eat today is the banana, but I don't want to think about that and the fact that if I don't get the job, hunger may be the least of my problems.

Resume in hand, I step out of the car. I'm about a half hour early, which is better than being late but not optimal. I was afraid I'd get lost without a GPS, so I left the library and headed over here as soon as the librarian explained where to go and gave me a local map. I didn't get lost, though, so now all I need is to walk over to that sleek, futuristic-looking front door and ring the doorbell.

Steeling my spine, I prepare to do exactly that when

the door swings open, revealing a tall, broad-shouldered man clad in a pair of dark jeans and a white button-up shirt with the sleeves rolled up to his elbows.

"Hi," I say, putting on a bright smile as I walk toward him. "I'm Chloe Emmons, here to interview for the..." I stop, my breath catching in my lungs as he steps out into the light and a pair of stunning hazel eyes meets mine.

Except "hazel" is too generic a term for them. I've never seen eyes like that. A rich, dark amber mixed with forest green, they're surrounded by thick black lashes and glitter with a peculiar fierceness, an intensity that wouldn't look out of place on a jungle predator. Tiger eyes, belonging to a man who himself is power and danger personified—a man so cruelly handsome my already-elevated heart rate goes supersonic.

High, wide cheekbones, a straight blade of a nose, jaw sharp enough to cut marble—the sheer symmetry of those striking features would've been enough for them to grace the covers of magazines, but when combined with that full, cynically curved mouth, the effect is absolutely devastating. Like his lashes, his eyebrows are thick and black, as is his hair, which is long enough to cover his ears and so straight it looks like a raven's wing.

Closing the distance between us with long, smooth strides, he extends his hand toward me. "Nikolai

Molotov," he says, pronouncing the name as a Russian native would—though there's no trace of accent in his deep, rough-silk voice. "It's a pleasure to make your acquaintance."

4

CHLOE

DUMBSTRUCK, I SHAKE HIS HAND. IT'S BIG AND STRONG, his lightly tanned skin warm as his long fingers wrap around mine and squeeze with carefully restrained power. A shiver ripples down my spine at the sensation, my body heating all over, and it takes everything I have not to sway toward him as my knees turn to jelly underneath me.

Get a grip, Chloe. This is a potential employer. Get a fucking grip.

With a herculean effort, I pull my hand away and reach for what remains of my composure. "It's nice to meet you, Mr. Molotov." To my relief, my voice comes out steady, my tone calm and friendly, as befits a person interviewing for a job. Taking a half-step back, I smile up at my host. "I'm sorry I'm a bit early."

His tiger eyes gleam brighter. "No problem. I've been looking forward to meeting you, Chloe. And please, call me Nikolai."

"Nikolai," I repeat, my stupid heartbeat accelerating further. I don't understand what's happening to me, why I'm having this reaction to this man. I've never been one to lose my mind over a chiseled jaw and washboard abs, not even when I was a hormonal teenager. While my friends were crushing on football players and movie stars, I dated boys whose personalities I liked, whose minds attracted me more than their bodies. For me, sexual chemistry has always been something that develops over time rather than being there from the start.

Then again, I've never met a man who exudes such raw animal magnetism.

I didn't know men like this existed.

Focus, Chloe. He's most likely married.

The thought is like a splash of cold water in my face, jerking me back to the reality of my situation. What the fuck am I doing, drooling over some kid's father? I need this job to *survive*. The forty-mile drive here ate more than a quarter tank of gas, and if I don't earn some money soon, I'll be stranded, a sitting duck for the killers coming after me.

The heat inside me cools at the thought, and when Nikolai says, "Follow me," and walks back into the house, my nerves jangle with anxiety instead of whatever it was that came over me at the sight of him.

Inside, the house is as ultra modern as it is on the outside. All around me are floor-to-ceiling windows with stunning views, modern-art-museum-worthy decorations, and sleek furniture that looks like it came straight out of some interior designer's showroom. Everything is done in shades of gray and white, softened in a few places by natural wood and stone accents. It's beautiful and more than a little intimidating, just like the man in front of me, and as he leads me through an open-layout living room to a spiral wood-and-glass staircase in the back, I can't help feeling like a mangy pigeon that's accidentally flown into a gilded concert hall.

Tamping down on the unsettling sensation, I say, "You have a beautiful house. Have you been living here long?"

"A few months," he replies as we go up the stairs. He glances at me. "What about you? You said in your cover letter you're on a road trip?"

"That's right." Feeling on firmer ground, I explain that I graduated from Middlebury College in June and decided to see the country before diving into the working world. "But then of course, I saw your listing," I conclude, "and it sounded too perfect to pass up, so here I am."

"Yes, indeed," he says softly as we stop in front of a closed door. "Here you are."

My breath hitches again, my pulse speeding up uncontrollably. There's something unnerving in the darkly sensual curve of his mouth, something almost… *dangerous* in the intensity of his stare. Maybe it's the unusual color of his eyes, but I feel distinctly uneasy when he presses his palm to an unobtrusive panel on the wall and the door swings open in front of us, spy-movie style.

"Please," he murmurs, motioning for me to enter, and I do so, doing my best to ignore the unsettling sensation that I'm entering a predator's lair.

The "lair" turns out to be a large, sunlit office. Two of the walls are made entirely of glass, revealing breathtaking mountain vistas, while a sleek L-shaped desk in the middle holds several computer monitors. To the side is a small round table with two chairs, and that's where Nikolai leads me.

Hiding a relieved exhale, I take a seat and lay my resume on the table in front of him. Clearly, I'm on edge, my nerves so frayed after the past month that I'm seeing danger everywhere. This is an interview for a tutor position, nothing more, and I need to get a hold of myself before I blow it.

Despite the admonition, my pulse spikes again as Nikolai leans back in his chair and regards me with those unsettlingly beautiful eyes. I can feel the growing dampness of my palms, and it's all I can do not to wipe them again on my jeans. As ridiculous as it is, I feel stripped bare by that gaze, all my secrets and fears exposed.

Stop it, Chloe. He knows nothing. You're interviewing to be a tutor, nothing more.

"So," I say brightly to hide my anxiety, "may I ask about the child I'd be tutoring? Is it your son or daughter?"

His face takes on an indecipherable expression. "My son. Miroslav. We call him Slava."

"That's a great name. Is he—"

"Tell me about yourself, Chloe." Leaning forward, he picks up my resume but doesn't look at it. Instead, his eyes are trained on my face, making me feel like a butterfly pinned under a microscope. "What is it about this position that intrigues you?"

"Oh, everything." Taking a breath to steady my voice, I describe all the babysitting and tutoring I've done throughout the years, and then I go over my internships, including my last summer job at a special-needs camp, where I worked with children of all ages. "It was a great experience," I conclude, "both challenging and rewarding. My favorite part of it, though, was teaching math and reading to the younger kids—which is why I think I'd be perfect for this role. Teaching is my passion, and I'd love a chance to work with a child one-on-one, to tailor the curriculum to his or her interests and abilities."

He sets the resume down, still without bothering to look at it. "And how do you feel about living in a place that's so removed from civilization? Where there's nothing but wilderness for dozens of miles around and only minimal contact with the outside world?"

"That sounds..." *Like a haven.* "...amazing." I beam at him, my excitement unfeigned. "I'm a big fan of the wilderness, and nature in general. In fact, my alma mater—Middlebury College—was chosen partly because of its rural location. I love hiking and fishing, and I know my way around a campfire. Living here would be a dream come true." Especially given all the security measures I spotted on the way in—but I don't say that, of course.

I can't appear to be anything other than a brand-new college grad looking for adventure.

He arches his eyebrows. "You won't miss your friends? Or family?"

"No, I—" To my dismay, my throat constricts with a sudden rush of grief. Swallowing, I try again. "I'm very independent. I've been traveling around the country on my own for the past month, and besides, there are always phones, videoconferencing apps, and social media."

He cocks his head. "Yet you haven't been posting on your social media profiles for the past month. Why's that?"

I stare at him, my heartbeat skyrocketing. He's looked at my social media? How? When? I have the highest privacy settings in place; he should be unable to see anything about me other than the fact that I exist and use social media like a normal person. Has he had me investigated? Hacked into my accounts somehow?

Who is this man?

"I actually don't have a phone right now." A trickle of sweat runs down my spine, but I succeed in keeping my tone level. "I got rid of it because I wanted to see if I could function on this road trip without all the electronics. A personal challenge of sorts."

"I see." His eyes are more green than amber in this light. "So how do you keep in touch with family and friends?"

"Email, mostly," I lie. There's no way I can admit that I haven't kept in touch with anyone and have no plans to do so. "I've been visiting public libraries and using the computers there once in a while." Realizing my fingers are laced tightly together, I unclench my hands and force a smile to my lips. "It's quite liberating, not being tied to a phone, you see. Extreme connectivity is both a blessing and a curse, and I'm enjoying the freedom of traveling around the country as people have done in the past, with only a paper map to guide me."

"A Gen Z luddite. How refreshing."

I flush at the gentle mockery in his tone. I know how my explanation sounds, but it's the only thing I can come up with to justify my lack of recent social media activity and, in case he looks at my resume closely, absence of a cell phone number. In fact, it's a good excuse for everything, so I might as well roll with it.

"You're right. I'm a bit of a luddite," I say. "That's probably why city life holds so little appeal for me, and why I found your job posting so intriguing. Living out here"—I motion at the gorgeous views outside—"and tutoring your son is the kind of job I've always wanted, and if you hire me, I will dedicate myself to it completely."

A slow, dark smile curves his lips. "Is that right?"

"Yes." I hold his gaze, even as my breath turns shallow and prickles of heat run over my skin. I really don't get my reaction to this man, don't understand how I can find him so magnetic even as he sets off all kinds of alarms in my mind. Paranoia or not, my instincts are screaming that he's dangerous, yet my finger itches to reach out and trace the clearly defined edges of his full, soft-looking lips. Swallowing, I wrench my thoughts away from that treacherous territory and say with as much earnestness as I can manage, "I'll be the most perfect tutor you can imagine."

He regards me without blinking, the silence stretching into several long seconds, and just when I feel like my nerves might snap like an overextended rubber band, he stands up and says, "Follow me."

He leads me out of the office and down a long hallway until we reach another closed door. This one must not have any biometric security, since he just knocks on the door and, without waiting for an answer, goes in.

Inside, another floor-to-ceiling window provides more breathtaking views. However, there's nothing sleek and modern about this room. Instead, it looks like the aftermath of a toy factory explosion. Colorful chaos is everywhere I look, with piles of toys, children's books, and LEGO pieces scattered all over the floor, and a child-sized bed covered by a Superman-themed sheet in the corner. The Superman-themed pillows and blanket from the bed are piled high in another corner, and it's not until my host says in a commanding tone, "Slava!" that I realize there's a little boy building a LEGO castle next to that pile.

At his father's voice, the boy's head jerks up, revealing a pair of huge amber-green eyes—the same mesmerizing eyes the man next to me possesses. In general, the boy is Nikolai in miniature, his black hair falling around his ears in a straight, glossy curtain and his child-round face already showing a hint of those striking cheekbones. Even the mouth is the same, lacking only the cynical, knowing curve of his father's lips.

"Slava, *idi syuda*," Nikolai orders, and the boy gets up and cautiously approaches us. As he stops in front of us, I notice he's wearing a pair of jeans and a T-shirt with a picture of Spider-Man on the front.

Looking down at his son, Nikolai starts speaking to him in rapid-fire Russian. I have no idea what he's saying, but it must have something to do with me because the boy keeps glancing at me, his expression both curious and fearful.

As soon as Nikolai is done speaking, I smile at the child and kneel on the floor, so we're on the same eye level. "Hi, Slava," I say gently. "I'm Chloe. It's nice to meet you."

The boy looks at me blankly.

"He doesn't speak English," Nikolai says, his voice

hard. "Alina and I have tried to teach him, but he knows we speak Russian, and he refuses to learn it from us. So that would be your job: teaching him English, along with anything else a child his age should know."

"I see." I keep my gaze on the boy, smiling at him warmly even as more alarms go off in my mind. There's something odd in the way Nikolai talks to and about the child. It's as if his son is a stranger to him. And if Alina—who I assume is his wife and the mother of the child—knows English as well as my host, why doesn't Slava speak at least a few words? Why would he refuse to learn the language from his parents?

In general, why doesn't Nikolai pick up the boy and hug him? Or playfully ruffle his hair?

Where's the warm ease with which parents usually communicate with their children?

"Slava," I say to the boy softly, "I'm Chloe." I point at myself. "Chloe."

He regards me with his father's unblinking stare for several long moments. Then his mouth moves, shaping the syllables. "Klo-ee."

I beam at him. "That's right. Chloe." I tap my chest. "And you're Slava." I point at him. "Miroslav, right?"

He nods solemnly. "Slava."

"Do you like comic books, Slava?" I gently touch the picture on his T-shirt. "This is Spider-Man, isn't it?"

His eyes brighten. "*Da,* Spider-Man." He pronounces it with a Russian accent. "*Ti znayesh o nyom?*"

I glance up at Nikolai, only to find him watching me with a dark, indecipherable expression. A tingle of unwelcome awareness zips down my spine, my breath hitching at a sudden feeling of vulnerability. On my knees is not where I want to be with this man.

It feels a lot like baring my throat to a beautiful, wild wolf.

"My son is asking if you know about Spider-Man," he says after a tension-filled moment. "I assume the answer is yes."

With effort, I tear my gaze away from him and focus on the boy. "Yes, I know about Spider-Man," I say, smiling. "I loved Spider-Man when I was your age. Also Superman and Batman and Wonder Woman and Aquaman."

The child's face brightens more with every superhero I name, and when I get to Aquaman, a mischievous grin appears on his face. "Aquaman?" He wrinkles his small nose. "*Nyet, nye* Aquaman."

"No Aquaman?" I widen my eyes exaggeratedly. "Why not? What's wrong with Aquaman?"

That draws a giggle. "*Nye* Aquaman."

"Okay, you win. Not Aquaman." I let out a sad sigh. "Poor Aquaman. So few kids like him."

The boy giggles again and runs over to a pile of comic books next to the bed. Grabbing one, he brings it back and points at the picture on the front. "Superman *samiy sil'niy*," he declares.

"Superman is the best?" I guess. "Your favorite?"

"He said he's the strongest," Nikolai says evenly,

then switches over to Russian, his voice taking on the same commanding tone.

The boy's face falls, and he lowers the book, his posture dejected.

"Let's go back to my office," Nikolai says to me, and without another word to his son, he heads for the door.

5

NIKOLAI

As I step out of the room, I can hear her saying goodbye to my son, her voice sweet and bright, and the painful thudding in my chest intensifies, anger mixing with the strongest lust I've ever felt.

Six months.

Six months, and I haven't gotten so much as a smile out of the boy. Alina has, though, and now so has this girl, this total stranger.

Slava laughed with her.

He showed her his favorite book.

He let her touch his shirt.

And the entire time I watched her with my son, all I could think about was how she'd look spread out naked underneath me, her sun-streaked hair freed from the tight bun confining it and her big brown eyes trained on me as I bury myself in her silky flesh, over and over again.

If I needed further proof that I'm unfit to be a father, here it is, in spades.

"Sit, please," I tell Chloe when we're back in my office. Despite my best efforts, my voice is tight, the roiling cauldron of emotions inside me too powerful to be contained. I want to grab the girl and fuck her on the spot, and at the same time, I want to shake her and demand she tell me how she worked her magic on Slava so quickly... why my son responded to her within minutes while I've been unable to get more than a few words out of him for months.

She sits down in the same chair as before, perching on the edge of the seat as delicately as a butterfly on a flower. Her eyes are locked inquisitively on my face, her expression perfectly composed, and if not for her small hands knotting together on the table, I would've thought she's as cool as she appears. But she's nervous, this pretty mystery of a girl, nervous and more than a little desperate.

I don't know why that is, but I'm going to find out.

"What did you think of my son?" I ask, my tone smoothing out as I lean back in my chair. Now that we're away from Slava, the strange tightness I often get in my ribcage around him is easing, the irrational anger and jealousy fading until it's only a faint pulse at the back of my mind.

So what if the boy likes this stranger better?

That means she might actually be able to do the job I'm about to hire her for.

I don't know when exactly I reached this decision,

at what point I decided my fascination with Chloe Emmons justifies the danger she might pose to my family. Maybe it was when she was glibly lying about why she stopped using social media, or as she was fearlessly holding my gaze after vowing to devote herself to the job. Or maybe it was when I came out of the house and those soft brown eyes landed on me for the first time, making every hair on my body stand on end with scorching awareness.

Attraction is too weak a word to describe the pull I feel toward her. My hands are literally twitching with the urge to touch her, to trail my fingers over her finely molded jaw and see if her bronzed skin is as baby soft as it appears. In pictures, she was bright and pretty, her radiance shining off the page. In person, she's all that and more, her smile full of unselfconscious warmth, her unflinching gaze speaking of both vulnerability and strength.

And underneath it all is desperation. I can see it, feel it... smell it. Fear, hopelessness—it has a scent, like blood. And like blood, it calls to the darkest parts of me, to the beast that I've been keeping carefully leashed. Worse yet, this inconvenient attraction isn't one-sided.

Chloe Emmons is drawn to me.

Masked by her bright, friendly smile is a purely feminine interest, a response as primal as my reaction to her. When I shook her hand, I felt a tremor run over her skin, saw her lips part on a shallow exhale as her delicate fingers twitched in my grip.

No, the girl is not indifferent to me at all, and that makes her fair game.

"I thought Slava was very bright," she answers, and my gaze falls to the tempting shape of her mouth. Her upper lip is a bit fuller than the lower, giving the impression of a slight overbite when she's not smiling. "I'm not sure why he refuses to learn English from you, but I'm confident I'll be able to teach him," she continues as I ponder if that small imperfection makes her features more or less appealing. More, I decide as she explains the teaching methods she intends to use. Definitely more, because all I can think about is how much I want to taste the plush softness of those lips and feel them on my body.

With effort, I refocus on her words.

"—and so we'll start with the—"

"What's your take on corporal discipline for children?" I interrupt, leaning forward. I've heard enough to know that she's capable of doing the job. There's only one other thing I need to know now. "Do you believe in spanking and such?"

She gives me an appalled look. "Of course not! That's the last thing—No, I would never condone that." Her eyes narrow fiercely as she leans in, slender hands balling into fists on the table. "Do *you*?"

"No. I don't."

She visibly relaxes, and I conceal a satisfied smile. For a second there, she looked like she was going to punch me with those tiny fists. And that reaction wasn't faked; every muscle in her body tensed at once, as if she'd been about to launch herself into battle. The mere possibility of my son getting spanked made her forget whatever is behind her desperation and ready to rip into me like a mama bear.

That's not the reaction of a woman who'd ever hurt a child. Whatever danger Chloe Emmons poses, it's not one of violent tendencies—at least none that would be directed at Slava.

The jury is still out about the true cause of her mother's death.

It's probably yet another sign that I'm unfit to be a parent, but a part of me is looking forward to the trouble she might bring. It's quiet here, in this remote corner of Idaho—beautiful and way too fucking quiet. The life I left behind is nothing like the one I've been leading for the past six months, and I can't deny that I miss the adrenaline rush of being at the helm of one of the most powerful families in Russia.

This girl with her intriguing lies and porn-doll mouth won't replace that for me, but one way or another, she'll provide some entertainment.

Leaning back, I lace my fingers over my ribcage and smile at her. "So, Chloe… when can you begin?"

6

CHLOE

I ALMOST JUMP UP AND SHOUT, "NOW! THIS MINUTE. This second." Only that would betray my desperation and ruin the whole thing, so I stay in my seat and say with some semblance of composure, "Whatever works best for you. I'm available right away."

Nikolai's eyes glint dark gold. "Excellent. I'd like you to start today. I assume you're okay with the salary stated in the ad?"

"Yes, thank you. It's adequate." By which I mean it's more money than I could've hoped to earn anywhere else, but all the interview books tell you not to appear too eager and to negotiate. I don't have the balls to do the latter, but I can attempt the former. Striving for a casual tone, I ask, "How often will I be paid?"

"Weekly. We'll count today as your first day, so you'll get the first paycheck next Tuesday. Does that work?"

I nod, too excited to speak. One week—or rather,

six and a half days—from now, I'll have money. Actual, real, substantial money, the kind that would provide me with food and gas for months if I have to run again.

"Excellent." He rises to his feet. "Come, I'll show you to your room."

I follow him, doing my best not to notice the way his designer jeans hug his muscled thighs and how his well-fitted shirt stretches over his powerful shoulders. The last thing I need is to lust after my employer, a man who's most likely married to a woman I have yet to meet. Which, come to think of it, is strange.

Why wasn't Slava's mother involved in this hiring decision?

Catching up to Nikolai, I clear my throat to get his attention. "Will I get to meet Alina soon?" I ask when his gaze lands on me. "Or is she away?"

He raises his eyebrows. "She's—"

"Right here." A stunning young woman steps out of the room we were about to enter. Tall and slim, she's wearing a red dress that could've come straight from a runway in Paris. On her feet is an elegant pair of nude-colored heels, and her long, straight, jet-black hair frames a strikingly beautiful face. Her full lips are painted red to match her dress, and a skillful application of black eyeliner emphasizes the cat-like tilt of her jade-green eyes.

Extending a perfectly groomed hand toward me, she says smoothly, "Alina Molotova. I take it the interview went well?" Like her husband, she speaks flawless American English, with only her pronunciation of her name betraying her foreign origins.

Recovering from the shock of her appearance, I shake her hand. "It's a pleasure to meet you, Mrs. Molotova." I say her name the way she did, with an "a" at the end; I remember from my Russian Lit course that Russian surnames are gendered. "I'm—"

"Chloe Emmons, I know. And please, call me Alina." She smiles, revealing a tiny gap between her front teeth —an imperfection that only enhances her striking beauty.

"Thank you, Alina." I smile back, even as an unpleasant ache tightens my chest.

Nikolai's wife is beyond gorgeous, and for some reason, I hate that fact.

Strangely, Nikolai doesn't look pleased with her either. "What are you doing here?" His tone is hard, his dark eyebrows knitting together in a frown.

Alina's smile turns catlike. "I was preparing Chloe's room, of course. What else?"

His response in Russian is swift and sharp, but she just laughs—a pretty, bell-like sound—and says to me, "Welcome to the household, Chloe."

With that, she walks away, her stride as graceful as a model's on a catwalk.

Exhaling a breath, I turn back to Nikolai, only to see him entering the room. I follow him in and find myself in a spacious, ultra-modern bedroom with a floor-to-ceiling window showcasing more breathtaking views.

"Wow." I walk over to the window and stare out at the snow-capped peaks of distant mountains veiled by a blueish haze. "This is… just wow."

"Beautiful, isn't it?" he says, and my pulse jumps as I realize he's come up to stand next to me, his gaze on the magnificent vista outside. In profile, he's even more stunning, his features as hard and perfect as if they'd been carved from the cliff we're perched on, his powerful body as much a force of nature as the unforgiving wilderness around us.

Dangerous.

The word whispers across my mind, and this time, I can't convince myself it's simply paranoia. He's dangerous, this mysterious employer of mine. I don't know how, I don't know why, but I can feel it. A month ago, the blinders I'd worn my whole life—the ones all normal people wear—were violently ripped away, and I can't unsee the darkness in the world, can't pretend it isn't there. And I see the darkness in Nikolai.

Underneath that stunning male beauty and those smooth manners lurks something savage… something terrifying.

He turns to face me, and it takes all my courage to remain in place and meet his tiger-bright gaze. My heart is thumping heavily in my chest, yet a white-hot current seems to leap between us, the air particles taking on an electric charge. My nerve endings sizzle with it, heating my skin and turning my breath shallow and uneven.

Run, Chloe.

Swallowing hard, I step back, Mom's voice ringing in my head as clearly as if she were here. And I desperately want to listen to it, but I'm down to a few dollars in my wallet and a quarter-tank of gas in my ancient clunker of a car. This man, who both attracts and terrifies me, is my only hope of survival, and whatever danger I face here can't be worse than what's waiting for me if I leave.

His eyes gleam with dark amusement as I take another step back and then another, and I again get the unsettling sensation that he's seeing right through me, that he somehow senses both my fear and my shameful attraction to him.

Forcing myself to turn away, I look around, feigning interest in my surroundings—as if anything around here could be as fascinating as he is. "So this will be my room?"

"Yes. Do you like it?"

"I love it." I look up at a large TV hanging from the ceiling over the bed, then walk over to a door across from the one opening into the hallway. It leads to a sleek white bathroom with a glass shower stall large enough to accommodate five people. Another door turns out to hide a walk-in closet the size of my college dorm room, all empty and waiting for my meager belongings.

It's luxury of the kind I've only seen in movies, and it adds to my unease.

Who are these people? Where did they get their

wealth? How did Nikolai know about my absence from social media when all my profiles are private?

Why do they need so much security in a place so remote?

I didn't want to think too deeply about any of this before—my focus was on getting the job—but now that I'm here, now that this is real, I can't help wondering what I've gotten myself into. Because there's one easy answer to all my questions, one word that, thanks to Hollywood, comes to mind when I think about wealthy Russians.

Mafia.

Is that what my new employers are?

7

CHLOE

Heart hammering, I turn to look at Nikolai. He's watching me with the same unsettling amusement, and I suddenly feel like a mouse being played with by a big, gorgeous cat.

Who may be in the mafia.

"So," I begin uncomfortably, "I should probably—"

"Give me your car keys." He walks up to me. "I'll have your things brought up."

"That's okay. I can do that myself. I'll just—" I shut my mouth because he extends his hand palm up, his expression uncompromising.

Fumbling in my pocket, I extract the keys and drop them onto his broad palm. "Here you go."

"Thank you." He pockets the keys. "Settle in and make yourself comfortable. Pavel will bring your bags in a minute."

"There's just one—a small suitcase in the trunk," I say, but he's already walking out.

Exhaling a breath I didn't realize I was holding, I collapse onto the bed. Now that the interview is over, the adrenaline that sustained me is dropping, and I feel wrung out, so completely drained that all I can do is lie there and stare blankly at the high ceiling. After a while, I recover enough to register the fact that the white coverlet underneath me is made of some soft, fuzzy material, and I spread my palms over it, stroking it as I would a pet.

A knock on the door jolts me out of my semi-catatonic state. Sitting up, I call out, "Come in!"

A man the size of a cave bear enters, carrying my suitcase, which looks more like a handbag in his enormous hand. Tattoos run up the sides of his thick neck, and his weathered face reminds me of a brick—hard, ruddy, and uncompromisingly square. His military-short hair is an indeterminate shade of brown liberally sprinkled with gray, and his hard gray eyes remind me of melted bullets.

"Hi," I say, mustering a smile as I get to my feet. "You must be Pavel."

He nods, his expression unchanged. "Where do you want this?" he asks in a deep, thickly accented growl.

"Right here is fine, thank you. I got this." I walk over to take the suitcase from him, and as I approach, I realize he must be the biggest man I've ever met, both in terms of height and width. More tattoos decorate the backs of his hands and peek out from the v-neck of the sweater that stretches tightly over his prominent pecs.

Trying not to gulp nervously, I stop in front of him and clasp the handle of the suitcase he's just set on the floor. "Thank you." I smile brighter, looking up. Very far up—my neck actually hurts from how far I have to bend it back.

He nods again, his thick jaw stiff, then turns and walks out.

Okay then. So much for befriending other staff members. What's the man-bear's job here, anyway? Bodyguard?

Mafia enforcer, maybe?

I push the thought away. Even though the guy fits the stereotype to a T, I refuse to dwell on this possibility. What would be the point? Even if my new employers are mafia, I'm safer here than out there.

I hope.

Shutting the door behind Pavel, I unpack—a process that takes all of ten minutes—and gaze longingly at the bed with its fuzzy white coverlet. I'm exhausted and not only from the interview. Between the nightmares that haunt me at night and the constant worry during the day, I haven't had more than four hours of sleep in weeks. But I can't just sleep the afternoon away.

I was hired to do a job, and I intend to do it.

To perk myself up, I take a quick shower in the enormous bathroom and change into a fresh T-shirt—my last one. I have to inquire about where to do laundry ASAP, but first things first.

It's time I got to know my young student.

The door to Slava's room is open as I approach, and I see Alina inside, talking to the boy in melodious Russian. Hearing my footsteps, she glances over at me and arches her eyebrows in a way that reminds me of her husband.

"Eager to start?"

I smile at her. "If you don't mind, I was thinking Slava and I could get to know each other this afternoon." I catch the child's gaze and give him a wink, earning myself a huge smile.

Alina's expression warms at her son's reaction. "Of course I don't mind. I was just explaining to him that you'll be living here and teaching him. He's quite excited about the idea."

"So am I." I crouch in front of the boy. "We'll have a great time, won't we, Slava?"

He clearly doesn't understand what I'm saying, but he grins regardless and rattles off something in Russian.

"He's asking if you like castles," Alina says.

"Yes, I do," I tell Slava. "Show me what you've got there. Is this your fortress?" I gesture at the partially built LEGO project.

The boy giggles and plops down among the LEGO pieces. Picking up two, he attaches them to the walls of the castle, and I help him by attaching two more. Only I apparently did it wrong because he shakes his head and takes off my pieces, then places them right next to where I attached them.

"Oh, I see. You're leaving room for windows. Windows, right?" I point at the giant window in his room.

He bobs his head. *"Da, okna. Bol'shiye okna."* Grabbing my wrist, he places another piece in my palm and guides my hand to the proper place on the wall. *"Nado syuda."*

"Got it." Grinning, I attach the next piece. "Like so, right?"

"Da," he says excitedly and grabs more pieces. We proceed in that vein, with him guiding me in castle assembly until Alina clears her throat.

"Seems like you two are on the same page, so I'll leave you to it," she says when I look up. "You have a half hour before Slava's snack time. Are you hungry by any chance, Chloe?"

My stomach responds before I can, emitting a loud growl, and Alina laughs, her green eyes lighting with amusement.

"I'm guessing that's a yes. Any food preferences or allergies?"

"I'm good with anything," I say, grateful that my darker skin tone conceals my embarrassed flush. I can't imagine Alina's elegant, long-limbed body ever emitting such an indiscreet noise—though, if she's human, it must upon occasion. Of course, jury's still out on the human part.

In those high heels and that stunning dress, Nikolai's wife looks too glamorous to be real.

Some of my embarrassment must show because her amusement deepens, her lips curving in a way that again reminds me disconcertingly of her husband. "How very accommodating of you. I'll let Pavel know."

Pavel? Is the man-bear their cook or something? Before I can ask, Alina turns to her son and says something in Russian, then strolls out, leaving me alone with my charge.

8

NIKOLAI

"So, tell me, brother... Did you acquire her for Slava or yourself?"

I pause in the middle of putting on my cufflinks and turn around to meet Alina's coolly mocking gaze. "Does it matter?" I have no idea how she sniffed out my interest in our new hire, but I'm not surprised.

My sister has always been able to read me better than anyone.

She leans against the doorframe of my walk-in closet, where I'm changing for dinner. "I guess I should've expected it. She's pretty, isn't she?"

"Very." I deliberately turn my back to her. Alina lives to get a rise out of me, but she's not going to succeed tonight. Nor is she going to shame me into staying away from Chloe.

The girl intrigues me too much for that.

"You know she spent the entire afternoon with Slava, right?" Alina strolls deeper into my closet and picks up my skinny black tie, the one I was just about to put on.

Resisting the impulse to reach for a different one just to spite her, I take the tie from her and put it on with practiced motions. "Yes, I do."

There are cameras in my son's room, and I spent *my* afternoon watching him play with his new tutor. They finished building the castle Slava was working on, ate the fruit-and-cheese platter Pavel brought, then played a game of tag, where Chloe chased him around his room and down the hallway, making him laugh so hard he was giggle-snorting. Afterward, Chloe read to him from some of his favorite comic books—the English-language ones, not the Russian translations Alina smuggled in to worm her way into the boy's good graces. As she spoke, Slava looked fascinated with his beautiful young teacher, something I can't blame him for.

I'd kill for her to sit next to me and read to me in that soft, slightly husky voice, to feel her hand play with my hair the way it so casually played with my son's when he snuggled up to her as if he's known her all his life.

"She's good with him," Alina continues as I finish buckling my belt and reach for my suit jacket. "Really good."

"I noticed."

"Yet you're still going to fuck her. Just like *he* would have."

I keep my tone level. "I never claimed to be any different."

"But you can be. Kolya…" She lays her hand on my arm, and when I meet her gaze, she says quietly, "We left. We came here. This is our chance to start over, to make ourselves into whoever we want to be. Forget our father. Forget all of it. You've put in your time; now it's Valery and Konstantin's turn."

A dry chuckle escapes my throat. "What makes you think I want to start over? Or be anything other than who I am?"

"The fact that you left. The fact that we're here, having this discussion." Her expression is earnest, open for once. "Let the girl be Slava's tutor and nothing more. Amuse yourself elsewhere. She's too young for you. Too innocent."

"She's twenty-three, not twelve. And I've just turned thirty-one—hardly an insurmountable age difference."

"I'm not talking about age. She's not like us. She's soft. Vulnerable."

"Exactly. And you brought her to my attention." I smile cruelly. "What did you think would happen?"

Alina's face hardens. "You're going to destroy her. But then again"—her lips twist in a bitter smile as she steps back—"that's the Molotov way, isn't it? Enjoy your new toy, Kolya. I can't wait to see you play with her at dinner."

And without another word, she walks out.

9

CHLOE

Holding Slava's hand, I approach the dining room, my knees all but knocking together. I don't know why I'm so nervous, but I am. Just the thought of seeing Nikolai again makes me feel like a rabid honey badger has taken up residence in my stomach.

It's the mafia question, I tell myself. Now that the idea has occurred to me, I can't get it out of my mind, no matter how hard I try. That's why my breath quickens and my palms grow damp each time I picture the cynical curve of my employer's lips. Because he might be a criminal. Because I sense a dark, ruthless edge in him. It has nothing to do with his looks and the heat that flows through my veins whenever his intense green-gold gaze lands on me.

It can't have anything to do with that because he's married, and I would never poach another woman's husband, especially when a child is involved.

Still, I can't help wondering how long Nikolai and

his wife have been together… whether he loves her. So far, I've only seen them together briefly, so it's impossible to tell—though I did sense a certain lack of intimacy between them. But I'm sure that was just wishful thinking on my part. Why wouldn't my employer love his wife? Alina is as gorgeous as he is, so much so they almost look alike. No wonder Slava is such a beautiful child; with parents like that, he's won the genetic lottery, big time.

I glance down at the boy in question, and he looks up at me, his huge eyes eerily like his father's. His expression is solemn, the exuberance he displayed when we played together gone. Like me, he seems anxious about our upcoming meal, so I give him a reassuring smile.

"Dinner," I say, nodding toward the table we're approaching. "We're about to have dinner."

He blinks up at me, saying nothing, but I know he's filing away the word, along with everything else I've said to him today. Young children are like sponges, absorbing everything adults say and do, their brains forming connections at dazzling speed. When I was in high school, I babysat for a Chinese couple. Their five-year-old spoke zero English when I met her, but after a few weeks of kindergarten and a dozen evenings with me, she was almost fluent. The same thing will happen to Slava, I have no doubt.

Already, by the end of this afternoon, he was repeating a few words after me.

No one's in the dining room yet, though Pavel

gruffly told me to be down here at six when he brought the fruit-and-cheese tray to Slava's room. However, the table is already set with all manner of salads and appetizers, and my mouth waters at the deliciousness waiting for us. While the afternoon snack quenched the worst of my gnawing hunger, I'm still starving, and it takes all of my willpower not to fall ravenously on the artfully arranged platters of open-faced caviar sandwiches, smoked fish, roasted vegetables, and leafy green salads. Instead, I help Slava climb up onto a chair that has a child's booster seat on it, and then I begin pointing out the names of the different foods in English. "We call this dish *salad,* and the green thing inside it is *lettuce,*" I'm saying as the *click-clack* of high heels announces Alina's arrival.

I look up at her with a smile. "Hello. Slava and I were just—"

"Why hasn't he changed?" Her dark eyebrows pull together as she takes in the child's appearance. "He knows we change for dinner."

I blink. "Oh, I—"

She interrupts with a stream of rapid-fire Russian, and I see the boy's shoulders tighten as he slinks down in his seat, as if wanting to disappear. Apparently realizing she's upsetting her son, Alina softens her tone and eventually gets what sounds like a chastised apology out of the child.

She faces me. "Sorry about that. Slava knows better than to come down like this, but he forgot in all the excitement."

My face burns as I realize that "like this" means his normal casual clothes, which are no different from the jeans and long-sleeved T-shirt I'm wearing. Nikolai's wife, on the other hand, has changed into an even more glamorous dress—a silver-blue ankle-length gown—and looks like she's on her way to a Hollywood premiere.

"I'm sorry," I say, feeling like a fanny-pack-wearing tourist who's stumbled into a Parisian fashion show. "I didn't realize there was a dress code."

"Oh, you're fine." Alina waves an elegant hand. "It's not a requirement for *you*. But Slava is a Molotov, and it's important that he learn the family traditions."

"I see." I don't see, actually, but it's not my place to argue with family traditions, however absurd they may be.

"And don't worry," Alina adds, taking a seat across from Slava. "If you wish to dress properly as well, I'm sure Kolya will buy you some appropriate clothing."

Kolya? Is that what she calls her husband?

"That's not necessary, thank you—" I begin, only to fall into a stunned silence as I catch sight of Nikolai approaching the table. Like his wife, he's changed for dinner, his high-end designer jeans and button-up shirt replaced by a sharply tailored black suit, crisp white shirt, and skinny black tie—an outfit that wouldn't look out of place at a high-society wedding… or the same movie premiere Alina's planning to attend. And while an average-looking man could easily pass for handsome in a suit like this, Nikolai's dark, masculine beauty is heightened to an almost unbearable degree. As I take in his appearance, my pulse goes through the roof and my lungs constrict, along with lower regions of my—

Married, Chloe. He's married.

The reminder is like a slap in the face, yanking me out of my dazzled trance. Forcing a breath into my oxygen-deprived lungs, I give my employer a carefully restrained smile, one that *doesn't* say that my heart is racing in my chest and that I'm wishing like hell Alina didn't exist. Especially since his striking gaze is trained on me instead of his gorgeous wife.

"You're late," she says as he pulls out a chair and sits next to her. "It's already—"

"I know what time it is." He doesn't take his eyes off me as he responds to her, his tone coolly dismissive. Then his gaze flicks to the boy at my side and his features tighten as he takes in his casual appearance.

"I'm sorry, it's my fault," I say before he can also reprimand the child. "I didn't realize we needed to get dressed up for dinner."

Nikolai's attention returns to me. "Of course you didn't." His gaze travels over my shoulders and chest, making me acutely conscious of my plain long-sleeved T-shirt and the thin cotton bra underneath that's doing nothing to hide my inexplicably erect nipples. "Alina is right. I need to buy you some proper clothes."

"No, really, that's—"

He holds up his palm. "House rules." His voice is soft, but his face could've been laid in stone. "Now that you're a member of this household, you must abide by them."

"I… all right." If he and his wife want to see me in fancy clothes at dinner and don't mind spending the money to make it happen, so be it.

Like he said, their house, their rules.

"Good." His sensual lips curve. "I'm glad you're so accommodating."

My breath quickens, my face warming again, and I look away to hide my reaction. All the man did was smile, for fuck's sake, and I'm blushing like a fifteen-year-old virgin. And in front of his wife, no less.

If I don't get a handle on this ridiculous crush, I'll be fired before the end of the meal.

"Would you like some salad?" Alina asks, as if to remind me of her existence, and I shift my attention to her, grateful for the distraction.

"Yes, please."

She gracefully ladles a serving of leafy green salad onto my plate, then does the same for her husband and son. In the meantime, Nikolai extends the platter with caviar sandwiches toward me, and I take one, both because I'm hungry enough to eat anything residing on bread and because I'm curious about the notorious Russian delicacy. I've had this type of fish roe—the big orange kind—in sushi restaurants a couple of times, but I imagine it's different like this, served on a slice of French baguette with a thick layer of butter underneath.

Sure enough, when I bite into it, the rich umami

flavor explodes on my tongue. Unlike the fish roe I've tasted, Russian caviar appears to be preserved with liberal amounts of salt. It would be too salty on its own, but the crusty white bread and mellow butter balance it perfectly, and I devour the rest of the small sandwich in two bites.

Eyes gleaming with amusement, Nikolai offers me the platter again. "More?"

"I'm good, thank you." I'd love another caviar sandwich—or twenty—but I don't want to seem greedy. Instead, I dig into my salad, which is also delicious, with a sweet, tangy dressing that makes my taste buds tingle. Then I try a bite of everything on the table, from the smoked fish to some kind of potato salad to grilled eggplant drizzled with a cucumber-dill yogurt sauce.

As I eat, I keep an eye on my charge, who's eating quietly beside me. Alina has given Slava a small portion of everything the adults are having, the caviar sandwich included, and the boy seems to have no problem with that. There are no demands for chicken fingers or French fries, no sign of the typical pickiness of a four-year-old. Even his table manners are those of a much older child, with only a couple of instances of him grabbing a piece of food with his fingers instead of his fork.

"Your son is very well-behaved," I tell Alina and Nikolai, and Nikolai lifts his eyebrows, as if hearing it for the first time.

"Well-behaved? Slava?"

"Of course." I frown at him. "You don't think so?"

"I haven't given it much thought," he says, glancing at the boy, who's diligently spearing a piece of lettuce with his adult-sized fork. "I suppose he conducts himself reasonably well."

Reasonably well? A four-year-old who sits calmly and eats everything served to him with zero whining or interruptions of adult conversation? Who handles utensils like a pro? Maybe this is a thing in Europe, but I've certainly never seen it in America.

Also, why hasn't my employer given his son's behavior much thought? Aren't parents supposed to worry about things like that?

"Have you been around many other children his age?" I ask Nikolai on a hunch, and catch his mouth flattening for a second.

"No," he says curtly. "I haven't."

Alina shoots him an indecipherable look, then turns to me. "I don't know if my brother has told you this," she says in a measured tone, "but we only learned of Slava's existence eight months ago."

I choke on a pickled tomato I've just bitten into and break into a coughing fit, the spicy, vinegary juices having gone down the wrong pipe. "Wait, what?" I gasp out when I can speak.

Eight months ago?

And did she just call Nikolai her *brother*?

"I see this is news to you," Alina says, handing me a glass of water, which I gratefully gulp down. "Kolya"—she glances at Nikolai, who's wearing a hard, closed-off expression—"hasn't told you much about us, has he?"

"Um, no." I set the glass down and cough again to clear the hoarseness from my voice. "Not really." My new employer hasn't said much at all, but I've made all sorts of assumptions, and wrong ones at that.

Alina is Nikolai's sister, not his wife. Which means the boy is not her son.

They didn't know he existed until eight months ago.

God, that explains so much. No wonder father and son act like they're strangers to each other—they *are*, for all intents and purposes. And I was right when I sensed a lack of lover-like intimacy between Nikolai and Alina.

They aren't lovers.

They're siblings.

Looking at the two of them now, I don't understand how I could've missed the resemblance—or rather, why the resemblance I did notice didn't clue me in to their familial relationship. Alina's features are a softer, more delicate version of the man sitting in front of me, and though her green eyes lack the deep amber undertones of Nikolai's stunning gaze, the shape of her eyes and eyebrows is the same.

They're clearly, unmistakably siblings.

Which means Nikolai is not married.

Or at least not married to Alina.

"Where is Slava's mother?" I ask, striving for a casual tone. "Is she—"

"She's dead." Nikolai's voice is cold enough to give

frostbite, as is the look he levels at Alina. Turning back to face me, he says evenly, "We had a one-night stand five years ago, and she didn't tell me she was pregnant. I had no idea I had a son until she was killed in a car accident eight months ago, and a friend of hers found a diary naming me as the father."

"Oh, that's..." I swallow. "That must've been very difficult. For you, and especially for Slava." I look at the boy at my side, who's still eating calmly, as if he has no care in the world. But that's not the case at all, I know that now. Nikolai's son has survived one of the biggest tragedies that can befall a child, and however well-adjusted he seems, I have no doubt the loss of his mother has left deep scars on his psyche.

I'm an adult, and I'm having trouble coping with my grief. I can't imagine what it's like for a little boy.

"It was," Alina agrees softly. "In fact, my brother—"

"That's enough." Nikolai's tone is still perfectly level, but I can see the tension in his jaw and shoulders. The topic is an unpleasant one for him, and no wonder. I can't imagine what it must be like to find out you have a child you've never met, to know you've missed the first years of his life.

I have a million questions I want to ask, but I can tell now's not the time to indulge my curiosity. Instead, I reach for more food and spend the next few minutes complimenting the chef—who, it turns out, is indeed the gruff, bear-like Russian.

"Pavel and his wife, Lyudmila, came with us from Moscow," Alina explains as the man-bear himself appears from the kitchen, carrying a large platter of lamb chops surrounded by roasted potatoes with mushrooms. With a grunt, he sets the food on the table, grabs a couple of empty appetizer plates, and disappears back into the kitchen as Alina continues. "Lyudmila is under the weather today, so Pavel is doing all the work. Normally, he does most of the cooking and cleaning, while she serves the food. Her main job, though, is looking after Slava."

"Are they the only two people living here besides your family?" I ask, accepting a lamb chop and a scoop of potatoes with mushrooms when she extends the platter toward me after giving a decent-sized portion to Slava—who again digs in without fuss.

"They're the only people residing in the house with us," Nikolai answers. "The guards have a separate bunker on the north side of the estate."

My heart jumps. "Guards?"

"We have a few men securing the compound," Alina says. "Since we're so isolated out here and all."

I do my best to conceal my reaction. "Yes, of course, that makes sense." Except it doesn't. If anything, the remote location should make it safer. From what I could see on the map, only one road leads up the mountain, and there's already an impenetrable-looking gate there, not to mention that ridiculously tall metal wall.

Only people with powerful, dangerous enemies would think it necessary to hire guards on top of all those measures.

Russian mafia.

The words whisper through my mind again, and my heartbeat intensifies. Lowering my gaze to my plate, I cut into my lamb chop, doing my best to keep my hand steady despite the anxious whirling of my thoughts.

Am I in danger here? Did I jump from the frying pan into the fire? Should I—

"Tell us more about yourself, Chloe."

Nikolai's deep voice cuts into my nervous contemplation, and I look up to find his tiger eyes on me, his lips curved in a sardonic smile. Once again, I have the disconcerting sensation that he's seeing straight into my head, that he knows exactly what I'm thinking and fearing.

Pushing the unsettling feeling away, I smile back. "What would you like to know?"

"Your driver's license says you reside in Boston. Is that where you grew up?"

I nod, spearing a piece of lamb chop. "My mom moved us there from California when I was a baby, and I grew up in and around the Boston area." I bite into the tender, perfectly seasoned meat and again have to give props to Pavel—it's the best lamb chop I've ever had. The potatoes with mushrooms are amazing too, all garlicky and buttery, so good I could eat a pound in a sitting.

"What about your father?" Alina asks when I'm halfway through the lamb chop. "Where is he?"

"I don't know," I say, patting my lips with a napkin. "My mom never told me who he is."

"Why not?" Nikolai's voice sharpens. "Why didn't she tell you?"

I blink, taken aback, until it dawns on me what he must be thinking. "Oh, she didn't hide the pregnancy from him. He knew she was pregnant and chose to walk away." Or at least that's what I've gathered based on the few hints my mom had dropped over the years. For whatever reason, she hated this topic, so much so that whenever I pushed for answers, she'd take to bed with a migraine.

Nikolai's tone softens a fraction. "I see."

"I think he wasn't ready for that kind of responsibility," I say, feeling the need to explain. "My mom was only seventeen when she had me, so I'm guessing he was very young as well."

"You're guessing?" Alina lifts her perfectly shaped eyebrows. "Your mom didn't even tell you his age?"

"She didn't like to talk about it. It was a difficult time in her life." My voice tightens as another wave of grief washes over me, my chest squeezing with an ache so intense I can barely breathe through it.

I miss my mom. I miss her so much it hurts. Though I saw her body with my own eyes, a part of me still can't believe she's dead, can't process the fact that a woman so beautiful and vibrant is gone forever from this world.

"Are you okay, Chloe?" Alina asks softly, and I nod, blinking rapidly to hold back the tears stinging my eyes.

"Are you sure?" she presses, her green gaze filled

with pity, and in a flash of intuition, I realize that she knows—and so does Nikolai, who's watching me with an unreadable expression.

Somehow, they both know my mom is dead.

A rush of adrenaline chases away the grief as my mind leaps into overdrive. There's little doubt now: They had me investigated prior to our interview. That's how Nikolai knew about my lack of posts on social media, and why Alina is looking at me this way.

They know all sorts of things about me, including the fact that I lied to them by omission.

Thinking fast, I give a visible swallow and look down at my plate. "My mom…" I let my voice break, like it wants to. "She died a month ago." Allowing the tears to flood my eyes, I look up, meeting Nikolai's gaze. "That's another reason I decided to go on the road trip. I needed some time to process things."

His eyes glint a darker shade of gold. "My deepest condolences for your loss."

"Thank you." I wipe away the moisture on my cheeks. "I'm sorry I didn't mention it earlier. It's not something I felt comfortable casually bringing up in an interview." Especially since my mom was killed and the men who did it are after me. I really hope Nikolai doesn't know about *that*.

Then again, he wouldn't have hired me if he did. It's not the sort of thing you want around your family.

"I'm very sorry for your loss," Alina says, a genuine expression of sympathy on her face. "That must've been difficult for you, losing your only parent. Do you have any other family? Grandparents, aunts, cousins?"

"No. My mom was adopted from an orphanage in Cambodia by an American missionary couple. They were killed in a car accident when she was ten, and none of their family wanted her, so she grew up in foster care."

"So you're all alone now," Nikolai murmurs, and I nod, the squeezing ache in my chest returning.

Growing up, I'd never minded the lack of extended family. Mom had given me all the love and support I could've wished for. But now that she's gone, now that it's no longer the two of us against the world, I'm painfully aware that I don't have anyone to rely on.

The friends I'd made in school and college are busy with their own, infinitely less fucked-up lives.

Realizing I'm drifting dangerously close to self-pity, I pull my gaze away from Nikolai's probing stare and turn my attention to the child at my side. He's finished his potatoes and is now industriously working on his lamb chop, his little face the very picture of concentration as he struggles to cut a bite-sized piece of meat using a fork and knife that someone left by his plate. Not a dull bread knife, either, I realize with a jolt.

An actual sharp steak knife.

"Here, darling, let me," I say, grabbing it from him before he can slice off his fingers. "This is—"

"Something he needs to learn how to handle," Nikolai says, reaching across the table to take the knife from me. His fingers brush over mine as he clasps the handle, and I feel it like an electric shock, the warmth of his skin igniting an answering furnace inside me. My insides tighten, my breath quickening, and it's all I can do not to yank back my hand as if scalded.

At least he's not married, an insidious little voice whispers in my head, and I shush it with vengeance.

Married or not, he's still my employer and thus strictly off-limits.

Biting my lip, I watch him hand the knife back to the child, who resumes his dangerous task.

"You're not worried he'll cut himself?" I can't keep the judgment out of my voice as I stare at the little fingers wrapped around a potentially lethal weapon. Slava is handling the knife with a reasonable degree of skill and dexterity, but he's still too young to be dealing with something so sharp.

"If he does, he'll know better next time," Nikolai says. "Life doesn't come with a safety lock."

"But he's only *four*."

"Four and eight months," Alina says as the boy succeeds in cutting a piece of lamb chop and, looking pleased with himself, forks it into his mouth. "His birthday's in November."

I'm tempted to keep arguing with them, but it's my first day and I've already pushed the envelope more than is wise. So I keep my mouth shut and focus on my food to avoid looking at the child wielding a knife next to me… or his callous, yet dangerously attractive father.

Unfortunately, said father keeps looking at me.

Each time I lift my gaze from my plate, I find his mesmerizing eyes on me and my heartbeat jumps, my hand tingling at the recollection of what it felt like to have his fingers brush against mine.

This is bad.

So bad.

Why is he looking at me like that?

He can't be attracted to me as well… can he?

10

NIKOLAI

If there was any doubt in my mind that I'm going to enjoy unraveling the mystery that is Chloe, it's gone by the time Pavel brings out dessert. Everything about her fascinates me, from the mixture of truth and lies falling so easily from her lips to the way she delicately and politely devours enough food to feed two NFL linebackers. And underneath my fascination is a primal attraction more powerful than anything I've experienced. I've never wanted a woman this much, and with so little provocation. She's not flirting, not doing anything to get my attention, yet from the moment I took my seat across from her, I've been hard, the sight of her plush lips closing around a fork turning me on more than the most erotic strip show in Moscow.

Even talking about Ksenia and the way she fucked me over with Slava couldn't cool the fire burning inside me.

"This has to be the most delicious thing I've ever had," Chloe says after trying a forkful of the Napoleon dessert, and I murmur my agreement, though I can barely taste the multilayered puff-pastry cake. My mind is occupied by how *she* will taste and feel when I take her to bed.

I have a feeling my son's new tutor will be the most delicious thing *I've* ever had.

"Don't, Kolya," Alina says quietly in Russian when Chloe turns to Slava and begins teaching him the English word for *cake*. "Please, I beg you, leave her be."

I glance at my sister in irritation. "I'm not going to force her." That's not my MO, and besides, after watching the girl sneak glances at me for the past hour, I'm even more sure this attraction goes both ways.

She'll be mine. It's only a matter of time.

"I'm beginning to think you may be worse than he was," Alina says in a low voice. "At least he tried to justify it with bullshit excuses. But you don't even try, do you? You just do whatever the fuck you want, regardless of who gets hurt in the process."

"That's right." I give her a hard smile. "And you'll do well to remember that."

If my sister thinks that comparing me to our father is going to change anything, she couldn't be more wrong. I know I'm like him. I always have been—which is why I never intended to have children.

Our little exchange in Russian catches Chloe's attention, and her eyes meet mine as she glances over at me. Immediately, she looks away, but not before I see her smooth throat move in a nervous swallow as her tongue flicks out to moisten her bottom lip.

Oh, yes, she's attracted to me. Attracted and worried about that fact.

I push away my half-eaten dessert and pick up my cup of tea to take a long sip. Catching her gaze again, I set the cup down and give her a slow, deliberate smile. "So, what did you think of your first Russian meal, Chloe?"

"It was amazing." Her voice is a touch breathless. "Pavel is a wonderful cook."

I let my smile deepen. "He is, isn't he?" He's even more skilled at other things, like knifework, but I'm not about to tell her that. She's already putting two and two together and coming up with four. I could see the way she reacted when I mentioned the guards. She suspects we're not just a wealthy family, and that makes her almost as nervous as her attraction to me.

I wonder if it's the natural wariness of a sheltered civilian, or if there's something more to it… like whatever secrets she's trying to hide.

The smart thing, the prudent thing, would've been to uncover those secrets before hiring her, but that would've taken time, and I didn't want to chance her slipping away and disappearing. Besides, after observing her throughout the meal, I'm even more convinced she doesn't pose a physical threat to my family. The way she snatched the knife from Slava betrayed not only her overprotectiveness of the boy but also her lack of skill with a blade. She held the knife like someone who's never used it as a weapon, either of the offensive or defensive variety, and I doubt that was an act—not when her fear for Slava was entirely real.

She thinks my son, a Molotov, needs to be protected from something as innocuous as a sharp blade.

The inexplicable tightness in my chest returns, and it takes all my strength not to glance at the boy. If I do, it'll only get worse. Instead, I keep my focus on Chloe and the way her lashes lower in response to my smile, her chest rising and falling in a faster rhythm. Her nipples are hard again, I note with savage satisfaction; whatever bra she's wearing under her shirt, if any, is quite revealing.

I can't wait to see her in a nice designer dress, her slender shoulders bared. Something slinky and cream-colored, to highlight the warm hue of her skin. She'll put it on for me before dinner, and I'll spend the entire meal fantasizing how I'll rip it off her later that night—not that I need her dressed in any particular way for those fantasies to manifest in my mind.

The cheap T-shirt and jeans she's wearing work for that purpose just fine.

"You should feel free to go to bed, Chloe," Alina says when Pavel brings out a tray with digestifs, then helps Slava out of his chair and takes him upstairs to get him ready for bed. "Don't feel compelled to stay here with us. I'm sure you're tired after such a long day."

"And I'm sure she can stay for a drink," I say before

Chloe can do more than give Alina a grateful smile. There's no way I'm letting the girl escape so quickly. "In fact," I continue, giving my sister a hard look, "weren't you saying *you're* tired? Maybe you should join Pavel in reading Slava a bedtime story and head to bed early yourself."

Alina wants to argue with me, I can see it, but even she knows it's not a good idea to push me further right now. She's become bolder since we left Moscow, freer with her sharp tongue. She thinks that because I temporarily handed over the reins to our brothers, I've softened, but she couldn't be more wrong.

The beast inside me is alive and well… and focused on a sweet new quarry.

"All right," she says after a tense moment. "In that case, good night. Enjoy your drink."

She gets up, and Chloe follows her example. "I think I will—"

"Sit," I say with a commanding gesture, and the girl sinks back down, blinking like a startled fawn as Alina strolls away with one final glare in my direction.

I wait until she's gone before gracing my quarry with a smile. "So tell me, Chloe…" I reach for the decanters on the tray. "Do you prefer cognac, brandy, or whiskey for your digestif?"

11

CHLOE

I STARE AT NIKOLAI, MY HEART THUDDING HEAVILY. AM I misreading the situation, or did he engineer it so we'd end up alone at the table?

"I… don't really drink," I say, my throat dry. The look in his richly colored eyes again makes me feel like a mouse trapped by a very large cat—except no mouse would feel such a pull toward a predatory feline.

I want to touch him almost as much as I want to run away.

He arches his dark eyebrows. "No alcohol ever? I find that hard to believe."

"That's not what I meant. It's just, you know, usually beer or wine at a party…" My voice trails off as he lifts one of the crystal decanters and pours two fingers' worth of amber-colored liquid into a whiskey glass, then slides it toward me.

"Try this. It's one of the finest cognacs in the world."

I hesitantly lift the glass and sniff its contents. I've

never actually had cognac. Vodka shots a bunch of times, yes. Tequila on a few memorable occasions, for sure. But not cognac—and judging by the strong liquor fumes hitting my nostrils, it's not something I should drink around Nikolai tonight or on any other night.

Not when I'm so confused about what's happening between us.

He pours himself a glass as well. "To our new partnership." He lifts the drink in a toast, and I have no choice but to clink my glass against his. Bringing it to my lips, I take a sip—and break into a coughing fit, my eyes watering as my throat and chest ignite with fire.

Damn, this stuff is *strong*.

Nikolai watches me, dark amusement glimmering in his gaze. "You really aren't much of a drinker," he says when I've finally caught my breath. "Try it again, but slower this time. Let it sit in your mouth for a few seconds before you swallow it. Absorb the taste, the texture… the burn."

This is a bad idea, I know, but I follow his instructions, taking another sip and holding it for a bit before letting it go down my throat. It still scorches my esophagus, but not as much as the first time, and in the wake of the fiery sensation, a pleasant warmth spreads through my limbs.

"Better?" he inquires softly, and I nod, unable to tear my gaze away from his hypnotic stare. Maybe it's the alcohol already messing with my inhibitions, or the fact that we're all alone, but this feels oddly like a date… like there's a sense of intimacy building between us. I want to reach across the table and trace the sensual curve of his lips, to lay my hand on top of his broad palm and feel its strength and warmth.

I want him to kiss me, and if I'm not misjudging the simmering heat in his eyes, that may be what he wants as well.

"Why did you ask me to stay for a drink?"

I want to take the words back as soon as they leave my mouth, but it's too late. A sardonic smile appears on his face, and he tips his head to one side, indolently swirling the cognac inside his glass. "Why do you think?"

"I don't..." I wet my lips. "I don't know."

"But if you had to venture a guess?"

My heartbeat kicks up higher. There's no way I can say what I'm thinking. If I'm wrong, this will go very poorly for me. In fact, I don't see how this could go well for me. If I'm right and he's attracted to me, that opens an enormous can of worms. And if I imagined it—

"Don't overthink it, *zaychik*." His voice is deceptively gentle. "This isn't one of your school exams."

Right. And I'd much rather it were—because then the only thing I'd have to worry about is a failing grade. The stakes are infinitely higher here. If I get this wrong, if I upset him, I could lose the job, and with it, any hope of safety.

Out there, beyond the confines of this estate, are monsters hunting me, and in here is a man who may be just as dangerous… and not just because he seems to enjoy playing this sadistic little game with me.

"What does that mean?" I ask cautiously. "Zay-something?"

"Zaychik?" Darkness glimmers in his smile. "It means *little hare*. A Russian endearment of sorts."

My face heats, my pulse taking on an uneven rhythm. The odds that I'm wrong are decreasing by the moment, and that makes me even more nervous. I'm no virgin, but I've never dated anyone remotely like this man. My boyfriends in college were precisely that—boys who started off as my friends—and I have no idea how to handle this dangerously magnetic stranger who's also my boss.

And who may be in the mafia.

It's the last thought that brings much needed clarity to the contradictory tangle of emotions in my head.

Steadying my jangling nerves, I rise to my feet. "Thank you for the dinner and the drink. If you don't mind, I'll go to bed now. Alina's right—it's been a long day."

For two long heartbeats, he doesn't say anything, just watches me with that mocking smile, and my anxiety spikes, my stomach tying itself into knots. But then he sets down his glass and says softly, "Sleep well, Chloe. I'll see you tomorrow morning."

And just like that, I'm free—and equal parts relieved and disappointed.

12

NIKOLAI

I toss and turn for two hours, trying to fall asleep, but nothing happens. Finally, I give up and just lie there, staring at the dark ceiling, my muscles tight and my cock hard and aching despite the relief I gave it with my fist.

What is it about this girl that's getting to me? Her looks? The mystery she represents? It was all I could do to let her go this evening, to back off and allow her to go to bed instead of reaching across the table to pull her to me.

What would she have done if I'd acted on that impulse?

Would she have stiffened, screamed… or would she have melted against me, her brown eyes turning soft and hazy, her lips parting for my kiss?

Swearing under my breath, I get up, throw on a robe, and walk over to my computer. It's late morning in Moscow, so I might as well catch up with my brothers on some business.

Anything is better than dwelling on Chloe and the frustrating ache in my balls.

Konstantin doesn't pick up my video call, so I try Valery. My younger brother answers right away, his face as smooth and expressionless as always. Despite the four-year difference between us, we look enough alike to be mistaken for twins—and often are, along with our older brother, Konstantin, and our cousin, Roman.

Molotov genes are a potent, toxic thing.

"Missing us already?" Valery's tone betrays nothing of his emotions—if he has any, that is. It's possible my brother feels as little as he shows. I've never seen him lose his temper, even as a child, and I've certainly never seen him cry. Then again, I was away at boarding school throughout most of his childhood, so I can't claim to be a Valery expert.

We're not close, my brothers and I; our father had ensured that.

"Did you get the sign-off on the manufacturing plant?" I ask in lieu of a reply. "Or is that still pending?"

Valery regards me with an unblinking stare. "It's on the President's desk as we speak. He promised to get it back to me by tomorrow."

"Good." It's a deal I worked on for several months before leaving Moscow, and I want to make sure it goes through. "What about the tax credit bill?"

"Progressing as hoped." My brother tilts his head.

"Why the late-night call? All this could've waited until tomorrow."

I shrug. "Just having some trouble sleeping."

Valery's gaze sharpens. "Something to do with Slava?"

"No." At least not in the way he thinks. "Where's Konstantin?" I want his team to do a deeper dive on Chloe Emmons, with a specific focus on the past month.

I need to know what she did and where she went while she was off the grid.

"Berlin," Valery answers. "Acquiring more servers."

"Again?"

It's his turn to shrug. In my absence, my brothers have divided up the responsibilities according to their interests and strengths, with technology falling squarely into Konstantin's domain. Not that it had ever been otherwise; even when we were in elementary school, our older brother could run circles around the nation's top programmers. The main difference now is Valery stays out of Konstantin's business, letting him do as he will, whereas when I headed up the family organization, I oversaw everything, Konstantin's dark web ventures included.

"Fine," I say. "I'll get in touch with him there. Now fill me in on the rest of it."

And Valery does. By the time we end the call, I feel like I'm back in the loop—or at least as much in the loop as I can be while being half a world away. So much of our business takes place in person, at the galas and opera houses and high-end restaurants frequented by the power brokers of Eastern Europe. You can't subtly bribe a politician over email, can't intimidate a supplier into giving you a discount over Skype. It's all about rubbing elbows with the right people, being in the right place at the right time—and not leaving traces, digital or otherwise, if you have to cross a line to get things done.

Shutting down my laptop, I throw off the robe and stride over to the window, where a half-moon caught partially behind a cloud provides just enough illumination to make out the tops of the trees on the mountainside. I'm still tense, every muscle in my body coiled tight. The call distracted me, as hoped, but now that it's over, I'm thinking about Chloe again. Wanting her again.

Fuck.

Maybe I shouldn't have let her leave the table. I enjoyed her nervousness, the wariness in her pretty brown eyes. She reminded me of a wild hare, ready to flee at the first sign of danger, and I wanted to chase her if she did.

But I didn't. I let her go. She looked tired, and not the kind of tired one gets from undersleeping for a night or two. It was exhaustion, deep-seated and total. Her clothes were loose on her, as if she's recently lost weight, and her delicate features were sharper than in the pictures, her eyes ringed by deep shadows. Whatever happened to her has brought her to the brink of a collapse, and at that moment, when she stood up from her seat, so fragile and brave, I felt a strange urge to comfort her… to protect her from whatever demons had etched those signs of strain into her face.

No, that's idiotic. I hardly know the girl. I didn't want to push her to the breaking point, that's all.

Walking over to my closet, I pull on a pair of running shorts and sneakers and head out of the room. Maybe it's just as well that I let her be tonight. Tomorrow, I'll get in touch with Konstantin and begin the process of uncovering her secrets. In the meantime, it doesn't hurt to let her rest, get her bearings… acclimate to the idea that I want her.

No matter what my cock thinks, there's no rush.

After all, she's here now, and she's not going anywhere.

13

CHLOE

"No!"

I land on all fours, panting, my entire body trembling and covered in sweat. It's dark and I'm naked, and I have no idea where I am or what's happening. Then I register the feel of the hardwood floor under my palms and the faint moonlight pouring in through the wall-sized window, and it all clicks into place.

I'm in my room at the Molotov estate, and none of what I saw is real.

It was another nightmare.

Wincing, I push up to my knees—which immediately scream in protest. I must've bruised them when I threw myself off the bed.

Slender brown arm in a pool of blood... Gun in a black-gloved hand... Huge pickup truck barreling toward me...

A fresh surge of adrenaline propels me to my feet

despite the pain. Sucking in air, I fumble in the darkness for a lamp switch. My hand lands on the bed, and I feel my way over to the nightstand.

The bedside lamp comes on at my touch, illuminating the room with a soft golden glow. My knees buckle with relief, and I sink onto the mattress, letting the light push away the lingering bits and pieces of the nightmare.

It was just a dream.

I'm safe.

They can't get to me here.

After a couple of minutes, I feel steady enough to stand, and I walk over to the bathroom to rinse off the sweat drying on my skin. Before doing so, I flick off the lamp, as I ran out of clean clothes to sleep in but couldn't figure out how to work the blinds on the window. There's probably a button hidden somewhere, but I was too tired to find it last night. As soon as I got to my room, I stripped off my clothes, hand-washed my shirt and underwear in the sink so I'd have something clean to wear in the morning, and passed out the second my head hit the pillow.

Even worries about my disturbingly attractive employer couldn't keep me awake.

Now, though, as I stand in the shower, my mind turns to him, and my heartbeat revs up, my breath quickening with a mixture of anxiety and excitement.

Nikolai wants me.

I think.

Maybe.

I could be wrong.

Or… not.

Heat pools low in my belly, my breasts tightening as I picture the darkly intent look in his eyes and replay the things he said… and how he said them. No, I'm not wrong. At least not about his attraction to me. It's possible he was just toying with me and has no intention of acting on said attraction, but I don't think so.

I think he intends to fuck me, and I have no idea how I feel about that.

Actually, that's a lie. My mind might be torn, but my body is very straightforward in its feelings. The heat inside me intensifies, an aching tightness coiling deep inside my core as I imagine what it would be like if he came up to my room at this very moment and knocked on my door… then, not getting a response, opened it and walked in.

If he was sitting on the bed, waiting, when I came out of the bathroom naked.

My eyes drift shut, my hands cupping my breasts, then sliding down my body as I picture him standing up and walking toward me… reaching out to touch me. My fingers slip between my thighs, where I'm slick and aching, and I imagine it's his hand, his cruelly sensual mouth down there. My breath hitches as the ache transforms into a heated throb, my leg muscles quivering with rising tension, and with a sudden burst of sensation, I come, my toes curling on the wet tiles as I lean against the glass wall of the stall, gasping for air.

Stunned, I open my eyes and pull my hand away, my heart racing madly in my chest.

I can't believe what's just happened. I've never been able to orgasm this way before, with only my fingers. Normally, I need a minimum of fifteen minutes with my vibrator—or for a guy to go down on me for a half hour—and even then, it's hit or miss, depending on how stressed or tired I am. Arousal is very much a mental thing for me, which is why I've never gone for casual hookups.

I have to know a man to get intimate with him.

I have to like and trust him.

Or at least that's what I'd always thought. I have no idea if I like Nikolai, and I certainly don't trust him.

So why does the mere thought of him bring me to the brink of orgasm?

Why am I drawn to a man who makes me feel like hunted prey?

The light falling on my face pulls me out of a sound sleep, and I groan, rolling over to escape it. But it's everywhere, bright and warm, and it dawns on me that it must be morning, even if it doesn't feel like it.

Forcing open my heavy eyelids, I sit up and rub my face. Though I went right back to sleep after my impromptu masturbation session, I still feel tired, as if

I've gotten only a few hours of shut-eye instead of the nine or ten I must've actually snoozed for. I have no idea what time it is now, but I'm pretty sure I went to bed before ten.

Must be all those sleepless weeks catching up with me.

Swinging my legs to the floor, I take in the gorgeous view outside the window. Despite the bright sunlight, traces of fog envelop the distant mountain peaks, and the whole thing looks like something out of a postcard. I'm tempted to sit and enjoy it for a minute, but I make myself get up and head into the bathroom to wash up. It's my first morning on the job, and I don't want to make a bad impression by showing up late. Not that I know what "late" is—we didn't discuss my work hours or Slava's schedule yesterday.

I'm clean from my nighttime shower, so my morning routine takes mere minutes. The shirt and underwear I hand-washed are still a little damp, but I throw them on anyway and make a mental note to talk to Pavel or someone about the laundry situation as soon as possible. Also, about my hours.

I need to understand what Nikolai's expectations are, so I can meet and exceed them.

My pulse begins to race at the thought of him, and I focus on gathering my hair into a bun to distract myself from the increasingly active butterflies in my stomach. I went to bed with my hair wet, so it's got all sorts of weird kinks in it, and in any case, it's more professional to keep my hair off my face.

Returning to the bedroom, I make the bed, pull on my sneakers, and square my shoulders.

I can do this.

I have to do this, no matter how my new boss makes me feel.

14

CHLOE

I DON'T SEE ANYONE IN THE DINING OR LIVING ROOM downstairs, so I walk around until I find the kitchen. Walking in, I see a curvy woman with bleached blond hair cut in a short, poufy bob. Dressed in a flowery pink-and-white dress, she's bent over a sink, washing a plate, so I clear my throat to warn her of my presence.

"Hi," I say with a smile when she turns around, drying her hands on a towel. "You must be Lyudmila."

She stares at me, then bobs her head. "Lyudmila, yes. You Slava teacher?" Her Russian accent is even thicker than her husband's, and her round, rosy-cheeked face reminds me of a painted matryoshka doll, one of those that have other dolls inside, like onion layers. I'm guessing she's in her mid-to-late thirties, though her skin is so smooth she could easily pass for ten years younger.

"Yes, hi. I'm Chloe." Approaching, I extend my hand. "It's nice to meet you."

She clasps my fingers cautiously and gives my hand a brief shake as I ask, "Do you know where Slava is, and if he's already had breakfast?"

She blinks uncomprehendingly, so I repeat the question, being careful to enunciate every word.

"Ah, yes, Slava." She points at the big window to my left, which turns out to look out over the front of the house, where I parked my car. Only the car isn't there. I frown, then realize Pavel must've re-parked it yesterday, when he brought up my suitcase.

I'll have to ask him where it is, along with my car keys. I don't think they ever gave them back to me.

Before I can pose the question to Lyudmila, I spot my young student. He's scampering up the driveway, with Pavel on his heels. The man-bear is carrying a huge fish on a hook, and the boy has an equally big smile on his face. The two of them must've done some early-morning fishing.

I steal a glance at the clock on the microwave and wince.

Nope, not early-morning. More like mid-morning.

It's nearly ten.

My stomach growls, as if on cue, and a smile splits Lyudmila's round face. "Eat?" she asks, and I nod, smiling back ruefully.

At least my stomach speaks a universal language.

"Is it okay if I take something?" I ask, gesturing at the refrigerator, but Lyudmila bustles over there herself and takes out a platter of what looks like stuffed crepes.

"This good?" she asks, and I nod gratefully. Picky eater I'm not, and if those crepes are anything like the delicious Russian food I had last night, I'm going to be in seventh heaven.

"Thank you," I say, walking over to take the plate from her, but she pops it into the microwave and gestures at the counter behind the sink.

"Go. Sit. I make for you."

I thank her again and sit down on one of the bar stools behind the counter. I don't want to be a burden, but with the language barrier, my polite protest might be misinterpreted as refusal or dislike.

"Tea? Coffee?" she asks.

"Coffee, please. With milk and sugar if you have it."

She gets busy making it, and I look around the kitchen. It's as modern as the rest of the house, with glossy white cabinets, gray quartz countertops, and black stainless-steel appliances. Part of the big kitchen island in the middle is occupied with a long row of potted herbs, and a wine rack with a variety of bottles hangs artfully above them.

The microwave pings after a minute, and Lyudmila brings the platter of crepes over to me, along with a clean plate, utensils, and a jar of honey.

"Wow, thank you," I say as she plates one of the crepes for me, drizzles honey onto it, and then mimes for me to cut and eat it. "That looks amazing."

I cut a piece of the crepe and examine its contents. It looks like ricotta cheese with raisins, and when I fork the bite into my mouth, I find it both sweet and savory—and even more delicious than I expected. My stomach growls again, louder, and Lyudmila grins at the sound.

"You like?"

"Oh, yes, thank you. This is so good," I mumble, my mouth already full with the second bite, and Lyudmila nods, satisfied.

"Good. You eat. So small." She moves her hands in the air, as if measuring the size of my waist, and tsk-tsks disapprovingly. "Too small."

I laugh uncomfortably and apply myself to the food as she goes back to doing the dishes. It's funny, her blunt criticism of my figure, but also true. I've always been slim, but after a month of sporadic meals, I've become downright skinny, the muscles on my body melting away along with what little fat I had. Even the booty I'd once deemed too prominent is barely there now; I'll probably have to do a million squats to get it back.

Which I will, once all of this is over.

If it's ever over.

No, not if. I refuse to think that way. I've come this far, eluding my pursuers against all odds, and now things are looking up. For the first time since this nightmare began, I've slept the whole night, I have a full belly, and I'm somewhere they can't ambush me. And in six days, I'll have my first paycheck, and with it, more options—including leaving here, if that's what I need to do to be safe.

If the darkness I sensed in Nikolai is anything more than a product of my imagination.

In this bright, sunlit kitchen, my fears about mafia feel overblown, irrational, as does my conclusion that he wants me. As Lyudmila pointed out, I hardly look my best, and I'm sure a man as rich and gorgeous as my employer is used to world-class beauties. The more I think about it, the more it seems my attraction to him might've led me to misinterpret the situation last night. The pet name, the probing questions, the low, seductive tone of his voice—it could've all been a case of cultural differences. I don't know much about Russian men, but it's possible they're always that way with women—just as it's possible that wealthy Russians are used to having guards due to high levels of corruption and crime in their country.

Yes, that's probably it. With all the stress of the past month, I've let my imagination run wild. Why would a mafia family settle here, in this remote wilderness? New York, sure; Boston, very likely. But Idaho? That makes no sense.

Shaking my head at my foolishness, I polish off the rest of the crepes and drink the coffee Lyudmila made. Then, feeling upbeat and hopeful for the first time in weeks, I get up, bring the dishes to the sink—where Lyudmila takes them despite my protests—and head out to find my student.

I can do this.

I really can.

In fact, I'm looking forward to it.

I'm rounding the corner to the living room, walking fast, when I run smack into a large, hard body. The impact knocks the air from my lungs and nearly sends me flying, but before I can fall, strong hands close around my upper arms, hauling me against said body.

Stunned, completely out of breath, I look up at my captor—and my heartbeat goes through the stratosphere as I meet Nikolai's tiger-bright gaze.

"Good morning, zaychik," he murmurs, his beautiful mouth curved in a mocking smile. "Where are you off to in such a rush?"

15

CHLOE

EVERY CELL IN MY BODY IGNITES WITH HEAT, MY PULSE jumping impossibly higher. My lower body is flush against his, my thighs pressed against the hard columns of his legs and my stomach molded against his groin. I can smell his cologne, something subtle and complex, with notes of cedar and bergamot, and underneath, the clean musk of warm male skin. And it *is* warm. Even with us both fully dressed, I can feel his animal heat—and, to my shock, the growing hardness pressing into my belly.

"Are you okay?" he murmurs, and I realize I'm staring up at him dazedly, like a rabbit caught in a trap. Which is pretty much how I feel. His long fingers completely encircle my upper arms, his grip unbreakable. And he's huge. Up until this moment, I hadn't realized just how tall and muscular he is. I'm of average height for a woman, but he dwarfs me in every way—and judging by the thickness of the bulge pressed against me, he's consistently big all over.

My skin heats another thousand degrees, and my insides contract on a sudden empty ache. "I'm… I'm fine." Only I sound anything but fine, my choked voice betraying my agitation. I can't think, can't process anything except the fact that his erection is pressing against me, and for whatever reason, he's not letting go of me.

He's holding me against him as if he might *never* let go, his gaze growing more intent by the second. Slowly, as if drawn by a magnet, his eyes move down to my lips and—

"Kolya." Alina's voice is tight. "Konstantin wants to talk to you."

Nikolai stiffens and raises his head, his fingers tightening on my arms to the point of pain. An involuntary gasp escapes my throat, and he loosens his grip—but still doesn't release me.

"Tell him I'll call him back," he tells his sister. His tone is cool and even, as if we were all sitting at a table instead of him holding me like we're about to tango. My face, on the other hand, is burning with embarrassment.

I can't even imagine what Alina's thinking right now.

"He wants to speak to you right away," she insists. "He's going into a meeting in a few minutes and will be busy afterward."

Nikolai mutters what sounds like a Russian curse

and finally releases me. Shaken, I stumble back on unsteady legs and turn to face Alina, who's watching her brother stalk off with a narrowed stare. Then her gaze swings to me, and her full red lips tighten.

"I ran into him," I blurt before she can accuse me of anything. "It was an accident. I would've fallen, but he—"

"My brother doesn't do accidents." Her eyes are like jade dipped in ice. "You'd do well to remember that, Chloe."

And with that, she walks off, leaving me more shaken than before.

After a few minutes, I've composed myself enough to resume my search for Slava—this time, at a much more sedate walking pace. When I get to his room, however, he's not there, so I go back downstairs to look for him.

I don't see him or Pavel in any of the common areas, so I return to the kitchen, hoping to find Lyudmila there. But she's also gone.

Maybe they're all outside?

Opening the front door, I step out into the bright sunlight. It's a gorgeous, cloudless day, the forest-scented breeze cool and refreshing on my face. Nobody's on the driveway, but I walk out there anyway, drawing lungfuls of fresh mountain air to further calm myself.

There's no reason to freak out.

Nothing happened.

Nikolai caught me when I would've fallen, that's all.

Except… something could've happened if Alina hadn't interrupted. I'm ninety percent sure Nikolai had been about to kiss me. And I definitely didn't imagine the hard bulge pressed against me.

He does want me.

There's no longer any doubt about that.

I take another deep breath, but my heart continues to pound, my palms sweating like crazy. Wiping them on my jeans, I walk around the side of the house, taking in mountain views in an effort to calm my racing thoughts.

It's fine. Everything's fine. Just because Nikolai is attracted to me doesn't mean anything is going to happen between us. I'm sure he realizes how inappropriate the whole thing is. No matter what Alina said, it *was* an accident, us bumping into each other. I don't know why she would imply otherwise. Maybe she thinks I was coming on to him? But no. It seemed almost as if she was warning me away from him, as if—

The sound of voices catches my attention, and as I round the corner, I see Pavel and Slava. They're standing by a tree stump some fifty feet away, with the big fish laid on top of it. As I approach, I see the man-bear slice it open halfway, then hand the sharp-looking knife to Slava.

What the hell? Is he expecting the child to finish the job?

He is. And Slava does. By the time I get there, the

boy is scooping out fish innards with his little hands and throwing them into a plastic bag Pavel is helpfully holding open for him.

Okay then. I guess they know what they're doing. I've cleaned fish a few times myself—my freshman-year roommate, a fishing-and-hunting enthusiast, taught me how—so I'm not grossed out, but it is unsettling to see a four-year-old doing it.

They're *really* not worried about him with knives.

Stopping in front of the stump, I put on my brightest smile. "Good morning. Mind if I join you?"

The boy grins up at me and rattles off something in Russian. Pavel, however, looks less than pleased to see me. "We're almost done," he growls in his thickly accented voice. "You can wait in the house if you want."

"Oh, no, I'm fine out here. Do you need any help with that?" I gesture toward the fish.

Pavel glowers at me. "You know how to remove scales?"

"I do." I'd actually rather not do it, lest I get my only clean clothes dirty, but I want to continue teaching Slava, and the best way to do that is to spend time with him, engaged in whatever activities he's doing.

In my experience, children learn best outside of a classroom—and so do most adults.

"Here then." Pavel thrusts a descaling knife at me. "Show the kid how to do it."

Judging by the smirk on his brick-like face, he thinks I'm bluffing—which is why it gives me great pleasure to take the knife from him and say sweetly, "Okay."

Taking care not to get any splatters on my shirt, I get to work, explaining to the boy the entire time what I'm doing and how. I tell him what every part of the fish is called and make him repeat the words, then let him try the descaling himself. He's as good at it as he was at the slicing, and I realize he's done it before.

When Pavel told me to show him, he was just testing me.

Hiding my annoyance, I let Slava finish the job and put the cleaned fish back into the bucket. Pavel carries it into the house, and Slava and I follow. The man-bear goes straight for the kitchen—probably to prepare the fish for lunch—and I tell him I'm taking Slava upstairs to get changed. Unlike me, the boy has fishy splatters all over his shirt.

Pavel grunts something affirmative before disappearing into the kitchen, and I shepherd Slava into the nearest bathroom. We both thoroughly wash our hands, and then I lead Slava up to his room.

To my surprise, Lyudmila is there when we walk in, presciently laying out a clean shirt and jeans for Slava on the bed.

"Thank you," I say with a smile. "He's in dire need of a change."

She smiles back and says something to Slava in Russian. He walks over to her, and she helps him out of the dirty clothes. I tactfully turn my back—the boy is old enough to be shy in front of strangers. When it seems like they're done, I turn around and find Lyudmila helping him with the buckle of his belt.

"All good," she announces after a moment, stepping back. "You teach now."

I grin at her. "Thank you, I will." Seeing her gather Slava's dirty clothes, I ask, "Is there a washing machine somewhere in the house? I need to do laundry."

She frowns, not understanding.

"Laundry." I point at the pile of clothes in her hands. "You know, to wash clothes?" I rub my fists together, mimicking someone doing laundry by hand.

Her face clears. "Ah, yes. Come."

"I'll be right back," I tell Slava and follow Lyudmila downstairs. She takes me past the kitchen and down a hallway to a windowless room about the size of my bedroom. There are two fancy washers and dryers—I guess to run multiple loads at once—along with an ironing board, a drying rack, laundry baskets, and other conveniences.

"This, yes?" She points at the machines, and I nod, thanking her. Returning to my room, I gather all my clothes and bring them down. Lyudmila is gone by then, so I begin loading the washers. In a half hour, I'll come down again to move the clothes over to the dryers, and by dinnertime, everything will be clean.

Things really are looking up, the situation with my boss notwithstanding.

My heart rate speeds up at the thought, the butterflies in my stomach roaring back to life. Slava and Pavel provided a much-needed distraction, but now that I'm away from them, I can't help thinking about what happened. My mind cycles through everything, over and over, until the butterflies turn into wasps.

I felt Nikolai's erection against me.

He looked like he was about to kiss me.

He didn't let go of me when his sister was there.

It's that last part that freaks me out the most, because it means I was wrong. He does intend to act on this attraction. If Alina hadn't insisted he take the call, he would've kissed me, and maybe more. Maybe at this very moment, we'd be in bed together, with his powerful body driving into me as—

I stop the fantasy before it can progress any further. Already, I feel overly warm, my breasts full and tight, my sex pulsing with a coiling ache. It must be some weird aftermath of my impromptu masturbation session last night; that's the only explanation for why I've suddenly acquired the libido of a teenage boy.

Taking slow, deep breaths to calm myself, I finish loading the laundry. The situation is undoubtedly tricky. An affair with my employer would be unwise on many levels, yet I'm less than certain of my ability to resist him. If I go up in flames merely thinking about him, what would it be like if he touched me? Kissed me?

Would my self-control evaporate like water on a frying pan?

There's only one solution I can see, only one thing I can do to prevent this disaster.

I have to avoid him—or at least, being alone with him—for the next six days.

Thus resolved, I set the washers to run, and turn around—only to freeze in place.

Standing in the doorway, golden eyes gleaming and mouth curved in a devastating smile, is the very devil who occupies my thoughts.

"There you are," he says softly, and as I watch, paralyzed in shock, he steps deeper into the room and shuts the door.

16

CHLOE

"I WAS LOOKING FOR YOU," NIKOLAI CONTINUES, approaching with a panther-soft stride. "Pavel said you were upstairs with Slava."

I swallow hard as he stops in front of me. "Yes, I just came down here for a moment to throw in some laundry. I hope that's okay." Despite my best efforts, my voice wavers, and it's all I can do not to step back in an effort to put more space between us. Not that he's overly close—at least three feet separate us—but now that I know the smell of his cologne, I can pick up the subtle cedar and bergamot notes in the air, and my memory fills in the rest, from the heat coming off his skin to the hard contours of his body pressing against me. And that big, thick bulge… My knees wobble, and I almost sway toward him but catch myself at the last moment, stiffening my legs and spine.

A dark heat invades his gaze, and I know he's

noticed my reaction. My cheeks burn and my heart hammers faster, icy-hot prickles running over my skin.

Why is he here?

Why was he looking for me?

Why did he shut that door?

"Yes, of course, that's not a problem." His voice is soft and deep, that unsettling heat still in his eyes. "You're living here now, so think of this as your home."

"I will, thank you." Dammit, now I sound all husky and breathless. Pulling myself together with effort, I give him my best model-employee smile. "I was actually going to ask you something. Do I have a work schedule? That is, are there any specific times you'd like me to work with Slava? Ideally, I'd like to teach him throughout the day, as opposed to having formal lessons, but if you prefer otherwise, I'm flexible."

There, that's better. I actually managed to steady my voice and sound semi-professional. Hopefully, that'll remind him I'm here to teach his son, not melt at his smoldering stare like—well, probably like every straight woman he's ever met.

Another wickedly sensual smile touches his lips. "It's up to you, zaychik. Your pupil, your methods. All I'm after are the results. The only thing I ask is that you join our family for mealtimes, so Pavel and Lyudmila don't need to cook and clean extra."

"Yes, of course. What time are breakfast and lunch?" Now I feel bad that I made Lyudmila give me those crepes; as late as I woke up, I could've waited until the next scheduled meal.

"We usually eat breakfast at eight and lunch at twelve-thirty. Does that work for you?"

"Absolutely." If there's anything I've learned over the past month, it's that food, anytime, anywhere, of any variety, works for me.

A full stomach is something I'll never take for granted again.

"Good. Then I'll see you at lunch today." He turns to walk away, and I exhale a shaky breath, again relieved and perversely disappointed—only to have my heart miss a beat as he stops and faces me again.

"Almost forgot," he says, eyes gleaming. "Your new clothes are getting delivered this afternoon. Pavel will bring them up to your room, and I'd appreciate it if you wore one of the dresses for dinner."

"Oh, sure. Thank you. I will." One of the dresses? How many did he buy? And how is he getting them delivered so fast? I'm dying to ask, but I don't want to prolong this nerve-racking encounter.

I'm still cognizant of that closed door.

"Good. Let me know if something doesn't fit." His gaze travels over my body, and the icy-hot prickles return, my breathing turning shallow as my nipples tighten in my bra. *Another thin cotton bra that's doing little to hide my reaction.* My face burns with the heat of a thousand suns, and as his eyes meet mine again, I feel the shift in the atmosphere, sense the air taking on that dangerously electric charge.

Mouth dry, I take a half step back, though what I really want is to lean toward him. The pull is so strong it's like a physical force—and judging by the way his jaw flexes as he watches my retreat, I'm not alone in experiencing it.

Run, Chloe. Get out.

Mom's voice is quieter this time, less urgent, but it clears away some of the haze in my brain. Gathering the withering shreds of my willpower, I take another step back and say as evenly as I can manage, "Thank you. I will."

His nostrils flare, and I again have the sense of being in the presence of something dangerous… something dark and savage that lurks underneath Nikolai's urbane veneer.

"All right," he says softly. "Good luck with your laundry, zaychik. I'll see you soon."

And opening the door, he walks out.

17

NIKOLAI

I ABSTAIN FOR ALL OF FIFTEEN MINUTES AFTER I GET TO my office. I check my email, pay a few invoices, fire off a reply to one of my accountants. Then, cursing under my breath, I turn up the sound on my laptop and bring up the camera feed from my son's room.

As expected, Chloe is there, having finished her task in the laundry. Hungrily, I watch as she plays cars and trucks with Slava, speaking to him the entire time as if he can understand her. Every once in a while, she points at something like a wheel and makes Slava repeat the English word after her, but for the most part, she just talks—and Slava listens to her raptly, as fascinated by her facial expressions and gestures as I am.

At one point, he laughs at the way his truck overtakes her car, and she grins and ruffles his hair, her slender fingers casually sliding through his silky strands. My chest squeezes painfully, my lust for her mixing with intense jealousy. I don't even know which of them I envy more—Slava, for experiencing her touch, or Chloe, for winning my son's affections. All I know is I want to be there, basking in her sunny smile, hearing my son's laugh in person instead of through the camera.

Fuck.

This is pathetic.

What am I doing?

I move to close down the feed but stop at the last second, hovering the cursor over the X. She's opened a book and is reading to Slava now, her voice a soft, slightly husky croon that makes me want to burst into my son's room, snatch her up, and carry her off to bed. I want to hear that voice moan my name as I drive into her tight, wet heat, to hear her plead and beg as I take her to the brink over and over before finally granting her the sweet mercy of release.

I want to torment her nearly as much as I want to fuck her, to make her pay for making me feel this way.

Clenching my teeth so hard I risk a toothache, I close the screen and propel myself to my feet. Despite the largely sleepless night I had, I'm brimming with restless energy. I need another hard run, or maybe a sparring session with Pavel.

I cast a glance at the clock above my office door.

Less than an hour before lunch.

Pavel is likely busy preparing food, and if I go for the kind of long, hard run I need, I won't have a chance to shower and change before it's time to join everyone at the table.

Exhaling a frustrated breath, I sit and open my inbox again. It's too soon to expect anything from Konstantin—I only asked him to do a deep dive on Chloe's missing month this morning—but I still check for his email.

Nothing.

Fucking hell. I really need a distraction. My fingers are itching to open up the camera feed again and watch her interact with my son. But if I do, this restlessness will only grow worse, my hunger for her more intense. Having held her this morning, I know how she feels pressed against me, how sweet and clean she smells, like wildflowers on a crisp spring morning. It took all of my strength to turn her loose, even with Alina there, and when I found her alone in the laundry room, every dark, primal instinct insisted that I take her, that I strip her naked and bend her over a washer, claiming her on the spot.

And I would've done exactly that if she'd leaned toward me.

If she'd done anything but back away, I'd be balls deep inside her instead of sitting here, wrestling with myself like a fool.

No, fuck this.

I launch to my feet.

I need a hard, bloody fight, and since Pavel's unavailable, the guards will have to do.

Arkash and Burev are out patrolling the compound when I get to the guards' bunker, but Ivanko, Kirilov, and Gurenko are sitting around a campfire out front with a few of our American hires. Like the barbarians they are, they're roasting a whole deer on a spit and trading their usual insults.

Ivanko spots me first. "Boss." Snatching up his M16, he jumps to his feet. "Something wrong?"

Kirilov and Gurenko are already on their feet as well, weapons ready, just like in our Crimea days.

"Easy, boys." Smiling grimly, I strip off my shirt and drape it over a nearby tree branch. "Everything's just right." Or it will be soon.

Three against one is exactly the type of odds I was hoping for.

18

CHLOE

To my relief, lunch with the Molotovs is a much more casual affair than dinner. Well, Alina is still dressed like she's at an upscale cocktail party, but Nikolai is wearing dark jeans with a white polo shirt, and nobody chides Slava for his shorts and T-shirt as we sit down at the table—which is again laden with all sorts of mouthwatering salads, cold cuts, and sides.

Do all Russians eat like czars, or just this family? If this is an every-meal thing, I have no idea how they're not fat. I'm still full, having had breakfast only a couple of hours ago, but there's no way I'm not going to gorge myself on this spread.

Everything looks so freaking good.

"How was your first night with us, Chloe?" Alina asks when we've all filled our plates. "Did you sleep well?"

I smile at her, relieved both by the innocuous question and the friendly tone. I was afraid she might still be mad at me after this morning's incident. "I slept very well, thank you." And it's true—the nightmare aside, it was the best sleep I've had in weeks.

"That's good," Alina says, cutting into what looks like a fancy deviled egg. "I thought I heard something from your room around three, but it must've been my brother returning from one of his middle-of-the-night runs." She shoots Nikolai a sidelong glance, and I busy myself with the food on my plate, grateful for the explanation.

I must've screamed out loud last night. That, or Alina heard me fall out of bed.

"I did go for a run," Nikolai says, "so that must've been it." When I look up, however, his gaze is trained on me, studying me with an unreadable expression.

Does he suspect something?

God, I hope *he* didn't hear me scream or fall.

Fighting the urge to squirm in my seat, I lower my gaze—and freeze, staring at his hands. He's holding a knife in one and a fork in the other, European style, but that's not what draws my attention.

It's his knuckles. They're red and swollen, as if he's been in a fistfight.

My pulse spikes as I look away, then sneak another look at his hands.

Yep. I didn't imagine it. Nikolai's knuckles are a mess. In general, his big, masculine hands look like they've seen a lot of action, with calluses on the edges of his thumbs and faded scars in a few places. Even his short, neatly groomed nails can't hide the truth.

These aren't the hands of a wealthy playboy. They belong to a man intimately acquainted with either hard manual labor or violence.

The suspicions I'd all but suppressed return, and this time, I can't pretend they're baseless. Something about the Molotovs unnerves me. Who are they? Why are they here? I can see a rich foreign family spending a couple of weeks in a place like this as a "nature detox," but to actually move here? Someone as glamorous as Alina belongs in Paris or Milan or New York, not a corner of Idaho where there are more bears than people. Same goes for Nikolai, with his smooth, cosmopolitan manners and insistence on *Downton Abbey* attire at dinner.

My new employers are the very epitome of the jet set—at least if one ignores Nikolai's street brawler hands.

I force myself to look away from those angry-looking knuckles and focus on the child next to me, who's again eating calmly and quietly. Disconcertingly so, I realize. What four- or five-year-old doesn't play at least a little with his food? Or demand adult attention on occasion? I know the boy can smile and laugh and play like any other child his age, so why does he turn into a kid-sized robot at mealtimes?

Feeling my gaze on him, Slava looks up, his big golden-green eyes strikingly solemn. I smile at him brightly, but he doesn't smile back. He just refocuses on his plate and resumes eating. I eat as well, but I continue watching him, my sense of wrongness intensifying by the second. There's something unnatural about my student's behavior, something deeply concerning. Maybe the boy is more traumatized by his mother's death than he seems on the surface, or maybe something else is going on… something far worse.

I steal another glance at Nikolai's knuckles, a horrible thought slithering into my mind.

To my infinite relief, the injuries look fresh, as if he's just pounded something or someone into the ground. Since Slava's been with me all morning, he couldn't have been that someone. Besides, only an impact of great force could've caused those types of contusions, and there's nothing about the way Nikolai's son is sitting or moving that would indicate he's been beaten so severely—or at all.

Whatever my employer is guilty of, it's not child abuse, thank God. I don't know what I'd do if that were the case. No, scratch that. I know. I'd call Child Protective Services and run, taking my chances with my mom's killers.

Which reminds me: I still don't have my car keys.

I'm about to ask Nikolai about them when Alina smiles at me and asks, "Have you always wanted to be a teacher, Chloe?"

I nod, setting down my fork. "Pretty much. I've always loved both children and teaching. Even as a child, I'd often play with kids younger than myself so I could cast myself in the role of their instructor." I grin, shaking my head. "I think I just liked having them look up to me. Stroked my ego and all that."

As I speak, I'm cognizant of Nikolai's eyes on me, intent and unwavering. A predator's stare, filled with both hunger and infinite patience. My skin burns under its weight, and it takes everything I have to keep my gaze on Alina and pick up my fork as if nothing is happening.

She asks about my choice of college next, and I tell her how I was lucky enough to get a full-ride scholarship there.

"I'd never even thought about applying to such an expensive school," I say between bites of delicious smoked fish and richly flavored beet salad. It helps if I concentrate on the food instead of the man staring at me. "My mom worked as a waitress, and money was tight for as long as I can recall. I was going to go to community college, then transfer to a state school, using a combination of scholarships, loans, and work-study to pay my way through. But just as I started my senior year of high school, I got an invitation to apply for this special scholarship program at Middlebury. It was for children of low-income single parents, and it covered one hundred percent of tuition, room, and board, in addition to providing an allowance for books and miscellaneous expenses. Naturally, I applied—and somehow got in."

"Why somehow?" Nikolai asks. "Weren't you a good student?"

I have no choice but to meet his penetrating stare. "I

was, but there were students in my circumstances who were far more qualified and didn't get it." Like my friend Tanisha, who'd gotten a perfect score on her SATs and graduated as our class valedictorian. I told her about the scholarship, and she applied to the program as well, only to be instantly rejected. To this day, I wonder why they chose me and not her; if it was a matter of surviving adversity, Tanisha had a "better" story, with her partially disabled mother raising not one but three children on her own, one of them—Tanisha's younger brother—with special needs.

"Maybe they saw something in you," Nikolai says, his eyes tracing over every inch of my face. "Something that intrigued them."

I shrug, trying to ignore the heat coursing under my skin. "Could be. More likely, though, it was just dumb luck." It had to have been, because a couple of months later, Tanisha got acceptance letters from every school she'd applied to, including Harvard, which she ended up attending thanks to a generous financial aid package. Not as generous as the scholarship I got—she graduated with seventy thousand dollars in student loans—but good enough that I stopped feeling guilty about taking the spot that should've been hers.

Being a nice person, she's never acted anything but happy for me, but I know how much the scholarship committee's rejection devastated her.

"I don't think it was dumb luck," Nikolai says softly. "I think you're underestimating your appeal."

Oh God. My heart rate jacks up, my face burning

impossibly hotter as Alina stiffens, her gaze bouncing between me and her brother. There's no mistaking his meaning, no waving it off as a casual compliment about my scholastic abilities, and she knows it as well as I do.

Still, I try. Pretending like it's all a joke, I grin widely. "That's very nice of you to say. What about you two? Where did you go to school?"

There. Change of topic. I'm proud of myself until I realize that if, for some reason, either of the siblings *didn't* go to college, my question could offend them.

Thankfully, Alina doesn't bat an eye. "I went to Columbia, and Kolya finished Princeton." She's composed again, her manner friendly and polite. "Our father wanted us to attend college in America; he thought it provided the best opportunities."

"Is that why you speak English so well?" I ask, and she nods.

"That, and we both attended boarding school here as well."

"Oh, that explains the lack of accent. I've been wondering how you both managed not to have it."

"We also had American tutors back in Russia," Nikolai says, a mocking half-smile playing on his lips. Clearly, he knows I'm trying to diffuse the tension, and he finds my efforts amusing. "Don't forget that, Alinchik."

His sister stiffens again for some reason, and I busy myself with clearing the rest of my plate. I have no idea what landmine I've stepped on, but I know better than to proceed with this topic. As I'm finishing up my food, I glance over at Slava and find him done as well.

"Would you like some more?" I ask, smiling as I gesture at his empty plate.

He blinks up at me, and Alina says something in Russian, presumably translating my question.

He shakes his head, and I smile at him again before looking over the other adults at the table. To my relief, they appear to have finished also, with Nikolai just sitting back, watching me, and Alina gracefully patting her lips with a napkin. Miraculously, her red lipstick leaves no traces on the white cloth—though I probably shouldn't be surprised, given that the bright color survived the entire meal without smearing or fading.

One of these days, I'm going to ask her to share her beauty secrets with me. I have a feeling Nikolai's sister knows more about makeup and clothes than ten YouTube influencers combined.

I'm about to excuse myself and Slava so we can resume our lessons when Pavel and Lyudmila walk in. He's carrying a tray with pretty little cups, a jar of honey, and a glass teapot filled with black tea. He sets it on the table while Lyudmila clears away the dishes.

"None for me, thank you," I say when he places a cup in front of me. "I don't drink tea."

He gives me a look suggesting I'm little better than a wild animal, then whisks my cup away and pours tea for everyone else, my student included. The delicate china looks ridiculous in his massive hands, but he handles the task deftly, making me wonder if he worked in some high-end restaurant prior to joining the Molotov household.

"Thank you for a wonderful meal. Everything was delicious," I tell him when he passes by me, but he just grunts in response, stacking the dishes that his wife didn't get to in a carefully arranged pyramid on top of the tray before carrying them all away. It's not until he's gone that I remember something important.

I turn to Nikolai, my face warming again as I meet his tiger gaze. "I keep forgetting to ask... Did Pavel repark my car somewhere? I didn't see it in front of the house. Also, I don't think I ever got my car keys back."

"Really? That's odd." Adding a spoonful of honey to his tea, Nikolai stirs the liquid. "I'll ask him about that." He hands the honey jar to Slava, who adds several spoonfuls into *his* cup—the boy must have a serious sweet tooth.

"That would be great, thank you," I say, picking up my glass of plain water—the only liquid besides coffee I like to drink. "What about the car? Is there a garage or something nearby?"

"At the back of the house, just underneath the terrace," Alina replies in her brother's stead. "Pavel must've moved it there."

"Okay, awesome." I grin, inexplicably relieved. "I was half-afraid you guys decided it's too much of an eyesore and pushed it into the ravine."

Alina laughs at my joke, but Nikolai just smiles and sips his honey-sweetened tea, watching me with an inscrutable expression.

19

CHLOE

The rest of the afternoon flies by. As soon as lunch is over, I find the garage—the entrance to it is at the back of the house, just past the laundry room—and verify that my car is indeed there, looking even older and rustier next to my employers' sleek SUVs and convertibles. Then, since the weather is beautiful—low seventies and sunny—I take Slava for a hike in the forested portion of the estate rather than teaching him in his room. We tromp through a wildflower-filled meadow, climb down to a small lake we find about a half mile to the west, and chase a dozen squirrels into the trees. Well, Slava chases them, giggling maniacally; I just observe him with a smile.

He's an entirely different boy out here than in the dining room with his family.

As we make our way through the woods, he chatters in Russian, and I reply in English whenever I can guess what he's saying. I also make sure to give him

English words for everything we encounter, and I do my best to learn the Russian words he teaches me.

"*Belochka,*" he says, pointing at a squirrel, only to break into giggles when I mangle the word in my attempt to repeat it. He, on the other hand, pronounces English words perfectly almost from the first try; I suspect he's either been watching English-language cartoons or he has perfect pitch.

Musically inclined kids tend to master accents faster than their peers.

"Do you like music?" I ask as we're returning home. I hum a few notes to demonstrate. "Or singing?" I do my best rendition of "Baby Shark," which causes him to whoop in laughter.

In case there was any doubt, I'm *not* musically inclined.

As we approach the house, Pavel comes out to greet us, a fierce glower on his face. "Where were you? It's almost five, and he hasn't had his snack."

"Oh, we were—"

"And your clothes have been delivered. They're in your room." Eyeing Slava's dirty shoes with disapproval, he picks up the boy and carries him into the house, muttering something in Russian.

Chagrined, I take off my muddy sneakers and follow them in. I probably should've cleared our hike with Slava's caretakers, or at least kept better track of time. I did bring a couple of apples for Slava to munch on if he got hungry—I grabbed them from the kitchen before leaving—but I guess that's not as complete of a meal as the cheese-and-fruit tray Pavel brought up yesterday.

When I get to my room, I wash my hands and fix my bun; a bunch of fine strands have escaped the confinement and are framing my face in a messy halo. Then I head into my closet to check out the delivery.

Holy shit.

The walk-in closet—ninety-five-percent empty after I unpacked my suitcase—is now packed to the brim. And it's not just the fancy gowns my employers mandate for dinner. There are jeans and yoga pants, tank tops and T-shirts and sweaters, casual sundresses and sleek pencil skirts, socks and pajamas and hats. And underwear, all kinds, from thongs to comfy cotton panties to sports bras and lacy push-up bras, all improbably in my size. There's even outerwear—lots and lots of outwear, ranging from light rain jackets and sleek wool coats to puffy parkas that would withstand arctic weather.

It's a closet for all seasons and all occasions, and judging by the tags, everything's brand-new.

Stunned, I turn over a tag hanging from a soft-looking white sweater.

$395.

What the fuck?

I grab a tag from the nearest parka, a pretty blue one with a fur-lined hood.

€3.499. Made in Italy.

"You like?"

I give a start and spin around to face Alina, who's standing at the entrance of the closet.

"Sorry, didn't mean to scare you," she says, flicking her glossy black hair over her shoulder. She's already changed into another stunning gown, a red ankle-length piece with a thigh-high slit that shows a sliver of one long, toned leg. She's also refreshed her makeup, extending the eyeliner to emphasize the feline quality of her tip-tilted eyes.

"I knocked, but no one answered," she continues, "so I figured you were exploring your new things."

"I was—I am." I glance over my shoulder at the packed hangers and shelves. "Is that… all for me?"

"Of course. Who else would it be for? I don't need any more, that's for sure." Strolling over to stand next to me, she pulls out a long yellow dress and holds it up to my chest, then hangs it up and pulls out a pale pink one.

"But it's way too much," I say as she holds the pink dress against me, only to reject it as well. "I don't need all of this. A few dresses for dinner, sure, but the rest—"

"That's my brother for you. Nikolai doesn't do half measures." She flips through the rest of the gowns with practiced speed and pulls out a shimmery peach number. *Versace,* the label on it states, and there's no price tag in sight—probably because the amount would be scary. Holding it up against me, Alina gives a satisfied nod. "Try this on." She thrusts it into my arms.

"Right now?"

She arches her eyebrows. "I can turn away if you're shy." Matching action to words, she gives me her back.

Suppressing an exasperated sigh, I quickly scramble out of my clothes and into the dress—which somehow fits perfectly, the gold-speckled peach chiffon draping over my body with stunning elegance. The A-line skirt falls gracefully to my feet, and the square-cut bodice has a built-in bra that lifts my modest B cups, giving me a hint of cleavage. The wide straps conceal my shoulders, but my arms and the upper portion of my back are left bare, exposing the scabs from where the shards of glass pierced my skin.

Dammit. I was hoping to avoid showing those until they've healed.

"Ready?" Alina sounds impatient.

"Just one sec." I twist my arm behind my back, trying to get the zipper all the way up. "Actually, do you think you could…?"

"Of course." She zips me up and steps back to give me a once-over. Instantly, her gaze homes in on the scabs. "What happened here?" she asks, a tiny frown creasing her smooth brow.

"It's nothing." I grimace, as if embarrassed by my clumsiness. "I tripped and fell on some broken glass."

The explanation must satisfy her because she lets it go and resumes her perusal. "Very nice," she finally declares. "But that bun has to go."

"Oh, no, that's okay—"

"Come." Grabbing my hand, she drags me out of the closet and into the bathroom, where she makes me stand in front of the mirror. "See? You need to wear your hair down with this. Also, makeup is a must."

I stare at my reflection in the mirror, messy bun, dark circles, and all. She's right. A dress this glamorous deserves the works. Unfortunately, I only have a tube of lip gloss with me, having trashed the majority of the items in my makeup bag when I was clearing out my dorm room after graduation. I figured I'd go shopping with Mom when I got home. She loved that sort of thing, and we always—

I stop that line of thought and inhale to clear the painful constriction in my chest. "I can take my hair down, but I don't really have—"

"Yes, you do." She pulls open one of the drawers next the sink, revealing a selection of tubes and bottles that would make a professional makeup artist proud. "I made sure Nikolai got all the necessities," she explains.

"You helped him buy all this?"

"Who else?" She grins, revealing that perfectly imperfect little gap between her straight white teeth. "None of my brothers know mascara from lipliner."

My ears perk up. "Brothers?"

She nods, reaching into the drawer. "There are four of us. I'm the youngest and the only girl." She uncaps a foundation bottle and grabs my hand, turning it palm up. Smearing a streak of bronze color on my inner wrist, she eyes it critically, then opens a slightly more golden shade and tests that.

"Where are your other brothers?" I ask, watching her work in fascination. I did just think it might be nice to get a lesson from her one day, and here we are. I've always had trouble finding the right foundation; most drugstore brands offer shades that are either too light, too dark, or too ashy. But the second color Alina tries blends into my skin perfectly—she definitely knows what she's doing.

"They're both in Moscow," she replies, capping the bottle. "Well, at this moment, Konstantin is on a business trip in Berlin, but you know what I mean." She sets the bottle on the counter in front of me, along with mascara, eyeliner, and a bunch of other stuff, including an egg-shaped sponge that she wets under the faucet. Meeting my gaze in the mirror, she asks, "Do you mind if I do your face? Or would you rather do it yourself?"

"No, please, go ahead." I'm more than eager for her to continue. Beauty lesson aside, this is a chance for me to learn more about my mysterious employers without Nikolai's darkly magnetic presence scrambling my brains.

"All right then, wash your face and come along."

I do as she says while she sweeps all the makeup she laid out into a little silver case. After I pat my face dry and moisturize with a fancy-looking face cream I find in yet another drawer, she leads me back into the bedroom, where she stands me in front of the floor-to-ceiling window—natural light is best, she explains. Placing the makeup case on the nightstand nearby, she steps in front of me and, bending her head with a look of intense concentration, begins applying foundation with the damp sponge.

"You always want to pat, not rub," she explains, dabbing at my cheeks. "The color blends in best that way."

"Good to know, thank you." I wait until she's done with my chin before asking, "So what made you and Nikolai decide to come here? I imagine it must be a big change from Moscow."

She pauses, her eyes meeting mine. "Oh, it is. Moscow is… a whole other world." Her red lips tilt up without humor. "Not always a nice world."

"Oh?"

She resumes her careful dabbing. "It's quiet here. Calm. And the nature is beautiful. Nikolai wanted that for his son."

"So you're here for Slava?"

"My brother is." She frowns, studying my face, and uses the pointed end of the sponge to add a little foundation under my eyes. The dark circles must be bugging her. "Me, I just needed a break," she continues as she moves on to the bridge of my nose, "a little timeout, if you will."

"From life in Moscow?"

"Something like that. Close your eyes."

I obey, silently digesting what I've learned as she sweeps eyeshadow onto my lids and applies mascara to my lashes. It makes sense that they'd be here for the boy—the timing of their move to this compound lines up with Nikolai's learning of his son's existence. And I suppose if quiet, calm nature is what you're after, you can't do much better than this place.

Still, something doesn't smell right. I'm sure there are spots of wilderness untouched by civilization in Russia and other countries nearby. Why move halfway across the globe if pretty nature is all you're after? The time difference alone must make it difficult to stay in touch with family, or conduct any type of business—assuming there *is* a business.

I wait until Alina is done tracing my lips with a pencil before opening my eyes to ask, "What do your brothers do, work-wise?"

"Oh, this and that." She carefully applies lipstick, has me close my lips on a tissue to smudge off some of the color, and repeats the process two more times. Finally satisfied, she puts the lipstick away and picks up a little container of blush and a long-handled makeup brush. "Our family owns a bunch of companies in various sectors—energy, technology, real estate, pharmaceuticals," she says, swiping the brush across the apples of my cheeks with quick, expert strokes. "Nikolai oversees it all... or he did until recently. When we learned about Slava, he handed over most of the responsibilities to Valery and Konstantin, so he could move here and spend time with his son."

I stare at her in disbelief. Is she talking about the same Nikolai? The coolly distant father who barely interacts with his son? I can't picture him leaving a business meeting early to be with Slava, much less stepping down as head of some major conglomerate.

I must be missing something. That or Slava is a convenient excuse for something shady.

"What about you?" I ask when she steps away and surveys her work with a critical eye. "Are you involved with the family business as well?"

She laughs, a light, trilling sound. "Oh, that's not for me." Taking half a step forward, she smooths my left eyebrow with her thumb. "Not bad," she declares. "Now we just need to do your hair. Come." Clasping my hand, she drags me back into the bathroom, where she takes out an entire array of styling products from another drawer while I gape at my reflection in the mirror.

I have never, ever looked this way before, not even when Mom shelled out fifty bucks to have my makeup professionally done for my high school prom.

The girl in the mirror is beyond pretty, her skin smooth and glowing, her brown eyes large and mysterious above delicately contoured cheekbones and soft, plump lips the color of dusky rose.

I don't look like Alina, with her bright red lips and dramatic cat-eye makeup. In fact, I don't look like I'm wearing makeup at all. Instead, it's as if I've been Photoshopped, all my imperfections blurred and smoothed out.

"Wow." I lift my hand to touch my face. "This is..."

Alina slaps my hand away. "Don't touch, you'll mess it up. In general, the less you touch your face, the better. You have nice, clear skin, but it'll be even better if you keep your hands off it. The oil and dirt on our fingers clog the pores, causing them to look larger over time."

"Right, okay." Chastened, I keep my hands at my sides as she goes to work on my hair, first freeing it from the bun, then misting it with water and applying various styling products to tease out the wave in my otherwise-limp strands.

"There, all done," she says after a few minutes. "Now you need shoes, and we'll be all set."

Oh, crap. "I don't think I have any—" I begin, but she's already walking out of the bathroom.

I follow and see her beeline for my closet. A second later, she emerges with a shoebox. *Jimmy Choo,* the logo on the box proclaims. Setting it down on the floor, she takes out a pair of strappy gold heels and hands them to me. "Try these."

They bought me shoes as well? Stopping my brain from doing the math on the not-so-small fortune that must've been spent on my wardrobe, I put on the heels—like the dress, they fit perfectly—and walk over to the full-length mirror hanging next to the closet.

"How do they feel?" Alina asks, coming to stand next to me. To my surprise, she's now only a couple of inches taller than I; those high heels she always wears have fooled me into thinking she possesses a model's height.

I experimentally shift my weight from foot to foot. "Surprisingly comfortable." Not as comfortable as my sneakers, obviously, but I can stand and walk in them better than in any dressy shoes I've worn before. Likewise, the peach gown doesn't pinch or scratch anywhere; all the seams are smooth and soft against my skin, the silky inner lining pleasantly cool.

No wonder Alina is able to dress like a queen at all times. If all her clothes are of this quality, looking glamorous is nowhere near as big of an inconvenience as I imagined.

"You just need one more thing," she says, smiling at my reflection. "Stay here. I'll be right back." She hurries out of the room, and I stay in front of the mirror, marveling at the way the shimmery gown drapes over my too-skinny body, giving the illusion of healthy curves.

I'll never be as beautiful as Alina, but I'm definitely the best version of myself.

She returns a minute later with a small jewelry box in her hand. Setting it down on the nightstand, she opens it and takes out a pair of diamond studs and a heart-shaped pendant on a thin gold chain.

"Thank you, but I couldn't possibly," I say as she comes toward me, holding the jewelry. "That looks really expensive."

"Don't worry. It's just a little trinket." Ignoring my protests, she drapes the gold chain around my neck and locks it into place, then inserts the diamond studs into my ears. "There, now the outfit is complete."

She steps back, and I turn to face the mirror again.

She's right. The jewelry has added that final touch of polish, the heart-shaped diamond glittering an inch above the faint hint of cleavage created by the bodice of the dress. I look equal parts elegant and sexy, like a modern-day princess about to attend a ball.

If Mom saw me like this, she'd be so proud. She'd make me take a million pictures in dozens of different poses, and she'd set up the best ones as her screensaver and phone background, so she could show them off to her coworkers at the restaurant. She'd—

I blink the sting out of my eyes and turn back to face Alina. "Thank you," I say, my voice only slightly strained. "I appreciate this."

"It's my pleasure." Her green eyes gleam as she gives me a final once-over. "Let's go down to dinner. I can't wait for Nikolai to see you like this."

And before I can wonder what she means, she heads out of the room, leaving me no choice but to follow.

20

NIKOLAI

"WHAT THE FUCK DO YOU THINK YOU'RE DOING?" MY voice is low and pleasant, my expression neutral as I address my sister in Russian. Across from me, Chloe has her head bent toward Slava, talking to him about the food on his plate as if he can understand her, and all I can think about is how much I want to reach across the table and rip that pendant off her smooth, slender throat—right after I throttle the person who gave it to her.

"You asked me to help her get dressed." Alina's tone matches mine, even as chilly amusement glitters in her eyes. "Don't you like the results?"

"Where did you get it?" I drop my voice further as Slava glances at us curiously. Unlike his American teacher, he understands exactly what we're saying, if not the context of it all. "I thought it was lost."

"Mom's favorite necklace? Hardly." Alina's smile is as icy bright as the diamond glittering on Chloe's chest.

"She gave it to me for safekeeping. Right before... you know." She waits for my response. Getting none, she flaps her lashes with exaggerated innocence. "Don't you like it on her? I thought it was just perfect for this dress—and for your pretty new toy."

My molars squeeze together, but my outward demeanor remains calm. I now understand what game Alina is playing, and I don't intend to let her win. "You're right. It *is* perfect, and so is she. Thank you for being so helpful."

Not waiting for her reaction, I turn my attention to Chloe, ignoring the white-hot rage streaking through my veins each time the glimmering stone catches my eye. That pendant is all I've been able to see since Chloe came to the table, so now I take in her actual appearance—and as I do, the burning fury inside me transforms into scorching lust.

She's beautiful. No, more than that. She's breathtaking, a painting of a Grecian goddess come to life. Like in the picture I saw earlier, her hair tumbles down to her slender shoulders in a cascade of sun-streaked brown waves, and her smooth skin glows with a mysterious inner light. Whatever my sister has done has enhanced the radiance that's captured me from the beginning, emphasizing Chloe's bright, tender beauty.

The kind of beauty that all but begs for a despoiling touch.

My gaze trails from her face to her fragile collarbones, then, determinedly skipping over the pendant, to the hint of shadow between her breasts, temptingly pushed up by the tight bodice of her dress. With vivid clarity, I imagine how her erect nipples will feel when I palm those small, delicious globes, how they'll taste when I suck them. She'll moan, her head arching back and her slender arms rising to—

I stop, the fantasy evaporating as I stare at the dark red scabs on her left bicep.

What the fuck?

They look like puncture wounds, deep ones.

"She said she fell on some broken glass," Alina murmurs in Russian, as uncannily tuned in to me as always. "Interesting, isn't it?"

It is indeed. While it's theoretically possible to fall on broken glass and end up with puncture wounds, one is far more likely to get sliced up—and I don't see any marks of that kind on her arm.

"I wonder if she was stabbed or caught some shrapnel," Alina continues, again echoing my thoughts. "What do you think? My bet is on the latter."

I force myself to sound disinterested, bored by the topic. "I think she fell on some broken glass." I haven't told my sister about the additional report I commissioned from Konstantin's team, and I'm not planning to do so.

Chloe is my mystery to unravel, my puzzle to solve.

My pretty toy to play with.

Her eyes meet mine, and she quickly looks away, her hand tightening on her fork as her small chest rises and falls in a faster rhythm. I smile darkly, watching her. I unsettle her, make her nervous, and it's not just the sexual tension that heats the air between us. I caught the way she looked at my banged-up knuckles during lunch, saw the questions in her eyes.

My zaychik is smart enough to be wary of me.

She knows, deep down, what kind of man I am.

I study her throughout the meal, feasting my eyes on her while she feasts on the fruits of Pavel's kitchen labor. She's still discreet and subtle about it, but at least three heaping portions of *plov*, Pavel's Georgian rice pilaf specialty, disappear from her plate in short order, followed by a serving of every salad and side dish on the table, along with an entire plate of lamb kebab, tonight's main dish.

Her off-the-charts appetite both amuses and upsets me because it reveals something important.

It tells me she's known real, true hunger in the recent past.

The realization adds to my frustration, as do the marks on her arm. Konstantin still hasn't come through with the report, and it's driving me mad. I want to know what happened to her. I *need* to know it. It's fast becoming an obsession—and so is she. This afternoon, when she went hiking with Slava, I found myself climbing walls because I couldn't watch her through the cameras. I want to know what she's doing every moment of every day, and no matter how hard I try to distract myself, she's all I'm able to think about.

As the meal draws to a close, I contemplate getting her to stay for an digestif with me, but when I catch her covering a yawn, I decide against it. Alina's skill with makeup has hidden the outward signs of Chloe's exhaustion, but she's still fragile, still breakable... too much so for all the dark, dirty things I want to do to her. Besides, I can't be certain of my self-control tonight.

The desire searing my veins feels too powerful, too savage for a smooth seduction.

Soon, I promise myself as I watch her walk out of the dining room and disappear up the stairs.

Soon I'll get to the bottom of what makes Chloe Emmons tick, and appease this hunger.

It's nearly two a.m. when I admit defeat and get up to go for a run. After barely sleeping last night and working off much of my restless energy by sparring with the guards, I should've been dead to the world. Instead, I lay awake for hours, my body burning with unfulfilled desire and my mind filled with restless thoughts. Each time I'd come close to drifting off, I'd see the fucking pendant dangling above me, and rage would flood my veins, jerking me awake.

My sister knew what she was doing when she hung that bauble around Chloe's pretty neck.

The night sky is clear when I exit the house, the light from the half-moon illuminating my path as I begin jogging down the driveway. Not that I need it—I have excellent night vision. As the forest thickens around me, I speed up until I'm sprinting down the road leading to the gate. Halfway there, I take a sharp right and enter into the woods, my sneakers crunching on leaves and twigs as I weave through the trees. It's darker here, more dangerous, with the uneven ground and fallen branches, but the challenge is what I'm after. Running like this forces me to focus, to exert myself both mentally and physically. At the same time, something about the night forest soothes me. The quiet rustling of wild creatures in the bushes, the hooting of an owl above my head, the loamy scent of decomposing vegetation—it's all part of the experience, part of what attracts me to this place.

I run until my lungs burn and my muscles feel like lead, until sweat runs down my face in rivulets. When my legs threaten to give out, I turn back and run up the mountain, pushing myself past the point of exhaustion, past the limitations of my body and the memories encroaching on my mind. I run until I can't think about anything, much less picture the heart-shaped pendant on Chloe's chest.

Finally, I stop and walk the rest of the way, letting myself cool down. By the time I enter the dark, silent house, my breathing has calmed and my legs are starting to feel like they're attached to me. Toeing off my dirty shoes, I lock the front door and make my way up the stairs, the weight of sleep deprivation descending on me like a layer of bricks. I can't wait to fall into my bed and—

A choked cry stops me short.

I freeze on top of the stairs, all my senses on high

alert as I scan the dark hallway.

A moment later, I hear it again.

A muffled scream, coming from Chloe's room.

Adrenaline blasts through my body. I don't stop to think, I just act. Soundlessly, I pad down the hallway, every muscle in my body coiled for battle. If someone's broken in, if they're hurting her… The mere thought of it paints my vision red. Only a lifetime of training keeps me from kicking down the door and rushing in. Instead, I stop three feet from her bedroom and press my palm against the wall, feeling for a tiny ridge. When I find it, I push in, and with a quiet whoosh, a small square of the wall slides away, revealing one of the mini arsenals I've hidden throughout the house.

Moving silently, I reach into the niche and grab a loaded Glock 17, then approach Chloe's door.

All is quiet again, but I don't let it fool me.

Something isn't right. I know it. I feel it.

Clicking off the safety with my right thumb, I carefully twist the knob with my left hand and open the door a crack.

Another cry rings out, followed by a choked sob.

Fuck it.

I push the door wide open and charge inside, prepared to do battle.

Only no one attacks me.

There are no flying bullets, no movement of any sort.

The faint moonlight reveals no one in the dark bedroom besides me and a small bundle underneath the covers on the bed—a bundle that jerks suddenly, emitting another one of those muffled cries.

Of course.

I lower the gun, the worst of the tension draining from my muscles. This must be what Alina heard last night. No wonder Chloe looked so uncomfortable when my sister brought up the topic.

She has nightmares. Bad ones.

I should leave now that I know she's safe, but I remain rooted in place, staring at that bundle of covers as my heartbeat takes on a hard, thumping rhythm. *She's here, sleeping only a couple of meters away.* The adrenaline in my veins transforms into a sharp, hot need, a hunger so fierce and potent I shake from the effort of containing it. I want to feel her smooth, warm skin under my fingers, smell her crisp, sweet wildflower scent… sink deep into her tight, wet heat… My pulse roars in my ears, my body so hard it hurts, and my legs move against my will, carrying me forward.

No. Fuck, no.

I stop half a meter from the bed, jaw clenched.

Move the fuck back. Now.

By some miracle, my feet obey.

One step.

Another.

A third.

I'm halfway to the door when the bundle on the bed jerks again and begins thrashing wildly, filling the air with raw, heartrending cries.

21

CHLOE

"No!"

My feet slip in the blood as I lunge forward, dropping to my knees over Mom's body. Her beautiful, expressive face is slack, her soft brown eyes glazed and unseeing. Her pink robe, my Christmas gift from last year, gapes open at the top, revealing her left breast, and her right arm is flung out to the side, blood from the deep vertical gash in her forearm pooling on the clean white tiles, seeping into the immaculately maintained grout. Her left arm is pressed against her side, but there's blood there too. So much blood...

"Mom!" I press my icy fingers to her neck. I can't feel a pulse, or maybe I just don't know where to find it. *Because there's a pulse. There's got to be. She wouldn't do this. Not now. Not again.* I'm simultaneously frantic and numb, my thoughts hurtling along at lightning speed even as I kneel there, stiff and frozen. *Blood. So much blood on the kitchen floor.* My head jerks up on autopilot, my eyes searching for a roll of paper towels on the counter. Mom will be so upset about the stains on the grout. I need to clean this up, need to—

Call 911. That's what I need to do.

I scramble to my feet, frenziedly patting my pockets as my gaze bounces around the kitchen.

My phone. Where is my fucking phone?

Wait, my purse.

Did I leave it in the car?

I spin toward the front door, breathing in shallow gasps. *Keys.* The car needs keys. *Where did I put my fucking keys?* My gaze falls on a little table by the entrance, and I race toward it, heart hammering so fast it makes me sick.

Keys. Car. Purse. Phone.

I can do it.

Just one step at a time.

My fingers close around my furry keychain, and I'm about to grab the door handle when I hear it.

The low, deep rumble of male voices in Mom's bedroom.

I turn to stone, every muscle in my body locking tight.

Men. Here in the apartment. Where Mom is lying in a pool of blood.

"—was supposed to be here," one of them is saying, his voice growing louder by the second.

Without thinking, I leap into the wall niche in the hallway that serves as our coat closet. My left foot lands on a pile of boots, my ankle twisting agonizingly, but I bite back the cry and yank the winter coats around me like a shield.

"Check the phone again. Maybe there's traffic." The other man's voice sounds closer, as do his heavy footsteps.

Oh God, oh God, oh God.

I slap both hands over my mouth, the keys I'm clutching digging painfully into my chin as I hold still, not daring to breathe.

The footsteps stop next to my hideout, and through the bulky layers of coats, I see them.

Tall.

Powerfully built.

Black masks.

A gun in one gloved hand.

Prickles of terror race up and down my spine, my vision dappling with dark spots from lack of air.

Don't pass out, Chloe. Stay still and don't pass out.

As if hearing my thoughts, the man closest to me pivots to face my hideout and yanks off his mask, revealing a shark's head. Baring his knife-like teeth in a macabre grin, he points the gun at me.

"No!"

I jerk back violently, only to get tangled in the coats. They're all over me, smothering me, holding me captive. I flail with increasing desperation, hoarse pleas and panicked sobs tearing from my throat as the black-gloved finger tightens on the trigger and—

"Shhh, it's okay, zaychik. You're okay." The coats constrict around me, only this time their weight is comforting, like being enveloped in a hug. They smell good too, an intriguing mixture of cedar, bergamot, and earthy male sweat. I inhale deeply, my terror easing as the shark's head and the gun recede into a foggy mist and awareness of other sensations trickles in.

Warmth. Smooth, hard muscle under my palms. A deep, rough-silk voice murmuring soothing nothings into my ear as powerful arms hold me tight, protecting me, keeping me safe from the horrors hovering beyond the mist.

My sobs quiet down, my jerky breaths slowing as the nightmare releases its hold on me. And it *was* a nightmare. Now that my brain is beginning to function, I know there's no such thing as a shark's head on a human body. My sleeping mind conjured that up, embellishing the memory, just as it's now embellishing—

Wait, this doesn't feel like a dream.

I stiffen, a spike of adrenaline sweeping away the lingering haze and bringing the realization that a big, warm, bare-chested, *very real* man is rocking me on his lap. My face is buried in the crook of his neck, my hands gripping the hard muscles of his shoulders as his large, callused palms stroke soothingly over my back. He's murmuring words of comfort in a mixture of English and Russian, and his soft, deep voice is terribly familiar, as is his beguiling male scent.

It can't be.

It's not possible.

And yet…

"Nikolai?" I whisper, feeling like I'm imploding on the inside—and as I lift my head from his shoulder and open my eyes, the weak moonlight streaming through the window illuminates the starkly carved lines of his face, giving me the answer.

22

CHLOE

A BIG, WARM HAND SETTLES ON MY NAPE, MASSAGING away the tension permeating every muscle in my body. "Are you okay, zaychik?" he murmurs, the pale moonlight reflecting in his eyes as his other hand strokes up and down my arm. "Is the bad dream gone?"

I can't find the words to respond. The shock is like a million tiny needles stinging my skin, my inner thermostat flipping from hot to cold and back again.

Nikolai and I are in bed.

Together.

He's holding me on his lap.

The thermostat dials up all the way to scorching, spiking my pulse and sending a dizzying spear of heat straight to my core. We're all but naked—my pajama tank and shorts are beyond flimsy, and he must be wearing only shorts or briefs as well because I can feel his bare thighs against mine. His skin is rough with hair, his leg muscles so hard they feel like stone.

And that's not the only stone-like hardness I'm feeling.

The entire world seems to fade away, replaced by the stark awareness of our intimate position and the dark, magnetic force that's pulled us toward one another from the start. My heart thuds violently in my ribcage, each beat reverberating in my ears as my breath stutters through my parted lips. His face is mere inches from mine, his powerful arms encircling me, holding me in an embrace that's equal parts protective and restraining.

"Chloe, zaychik…" A strained note enters his deep voice. "Are you okay?"

Okay? I'm burning up, dying from the firestorm of need inside me. He's so close I can feel the warmth of his breath, smell a hint of minty toothpaste mixing with the sensual notes of his cologne and the salty undertones of clean, healthy male sweat. His eyes gleam with moonlight speckled with shadows, his black hair blending with the night, and I have the surreal thought that *he* is made of darkness… that like a creature of the underworld, he exists out of the reach of light.

Trepidation curls through me, mixing with the heat burning in my veins, intensifying it in some peculiar, unsettling way. My nipples harden, my inner muscles clenching on a growing empty ache, and my body acts on a long-simmering impulse, my fingers tightening on the hard muscles of his shoulders as my lips press against his.

For a brief moment, nothing happens, and I have the horrifying thought that I've misjudged the situation, that the attraction is one-sided after all. But then a low, rough sound rumbles in his throat, and he kisses me back with savage hunger, his arms tightening to form an iron cage around me. His lips devour mine, his tongue stabbing deep, tasting me, invading me in a blatant imitation of the sexual act, and my mind goes completely blank, all thoughts and fears evaporating under the brutal lash of desire.

I've never known a kiss so raw and carnal, have never felt arousal so intense it hurts. My skin burns, my heart beats like a fist against my ribcage, and my core pulses with a desperate, coiling need. He bears me down to the bed, pinning me under his heavy weight, and all I can do is moan helplessly into his mouth as my nails dig into his shoulders and my legs wrap around his hips, grinding my throbbing clit against the hard bulge of his erection.

A ragged groan escapes his throat, and he sweeps a hand down my body, his touch trailing fire in its wake. Roughly, he pulls up my tank top, and his callused palm closes over my left breast, kneading it with hungry pressure as his lips crush mine, his kiss consuming me, stealing every exhalation from my lungs. Breathless, dizzy, I strain against him, my hands sliding up to grip fistfuls of his silky hair. The feel of his hot palm on my nipple is equal parts relief and aggravation; it soothes the feverish craving for his touch while intensifying the rapid build of tension. Like a loaded spring, the pressure coils ever tighter in my core, each grinding movement of my hips bringing me closer to the edge, to the relief I'm so desperately seeking.

I'm going to come. The realization sweeps through me a heartbeat before the climax does. My back bows, my legs tighten around his muscled ass, and a choked cry bursts from my throat as heated pleasure rockets through my body. The release is so powerful it wipes away all thought, all reason, and it's only as I come down from the high and open my eyes that I realize he's stilled on top of me, his head turned toward the door and his powerful body all but vibrating from tension.

A split second later, I realize why.

"Chloe, is that you? Are you—" Alina freezes in the doorway, her negligée-clad figure outlined by the light streaming in from the hallway.

A light she must've turned on when she heard us.

Or more specifically, heard *me*.

A hot flush sears my face and neck as I realize exactly what she heard—and what she's seeing.

Me, in bed with her half-naked brother in the middle of the night, my pajama top hiked up to my armpits.

There's no spinning this as an accident, no mistaking it for anything other than what it is.

"Excuse me." Alina's tone turns chilly. "The door was open. I didn't mean to intrude."

She disappears into the hallway, and Nikolai mutters something that sounds like a Russian curse. Rolling off me with an explosive motion, he strides to the wide-open door and slams it shut, plunging us back into darkness.

I scramble to a sitting position, yanking down my tank top as I hear his returning footsteps. *Fuck. Fuck. Fuck. What am I doing?* My hand pats frantically along the nightstand in search of the bedside lamp switch, and the light flips on just as the mattress dips under his weight.

For a few beats, we just stare at each other, and I register all sorts of panty-melting details, like the way his straight black hair is mussed from my fingers and how his sensual lips are red and swollen, glistening from our rough kisses. Mine must look the same because I can feel them, damp and throbbing, aching for more of his addictive touch and taste. He's wearing only a pair of running shorts, and his chest and shoulders are all lean muscle, his abs sharply defined. Unlike the powerful trunks of his legs, which are sprinkled with crisp, dark hair, his torso is smooth, his lightly tanned skin marred only by a pale, puckered scar on his left shoulder.

My heart rate kicks up.

Bullet wound.

I've never seen one, but I'm certain I'm right. It's either that, or a drill bit went through his shoulder.

The lingering glow of orgasm dissipates as fear born of clearer thinking filters in. Who is he, this gorgeous man who appears to be so intimately acquainted with danger?

Why is he in my bedroom, on my bed?

Slowly, I scoot away, not taking my eyes off his. The bullet wound, the bruised knuckles, the wall around the compound, and the guards… There's a story here, and it's not a good one. Violence, in some shape or form, appears to be part of my new employer's life, and I want nothing to do with it, no matter how much my body longs for us to finish what we started.

What *I* started, by kissing him so thoughtlessly, so brazenly.

At my retreat, his tiger eyes narrow, and I feel his frustration, the simmering fury of a predator witnessing the inevitable escape of his prey. Except it's not inevitable in our case—with his superior size and strength, he can stop me at any point, and the fact that he remains still despite the tension evident in his powerful muscles is more than a little reassuring.

He must realize what I'm thinking because his expression smooths out, his posture taking on a relaxed, almost lazy vibe. "Don't worry, zaychik. I'm not going to pounce on you." His voice is soft, his tone gently mocking. "If you don't want this, just say so. I'm not in the habit of bedding the unwilling… or anyone pretending to be that."

My face feels like someone is burning coals under my skin. He's no doubt referring to my impromptu orgasm, something I haven't let myself think about yet. Because as shameless as my behavior tonight has been, nothing beats dry-humping him like a bitch in heat—and coming from it.

"I'm not—" I stop, realizing I was about to launch

into childish denials. "You're right," I say in a more level tone. "I apologize. I shouldn't have kissed you. That was completely inappropriate and—"

"And it's going to happen again." His eyes are like amber jewels in the warm light cast by the lamp. "You're going to kiss me, and we're going to fuck, and you're going to come again and again. You'll come on my fingers and my tongue, and with my cock buried deep inside your tight, wet pussy. You'll come as I fuck your throat and your ass. You'll come so fucking much you'll forget what it feels like not to come—and you'll still beg for more."

I stare at him, my throat dry and my underwear soaking wet. My clit pulses in tune with his softly spoken words, my heart hammering like a woodpecker even as my lungs struggle to draw a single breath. I've never had a man speak to me this way, never knew dirty talk could simultaneously turn me on and make me burn with shame.

"That's not... I'm not..." I drag in oxygen. "It's not happening."

"Oh, but it is, zaychik. You know why?"

I shake my head, not trusting myself to speak.

"Because this is inevitable. From the moment I saw you, I've known it's going to be like this... hot and wild and raw, completely uncontrollable. And you've known it too. That's why you can barely look at me at mealtimes, why being alone with me makes you so scared." He leans in, eyes gleaming. "You want me, Chloe... and believe me, I want you too."

I search for something to say, but nothing comes to mind. Where thoughts should be is a big, blank gap. At the same time, my body thrums with electric awareness, each nerve ending viscerally conscious of his nearness and the dark heat in those leonine, hypnotic eyes. This is so far beyond my realm of experience that I have no playbook for this, no clue how to react, much less act. He's my employer, the father of my student, and even if he weren't, there'd still be that aura of danger, of violence, that he wears like a lethal halo. The only sane solution is to shut this down, deny that I want him, but I can't bring myself to voice the obvious lie.

He waits for me to speak, and when I don't, his lips tilt up in a mocking half-smile. "Think about it, zaychik," he advises softly, the muscles in his powerful body rippling as he rises to his feet. "Think about how good it'll be when you come to me."

By the time I finally formulate a reply, he's gone, leaving a faint trace of bergamot and cedar on my sheets—and utter turmoil in my mind and body.

23

NIKOLAI

It takes every bit of the self-control I've cultivated over the years to walk into my bedroom and close the door behind me. Lust, dark and potent, pulses through me, demanding I get back to Chloe and continue where we left off.

I head into my bathroom instead. Stripping off my sweat-soaked shorts, I turn on the shower and set the temperature all the way to cold. Then I step under the spray, letting the chill of the water cool the fire raging in my blood.

Too fucking soon.

I could've pushed her further, I know, but it would've been too soon. She's not ready for this, for me. The nightmare made her lower her guard, but my sister's untimely interruption reminded her of all the reasons she shouldn't want me, all the reasons she thinks this is wrong. Her body may want me, but her mind is fighting the attraction. It frightens her, the intensity of what simmers between us, and I can't blame her.

It almost frightens me.

There's something different about my desire for the girl, something both tender and violent… a possessiveness that goes beyond simple lust. When I thought she was in trouble, all I could think about was getting to her, protecting her, destroying anyone who'd hurt her. And when she started thrashing around in the throes of her nightmare, the need to comfort her had been too powerful to deny. I retained just enough presence of mind to lay the gun down in the hallway, and then I was there, holding her as she shook and sobbed, her obvious terror tearing at me, filling me with frustration and helpless fury.

She's been traumatized, hurt by someone or something, and I don't know who or what.

I don't know, and I need to know.

I need it, so I can protect her.

I need it because in my mind, she's already mine.

I still under the cold spray, a dark realization threading through me.

Alina is right to fear for Chloe.

I *am* a danger to her, though not for the reason my sister imagines. She thinks I want the girl as a disposable fuck toy, a casual plaything, but she's wrong. As much as I want to bury myself in Chloe's tight little body, I want to get inside her mind even more. I want to know every thought behind those brown eyes, to lay bare her every want and need… every scar and wound.

I want to dig deep into her psyche, and not just because of the secrets she's hiding.

I don't just want to unravel the mystery she represents.

I want to unravel *her.*

I want to take her apart and understand what makes her tick.

I want that so I can make her tick solely for me, so she can be mine alone.

I want her the way my father must've once wanted my mother… a lifetime ago, before their love turned to hate.

For one long, stomach-hollowing second, I contemplate doing the right thing. I consider walking away, or rather, letting Chloe do so. First thing tomorrow, I could give her two months' pay, free of strings, and send her on her way… watch her drive out of here in her rundown Toyota.

I consider it, and I dismiss it.

It may be too soon for Chloe to occupy my bed, but it's too late for me to do the right thing.

It was too late the moment I laid eyes on her… maybe even the moment I was born.

I meant what I said to her tonight.

This *is* inevitable. I feel the certainty of that deep in my bones.

She'll come to me, drawn by the same dark, primal need that writhes under my skin.

She'll give herself to me, and it'll seal her fate.

Shutting off the cold water, I step out and towel off,

then pad silently into my bedroom. The recessed lights in the headboard are lit, casting a soft glow on the white silk sheets, but the bed doesn't feel welcoming. Not the way *her* bed felt, with her small, warm body in it. Not the way *she* felt, writhing against me, not asking but taking her pleasure from me, her lips like honey and sin, her taste like innocence and darkness combined.

My cock hardens anew, a wave of burning lust chasing away the chill lingering from the shower. Sitting down on the bed, I pull open my nightstand drawer and look at a pair of keys on a furry pink keychain—the ones Pavel gave me last evening, right after he re-parked Chloe's car.

Carefully, reverently, I pick them up and bring them to my nose. The keys themselves smell like metal, but the pink fur holds a faint trace of wildflowers and spring, the fresh, delicate sweetness of her. I inhale deeply, absorbing every note, every nuance.

Then I drop the keys back in the drawer and slide it shut.

24

CHLOE

Groaning, I roll over onto my back and throw an arm over my eyes to shield them from the sunlight. It took me hours to fall asleep after Nikolai left, and I feel like a total wreck. All I want to do is shut out the stupid sunlight and—

Wait, sunlight?

I jerk upright, squinting at the bright light streaming through the window.

Dammit.

Am I late to breakfast?

I cast a frantic glance around the room, but there's no clock. There is, however, the TV hanging from the ceiling, and I spot a remote lying on top of my nightstand. I grab it and press the power button, hoping it's not one of those complicated home theater setups that requires a computer science degree to operate.

The TV comes on, conveniently tuned to a news

channel, and I exhale a relieved breath.

7:48 a.m.

If I hurry, I'll make it downstairs in time.

I dash to the bathroom and speed through my morning routine, then beeline for my closet. The TV is still on, the newscaster droning on about the upcoming elections as I grab one of my new pairs of jeans and a soft-looking long-sleeved shirt, another new purchase. According to the informative blue strip on the bottom of the TV screen, the temperature is in the high fifties this morning, significantly cooler than yesterday. Besides, it doesn't hurt to cover up those still-healing scabs on my arm—I saw Nikolai eyeing them last night.

I emerge from the closet fully dressed at 7:55 and, as a last-minute thought, grab the jewelry box with the pendant and earrings and slip it into my pocket, so I can return it to Alina. The news program is now showing a clip from last night's presidential primary debates, in which one of the frontrunners, a popular California senator, is decimating his opponents with a barrage of cleverly worded facts and figures. I don't really follow politics—my mom thought all politicians were the scum of the earth, and her opinions have rubbed off on me—but this guy, Tom Bransford, is prominent enough that I know who he is. At fifty-five years of age, he's one of the youngest candidates in the presidential race, and is so good-looking and charismatic he's been compared with John F. Kennedy. Not that he's got anything on my employer.

If Nikolai ran for president, the entire female

population of the United States would need a change of panties after each debate.

The time on the screen changes to 7:56, and I power off the TV. Maybe tonight I'll have a chance to watch something, preferably a light, funny comedy. Nothing romantic, though—I need to take my mind off Nikolai and the confusing situation between us, not be reminded of it.

I don't want another sleepless night where my body aches with arousal and my thoughts loop in an X-rated reel, replaying his dirty promises and the dark, heated images they conjure up.

To my surprise, Nikolai isn't at the table when I get down there at 7:59 on the dot. His sister is, though, and so is Slava. The child gives me a bright grin that contrasts with Alina's much cooler smile, and I smile back at them both, even though the thought of what Alina saw last night makes me want to slink away and never show my face in this house again.

"Good morning," I say, taking my usual seat next to Slava. It's tempting to avoid Alina's gaze, but I'm determined not to give in to my embarrassment.

So what if she caught me making out with her brother? It's not like I'm a governess in Victorian times who was seen canoodling with the lord of the manor.

"Good morning." Alina's tone is neutral, her

expression carefully controlled. "Nikolai is on a call, so he won't be joining us for breakfast."

"Oh, okay." I again experience that strange mixture of disappointment and relief, as if a hard test I've been studying for has been rescheduled. Though I've tried not to think about Nikolai this morning, I must've been subconsciously psyching myself up for seeing him here because I feel deflated despite the easing of the tension in my shoulders.

Slipping my hand into my pocket, I take out the little jewelry box and hand it to Alina. "Thank you for loaning me this last night."

Her long black lashes sweep down as she takes it from me. "No problem. Some *grechka?*" she asks, gesturing at a pot of dark-colored grain sitting next to her. Breakfast here appears to be a much simpler affair, with only a jar of honey and a few platters of berries, nuts, and cut fruit accompanying the main dish.

Nodding gratefully, I hand Alina my bowl. "I'd love some, thank you." I'm beyond happy she's acting normally. Hopefully, it'll continue.

When she hands the bowl back to me, I try a spoonful of the grain she called "grechka." It turns out to be surprisingly flavorful, with a rich, nutty taste. Mimicking what Alina is doing, I add fresh berries and walnuts into my bowl and drizzle the whole thing with honey.

"It's roasted buckwheat," she explains as I dig in. "Back home, it's usually eaten as a savory side, often mixed with some variation of pan-fried carrots, mushrooms, and onions. But I like it this way, more like oatmeal."

"I think it's tastier than oatmeal."

Alina nods, ladling Slava his portion of the grain. "That's why I like it for breakfast." She tops Slava's bowl with berries, nuts, and a generous drizzle of honey and places it in front of the boy, who immediately sticks his spoon in. Instead of eating, however, he starts chasing a blueberry around the bowl while making engine noises under his breath.

I grin, realizing I'm finally seeing him play with his food like a normal kid. Catching his gaze, I wink and start stacking my blueberries on top of each other, like I'm building a tower. I make it only to the second level before the berries roll off each other, landing in the portion of the grain made sticky by the honey.

I grimace, feigning dismay, and Slava giggles and starts building a berry tower of his own. It turns out much better than mine since he uses honey as glue and props up his blueberries with cut strawberries.

"Very good," I say with an impressed expression. "You really are a natural-born architect."

He beams at me and proudly scoops up a spoonful of the grechka along with a chunk of his berry creation. Stuffing it into his mouth, he chews triumphantly while I praise him for being so clever. Encouraged, he builds another tower, and I make him laugh again by having one of my blackberries chase a blueberry that keeps rolling away from my spoon.

"You really do like children, don't you?" Alina

murmurs when Slava and I tire of the game and resume eating. Her expression is decidedly warmer, her green gaze filled with a peculiar wistfulness as she glances at her nephew. "It's not just a job to you."

"Of course not." I smile at her. "Children are amazing. They can make us see the world as we once did… make us feel that sense of joy and wonder that the passing years steal from us. They're the closest thing we have to a time machine—or at least a window to the past."

Her lashes sweep down again, concealing the look in her eyes, but there's no missing the sudden tension bracketing her mouth. "A window to the past…" Her voice holds a strangely brittle note. "Yes, that's exactly what Slava is."

And before I can ask what she means, she changes the topic to today's cooler weather.

25

NIKOLAI

"We have a problem," Konstantin says in lieu of a greeting as his face—a leaner, more ascetic version of mine, with black-rimmed glasses perched high on his hawkish nose—fills my laptop screen.

I lean closer to the camera, my pulse speeding up with anticipation. "What did you find out?"

Konstantin frowns. "Oh, about the girl? Nothing yet. My team's still working on it." Oblivious to the sharp sting of disappointment he's just delivered, he continues. "It's my nuclear project. The Tajik government has just pulled our permits."

I inhale and slowly let the air out. At times like this, I want to strangle my older brother. "So what?" He has to know I don't give two fucks about his pet projects, especially ones that verge on science fiction.

Then again, maybe he doesn't. Despite his genius-level IQ—or possibly because of it—Konstantin can be remarkably unaware of what's going on around him, especially if it involves people instead of zeroes and ones.

"So Valery thinks it's the Leonovs," he says, eyes gleaming behind the lenses of his glasses. "Atomprom is bidding against us, and Alexei was spotted having lunch with the head of the Energy Commission in Dushanbe."

Fuck. It's all I can do to hide the flare of rage searing through me.

I was wrong. My brother is very much aware of what he's doing by involving me in this. If it were anyone but the Leonovs, I *wouldn't* give two fucks—business is business—but there's no way I'm letting their interference slide.

Not after Slava.

"Did Valery—" I begin grimly, but Konstantin is already shaking his head.

"The Energy Commission refused to talk to him. Some bullshit about avoiding undue influence. Valery has a few ideas on how to proceed, but I figured I'd speak with you before we go down that path."

I take another steadying breath and force my tense shoulders to unclench. "You did the right thing." The persuasion tactics our younger brother likes to use might draw unnecessary attention, and after the stunt the Leonovs pulled two years ago, we're already on thin ice with the Tajik authorities.

A more delicate touch is required, which is why Konstantin has come to me with this.

"I'll call the Commission head and set up a meeting,"

I say. "We were in boarding school together. He'll see me."

Konstantin dips his head. "I'll meet you in Dushanbe. How soon can you be there?"

"Tomorrow. I'll fly out this morning." The sooner I get this bullshit over with, the sooner I get back here.

For the first time since I've left Moscow, this quiet retreat in the wilderness excites me more than any city in the world.

26

CHLOE

By the time we're done with breakfast and I get Slava to myself, gray clouds replace the bright sunshine that woke me up, and the temperature drops further as a light rain begins. According to Alina, we're supposed to get thunderstorms by noon, so I scrap the idea of taking my student on another hike.

Instead, I let Slava choose what he wants to do indoors, and I join him in that activity—which happens to be more LEGO tower assembly. That works well for me, since it lets us practice some of the words he's learned. When he gets bored with that, we build a fort out of pillows and blankets and play campers and bears, where I growl as I chase him all around the house, earning us vaguely disapproving stares from Lyudmila and Pavel, who are prepping for the next meal in the kitchen. Afterward, I read him his favorite comic books, and we play with cars and trucks, our chosen vehicles racing against each other while I commentate like a NASCAR sportscaster.

The boy really is bright and funny; it's a pleasure to teach him. Yet no matter how engaging our games are, I can't concentrate on them, or on him, fully. A part of my mind is elsewhere, on a different pair of golden eyes. After Nikolai left, I lay awake for hours, my skin flushed and my heart racing. Each time I closed my eyes, I heard his deep, soft voice making those carnal promises, and the throbbing ache between my legs returned, making me slick and swollen and so sensitive I could barely tolerate the touch of my pajama shorts. It wasn't until I gave in and used my fingers to reach another orgasm that I was able to drift off—and even then, my sleep was fitful, filled with hazy sex dreams interspersed with fragments of nightmares.

But not my usual nightmares.

In these, there was only one man in a mask, and he didn't want to kill me.

He wanted to capture me.

He wanted to make me his.

Slava and I are lounging on our stomachs on his bed, flipping through a book about the ABCs, when I become aware of a tingling sensation between my shoulder blades. I cast a curious glance over my shoulder—and heat suffuses my entire body as I meet Nikolai's gaze.

He's leaning against the doorframe, watching us, his expression carefully veiled. I have no idea how long he's been standing there, but I don't remember hearing the door open, so it must've been a while.

"Go ahead, finish what you're doing," he murmurs. "I don't want to interrupt the lesson."

Swallowing hard, I return my attention to Slava and the book. He's also spotted his father, but his reaction is much tamer. He's slightly subdued as we resume naming letters and the objects that start with them, but by the time we get to P and I make *oink-oink* noises to go with the illustration of the piggy, he's back to being his animated, giggling self.

Unable to help myself, I sneak another glance over my shoulder—and my heart stutters for a beat. Nikolai is not looking at me now but at his son, and there's something soft and pained in his eyes... a strange, despairing sort of yearning.

I blink, and just that fast, his attention shifts to me, the odd expression disappearing, replaced with the familiar scorching heat. Flushing, I look away and resume the lesson, my pulse pounding unevenly. I must've imagined that look, or misinterpreted it somehow. It doesn't make sense for Nikolai to yearn for a son who's right in front of him. If he wants to be closer with the boy, all he has to do is reach out to him, smile at him, talk to him... get to know him.

He can try to actually *be* a dad instead of this distant authority figure that Slava doesn't seem to know what to do with.

Then again, I've always found it easy to relate to children. That's why I chose this career path. If Nikolai's had minimal exposure to kids prior to learning of his son's existence, maybe he's just feeling lost and uncertain—as hard as it is to believe of a man this powerful and self-assured.

On impulse, I twist up to a sitting position facing him. "Would you like to join us? Maybe the two of us can finish going over the last few letters with Slava."

A peculiar stillness steals over him. "The two of us?"

"Or you can do it yourself if you'd rather." I'm beginning to feel foolish. It's highly likely I've misread the whole thing, ascribing thoughts and emotions to Nikolai that reflect my own wishful thinking. Just because I've secretly dreamed of meeting my father and growing close to him doesn't mean every parent-child relationship needs to adhere to a specific dynamic or—

"I'll join you." Nikolai pushes away from the doorframe and approaches the bed with those long, graceful strides that remind me of a jungle cat.

I scramble back as he sits down on the mattress next to me, but with Slava stretched out between me and the wall, I can't go far. Nikolai is so close to me we're almost touching, and my breath catches in my throat as his sensual cedar-and-bergamot scent envelops me, reminding me of last night. Vivid sexual images invade my mind, and more heat surges through me, dampening my underwear and sending my heart into overdrive. Uncomfortably aware of Slava's wide-eyed gaze on us, I try to tamp down on my arousal, but the heat doesn't dissipate, my pulse refusing to settle into a steadier rhythm.

This was a bad idea. A very bad idea. I should be keeping my distance from my employer, not issuing what amounts to an invitation to cuddle on a twin-sized bed. There's barely enough room for me and Slava. The only way for us all to fit is if—

"Lie down, zaychik," Nikolai says softly, a wicked half-smile curving his lips as he reaches around me to pick up the book. "So I can properly join you."

The blood flowing to my face feels like lava as I reluctantly obey, turning to lie on my stomach next to Slava—who seems fascinated by what's happening. Nikolai stretches out next to me, his big, hard body flush against mine, and it belatedly occurs to me that Slava should be in the middle, serving as a buffer. Before I can suggest it, Nikolai drapes a heavy arm over my shoulders, pinning me in place, and places the book in front of me.

"Go ahead," he murmurs in my ear, his warm breath sending goosebumps down my arm. "Let's see you work your teaching magic."

Magic? The only magic around here is that I'm somehow intact and not a puddle of goo on the sheets —which is what my body feels like as I lie in what amounts to his embrace. My pulse is pounding in my temples, my breath sawing through my lips as my underwear grows even slicker, and only the presence of the child next to us keeps me from repeating last night's mistake by giving in to the dangerous, hypnotic pull Nikolai exerts on me.

Instead, I attempt to concentrate on the task at hand. Clearing my throat, I read, "T is for train: *choo-choo*. Also for truck." My voice is a shade too husky, but I'm just glad my brain is functioning enough to make out the words on the page. Luckily, Slava doesn't seem to notice anything amiss as I continue, pointing at the picture of the truck with a slightly unsteady finger.

Casting curious looks at his father, he repeats the words after me, his voice quiet and subdued at first, then increasingly livelier, and by the time we get to Z, he's laughing at the stripes on the zebra and purposefully mispronouncing the word, having forgotten all about the large man in bed with us.

After his third incorrect attempt, I tsk-tsk with mock disappointment and glance at Nikolai. "Why don't you try saying it?" I suggest, ignoring the way my pulse spikes as I meet his gaze. "Maybe you'll have better luck."

Nikolai's expression doesn't change, but the arm draped over my shoulders stiffens slightly. "All right," he says in a measured tone, and looking down at the book, he says in a thick, exaggerated Russian accent, "Zye-bruh."

Slava's eyes round. He clearly wasn't expecting his father to have trouble with the English word. I tsk-tsk again, shaking my head as if disappointed by Nikolai's attempt, and after a brief, tension-filled moment, Slava bursts out laughing.

"Zebra," he corrects through the giggles, his pronunciation as perfect as mine. "Zebra, zebra."

"Oh, I see." Nikolai glances at me, a mischievous gleam in his eyes. "So… zee-bro?"

Slava is all but dying from laughter now, and I can't help grinning as well. This is a side of my employer I've never seen before, and judging by Slava's reaction, neither has he. Giggling, he corrects his father's pronunciation, and Nikolai bungles it again, sending the boy into fresh peals of laughter. Finally, Slava succeeds in "teaching" Nikolai how it's done, and we triumphantly close the book, having covered the entire alphabet.

Immediately, the tension between me and Nikolai returns, the air crackling with a sexual charge. I've been doing my best to ignore the feel of him pressed against my side, but without the distraction of the book, it's impossible. His big body is warm and hard next to me, his arm heavy over my shoulder blades, and though we're both fully clothed, the intimacy of lying together like this is undeniable.

To my relief, Nikolai removes his arm and sits up. I do the same, quickly scooting back to put some distance between us—a retreat he observes with dark amusement before saying something in Russian to his son.

The boy nods, still flushed from excitement, and Nikolai rises to his feet.

"Let's go to my office," he says to me. "There's something I'd like to discuss."

27

NIKOLAI

I SIT AT THE SMALL ROUND TABLE IN MY OFFICE, AND Chloe sits across from me, regarding me with those pretty, wary brown eyes. Her hands twist together on the table as she waits for me to initiate the conversation, and I let the moment stretch on, enjoying her nervousness. Lying next to her on Slava's tiny bed had been torture; if not for my son, I wouldn't have been able to control myself. As is, I'm still hard from being next to her, feeling her warmth and breathing in her crisp, sweet scent. It takes everything I have not to reach over and grab her right here and now, spreading her out on this very table.

With effort, I rein myself in. It's too soon, especially since I'm leaving in a half hour and won't be back for several days. A quick fuck isn't what I'm after. It won't be anywhere near enough.

Once I get Chloe into my bed, I intend to keep her there for hours. Maybe even days or weeks.

Besides, that's not why I called her into my office.

Placing my forearms on the table, I lean forward. "About last night..."

She stiffens, the pulse in her neck visibly quickening.

"... was it about your mother?"

She blinks. "What?"

"Your nightmare. Was it about your mother's death?" The question has been tormenting me all morning, and since Konstantin hasn't come through with the report, there's only one way I can learn the answer.

At the word "death," her chin wobbles almost imperceptibly. "It's... yes, in a way, it's about her..." She swallows thickly. "Her death."

"I'm sorry." Whatever she's hiding, her pain is unfeigned, and it tugs at me like a dull fishing hook. "How did she die?"

I know what the police report said, but I want to hear Chloe's take on it. I've already dismissed the possibility that she might've killed her mother—the girl I've observed for the past two days is no more a killer than I'm a saint—but that doesn't mean something *didn't* go down. Something that made her drop off the grid and sent her on a cross-country trip in a car that should've been junked a decade ago.

Chloe's hands lace tighter together, her eyes glittering with painful brightness. "It was ruled a suicide."

"And was it?"

"I… don't know."

She's lying. It's clear as day that she doesn't believe a word of that police report, that there's something she's not telling me. I'm tempted to press her harder, force her to open up to me, but it's too soon for that as well. She has no reason to trust me yet; if I push too hard, it'll only backfire.

The last thing I want is to frighten her, make her want to run while I'm gone.

"That's tough," I say softly instead. "No wonder you have nightmares."

She nods. "It has been kind of tough." Cautiously, she asks, "What about your parents? Are they back in Russia?"

"They're dead." My tone is overly harsh, but my family is not a topic I care to delve into.

Chloe's eyes widen before filling with expected sympathy. "I'm really sorry—"

I hold up a hand to stop her. "You don't have a phone or a laptop or any kind of tablet, right?"

She looks taken aback. "Right. I didn't bring any with me on the trip."

I get up and walk over to my desk. Opening one of the drawers, I take out a brand-new laptop, still sealed in a box, and bring it back to the table.

"Here." I place it in front of her. "I'm leaving for Tajikistan in"—I consult my watch—"fifteen minutes. I don't know how long I'll be gone, but it'll be at least three to four days, and I want you to keep me posted on Slava's progress."

"Yes, of course." She stands as well, her brown eyes gazing up at me. "Would you like me to send you a daily email or...?"

"I'll videocall you. Ask Alina to set up an account for you on the secure platform we use. Also"—I pull out my business card and hand it to her—"here's my cell number in case of emergencies."

I plan to watch her through the cameras in Slava's room as well, but it's not going to be enough. I already know that. I need more contact with her, need to hear her talking to *me,* see her smiling at *me,* not just my son. The videocalls won't be enough either, but it's the best I can do short of bailing on the trip altogether, and I'm not that far gone yet.

No, this will have to do, and keeping up to date on Slava's progress makes as good of an excuse for these calls as anything.

My chest tightens again at the thought of my son, but this time, the ache is accompanied by an unsettling sort of warmth. Slava laughed with me, looked at me with something other than wariness this morning... and it was because of her, because she was there, lending me her sweetness, her radiant magic.

I want more of it.

I want to take all of her sunshine, use it to light every dark, hollow corner of my soul.

Slowly, taking care not to spook her, I step closer and gently curve my palm over her silky-smooth cheek. She stares up at me, unmoving, hardly breathing, those soft, pouty doll lips parted, and my guts clench on a violent surge of need, a hunger as intense as it is dark. As much as I want to fuck her, I want to possess her even more.

I want to own her inside and out, to chain her to me and never let her go.

Something of my intent must show because her breath hitches, her throat moving in a nervous swallow. "Nikolai, I…"

"Keep the laptop on in the evenings," I order softly, and dropping my hand, I step back before I can give in to the dangerous maelstrom inside me.

To the beast that no amount of refinement can hide.

28

CHLOE

HEART POUNDING, I WATCH THROUGH THE WINDOW IN Slava's room as Pavel loads a suitcase into the backseat of a sleek white SUV and gets behind the wheel. A minute later, Nikolai approaches the car. Dressed in a sharply tailored gray suit and pin-striped white shirt, with a laptop bag slung over one shoulder, he looks every inch the powerful businessman. Moving with his customary athletic grace, he climbs into the front passenger seat and shuts the door.

I let out a shaky breath, my pulse slowing as the car pulls away and disappears down the winding driveway. I have no idea how I feel about his departure or what happened in his office. Had he been about to kiss me? If I hadn't said his name, would he have—

"Chloe?" a small, high-pitched voice pipes up, and I turn with a smile, putting all thoughts of my employer on hold.

"Yes, darling?"

Slava holds up a box of LEGO pieces. "Castle?"

I grin. "Sure, let's do it." I love that he remembered the word, and that he feels comfortable enough to call me by my name. He really is one of the brightest kids I've ever met, and I have no doubt I'll have a lot to report to Nikolai when he calls me.

My heart rate speeds up again at the thought of talking to him on video, and I busy myself by taking the LEGO pieces out of the box. A part of me is glad that Nikolai is gone… that for the next few days, I won't have to contend with his dangerous, magnetic presence. But another, weaker part of me is already mourning his absence. The overcast sky outside feels darker, grayer, the house emptier and colder.

It's as if something vital has disappeared from my life, leaving behind a strangely hollow feeling.

I spend the rest of the morning with Slava, playing various educational games, and then we eat lunch in the dining room, just the two of us, with Lyudmila bringing out all the dishes.

"Headache," she informs me when I ask about Alina. "You eat yourself, okay?"

I nod, biting back a laugh at the unfortunate phrasing. Maybe Pavel's wife would be open to some English lessons while I'm here? I'll have to ask her at some point. For now, I concentrate on giving Slava a generous serving of everything on the table and then doing the same for myself while Lyudmila disappears into the kitchen. I don't see her again until dinner—which Alina also skips, leaving me to dine alone with my charge.

I don't mind it. In fact, it's a relief. Despite the fancy clothes Slava and I put on as per the "house rules," the dinner feels infinitely more casual with just the two of us, the atmosphere lacking all the strain and tension that the Molotov siblings bring with them. I play with my food, making Slava giggle like crazy, and I continue teaching him words for various food items, along with basic mealtime phrases. Before long, he's asking me in English to pass him a napkin, and by utilizing a lot of gestures and facial expressions, we succeed in discussing which foods he likes the most and which ones he dislikes.

It's not until Lyudmila takes Slava away to put him to bed and I go up to my room that I realize I need Alina. She's the one who's supposed to set up an account for me on the secure videoconference platform. I doubt Nikolai will call me tonight—he's most likely still in the air—but he could easily call me tomorrow morning. Or in the middle of the night, if that's when he lands.

Still, I don't want to bother her if she's not feeling well.

I decide to begin by setting up the computer itself. It's a sleek, high-end MacBook Pro, and as I unpack it from the box, I realize I've never had a laptop this expensive. It's hard to believe Nikolai just had it sitting in his desk drawer like a spare pen.

Then again, why am I surprised? This family clearly has money to burn.

I boot up the laptop and go through the new computer setup routine. But when I try to get on Wi-Fi, I can't—it's password protected. I need Alina for this too. I suppose I can ask Lyudmila, but she's putting Slava to bed right now, and there's no guarantee she'd know the password, given how paranoid the Molotovs are about security, digital and otherwise.

Blowing out a frustrated breath, I close the laptop. Without internet, it's pretty much useless.

I guess tonight I get to laze around and watch TV.

I change out of my evening gown and into a pair of butter-soft leggings and a long-sleeved cotton tee—both new acquisitions—and make myself comfortable on the bed. Turning on the TV, I locate a nature show and spend the next hour learning about the plains of the Serengeti. The David Attenborough narration is as magnificent as always, and I find myself completely absorbed by the story unfolding on the screen, my mind calm for the first time in weeks. It's only when I'm watching a lion stalk a gazelle that my thoughts turn to the killers hunting me, and my disquiet returns.

I still don't know who those men are or what they wanted with my mom—why they killed her and made it look like a suicide. The most logical possibility is that she walked in on them while they were burglarizing the apartment, but then why was she wearing her robe like she was relaxing at home? And why didn't the police notice signs of forced entry or things missing?

At least I assume they didn't notice it. If they did and ruled her death a suicide anyway… well, that raises all kinds of other questions.

The other possibility, a likelier and much more disturbing one, is that they came specifically to kill her.

Turning off the TV, I get up and walk over to the window to stare out at the rapidly darkening landscape. My chest is tight, my mind churning anew. I've racked my brain ever since it happened, trying to think of reasons why someone might want to kill my mom, and I can't come up with a single one. Mom wasn't perfect—she could be sharp-tongued when tired, and she was prone to bouts of depression—but I'd never seen her be deliberately mean or unkind to anyone. For as long as I can remember, she'd worked two or more jobs to support us, leaving her with little time and energy to socialize and make friends—or enemies. To the best of my knowledge, she didn't even date, though men hit on her all the time.

She was beautiful… and barely forty when she died.

My throat cinches tight, a stinging pressure building behind my eyes. Not only have I lost the only person in the world who loved me unconditionally, but her murderers are out there, free. The police didn't believe a single word I told them, the reporters I contacted didn't reply to my emails, and nobody is looking for my mom's killers. Nobody is hunting them like the rabid animals they are.

Instead, the killers are hunting me.

Fuck this shit.

Pivoting on my heel, I stride to the bed and grab the laptop. I can't sit around, watching TV like my world didn't crumble a month ago. Not when I'm finally safe and have a computer on which I can do research at my leisure. For weeks, I've lurched from one crisis to another, all my energy focused on survival, on escape, but things are different now. I have a full belly, a safe place to rest my head, and—if I can only get that Wi-Fi password—an internet-connected laptop. No more sneaking into a library in some small town to huddle over their slow, ancient desktops while looking over my shoulder every minute; no more dashing off hastily composed emails before running to my car.

Here, in the privacy of my room, I can take my time and look for evidence to back up my claims, for some kind of proof to take to the police.

I can try to solve the mystery of Mom's murder and turn the tables on her killers, make them be the ones who have to run.

29

CHLOE

I don't know which room is Alina's, but it has to be close to mine for her to have heard me both nights. Holding the laptop against my chest, I knock on the door closest to my bedroom, and when I don't get an answer, I move on to the next one.

Still no luck.

I try three more bedroom doors, plus Nikolai's office, with the same lack of results. The only room that's left is Slava's, and since all is quiet there, he must already be asleep.

Suppressing my frustration, I go downstairs. I'm pretty sure Lyudmila and Pavel's room is near the laundry; I heard their voices coming from there when I was taking my clothes out of the dryer yesterday. Hopefully, Lyudmila hasn't gone to bed yet, and can either provide the password or locate Alina for me.

Nobody answers that knock either—nor is Lyudmila in the kitchen or any of the other common areas downstairs. I'm about to give up and go back to my room when a distant peal of laughter reaches my ears.

It's coming from outside.

Finally.

Leaving the laptop on a coffee table in the living room, I hurry to the front door and step out into the cool, misty darkness. It's no longer raining, but the air still holds a damp chill, with thick clouds blocking all hint of moonlight. If not for the light spilling from the windows and the solar path lights lining each side of the driveway, it would be too dark to see. As is, it's still more than a little creepy, and I wrap my arms around myself to stop from shivering as I walk toward the back of the house, following the sound of voices.

I find Alina and Lyudmila sitting on a pair of boulders near the edge of the cliff, a small fire crackling merrily in front of them. They're laughing and talking in Russian—and, I realize as I get closer, sharing a joint.

The grassy smell of pot is unmistakable.

At my approach, they fall silent, Lyudmila regarding me with open dismay and Alina wearing her usual enigmatic expression. Taking a deep drag, Nikolai's sister slowly blows out the smoke and holds out the joint to me. "Want some?"

I hesitate before gingerly taking it from her. "Sure, thanks." I'm no stranger to pot, having smoked more than my fair share my freshman year of college, but it's been a while since I've had any.

It used to help me relax, though, and I could use that tonight.

I sit on a boulder next to Alina and inhale a lungful of smoke, enjoying the acrid, grassy taste, then pass the joint to wary-looking Lyudmila. Alina murmurs something to her in Russian, and the other woman visibly relaxes. Taking a drag, she passes the joint to Alina, who takes a drag and passes it to me, and we go like that in a circle, smoking in companionable silence until only a small, useless stub remains.

"I told her you won't rat us out to my brother." Alina drops the stub into the fire and watches the resulting explosion of sparks. "Or her husband."

"They don't like pot?" My voice is raspy and mellow, my mind pleasantly fuzzy. Even the prospect of upsetting my employer doesn't faze me right now, though I know it should. Besides, Alina is technically my employer too, and she offered me the joint, so I'm not at fault. Or am I? Maybe only Nikolai is my employer, after all?

It's hard to think straight.

"Nikolai can be… uptight about certain things. And Pavel doesn't keep secrets from him." Alina nudges a glowing ember with the tip of her shoe, and I hazily register the fact that she's wearing stilettos and a blue cocktail dress that would be perfect for an art gallery opening. Her only concession to the wilderness surrounding us is a white faux fur draped around her slender shoulders—presumably to keep out the chill. She's also wearing her usual lipstick and eyeliner.

"Lyudmila said you had a headache," I say before I can think better of it. "Do you dress up and put on makeup even when you're sick?"

Alina laughs softly and lights another joint. Taking a drag, she offers it to Lyudmila, who does the same and offers it to me. I start reaching for it but change my mind. I know from experience that I'm about as mellow as I'm going to get; anything more will just make me slow-witted. Not that I'm not already—that first joint was potent stuff, as strong as anything I've tried. Besides, there was a reason I came out here, and it wasn't to get stoned.

"I'm good, thanks," I say, pulling my hand back, and with a shrug, Lyudmila returns the joint to Alina.

I watch the flames crackle and dance while the two of them smoke and converse in Russian. I wish I spoke the language so I could understand them, but I don't and the smooth rhythm of their speech reminds me of a burbling mountain stream, the words flowing into one another, defying comprehension.

Is that what it's like for Slava when I speak? Or for Lyudmila?

Is that what it was like for my mom when she was first brought to America from Cambodia?

She'd never spoken much about her early years; all I know is that she was adopted by the missionary couple when she was around Slava's age. I'd never pressed her for details, not wanting to evoke any bad memories. I'd figured we'd have a lifetime to talk about whatever, and she'd tell me eventually, if there was anything to tell.

I was a short-sighted idiot.

I should've learned everything there was to know about my mom when I had the chance.

Alina's laughter catches my attention, and I shift my gaze from the dancing flames to her face, studying each striking feature. It would be easy to envy her, both for her extraordinary beauty and her wealth, but for some reason, I don't get the impression that Nikolai's sister is particularly happy. Even now, when she must be more than a little high, there's a brittle edge to her laughter… a peculiar fragility underneath her glossy façade. And maybe it's the glow of firelight softening the porcelain perfection of her skin, but tonight, she seems younger than the mid-to-late twenties I pegged her for.

Much younger.

"How old are you?" I blurt, suddenly worried I might've accepted pot from a teenager. A split second later, I recall that she finished Columbia, so she has to be at least my age, but it's too late to take back my overly personal question.

To my relief, Alina doesn't seem to think it inappropriate. "Twenty-four," she replies in a dreamy tone. "Twenty-five next week." Her eyes slightly out of focus, she reaches over and touches my hair, rubbing one strand between her fingers. "Anyone ever mention you look a bit like Zoë Kravitz?" Not waiting for a reply, she trails her fingertips over my jaw. "I can see why my brother wants you. So pretty… so sweet and fresh…"

Laughing awkwardly, I swat her hand away. "You

are so stoned." I can feel Lyudmila's gaze on us, curious and judging, and my face warms as I reflect on how much of Alina's words she's understood—and what she already knows. These two seem to be good friends, and I wouldn't be surprised if at least some of their earlier laughter was at my expense.

"Extremely stoned," Alina agrees, throwing the second stub into the fire. "But that doesn't change the facts." Propping her elbows on her knees, she leans in, firelight dancing in her eyes as she says quietly, "Don't fall for him, Chloe. He's not your white knight."

I draw back. "I'm not looking for a—"

"But you are." Her voice stays soft, even as her gaze sharpens to a knife's edge, all haziness disappearing. "You need a white knight, noble and kind and pure, a protector to cherish and love you. And my brother can't be that for you, or for anyone. Molotov men don't love, they possess—and Nikolai is no exception."

I stare at her, my stomach turning hollow as the pleasant state of chemically induced non-worry dissipates, my head clearing more by the second. I don't understand what she means, not fully, but I don't doubt that she's sincere, that her warning is meant to protect me.

Drawing back, Alina lights a third joint and extends it toward me. "More?"

"No, thanks. I, um…" I clear my throat to rid it of residual hoarseness. "I actually need the Wi-Fi password. That's why I came out here to look for you. Also, Nikolai wanted you to set me up on your videoconference platform—if you're feeling up to it, that is."

She takes a deep drag and slowly blows out the smoke at my face. "I suppose that can be arranged." Handing the joint to Lyudmila, she rises to her feet. "Let's go."

And with a gait that's only slightly unsteady, she leads me back to the house.

When we get to the living room, I hand her the laptop and watch, with no small degree of amazement, as she navigates to the settings and inputs the password, her elegant fingers flying over the keyboard. If not for the strong smell of pot clinging to her hair and clothes—and if I hadn't personally witnessed her smoking the majority of those two joints, plus however many she'd shared with Lyudmila prior to my arrival—I would've never known she's high.

She's just as unerring with her installation of the videoconference software and setup of the account, her red-tipped fingers moving at a speed that would do a hacker proud.

"You're really good at this," I say after she hands the laptop to me and explains the basics of the software. "Did you major in computer science or something along those lines?"

"God, no." She laughs. "Economics and PoliSci,

same as Nikolai. Konstantin's the geek in the family—the rest of us are proficient at best."

"Gotcha. Either way, thanks for this." I close the laptop and tuck it under my arm. "I'm going to head to bed. Are you…?" I wave in the general direction of the front door.

She nods, one corner of her mouth lifting in a half-smile. "Lyudmila's waiting for me. Goodnight, Chloe. Sweet dreams."

30

CHLOE

Back in my room, I take a shower to clear the remaining haziness from my mind and change into my pajamas. Then, brimming with anticipation, I get comfy on the bed, open the laptop, and bring up a browser.

I start by looking for news coverage of my mom's death. There isn't much, just an obituary and a short article in a local paper reporting that a woman had been found dead in her East Boston apartment. Neither goes into details, tactfully omitting any mention of suicide. I'd already read both the article and the obituary when I stopped at a library in Ohio a couple of weeks back, so I don't spend much time on them. Instead, I make a note of the reporter's name and look up her contact info, then log into my Gmail and send her a long, detailed email outlining exactly what happened on that June day.

Maybe I'll have better luck with her than with the

other journalists I've contacted so far. None of them have bothered to reply—probably dismissing me as a mental case, just as the police had. But those were reporters at major news outlets, and they undoubtedly get harassed by all sorts of crazies. In the movies, it's always the small-time reporter who gets intrigued enough to investigate, and maybe that will be the case here too.

One can always hope.

Next, I type Mom's name into Google and see what else I can pull up. Maybe somewhere out there is a mention of her leading some secret double life, something that would explain why someone would want to kill her.

And maybe pigs will hop on a spaceship and fly to the moon.

I find exactly what I expected: a big fat nothing. The only thing my search brings up is Mom's Facebook profile, and I spend the next half hour reading her posts while fighting back tears. Mom didn't love the idea of putting her life on display, so her friend count is in the low double digits and her posts are few and far between. A photo of the two of us dressed up to go clubbing for my twenty-first birthday, a snapshot of the bouquet of flowers her co-workers at the restaurant gifted her for her fortieth, a video of me feeding lettuce to a giraffe during our recent vacation in Miami—her profile barely touches on the highlights of our lives, much less reveals anything I didn't already know.

Still, I diligently review all of her Facebook friends' profiles on the off chance that one of them may be a drug dealer who's stupid enough to announce it on social media. Because that's the best theory I can come up with.

Mom witnessed something she shouldn't have, and that's why those men came after her—just as they're now coming after me because I saw them and know her death wasn't a suicide.

Admittedly, the evidence for this theory is nonexistent, but I can't think of a reasonable alternative. Well, I can—a burglary gone wrong—but there are way too many issues with that idea. I mean, guns with silencers? What burglars carry those?

The more I think about it, the more convinced I become that those men came to kill her.

The big question is: why?

Three hours later, I delete my browser's history and clear the cookies—just in case I have to give back the computer unexpectedly—and close the laptop. My eyes feel like they've been rubbed with sandpaper from all the reading on the screen, and the mellowing effects of pot have long since worn off, leaving me tired and dispirited. I've googled just about everything I could think of in connection with Mom's life and death, have scoured the local papers for reports of other crimes around the same time—in the unlikely case that Mom's murderers were two serial killers working together—and have stalked each of her Facebook friends and restaurant co-workers with the perseverance of the most dedicated online troll. I've even looked into the death of her adoptive parents, in case there was something more to their car accident than I'd been told, but it seems to have been a straightforward case of a drunk driver ramming into them on the highway.

There's nothing, absolutely nothing to take to the cops. No wonder they didn't believe me when I burst into the station that day, shaking and hysterical.

I should probably call it a night and think about everything with a fresh head tomorrow, but despite my tiredness, my mind is buzzing with all sorts of unsettling questions—only some of which have to do with Mom's death. Because there's another mystery I haven't let myself think about yet, one that may have just as much bearing on my safety.

Who exactly is Nikolai Molotov, and what did Alina mean by her strange warning?

I look at the pillow, then at the computer. It's late, and I should really go to sleep. But the odds of being able to drift off while I'm this wired are low, almost nonexistent.

Screw it. Who needs sleep?

Opening the laptop, I type "Nikolai Molotov" into the browser and dive in.

31

NIKOLAI

THE FIRST THING I DO UPON ARRIVAL AT MY HOTEL IS power up my laptop, open the video feed from Slava's room, and check that my son is peacefully asleep.

He is. The car-shaped nightlight he likes us to leave on illuminates his sleeping features, revealing a tiny fist tucked underneath his sweetly rounded cheek. My heart thumps harder at the sight, a now-familiar ache spreading through my chest. I don't understand it any more than I understand my growing obsession with his tutor, but I can't deny it's there, as real and concrete as my hatred for the woman who gave birth to him.

For Ksenia, and the entire Leonov viper clan.

Rage kindles in my stomach, and I wrench my thoughts away from them. Tomorrow will be soon enough to deal with their latest sabotage; tonight, I have more pleasant things to think about.

Opening a new window, I bring up the feed from the webcam on Chloe's laptop, and a warm glow spreads through me as her pretty face fills the screen. Despite the late hour, she's awake, her smooth forehead creased in a frown as she peers intently at her computer. She must be doing something online because I can see her browser being active, and when I go into her search history, I'm pleased to find her researching me.

I was hoping she'd be thinking about me, just as I'm thinking about her.

She has no idea I can see this, of course. The laptop I gave her is from a special batch altered by one of Konstantin's shadier ventures. It looks like a regular brand-new Mac but comes pre-installed with undetectable spyware that allows us to keep an eye on all sorts of influential businesspeople and politicians.

Many a business deal was pushed through thanks to this handy software and the secrets it has revealed.

I watch her for a few minutes, amused by her attempts to read an article from a Russian newspaper using free web translation tools. She wrinkles her nose in the most adorable way when puzzled, and her eyes go from wide to narrow and back, her teeth frequently tugging at her lower lip. I want to bite that plump lip and soothe it with a kiss, then do the same all over her delicious little body.

My cock stirs at the thought, and I take a breath to distract myself from the heat building inside me. As enjoyable as it is to observe her, what I want even more is to talk to her, to hear her soft, husky voice and see her sunny smile. I miss that smile.

Fuck, I miss *her*.

It's ridiculous, I know—I just met her this week, and we've been apart less than a day—but that's the way it is, that's the inevitability of it all. Fate brought her to me, and now she's mine, even if she doesn't know it yet. If not for this trip, she'd already be in my arms, but the Leonovs stuck their dirty paws into our business and here we are.

Drawing in another settling breath, I open Konstantin's video software and place the call.

32

CHLOE

I'M IN THE MIDDLE OF PAINSTAKINGLY COMPARING THE Bing translation of the Russian article to the Google version in the hopes of making sense of three particularly confusing sentences when a soft chime sounds and a videocall request pops up, with Nikolai's picture in it.

My heart rate shoots up, my breathing quickening uncontrollably. It's like he's the proverbial devil, summoned by my thoughts—or my research. Is that possible? Does he somehow know I'm reading about him at this very moment?

Is that why he's calling so late? To fire me for snooping?

No, that's crazy. He probably just landed, saw on the videoconference app that I'm online, and decided to check in.

Pulling in a shaky breath, I smooth my hair with my palms and click "Accept."

His gorgeous face fills the screen, making my heart pound harder. "Hi, zaychik." His voice is soft and deep, his gaze mesmerizing even through the camera. In general, the quality of the video is insane; it's like a movie in HD. I can see everything, from the artful swoops in the abstract painting hanging on the wall a few feet behind his chair to the forest-green flecks in his amber eyes. He must've just arrived because he's still wearing the shirt and tie I saw him leave in, but instead of looking tired and rumpled, as a normal person would after a transatlantic flight, he's the very picture of effortless elegance, every glossy black hair in place.

Realizing I'm staring at him like a star-struck groupie, I force my vocal cords into action. "Hi." My throat is still a bit raw from smoke, but I'm hoping he ascribes the raspiness in my voice to the late hour. "How was your flight?"

His sensuous lips curl in a warm smile. "Uneventful. Why are you still awake? It's past midnight over there."

"Just… not sleepy." Especially now that I'm talking to him. Getting this call was like downing five shots of espresso; even my tiredness is gone, replaced by a jittery sort of excitement—one that's only partially related to what I was reading.

As I suspected, the Molotovs are filthy rich and a huge deal in Russia. "One of the most powerful oligarch families" is a Google-translated quote from one Russian article, and there are plenty of mentions of Nikolai and his brothers—and before that, of Vladimir, their father—in the Russian press. I even found a photo from last year in which Nikolai is sitting next to the Russian president at some black-tie event in Moscow, looking as cool and comfortable as at his family dinners.

What I didn't find, to my huge relief, is anything about the Molotovs being mafia or having criminal affiliations, though maybe I just didn't dig deep enough. Even with the help of web translation tools, it's hard to come up with the right search terms in Russian, and there's surprisingly little written about Nikolai's family in English—a passing mention on CNN of a pipeline in Syria laid by one of their oil companies, a paragraph on Bloomberg about a new cancer drug developed by one of their pharmaceutical companies, a line about Vladimir Molotov in a *New York Times* article discussing the enormous wealth in Russia. There are no Wikipedia entries on them, nothing in the tabloids. They don't even appear on any *Forbes* lists, though several Russian billionaires do, and the Molotovs sound even richer.

Of course it's possible I couldn't find anything because of all the Molotov cocktail references clogging up search results. I'll have to ask Nikolai or his sister if they're any relation to the Soviet foreign minister the homemade explosives are pejoratively named after.

At my reply, Nikolai frowns into the camera, looking concerned. "You didn't have another nightmare, did you?"

I shake my head with a smile. "I just haven't gone to sleep yet."

Maybe it's the lack of any alarming discoveries in my search, or the simple reality that he's not here to make my body hum with physical awareness, but I feel calmer talking to him tonight… safer. After all, it's possible that my experiences over the past month have shredded my nerves, leading me to see danger where none exists, and all the supposed red flags—his bullet wound scar and busted knuckles, the guards and all the security measures—have innocuous explanations. In fact…

"Were you ever in the military?" I ask impulsively, and more tension leaves my shoulders as Nikolai nods, a faint smile dancing on his lips as he leans back in his chair.

"My family has a long history of distinguished service to the country, and my father insisted my brothers and I follow the tradition. All three of us enlisted at eighteen and served for several years." He tilts his head, regarding me thoughtfully. "Were you wondering about this?" He touches his left shoulder.

"I was," I admit sheepishly. I'm beginning to feel like an idiot for letting my imagination run wild before. "What happened? Were you shot?"

He nods. "A sniper sent a bullet my way. Luckily, he missed."

"Missed?"

His white teeth flash in a grin. "I'm not dead, am I?"

"No, thank God." Still, my chest squeezes as I

picture that scar and the pain he must've experienced as the bullet tore through his flesh. "Did it take you long to recover?"

"A few weeks. I was only twenty at the time, which helped."

"Still, I can't imagine it was fun." Unable to resist the temptation, I ask, "Do you keep up with your training to this day? Like… fighting and stuff?"

I'm trying to be subtle, but he sees right through me anyway.

Grinning wickedly, he holds up his hands, turning them to show the bruised knuckles to the camera. "You're asking about these, I assume? That's from sparring with a few of my guards. They're from my former unit, and we go at it once in a while—at least when Pavel can't oblige me."

I grin back at him, so relieved I could cry. Of course his guards are his army buddies; that makes so much sense, and speaks volumes about his character. "Was Pavel in the army with you as well?" I can easily picture the man-bear in army fatigues, toting an M16 and maybe carrying a tank on his shoulders.

To my surprise, Nikolai shakes his head. "He actually served with my father. He enlisted at fourteen, and they let him, since he was already his current size and looked all of twenty-five."

"Oh, wow. So he's known your family since before you were born?"

"Long before," Nikolai confirms. "My father hired

him straight from the army, and he's been with our family ever since."

"Lyudmila too?"

"No, they've only been married for about ten years." He laughs. "Alina just about had a fit when he first introduced Lyudmila to us. I think my sister was under the impression that Pavel was her exclusive property."

My eyes widen. "She had a crush on him?"

"Not precisely, no. I think she thought of him more as a second father." His smile fades, and something bleak flickers in his eyes before his lips take on their usual darkly sensual curve—that cynical, seductive smile that, I'm now realizing, hides his true emotions. Leaning closer to the camera, he says softly, "Enough about them. Tell me about your day, zaychik. What did you and Slava do while I've been gone?"

Right, that's why he's calling: to get a report on his son. Concealing an irrational pang of disappointment, I put on my tutor hat and fill him in on our activities and the progress Slava's making. He listens attentively, interrupting occasionally to ask follow-up questions, and as our conversation continues, I realize I have to revise yet another negative opinion I had of him.

Nikolai does care about his son. A lot.

I caught a glimpse of it this morning, when Slava and I lay there on the bed, and I see it now in the way his face softens when I talk about the boy. I don't know why he refuses to protect his son from such obvious dangers as a sharp knife, but it's not because he doesn't love him. He does—though judging by the way he is around Slava, I wouldn't be surprised if he has trouble admitting it.

I think Nikolai wants to be closer to his son but doesn't know how.

I think… he may be a good man, after all.

Alina's warning intrudes on my mind again, but I push it away. She was high, and there's clearly tension between brother and sister, some kind of history I'm not privy to. Besides, I don't know what she thinks is happening between me and Nikolai, but love is nowhere on the table. Sex, maybe—I'm realistic enough to admit that my determination not to sleep with my boss is proving to be no match for the powerful attraction between us—but love is a whole other game. I'd be an idiot to fall in love with a man like Nikolai, who's undoubtedly used to the most beautiful women in the world throwing themselves at him. If we slept together, it wouldn't mean anything to him—and I can't let it mean anything to me.

Better yet, we shouldn't sleep together.

That way, nobody gets hurt.

We talk about Slava for another twenty minutes before the late hour catches up with me and a yawn overtakes me in the middle of a sentence. I stifle it right away, but Nikolai isn't fooled.

"You're exhausted, aren't you?" he murmurs, eyeing me with concern. "You should've said something, zaychik. I didn't mean to keep you up."

"No, no, it's fine. I'm just…" Another uncontrollable yawn interrupts my words, and I cover it with the back of my hand before giving him a rueful smile. "Okay, yes, it's sleepy time for me. How are you so awake? You must be jet-lagged on top of everything."

The green flecks in his eyes gleam brighter. "I don't need much sleep."

Of course he doesn't. I wouldn't be surprised if he was part superhuman—that would explain those extraordinary good looks he shares with his sister.

"Well, goodnight anyway," I say, fighting another yawn. "And good luck with whatever business you have there."

"Thank you, zaychik." His smile holds a tender note. "Sleep well. I'll call you tomorrow evening."

He hangs up, and as I put away the laptop, I'm cognizant of my heart beating in a new, uneven rhythm, my chest filled with a warmth I don't dare examine.

33

NIKOLAI

I CLOSE MY EYES AFTER WE DISCONNECT, TRYING TO hang on to the unaccustomed feeling of well-being talking to Chloe has generated, but it's fading fast. In its place is grim awareness of what I must do today, mixed with dark anticipation.

It's been six months since I've been in this world. Six months since I've let myself get involved in our business on any level beyond the most superficial. And while I'd like to say that I hate being back, I can't deny that a part of me revels in it all… that my blood is pumping faster through my veins.

Opening my eyes, I close the laptop and rise to my feet.

Time to get to work.

Pavel is already waiting in the hotel lobby, and we walk out together. Our destination is a small tavern a few blocks away, or more specifically, its basement.

The sight that greets us when we descend isn't pretty. A man is hanging by his wrists from a chain bolted into the ceiling, the toes of his booted feet just barely scraping the bare concrete floor. His pale face is bruised and swollen, the area under his off-center nose crusted with dark blood. Two of Valery's men stand next to him, their faces hard and eyes emotionless.

"Any luck?" I ask one of them, and he shakes his head.

"Claims he doesn't have the entrance code. It's a lie. We saw him use it."

"Hmm." I approach the captive and make a slow circle around him, noticing how his breathing picks up as I do. An acrid urine scent emanates from his crotch area, and there are dirt and blood stains on his beige Atomprom uniform.

The poor guy knows he's fucked.

"What's your name?" I ask, stopping in front of him.

He stares at me, mouth trembling, then bursts out, "I don't know the code. I don't!"

"I asked for your name. You know that, don't you?"

"Iv—" His voice cracks, as if he were a teenage boy instead of a twenty-something man. "Ivan."

"Okay, Ivan. Tell you what: I know you don't want to piss off your employer, but you don't really have a choice." I give him a sympathetic smile. "You see that, don't you?"

"I don't know the code!" Beads of sweat form on his forehead. "I swear—I swear on my mother's life."

"But she's dead, Ivan. She died in a factory fire when you were fifteen. That was tragic, I'm sorry."

His face goes linen white, and I continue in the same sympathetic tone. "Look, you're not a bad guy, Ivan. You've had a rough life, and you've done all you can to help out your family and take care of your younger sister. She's what, in tenth grade now?"

"Y-you…" He's shaking almost too hard to speak. "You fuckers!"

I tsk-tsk. "Insults will get you nowhere. Now listen to me, Ivan. I can let them"—I gesture at the emotionless guards—"beat the answer out of you. And if they fail, there's always my associate"—I glance at Pavel, who's quietly standing in a corner—"and his skill with knives. Not to mention all sorts of other, less savory tactics that my brother likes to use. But why go there when we can make a deal, you and I?"

His Adam's apple moves in a nervous swallow. "W-what kind of deal?"

I smile at him gently. "You're afraid of the Leonovs, aren't you? That's why you're being so brave. You couldn't care less about the plant you're guarding. What's it to you if we get the entrance code, right? But the Leonov family…" I make another slow circle around him. "… they can do things to you, to your loved ones. To your baby sister." I stop in front of him. "Nod if I'm on the right track."

He dips his chin in a barely perceptible nod, sweat running down his face.

"That's what I thought." I pull out a tissue from my pocket and dab at his forehead. "So how about this: You tell us the entrance code and share everything you know about the security protocol at the plant where you work, and we put you and your family on the nearest flight to a destination of your choice. It can be any place: Zimbabwe, Fiji, Thailand… the Cayman Islands. Name it, and we send you there with a new identity and a hundred grand in cash as a relocation bonus. How does that sound?"

Breathing raggedly, he stares at me, hope warring with fear in his eyes.

"I know what you're thinking, Ivan," I continue softly, letting the soiled tissue drop to the floor. "How can you trust me to hold up my side of the bargain? What's to stop us from killing you as soon as you tell us what we want to know, right?"

He swallows again. "R-right."

"The answer is nothing." I let a hint of cruelty seep into my smile. "Absolutely nothing. But that doesn't matter, because trusting me is the only option you have. If you don't, you'll tell us everything the hard way—and when the Leonovs learn of the breach at the plant, they'll look for the culprit. When they discover it's you, they *will* come after your family. Do you understand, Ivan? Do you understand what you have to do if you want your sister to live?"

His chin quivers as he stares at me, tears leaking

from the corners of his eyes. Finally, he bobs his head in defeat.

"Good. Now tell these gentlemen what they want to know."

Turning away, I nod at Valery's men, and they promptly step up, pulling out their phones to begin recording.

"You didn't have to do this personally, you know," Pavel says in a low voice as we walk out of the tavern. "They could've gotten the answers out of him. If not, I would've stepped in. Would've been cheaper that way."

"Maybe. But this way, we know he's not bullshitting us to make the pain stop." I glance at my lifelong bodyguard, whose gaze is restlessly sweeping our surroundings despite the fact that Valery's guards have already secured the perimeter. "Numerous studies have shown that information obtained under torture is unreliable."

"Not the information I obtain," he says darkly, and I chuckle.

"Afraid your knife's getting rusty?"

Pavel doesn't deny it. He misses being in the thick of things, just like I do—or did. Right now, I'd much rather be in Idaho with Chloe. I want to be there in case she has another nightmare. I want to hold her, soothe her, comfort her… and eventually, seduce her. Her resolve is already wavering, I can feel it—which is why I decided to reassure her about the bruises on my knuckles and the scar on my shoulder.

I don't intend to lie to her about the kind of man I am, but I don't want her to fear me.

I won't hurt her… not in that way, at least.

"Did you already set up a meeting with the head of the Energy Commission?" Pavel asks as we stop at an intersection, and I nod, pulling my thoughts away from Chloe.

"I'm meeting him for lunch on Monday," I say, stepping onto the street as the light in front of us turns green. It took three phone calls to get through to the guy, but I succeeded, as I knew I would. "That's another reason I went this route with Ivan," I continue. "There was no time to break him properly—we needed that code ASAP."

"Wouldn't have taken me long either," Pavel mutters, and I laugh—just as a motorcycle roars around the corner and barrels straight at me.

34

NIKOLAI

I REACT IN A SPLIT SECOND, BUT PAVEL IS EVEN FASTER. He shoves me just as I dive to the side, and we both hit the ground hard as the bike roars past us, so close I feel a whoosh of hot air on my face.

Adrenaline propels me to my feet straight away, but the biker is already halfway down the block, weaving through the traffic with race car speed. All I can tell from this distance is that it's a man wearing a black leather jacket and a helmet.

Pavel is already on his feet as well, jaw taut with fury. "Did you see his face?"

"No." I straighten my jacket and tie and brush the dirt and gravel off my scraped palms. My shoulder throbs from landing on it, and cold rage burns inside me, but my voice is calm. "His helmet had a mirrored visor. Maybe one of Valery's guys caught his license plate." I take in the gathering crowd of eyewitnesses, some of whom are pulling out their phones, presumably to call the police. "We better get out of here."

Pavel nods grimly, and we swiftly make our way to the hotel.

Levan Abkhazi, Valery's local security chief, meets us in my room an hour later. A burly Georgian about Pavel's age, he's completely bald but sports a thick black unibrow and a matching beard.

Pulling out a folder, he lays out a series of grainy photos on the desk. "This is all we were able to pull from the nearby store and traffic cameras," he reports in heavily accented Russian. "The team stationed on the rooftops didn't have a good angle on the license plate at any point, and there were too many civilians to risk taking a shot at him."

Pavel and I examine the photos. On one of them, it's possible to make out a portion of a digit, but the other pictures show a corner of the license plate at best. The biker is either the luckiest son of a bitch to ever walk the earth, or he knew where Valery's team was stationed.

I look at Pavel. "Thoughts?"

"A pro, definitely." His face is set in harsh lines. "He didn't slow down, didn't react in any way to almost running you over. And he knew how to handle that bike—and how to avoid the cameras."

Abkhazi's unibrow bunches in a frown. "You don't

think it could've been an accident? If the guy's a pro, he should know that running someone down in the street is not the most efficient way to carry out a hit."

"That depends on whether you want to make it look like an accident or not," Pavel says. "Besides, it wasn't a hit."

The Georgian gives him a confused look. "What was it then?"

"A message," I say, placing the photos back in the folder. "From our friends, the Leonovs. They wanted me to know that they know. The question is: know what?"

35

CHLOE

I WAKE UP SMILING, AND FOR A COUPLE OF MINUTES, I just lie there, eyes closed, floating in that blissful state between dreams and full wakefulness.

And what dreams they were.

My hand slips between my thighs, and I press on the sweet ache that lingers there, trying to remember the sensual scenes that played in my head all night. I only recall fragments of them now, but I know all of them featured Nikolai… his wicked smile… his deep, smooth voice… Best of all, they were the only dreams I had last night.

The nightmares that have plagued me since Mom's death stayed away.

Smile broadening, I open my eyes and sit up. It's bright and sunny, so I've probably overslept. I'm not too worried, though. Nikolai isn't here to enforce the mealtimes, and in any case, now that I know him better, I don't think he'll fire me for such a minor transgression.

Still, I don't want to take advantage, so I hop out of bed and turn on the news. They're again reporting on the primary debates, but all I care about is the time—9:20 a.m. It also happens to be a Saturday, I realize, looking at the date. I wonder if that means I get a day off.

I should probably ask Nikolai about that the next time we talk.

A warm glow fills my chest at the thought of him calling me again and the two of us talking late into the night—almost like a dating couple. Because that's how that videocall last night felt: like the kind of thing you do with your boyfriend while he's away, a long-distance date of sorts. Though we spent most of the time talking about Slava, as befits our employer-tutor relationship, there'd been a definite softness in the way Nikolai looked at me and the way he spoke… an undercurrent of tenderness that makes my heart skip a beat each time I think about it.

It's almost as if he's starting to care for me, as if there's something more between us than animal attraction.

I try not to think about it as I go about my day because it's such a foolish notion. There's no way Nikolai is developing feelings for me. Not only is it way too soon, but I'd be an idiot to imagine that a man like that would be interested in me for any reason other than proximity. I *am* the only available woman here; he can't exactly hook up with Lyudmila or his sister. So what if he called me as soon as he landed yesterday? That doesn't mean he was thinking about me during the long flight.

He could've just been concerned about his son.

Still, that warm glow stays with me as I sneak into the kitchen to grab myself a late breakfast—the official breakfast being over—before taking Slava for a nice long hike. And it persists through lunch despite Alina's presence at the table reminding me of her strange warning.

"How's your headache?" I ask when we sit down to eat, and she waves away my concern, claiming that she's fully recovered. However, I can't help but notice that she's quiet and oddly distant, frequently staring off into space during the meal. It makes me wonder if she's high again, but I decide not to ask.

Last night, the campfire and the pot lowered everybody's inhibitions, creating a false sense of intimacy, but today, she feels like a stranger again. So does Lyudmila, who doesn't even smile at me as she brings out the food. Maybe she's embarrassed I saw her stoned? Either way, I hurry through the meal, and as soon as Slava is done eating, I take him to his room for our play lessons.

We build another castle and review the alphabet, and I teach him how to count to ten in English.

Afterward, we play hide-and-seek and read some books, including, at Slava's request, a story about a family of ducks. Before we begin, he proudly shows me a book in Russian that appears to be a translation of it, and I realize he's trying to apply his knowledge of the plot and characters to better understand the English words and phrases I read out loud to him.

"You're such a clever boy," I tell him, and he beams at me. Though I doubt he understands exactly what I'm saying, my tone of approval is unmistakable.

I sit on the floor, my back leaning against the bed, and Slava climbs into my lap as we start the story—which turns out to be surprisingly complex for a children's book. The duck family isn't all happy and go-lucky; they squabble and have conflicts, and at one point, the main hero, a young duckling, runs away from home. When he returns, he finds Mama Duck gone, and he cries, thinking that he caused her to leave.

I keep an eye on Slava during this part, worried that this might bring up memories of losing his mother, but the boy's expression remains curious and relaxed. However, when we get to the part where the young duckling has to stay with his grandfather, Slava stiffens and insists on skipping over the next three pages.

"You don't like Grandpa Duck?" I guess, and the child shrugs, avoiding my gaze.

"Okay. We don't have to read about him. Forget Grandpa Duck." Smiling, I ruffle his hair and move on to a less problematic section of the book.

Alina doesn't join us for dinner—another headache, Lyudmila tells me gruffly—so Slava and I have another relaxed meal before I go up to my room for the evening. Changing out of the formal dinner attire, I make myself comfortable on the bed and open the laptop—to do some more research, I tell myself. Not to wait for Nikolai's call like some lovesick girlfriend. So what if he promised he'd call? Maybe he will, or maybe he won't.

I shouldn't care either way.

Determined not to sit there biting my nails, I resume my research into Mom's death. The reporter I emailed last night hasn't replied, so I find the contact info of a few more Boston-area journalists and message them. I also research the owner of the restaurant where Mom worked, as well as the corporation behind the upscale hotel where the restaurant is located.

There has to be a reason those men killed my mom.

I find the same thing as yesterday: nothing. What I really need is a private investigator, but there's no way I can afford one right now. Although… it doesn't hurt to get some rate quotes. Come Tuesday, I'll have money, and if I'm staying here—which I don't see why I wouldn't—I might as well use that money to get some answers.

Yes, that's it.

That's exactly what I'll do.

Encouraged, I look up a few promising leads and email them for a quote. Then, feeling accomplished for the evening, I switch over to my other project: learning everything I can about Nikolai.

I've thought of a few more phrases I can translate into Russian, and my search turns up several tabloid photos. One is of Nikolai at a Warsaw charity gala with a tall blond beauty on his arm; another is of him at a Moscow fashion show, sitting next to a bored-looking Alina. A couple more show him vacationing at various exotic destinations, invariably with some leggy model at his side staring at him with adoration.

I was right. He's all but drowning in gorgeous women. For all I know, he might be in bed with some stunning model at this very moment, having picked her up at some VIP nightclub last night.

The thought is like a splash of boiling water on my chest. I have no right to feel this way, but I suddenly want to rip out every hair on the head of this imaginary woman—right before I do the same to Nikolai.

Setting the laptop aside, I jump off the bed and start to pace.

Why isn't he calling?

He said he would.

He promised.

He has to know it's getting later here by the minute.

Is it because he's busy with work—or with some woman? I picture her glossy red lips wrapped around his cock, her eyes peering up at him through skillfully applied fake lashes as she—

A soft chime sounds from the bed, and I lunge toward the open laptop, my pulse skyrocketing. Plopping down on my stomach, I pull the computer toward me and, with an unsteady finger, hit "Accept" on Nikolai's videocall request.

His face fills the screen, his hotel room visible behind him, and I exhale a shaky breath, my irrational jealousy fading as I see the tender look in his tiger eyes.

"Hi, zaychik," he murmurs, his deep voice so velvety I want to rub it against my cheek. "How was your day?"

"It was good. How was yours? I mean, your morning—or your day yesterday?" I sound out of breath, but I can't help it. My heart is pounding in a techno beat, and every cell in my body is vibrating with excitement. As pathetic as it is, I've been looking forward to this call all day. Even when I wasn't consciously thinking about it, it was lurking at the back of my mind.

He gives me a wry smile. "My morning was okay, and so was the rest of yesterday. Some meetings, some bullshit—business as usual."

"What kind of business?" Realizing how nosy that sounds, I open my mouth to take back the question, but he's already answering.

"Clean energy. Specifically, nuclear energy. One of our companies has developed a proprietary technology that allows for small, portable nuclear reactors that can be used to provide low-cost electricity in small villages and other remote settlements."

"Wow. And they're safe? Not like—what was that famous one in Ukraine?"

"Chernobyl? No, they're nothing like that. For one thing, each reactor is only about the size of a car, so even if there was an accident, the amount of radiation released would be much less. More importantly, our engineers have added so many redundancies that an accident is next to impossible. Our moto is *Safety First*—unlike our rivals.'" His voice hardens on the last part.

"There are other companies doing the same thing?" I ask, fascinated by this glimpse into a world I know nothing about.

His eyes glint darkly. "One. They're bidding against us for a huge contract with the Tajik government. Whoever wins it will dominate this nascent industry in Central Asia—which is why my brother asked me to get involved."

"Oh?"

"The head of the Tajikistan Energy Commission was a classmate of mine at boarding school, and my brother's hoping I'll have better luck making our case to him." A wry smile touches his lips. "As you've probably guessed, personal connections are very important in business."

I widen my eyes exaggeratedly. "No! Really?"

He laughs. "I know. Hard to imagine, right? I have a lunch meeting with him on Monday, and then I'll hopefully be able to fly back."

"So you'll be back by Tuesday?" I'm already counting down the days until my first paycheck, and now I'll have another reason to wish I could put the next fifty hours on fast-forward.

"I should be, yes." He pauses, then says softly, "I miss you, zaychik."

My breath stops, literally, even as my heart hammers faster and my skin tingles with a flush. Regardless of what I thought I saw in his eyes last night—what I hoped he might feel—I never dreamed that I'd hear him say that to me tonight so casually… so openly.

Like a boyfriend.

He's looking at me, patiently waiting for my response, so as soon as my breathing resumes, I force myself to speak. "I… I miss you too. And Slava. He misses you. We both miss you. He really does." I know I'm not making any sense, but I can't help it. I've never had trouble expressing my feelings with the guys I've dated, but I've never dated anyone like Nikolai before—not that we're dating. Or are we? Maybe he just misses me in the friend sense? Or son's tutor sense?

God, I have no idea what's happening.

The corners of his sensuous lips twitch with suppressed amusement, and I once again have the unnerving suspicion that he's looking straight into my brain and seeing the confusion there. "Tell me more, zaychik," he murmurs, leaning closer to the camera. "What has my son been up to today?"

Slava, that's it. I grab on to the topic like a drowning man latching on to a buoy, and launch into a detailed description of everything Slava and I have done and learned. Nikolai listens raptly, his gaze filled with that special softness he reserves for his son. However, when I get to the book Slava and I read last—the story about the ducklings—and I laughingly mention Slava's apparent dislike for Grandpa Duck, all traces of softness disappear from Nikolai's expression, his eyes taking on a hard, sharp gleam.

"Did he say anything?" he demands. "Explain it in any way?"

"No, I… I didn't ask." I draw back at the look on his face, an expression so dark and cold it sends a chill through my body. This is a side of Nikolai I've never seen, and suddenly, my earlier concerns about mafia don't seem quite as foolish.

I can picture this man ordering a hit—even pulling the trigger himself.

In the next moment, however, his features smooth out, the chilling look disappearing as he asks me to continue, and I'm again left wondering if my unruly imagination played a trick on me. Maybe I read too much into that brief change of expression… or maybe I just got a peek into some Molotov family drama. It could simply be that Nikolai doesn't get along with Slava's grandfather—assuming there is one on his mother's side.

There's still a lot I don't know about this family.

Deciding to remedy that, I finish my report on Slava's progress by going over what I taught him at dinner, and then I carefully—very carefully, lest I step on any landmines—ask Nikolai to tell me about his brothers.

Thankfully, my request doesn't upset him. "I'm the second oldest," he tells me. "Valery is four years my junior, and Konstantin—the genius of the family—is two years older than me. He runs all of our tech ventures, while Valery oversees the entire organization."

"Which you used to do, right?" I ask, recalling what Alina told me.

"That's right." He doesn't look surprised that I know. "But it's hard to do remotely, so I asked Valery to step in while I'm away."

"Why *are* you away?" I ask, unable to resist the question that's been on my mind for so long. "What brought you to this corner of the world?"

He smiles at my blatant curiosity. "I know. It's odd, right?"

"Extremely odd." So odd, in fact, that I've concocted a crazy mafia story in my head, but I'm keeping my mouth shut about that.

He leans back in his chair, the smile fading until only a trace of the sensual curve remains. "It's a long story, zaychik, and it's getting late. You should go to sleep."

"It's okay, I'm not tired." And even if I were, I'd deny it because I'm dying to hear this story, whatever length it may be. Sitting up straighter, I arrange the computer more comfortably on my lap and give him my best puppy eyes, fluttering lashes and all. "Please, Nikolai… tell me. Pretty, pretty please."

I meant it as a joke, a light flirtation at best, but his face goes taut, his gaze darkening as he leans toward the camera. "I like hearing my name on your lips." His voice is a low, honeyed purr. "And I really, really like it when you beg."

My mouth goes Sahara dry, my heartbeat uneven as fire streaks through my veins and centers low in my core. With him so far away and our video chats staying mostly on safe topics, I've somehow let myself forget about the sexual tension that smolders between us, ready to ignite into a conflagration at the slightest spark. I've convinced myself that I imagined that feeling of being hunted prey… that alarming, yet strangely exciting awareness that I'm at the mercy of this dangerously alluring man.

"Is that—" I swallow, uncertain if I should venture there. "Is that your thing? Women begging?"

The dark heat in his eyes intensifies. "My *thing*, zaychik, is you. I want you in every way possible… sweetly and roughly… on your knees, and on your back, and on top, riding me… I want to eat your pussy for dessert after each meal and pour my cum down your throat every morning. I want to fuck you so hard you scream, and then I want to cuddle you for hours. Most of all, I want to drown you in pleasure… so much pleasure you won't mind the occasional bite of pain… In fact, you'll beg for it."

Oh. My. God.

I stare at him, my breaths short and shallow, my clit throbbing and my nipples pebble hard. My body feels like one of his nuclear reactors in meltdown, the heat under my skin so scorching I might spontaneously combust. *Or come.* If I put any pressure on my clit right now, I could definitely come.

I wet my lips, trying to ignore the pulsing ache between my legs. "So… you *are* into stuff. Like, kinky stuff."

As soon as the words leave my mouth, I cringe at how juvenile and vanilla I sound. And I'm not vanilla. At least I don't think I am. My sexual fantasies have always had a darker tinge to them, and I've had a boyfriend tie me up once or twice—and another time, spank me. None of that turned me on, but then again, my boyfriend wasn't really into it. It felt awkward and forced with him… childish, somehow.

I have a feeling it'll be nothing of the sort with Nikolai.

The man doesn't know the meaning of childish and awkward.

Sure enough, his lips curve in another darkly sensual smile. In a voice like heated silk, he murmurs, "Chloe, zaychik… I'm into everything—as long as it's with you."

This time, it's my heart that goes into meltdown mode. Because it sounds a lot like… "Are you saying you don't want to see other women?" I blurt, and immediately want to kick myself for once again sounding like I'm in high school. He's just flirting, not making any kind of exclusivity commitment. We haven't even—

"I don't," he says softly, bringing my thoughts to a screeching halt. "I don't want anyone but you. I haven't since the moment we met."

"Oh." I stare at him, unable to come up with anything else to say.

This is big.

Huge, really.

There's no possible misunderstanding here, no chance that I'm being a foolish romantic.

Nikolai is telling me that he wants me and no one else… that essentially, we *are* exclusive.

"Does this scare you?" he asks, disconcertingly astute. "Is this too much for you?"

It is. Way too much. And yet… "No," I say, gathering my courage. "It's not. And I—I don't want to see anyone else either."

His nostrils flare. "Good. Once you're mine, I won't deal kindly with any man who tries to steal you."

A startled laugh escapes my throat, but Nikolai doesn't smile in response. His gaze remains fixed on me, his expression darkly intent, and to my shock, I realize that he means it, that it's not a joke at all.

I attempt to make it into one anyway. "Possessive much?"

"With you," he says, his gaze unwavering, "very much."

My heart stutters to a halt again. "Why me?" I ask when I recover my voice. "Is it because I'm the only woman here, within arm's reach? Is it a convenience thing or…" I trail off as amusement brightens the dark gold of his eyes, highlighting the flecks of forest green.

"If I were so inclined," he says gently, "I could have a different woman flown in every week—and I often did before you came. There's no lack of candidates willing to make the trip, believe me, zaychik."

Oh, I believe him. Even before I came across those tabloid photos, I knew he must have a stable of gorgeous women at his beck and call. How could he not, with his looks, wealth, and sex appeal?

The wonder is not that women are willing to fly in, it's that they're not camped out in the woods.

"Why then?" I ask unsteadily. "Why me?"

He cocks his head. "Do you believe in fate, zaychik?"

"Fate? Like God or destiny?"

"Or predestination. All of us being connected, like threads in a tapestry that was woven long before our births."

I stare at him, bemused. "I don't know. I've never given it much thought."

His lips curve in a faint smile. "I have. And I think at some point in the weaving of this tapestry, your thread was joined to mine. Our paths were bound to intersect, our meeting date set long before I saw you. Everything that had happened in our lives had brought us to that point, to that place and time… all the good things and the bad." His voice roughens. "Especially the bad."

Like my mom's death. If not for that, I would've never been on this road trip, never seen the job listing, never met him. Not that it means this is fated. But Nikolai seems to believe that, and I have to admit that we wouldn't be here today without the violent upheaval in my life. And, it sounds like, without some upheaval in his.

"What bad things happened to you?" I ask softly. "Or is that the long story you keep promising me?"

His smile takes on a rueful edge. "More or less. Unfortunately, zaychik, you need to go to sleep, and I have to go meet my brother. How about I call you tomorrow around the same time, and we'll talk some more?"

"Oh, sure. I didn't mean to hold you up."

"You didn't." That tender look is in his eyes again, making my heart pound in an erratic, joyous rhythm. "If I could, I'd talk to you all day."

"Me too," I admit with a shy smile.

His answering smile is dazzling. "Until tomorrow then. Sleep well, zaychik."

And as he disconnects the call, I push the computer off my lap and do a dance around the room, grinning so hard my cheeks hurt.

36

NIKOLAI

"YOU'RE IN A GOOD MOOD FOR SOMEONE WHO WAS almost killed yesterday," Konstantin says after we place our orders with the waiter, and I realize I've been smiling so much even my socially oblivious brother has noticed. And it's all because of her.

Chloe.

She's fast becoming my feel-good drug.

I love that she's beginning to trust me, to accept what's happening between us. I didn't want to come on too strongly on our call today, but it was time she knew my intentions—and now she does. More importantly, I got her to admit that she reciprocates my feelings.

Her sweetly murmured "me too" is still playing in my mind on a loop.

"Do you have the report?" I ask, ignoring Konstantin's comment. It's none of his business what kind of mood I'm in or why. Besides, there's nothing like almost dying to make one appreciate life and all of its wonderful possibilities—such as taking Chloe to bed as soon as I get back home.

"Not yet," Konstantin says, picking up his cup of chamomile tea. "Hopefully, either later today or tomorrow. But we have verified the info the security guard provided, and it all checks out. The operation is a go for tonight."

"What's taking so long? Your hackers usually come through within hours."

He blinks behind the lenses of his glasses. "You're still talking about the report on the girl?"

I grit my teeth. "What else?"

"My team's been busy, and it's not an easy task you've assigned them."

"How so? All I've asked is for you to look into her mother's death and her movements for the past month. How difficult is that? I know she's been off the grid, but there's got to be traffic cameras, gas station cam—"

"There seems to be some interference." He sips his tea. "A few of the security tapes my guys have pulled have been damaged or wiped clean."

I still. "Wiped clean?"

"A professional job, from the looks of it." He sets down his cup. "You said she's just a civilian, right? No affiliation?"

"None that I'm aware of," I say evenly.

Is it possible?

Could she have fooled me?

Is sweet little Chloe involved with the mob… or worse, the government?

"Why didn't you tell me this before?" I ask Konstantin, who, once again oblivious to the bombshell he's delivered, is calmly spreading sundried tomato pesto on a piece of freshly baked rye bread. "Don't you think it's important for me to know?"

He bites into the bread and chews leisurely. "I'm telling you now," he says after he swallows. "Besides, my guys only realized what's going on last night. A couple of damaged tapes could be just shit luck. But several—that's a pattern."

"So let me get this clear. You're telling me someone's erasing all the security tapes where she appears."

"Not all the tapes." He reaches for another piece of bread. "My team's been able to reconstruct her movements for the majority of the past month. Just certain tapes... ones I suspect may hold the answers you're after."

Fuck.

This is big.

I don't know what I thought Konstantin's hackers would uncover, but it wasn't this.

A thought slithers into my mind, a suspicion so awful my stomach turns over. "Do you think it's the—"

"Leonovs?" Konstantin sets down his bread. "I doubt it. My guys have come across their hackers' work before, and this doesn't feel like it."

"Feel like it?"

Light glints off the lenses of his glasses. "It's hard to explain to a non-techie, but yes. There's a certain sloppiness to the way this was done that doesn't fit the Leonovs."

"I thought you said it was professionals."

"There are different levels of professionalism. My guys are top notch, the Leonovs' team isn't far behind, and many are way, way worse. These guys are somewhere in the middle, which is why I think my team's going to come through for you. They just need more time."

I take a breath and let it out slowly. Just the possibility that Chloe could've been hired by my enemies is enough to spike my blood pressure. But Konstantin knows what he's talking about, and if he doesn't think it's them, I have to lay that suspicion to rest for now. Besides, if the Leonovs knew enough to plant Chloe in my compound, I doubt they would've sent a guy on a motorcycle as a warning.

There would've been no warning, just straight-up war.

"About the biker," I say. "Any luck tracking him down?"

"No. And that does have Leonov fingerprints all over it. If I had to guess, Alexei's pissed that you're here, interfering with his bid."

"You're probably right." I fall silent as the waiter brings out our food. Once he leaves, I continue. "He must've found out about my meeting with the Commission head."

"Valery's doubling your security until then, just in case. Now"—Konstantin drizzles dressing onto his

Greek salad—"let's discuss your talking points for tomorrow."

And as he goes over the technical specifications of our product, I do my best to focus on his words instead of the growing number of questions about Chloe and my increasing obsession with her.

37

CHLOE

I'VE NEVER FELT AS GIDDY AS I DO THIS SUNDAY. ALL DAY long, I catch myself smiling uncontrollably and walking around like I'm floating on a cloud. It's embarrassing, really, but I can't stop. Each time I think about last night's call, my pulse races with excitement.

Nikolai wants me.

He misses me.

He wants us to be exclusive.

I feel like a teenager whose movie star crush just asked her out on a date. Which, in a way, is what's happening.

Nikolai wants us to date, or more precisely, to be in a relationship.

It should seem crazy, and on some level, it does. We've known each other less than a week, and for the past couple of days, he hasn't been here in person. It's way too soon to be talking about exclusivity, much less destiny and fate. But I can't deny the strength of the attraction that burns between us, of that powerful, magnetic force that's terrified me from the start. It wasn't the attraction itself I feared, though—it was getting hurt. I was afraid of falling for a man who, at best, thought of me as a few nights of entertainment. But that's not how it is for Nikolai. He made that clear last night, and though it may be naïve of me, I believe him.

I see no reason for him to lie to me.

There are other obstacles to our relationship, of course—like his status as my employer and the fact that I'm on the run from a pair of ruthless killers. At some point soon, I'll have to disclose that, and I have no idea how he'll react. But that's a worry for another day.

Right now, all I want to think about is seeing him on my computer screen tonight.

"Someone chasing you?" Alina inquires at dinner, and I freeze, my heart stopping for a second before I realize she's referring to the speed with which I'm devouring my food.

"Just hungry," I say after I swallow. "Sorry if I'm being rude."

She shrugs her graceful shoulders, which are left bare by her strapless evening dress. "I don't care. Just curious why you're in such a rush."

I'm in a rush because I'm dying to get up to my

room in case Nikolai calls early, but there's no way I'm telling her that. "No reason other than yummy food."

Slava giggles at my side. "Yummy. I like yummy in my tummy."

I beam at him. "Yes, you do." We've spent all day learning various words and phrases, including this little rhyme, and I'm beyond pleased he remembers it.

"At this rate, you're going to have him speaking English in a week," Alina says, cutting a piece of chicken and placing it on his plate.

I grin at her. "I hope so—but more realistically, in a couple of months."

She smiles back at me and resumes eating, and I do likewise, eager to be done and ensconced comfortably in my bed with the laptop. Like Alina, I'm wearing an evening gown, and I'm looking forward to changing into my pajamas. Although... maybe I shouldn't. Nikolai might enjoy seeing me like this, even through the camera.

In fact, I should probably refresh my makeup before he calls.

"Want to race?" I ask Slava, and make engine-revving noises to remind him of our racing game with toy cars. "See who can eat faster?"

He blinks, not understanding, so I pick up my fork and begin shoveling food into my mouth with exaggerated speed. Catching on, he does the same, and we clean our plates in record time. Alina, who's eating at a normal pace, watches our race with amusement, and by the time we're done, she pushes away her half-eaten chicken.

"I guess I'm done as well," she says dryly. Louder, she calls, *"Lyuda, Slava gotov!"*

Lyudmila appears from the kitchen, wiping her hands on her apron. I smile and thank her for the delicious meal—though, truth be told, it was nowhere near as good as what her husband makes. The chicken was on the dry side, the potatoes were too salty, and most of the appetizers and side dishes were leftovers. But I'm not about to quibble: Food is food, and I'm grateful to have it.

Smiling back at me, Lyudmila picks up Slava, and just like that, my evening is free.

As soon as I get to my room, I completely redo my makeup—all I had on at dinner was a light layer of foundation and a coat of mascara—and fix up my hair. I still don't look nearly as polished as when Alina did this for me, but hopefully, Nikolai won't mind.

I was barefaced and in my PJs on our last two calls, so this is a definite improvement.

Feeling giddy again, I grin at my reflection. I look much better than when I first got here. My cheeks are no longer painfully hollow and the dark circles under my eyes have faded, as has the look of desperation in them. Last night was another one with no nightmares, only sex dreams, and I have Nikolai to thank for that. I may have woken up wet and aching, with my hand pressed between my thighs, but at least I slept through the night.

God, I can't wait to talk to him.

Hurrying over to my bed, I sprawl on my stomach and grab the laptop, willing him to call at this very moment.

He doesn't. I guess my mental powers aren't up to snuff.

Sighing, I go into my inbox to check for any replies from the journalists. There's nothing, naturally—though there *is* a quote from one of the PI firms, detailing their hourly rates and retainer fees.

I skim it and wince. It's a lot, way more than I can hope to cover with my first week's paycheck, at least given the number of hours I anticipate they'll have to spend. I'll need at least a couple weeks' pay for the retainer alone. Maybe the other PIs will be cheaper, but they haven't responded yet, so I have to wait.

Like I'm waiting for Nikolai, *who's still not calling.*

Taking a breath, I remind myself to be patient. He said he'd call me around the same time as yesterday, and it's nowhere near that. For now, I need to distract myself with something, so I begin researching my mom's friends and co-workers again on the off chance I missed something the first time.

I'm scrolling through the pictures of her manager's daughter's quinceañera when the call request pops up, sending my pulse skyrocketing.

Beaming, I smooth my hair and click "Accept."

38

NIKOLAI

Chloe's smile is so radiant I feel like I've stepped out of an underground bunker onto a sunlit beach. "Hi," she says, slightly breathless as she sits back against a stack of pillows and places the computer on her lap. "How's it going? How's your nuclear bidding thing?"

I smile back at her, pleasure spreading through me like molten honey. "It's good, zaychik, thank you."

And it is. Valery's operation has gone off without a hitch, and the Energy Commission is already swarming around the Atomprom plant, seeking to contain the fallout from the reactor that exploded overnight. The radiation leakage is minimal, as expected, but the damage to Atomprom's reputation is significant—which sets us up well for my lunch meeting with the Commission head today.

More importantly, for the past hour, I've been watching Chloe's online activities and examining her browser history from yesterday, and I've concluded that she's unlikely to be affiliated with any government or rival organization. If she were a plant, she'd know everything about me already and wouldn't need to translate Russian articles with the aid of free online tools. Nor would she be researching her mother's friends and co-workers using nothing more than their public social media—or looking into PI firms.

Something else is going on with Chloe, something I find both worrisome and intriguing.

My best bet is to get her to open up to me, to tell me the truth, but if I press her on it now, she might get spooked and try to run—and I don't want that. Not when I'm an ocean away. The next best option is to get Konstantin's team to hack her Gmail; the spyware allows me to see what sites she's on but not the content of them, like individual emails.

Either way, I'm going to get the answers. I just need to be patient a little longer.

"How was your day?" I ask, settling more comfortably into my chair. "What did you and Slava do?"

Her smile turns impossibly brighter, and she tells me all about my son's amazing progress, her small face so animated I can't take my eyes off it. She sounds as proud as any parent, and for the first time since I've learned of Slava's existence and Ksenia's death, my chest doesn't feel as painfully tight when I think of him and the future that awaits him because of the tainted blood running through his veins. Instead, I feel a sliver of hope as I picture Chloe with Slava, playing with him, cuddling him, loving him… giving him what his mother can't.

What *I* can't.

And that's part of it, I realize, part of why I want her so badly. I want her not just for myself but for my son. I want her sunshine to touch him, to warm him… to keep away the darkness of his heritage for as long as possible. I want her the way I've seen her through the cameras in Slava's room, gracing my son with her radiant smile, making him feel like he's the most important person in the world to her.

And I want him to be that.

I want her to love Slava even more than I want her to love me.

Hungrily, I listen to her talk about him, absorbing every word, drinking in every expression. She's wearing one of her new evening dresses, a pale-yellow number with thin straps that bares her delicate shoulders. Her brown eyes sparkle, and even through the camera, her bronzed skin glows in the golden light cast by her bedside lamp. She's breathtaking, this sweet mystery of a girl—and mine. All mine. I might not have claimed her physically yet, but it doesn't change the facts. She was made for me, her light the perfect foil to the dark void inside me, her warmth filling every cold, empty crevice in my heart. I don't care who she turns out to be or what secrets she's hiding.

Criminal or victim, she belongs to me, no matter what.

When she's done telling me about Slava, I ask her

about her favorite books and music, and we bond over our mutual love of eighties bands and Dean Koontz novels. I'm not surprised that we have things in common; that's how it often works when you find your other half, the puzzle piece that completes you. She's my opposite in so many ways, yet there are threads that connect us, that bound us together long before we met.

We talk for a solid hour, and I find out more about her childhood and teenage years, about her young mother and how hard she worked to raise Chloe by herself. She tells me about hanging out downtown with her friends and vacationing in Florida with her mother, about struggling with calculus in high school and working two jobs for three summers straight to buy her rickety Corolla on her own.

"It's almost as old as I am," she says fondly, "but it still runs. Even after all the miles I put on it driving across the country. Speaking of which, did you ever have a chance to ask Pavel about my car keys? I still don't have them."

I veil my expression, concealing the beast that stirs inside me at the thought of her getting into her rust bucket of a car and leaving. "He said he couldn't find them. We'll look for them when we get back."

It's a lie, but I can't tell her the truth. She wouldn't understand. I don't fully understand it myself. All I know is that I sleep better knowing the keys on that furry chain are in my possession, that my zaychik is safe and sound under my roof.

A tiny frown creases her forehead. "Oh, okay. But he'll find them, right?"

"I'm sure he will. If not, I'll buy you another car."

She laughs, clearly thinking it's a joke, but I'm completely serious. I *will* buy her a car, something better, safer than the Corolla. It's a miracle it hasn't broken down on some deserted road, leaving her stranded with no phone, at the mercy of any murderer or rapist who might be passing by.

Just the thought of her in that situation makes me break out in a cold sweat.

"I'll just call a locksmith," she says when she stops laughing. "There are locksmiths in Elkwood Creek, right?"

"I'm sure there's at least one." And I'm just as sure he's getting nowhere near Chloe's car. The more I think about her driving across the country all alone, the darker my mood turns. Anything could've happened to her, absolutely anything—and for all I know, it did.

Her nightmares could have nothing to do with what happened to her mother and everything to do with some lowlife assaulting her on the road.

Rage burns inside me as I picture her getting attacked, hurt and traumatized, and it's all I can do not to demand that she tell me the truth right now, so I can exterminate those responsible. Only the fear that she might pull back and try to leave keeps me silent. That and the recollection of those damaged tapes, the ones that indicate that something more is going on, that she's involved with someone or something with the resources to conceal her movements.

Oblivious to the storm inside me, she grins and says, "All right then. You can tell Pavel not to stress about it. I'm guessing he's upset he lost them?"

"I'll talk to him, don't worry." And I will. I need to explain the situation and ask him to apologize to Chloe. Right now, he has no clue that anything's amiss. "As to the—"

A soft chime interrupts me, and to my disappointment, I see it's time to head to my meeting. I set an alarm on my phone so I wouldn't be late.

"Do you have to go?" Chloe asks astutely, and I nod, buttoning my jacket.

"This is the meeting I'm here for. The good news is, if all goes as expected, I'm getting on a plane home right after."

Her eyes brighten. "Really? What time does your flight leave?"

"When I tell it to. It's my plane." Leaning into the camera, I murmur, "I can't wait to see you in person."

She gives me a sweet smile. "Same here. Good luck at your meeting and fly home safe."

"Thank you, zaychik." Voice roughening, I advise, "Sleep well tonight—you'll need it."

And as her lips part on a startled inhale, I hang up, eager to conclude the meeting so I can be in the air, on the way to her.

I'm already at the table when Yusup Bahori walks into Al Sham, one of the best Middle Eastern restaurants in Dushanbe and, according to Konstantin's research, a favorite spot of Yusup's. After the obligatory half hour of catching up on our favorite school memories and discussing our classmates and other mutual acquaintances, I shift the conversation toward our permits and the bidding for the contract with the Tajik government.

"Nikolai, you know I can't—" he starts, but I hold up my hand, stopping the bullshit in its tracks.

"Let's not play games. You and I both know our product is superior to Atomprom's. So why were our permits pulled?"

He blinks, not expecting me to be that direct. "Well, there were safety concerns and—"

"We've never had a meltdown or a leak. Our safety protocols go above and beyond any government requirements, and best of all, our reactors can provide cheap, clean energy to every settlement and village, no matter how inaccessible or remote."

He sighs, pushing away his half-finished kebab. "Look, I don't know the particulars, but if our inspectors—"

"Are these the same inspectors that greenlit Atomprom's bid? If so, for how much?"

He has the grace to flush. "We've just begun the investigation of last night's accident," he says stiffly. "If it turns out there was any improper conduct, we'll take appropriate measures. We don't tolerate corruption and bribery. The safety of our citizens and the environment is of utmost importance to us."

I nod, picking up my fork. "Which is why Atomprom was never the right company to partner with you. Their safety record is abysmal."

Calmly, I eat two bites of falafel, letting him mull it over, and I'm not the least bit surprised when he says abruptly, "Fine. I can look into the permits for you. Maybe some inspector did get overzealous."

"That would be much appreciated. And if it does turn out there's been a misunderstanding, we would be grateful if you reversed the decision and put in a good word for us during the bidding."

He licks his lips. "I understand."

Of course he does. Gratitude from the Molotov organization is a very lucrative thing. As is gratitude from the Leonovs—but he's already received it.

His new mansion in Khujand is proof of that.

It would be easy to point that out, to use the evidence of corruption Konstantin's hackers have uncovered to get him to do what we want, but unlike Valery, I believe in waving the carrot before grabbing the stick.

Things tend to go smoother that way.

Goal achieved, I return to neutral topics, and the rest of the meal passes in pleasant conversation. He doesn't bring up the specifics of our "gratitude," and neither do I. Let him have plausible deniability when our payment lands in his offshore account; it doesn't hurt us in the least.

When we're done, he heads out to his car, and I stop by the restroom before the long drive to the small airport where my jet is waiting. I'm washing my hands when the door opens and a tall, athletically built man about my age steps in.

A man I instantly recognize.

"Well, if it isn't the missing Molotov brother," Alexei Leonov drawls, leaning against the door and folding his tattooed arms across his chest. "Fancy running into you here."

39

NIKOLAI

I CASUALLY WIPE MY HANDS ON A PAPER TOWEL AND DROP it in the trash. In the process, I scan my enemy for any visible weapons. None are in sight, but that doesn't mean anything. He could have a gun strapped to his ankle or tucked into the back of his jeans. And there's definitely a knife or two in his biker boots.

Alexei Leonov is known for his appetite for violence.

"Coincidence is a funny thing," I say calmly, preparing to reach for the Glock strapped to my chest under my jacket. "What brings you to Dushanbe?"

He grins sharply. "Same thing as you, I imagine." Uncrossing his arms, he pushes away from the door and approaches me. Stopping in front of me, he asks, "How's life in… where is it you are these days? Thailand? The Philippines?" Even up close, his dark brown eyes look almost black, matching the hue of his hair.

"Life's great. How's your old man?" If he thinks I'm going to blurt out my location after all the trouble Konstantin's gone through to hide it, he's got another thing coming. "Still alive and kicking?"

His smile is all teeth. "You know how these old men are. Practically indestructible. You have to *really* try to get them to croak."

I don't take this bait either. "Say hello to him for me. And to your brother."

His eyes glint harshly. "Not my sister? Oh, yeah, she's fucking dead."

It takes everything I have to keep a poker face. "I've heard. I'm sorry." It's a lie—Ksenia deserves to rot with the worms—but anything more than the most neutral response may tip my hand, and he already seems to harbor some suspicions.

His savage grin returns. "Speaking of sisters… how's my intended?"

Now this I can't let slide. I hold his gaze, letting him see the ice in my eyes. "Alina's not yours. Never was, never will be."

"That's not what our betrothal contract says."

"That contract was voided by my father's death, and you know it."

"Do I?" He leans in until we're almost nose to nose. No hint of humor remains on his face, stamping his hard features with an unmistakable patina of cruelty. In a lethally soft tone, he says, "Tell Alina it's time. I'm done being patient."

And stepping back, he exits through the door.

Red-hot fury still burns in my chest when Konstantin's Tesla pulls up to the plane.

"Thanks for waiting," he says, climbing out. "I figured it'd be better to give this to you in person." He hands me a flash drive.

"Chloe?"

He nods. "It's a doozy. You were right to have me dig deeper. The girl isn't who she seems."

Fuck. "Mafia?"

"Maybe. Watch the video. My guys are doing their best to learn more."

Motherfucker. I want to demand all the answers, now, but the plane is ready to depart, and I need to fill him in on my encounter with Alexei. Swiftly, I do so, and when I get to the part about Alina, I see the same fury reflected on his face.

"I'll kill him if he so much as breathes her way," Konstantin says savagely. "If he thinks we're going to honor that fucking medieval contract, made when our sister was barely fifteen, he's—"

"I doubt he was serious. Most likely, he was trying to provoke me as payback for the explosion at their plant. Either way, he doesn't know for sure she's with me. He was shooting in the dark."

Konstantin takes a breath, visibly composing himself. Of the three of us, he's closest to Alina, having spent time babysitting her during school holidays and summer breaks. I never had that luxury; our father had decided early on that I was the son best suited to assume the mantle of leadership in our organization, and all of my childhood and teenage years were spent learning the family business.

"You're right," he says in a calmer tone. "He's pissed, and he wants to piss us off. Just in case, though, tell Alina to be on her guard."

"I don't think that's a good idea. She's been… having some trouble the last couple of days."

His eyebrows pull together. "The headaches are back?"

I nod grimly. "Lyudmila says she's been hitting the medications pretty hard while I've been gone. Pot, too."

Alina thinks I don't know about that last part, but I do—and I've asked Lyudmila to keep her company whenever she wants to smoke. I'm not a fan of mind-altering substances, but I know why my sister needs it, and weed is preferable to some of the prescriptions in her bedside drawer.

Konstantin's frown deepens. "She's spiraling again."

"Let's hope not." But if she is, that's another reason for me to hurry back. Though Alina and I barely get along, something about my presence keeps her on an even keel—maybe even the friction that exists between us. It gives her an external focus, a distraction from her inner turmoil.

With me, she has a clear and present target instead of the shadows lurking in her mind.

"Listen," I tell Konstantin, "I have to go. I'll let you know how she is when I see her in person. Just tell your team to keep doing what they're doing—Alexei can't find out where we are."

His jaw tightens. "Don't worry. He won't."

"Thanks."

With one last glance at my brother, I board the plane.

Pavel is waiting for me on the couch in the jet's main cabin, a laptop open on the coffee table in front of him. Wordlessly, I take a seat next to him and stick the flash drive into the computer.

There are two files on it, one titled "Updated report" and the other "Store camera, Boise, July 14."

My heart rate picks up as tension pervades my body.

That's the same day she applied to be Slava's tutor.

I click on the video.

The grainy recording shows a nondescript street with a few stores, a coffee shop, some parked cars, and occasional pedestrians. The time stamp in the corner tells me it's just after ten in the morning.

At first, it seems like nothing is going on, but after about thirty seconds, I catch sight of a familiar slender figure. Dressed in a T-shirt and a pair of jeans, Chloe is walking briskly down the street.

She's passing by a clothing boutique when it happens.

With a sharp *pop,* the display window to her left explodes.

Pavel emits a startled expletive, but I ignore him, all my attention on Chloe's small, frozen figure. Every muscle in my body is locked tight, fear and fury pulsing through me in sickening waves. Even on the blurry video, I can see the shock on her face as her wide eyes scan the street uncomprehendingly. Then screams about gunshots and 911 begin, and she lurches into a sprint—just as another *pop!* rings out and more glass around her goes flying.

Within seconds, she's gone from view, and the video cuts off.

"Motherfucker," Pavel mutters, but I'm already opening the other file.

The updated report.

40

CHLOE

I don't sleep well. At all. Who would, with that kind of warning?

Sleep well tonight—you'll need it.

I can't think of anything Nikolai could've said that would've been *less* likely to make me get my zzzs. He might as well have told me that he intends to fuck me to exhaustion as soon as he returns home.

Actually, he did tell me that, more or less, before he left. His dirty promises have provided ample fodder for my wet dreams and shower masturbation sessions—including the lengthy one after our call last night.

I figured a couple of orgasms might relax me, but they actually made things worse. The entire time I played with myself, I kept thinking of what he'll do to me when he returns… how his hands and lips will feel on me… how his cock will feel inside me. My imagination went wild, painting all sorts of X-rated, non-PC scenarios, and they're still playing in my mind now, in the bright light of the morning, dampening my underwear and keeping my pulse racing.

It doesn't help that Alina is again nowhere to be seen. She doesn't come down for breakfast or lunch, and when I ask Lyudmila about that, she tells me Nikolai's sister has another headache.

"Does she get these a lot?" I ask at lunch, concerned, and Lyudmila nods, her face tight as she averts her eyes.

I wonder about that, but Lyudmila isn't exactly chatty around me, so I decide against questioning her further. Instead, I spend the afternoon teaching Slava and counting down the minutes until dinnertime, which is when Nikolai is expected to arrive.

My student is equally impatient. Lyudmila must've told him that his father is coming back today because he keeps jumping up and running over to the window as we're reviewing the alphabet.

"Do you want to surprise your daddy?" I ask when he returns from his expedition for the fifth time. "Make him happy?"

Slava's brows furrow. "Happy?"

"Yes, happy." I draw a smiling face with a yellow crayon. "Do you want your daddy to be happy?"

He nods, plopping down on the floor next to me.

"Then repeat after me: 'Hi, Daddy.'"

Slava is silent. He knows both of those words from the books we've been reading, and he's been repeating phrases after me when I request it, so I know it's not a comprehension issue.

Gently, I try again. "Hi, Daddy."

He stares at his sneakers. "Hi, Daddy." His voice is barely above a whisper, but the words are clear, as is the wariness in his large golden eyes when he lifts his gaze.

He's hesitant, and I can't blame him. Despite the small bit of progress we made with our joint reading session the other day, father and son are still virtual strangers.

I reach over to take his hands in mine. "I'm very proud of you. You're being brave and strong, like Superman."

His small face brightens. "Superman?"

"Superman," I confirm, squeezing his hands gently before releasing them. "Brave and strong."

"Brave and strong," he whispers, trying out the words. He points at his chest. "Brave and strong?"

I beam at him. "Yes, you are brave and strong, just like Superman. And you'll make your daddy very happy."

He gives me a big grin. "Happy, yes." He points at the smiley face drawing and puffs out his thin chest. "Very happy."

He's so adorable that I can't resist giving him a hug, and my heart melts when his short arms go around my neck, squeezing tightly. This, here, is why I love children so much. All they want is love and affection, and once they have it, they return it in spades.

Nikolai doesn't understand that about his son yet, but he will.

It's just a matter of time and a little effort on my part.

An hour before dinner, I leave Slava with Lyudmila and go to my room to change and get ready. I'm so excited and nervous I can barely keep my hands from shaking as I apply my makeup and smooth my hair into a semblance of the polished waves Alina was able to create for me. If she were feeling well, I'd ask her to repeat her magic, but since I haven't seen her at any point this afternoon, I have to assume she's still down with the headache.

Poor girl. I hope she feels better soon.

Once my hair and makeup are done, I flip through my ridiculously large collection of evening dresses to find the absolute best one. Without Nikolai here, I've been grabbing whichever one seems most comfortable and easiest to put on, but tonight, I want to put in extra effort.

I want to see his breath catch and his eyes kindle with that dark, savage heat that both excites and alarms me.

I settle on a delicate ivory gown that has subtle threads of gold woven in. Made of some diaphanous material, it's strapless, with a heart-shaped, corseted bodice that pushes up my breasts and defines my waist. The form-fitting skirt skims over my hips in the most flattering manner imaginable, and when I walk, a thigh-high slit on the left side reveals flashes of my leg. I pair the dress with the gold Jimmy Choos I wore on my first formal evening here, and I'm ready.

Ready to see Nikolai and take our relationship further.

The car pulls up as I'm coming down the stairs. I catch a glimpse of it in one of the large windows, and my heart beats faster. Lyudmila and Slava are already standing in the living room, with the boy dressed in his evening best. As I approach, he smiles up at me shyly, and I give him an encouraging shoulder squeeze.

"Remember, brave and strong, like Superman," I whisper, trying to control my own nervousness, and he giggles—only to fall silent at the sound of the front door opening, followed by footsteps heading in our direction.

Pavel appears first, but his house-sized frame barely registers in my vision. All my attention is on the tall, darkly beautiful man behind him, whose tiger-bright gaze homes in on me with an intensity that scorches my flesh and stills my lungs.

In the span of the past couple of days, I've forgotten what it's like to be near him, to experience the devastating impact of his presence. I don't just see him, I *feel* him with every inch of my skin, every cell of my being. Helplessly, my eyes trace over his features, taking in the uncompromising angles of his jaw and the sensuous shape of his lips, the startling thickness of his jet-black lashes and the way his raven's wing hair is brushed back from his forehead, revealing those high, wide cheekbones. He's dressed more casually than when he left, with a blue button-up shirt tucked into tailored slacks, and he looks so mouthwateringly hot that it's all I can do to remain standing. My heart races, my entire body buzzing as if a network of live wires resides under my skin, and I'm only peripherally aware of Lyudmila stepping up to embrace her husband while chattering excitedly in Russian.

Nikolai must be caught in the same potent spell because for a long moment, he stands still, eyes glittering as he takes in my appearance.

Then he comes toward me.

Breathless, I stare up at him as he stops in front of me. He's so much more up close than on a computer screen. Bigger, taller… more dangerously, primitively male. With his seductive charm and fine clothes, it's possible to forget that raw, animal quality he possesses, the sense that something feral lurks underneath his beautiful façade… something that draws me to him even as it makes the fine hair on the back of my neck stand up in warning.

At a distance, it was easy to dismiss my imaginings about him being dangerous.

Up close, it's infinitely harder.

"Hi, Daddy."

The sound of that small, high-pitched voice jolts me out of my trance—and it has an even stronger effect on

Nikolai. Every muscle on his face tightens as his gaze jumps to the boy standing bravely at my side.

For a moment, father and son just stare at each other. Then Nikolai slowly goes down on one knee.

"Hi," he says hoarsely as a medley of emotions plays across his face. "Hi, Slavochka."

My heart clenches with a surge of warmth. That version of the boy's name is an endearment; I've heard enough Russian over the past few days to know that.

Slava smiles uncertainly at his father before looking up at me.

"You did good," I say huskily, smoothing my palm over his silky hair. "Just like Superman." Smiling, I catch Nikolai's gaze. "Tell him he did well."

His face twists, something dark and agonizing flashing in his eyes before he regains control. "You did well," he says to the boy tonelessly, and rising to his feet, he steps back, his expression shuttered once more.

Confused, I start to speak, but he beats me to it.

"I need to talk to you," he tells me in a hard voice, and taking my hand in an inescapable grip, he leads me to his office.

41

CHLOE

My stomach churns and my pulse is sickeningly fast as he takes a seat across from me at the round table, his eyes filled with a darkness I can no longer convince myself stems solely from my imagination. No trace remains of the tender, seductive man I spoke to for so many hours over video, a man who was so open about his feelings for me. In his place is a beautiful, terrifying stranger, his face taut with fury.

The worst part is I have no idea what I've done, what happened to upset him so. Was it what Slava said? Or my clumsy suggestion that he praise the boy for—

"You lied to me, zaychik," he says in a lethally soft tone, and my heart plummets to my feet.

I was wrong.

This has nothing to do with Slava.

It's infinitely worse.

I gulp in a breath. "Nikolai, I—"

He holds up a hand, then opens a laptop that I just

now notice is on the table. "Watch this," he orders, turning the screen toward me.

I watch—and what I see turns my blood to icy slush.

It's me, that day in Boise.

The day they openly shot at me.

There's nothing more damning that Nikolai could've come across, no incident that speaks more clearly of the danger I pose to his family—a danger I haven't let myself think about in any real way, focusing instead on *my* situation, *my* survival. It's only now, with that grainy video in front of me, that I comprehend just how thoughtless, how selfish I have been.

I have two violent killers after me, and here I am, playing dress-up in the clothes he bought for me, pretending I'm safe in a compound he built for his son, a bright, sweet child I've already grown to adore.

A child who's in danger every second I'm here.

I'd blocked that out of my mind somehow, along with the crushing terror of that day, but I can do so no longer. Trembling, sick inside, I rise to my feet. "Nikolai, I'm so, so sorry. I'll leave. I'll go right now—"

"Sit." His voice is even softer, a frightening contrast to the savage ferocity in his eyes. "You're not going anywhere."

"But—"

"Sit."

My knees buckle underneath me, obeying his command.

He leans in, his gaze pinning me in place. "I want the truth. The full truth. Understand?"

I nod, even though I'm crumbling on the inside, all my hopes and dreams crashing around me.

I will tell him.

I will tell him everything.

After all the lies, he deserves the truth.

42

CHLOE

"It all started when I drove home after my college graduation," I say, trying—and failing—to keep my voice steady. "I was supposed to arrive in time for dinner, but the traffic was unusually heavy and I was almost an hour late. As soon as I found a parking spot in front of our building, I ran to the apartment, leaving my suitcase in the car. I figured I'd come back for it after we ate.

"I had my keys, so I came in and went directly to the kitchen, where I thought Mom was warming up some of the food. But when I got there—" I stop to swallow the lump threatening to overtake my throat.

"She was dead," Nikolai guesses grimly, and I nod, hot tears stinging the back of my eyes.

"She was lying in a pool of blood on the kitchen floor, her wrists slit. I couldn't feel a pulse, so I ran to get my phone—I was in such a rush I forgot my purse with the phone in the car. But before I could exit the apartment, I heard voices, male voices, coming from Mom's bedroom."

His eyes narrow dangerously. "They were there? In the apartment with you?"

"Yes. I jumped into the little closet niche by the door and hid behind the coats there. I saw them then. Two big men in ski masks. They exited the apartment, then immediately came back in. I heard them go back into the bedroom, and since I was right by the door, I ran. I ran down all five flights of stairs, and then I kept running until I got to my car." I drag in a shuddering breath, shoving down the recollection of that mind-numbing panic, of hyperventilating and sobbing as I fought to jam my keys into the ignition.

Nikolai gives me a moment to compose myself. "What happened next?"

"I called 911 and drove to the nearest police station. I told them what happened, and they dispatched a unit to my apartment. But the killers were gone by then, and the police, they ruled it—" My voice breaks. "They ruled it a suicide."

His eyebrows snap together. "I don't understand. You told them about the two men? As in, filed an official police report?"

"I did. I told them about the masks and the guns with silencers and—"

"Guns with silencers?"

I nod, wrapping my arms around myself. I'm so cold my teeth are beginning to chatter. "I saw them, through the coats in the hallway. Well, technically, I spotted just one gun, but later, when I saw them again, there were two, so I assume—"

"Later?" His jaw flexes. "You saw them up close again?"

"Not up close, no. They were about a block away. It was after this." I jerk my chin toward the laptop. "They ran after me, and I saw them. They each had a gun."

"Ski masks too?"

"Yes." I strain to recall the two figures, but other than their general size and the guns in their hands, they're blurry in my mind. "At least I'm pretty sure."

Nikolai's gaze sharpens. "But not certain?"

"I… no." Which is stupid of me. I should've been paying attention, should've memorized every tiny detail so I could—

"Was that the only other time you saw them? The only time they came after you?"

"No." A shiver racks my body. "Not even close."

His face is a mask of barely restrained fury. "Tell me everything."

So I do. I tell him about the black pickup truck with tinted windows that nearly ran me down as I was coming out of the police station, and how it happened again in a Walmart parking lot barely an hour after I reported the first attempt. I tell him about the fire at the local motel where I booked a room to avoid sleeping in the apartment, and about a van that nearly ran me off the road once I was already on the run. I tell him about my narrow miss at an Airbnb in Omaha, where I stopped for some much-needed rest a couple of weeks ago, only to end up escaping through the window in the middle of the night when I heard scratching noises at the door.

"The lock. They were picking it." Nikolai's jaw is clenched tight. "If you hadn't woken up—"

"Yes. And there were other instances where I thought they might've been close, like the time I spotted a black pickup with tinted windows pulling up to a gas station just as I was pulling out. I was so paranoid by then, though, that it could've been my imagination. Or maybe not. Maybe it was them. I don't know. All I know is they kept coming after me, and the only thing I could do was keep moving. That is, until I ran out of money."

"Which is when you came across my ad."

"Yes." I swallow thickly. "I'm sorry, Nikolai. I really am. I wasn't thinking straight when I applied for the position. I was down to a few dollars, and I was terrified because they'd just found me again, and they were getting bolder, shooting at me in broad daylight. I'll leave, I swear I will. You don't even need to pay me for the week. I'll find another job and—"

"What the fuck are you talking about?" Jerking up to his feet, he props his fists on the table and leans in. His voice is harsh. "I told you, you're not going anywhere."

I scramble to my feet and back away. "Nikolai, please. I really *am* sorry. I didn't mean to endanger your family. I'll go today. Right now. Before they figure out I'm here and..." My heart climbs into my throat as he advances on me, eyes like fire and brimstone. "Please. I swear I—"

His hands close around my upper arms in an iron grip. "You're not leaving," he growls, and yanking me toward him, he crushes his lips to mine.

43

NIKOLAI

I DEVOUR HER MOUTH WITH ALL THE FURY AND FEAR inside me, all the hunger I've been holding back. So much makes sense now: her starved appearance and her lumberjack appetite, the puncture wounds on her arm and the nightmares that assault her every night. For weeks, they've hunted her, seeking to exterminate her, snuff her out of existence, and on that day in Boise, they nearly succeeded.

A couple of inches to the right, and the bullet would've torn through her skull.

The entire flight home, I shook with rage, and that was before I knew the rest of it. Before I knew how many times she came close to dying. If she hadn't woken up to hear the locks getting picked, or jumped out of the way of that pickup truck… Fuck, if she'd just so much as breathed louder in that coat closet, she wouldn't be here today.

I wouldn't be holding her, tasting her.

I wouldn't know what it's like to have found the other half of my soul.

Her head falls back under the brutal pressure of my lips, her hands clutching desperately at my arms, and I know I should slow down, be gentle, but I can't. Whatever restraint I'd possessed is gone, burned to ash in the fires of my fury, decimated by my fear for her.

There was so little of what she told me in Konstantin's report, so many suspicious blanks in the police files he'd pulled for me. No mention of the two masked men in her mother's apartment, nothing about the attempted hit-and-runs. Even her emails to the journalists, the ones Konstantin's hackers found in her sent folder, don't appear to have reached their destination, as if someone has had her messages blocked or marked as spam. And then there are all the erased and damaged tapes, likely those that would've served as proof of the other attempts on her life.

Someone went to enormous trouble to kill her mother and cover their tracks, someone with massive resources, and the fact that I don't know who it is eats at me like acid.

Breathing hard, I wrench my mouth away from hers and meet her dazed gaze. "You're not leaving."

I wasn't going to let her go before, but now that I know she's in mortal danger, I will do whatever it takes to keep her here. I will literally chain her to me if I have to.

She blinks up at me, her kiss-swollen lips parting. "But—"

"But nothing. I don't want to hear it again. You're mine now, understand?" My voice is harsh, guttural. I'm frightening her, I can see it, but I can't stop myself, can't place the beast back on its leash.

She opens her mouth to respond, but I don't let her. Roughly, I slide my hand into her hair and grip a fistful, holding her still as I swoop in for another deep, marauding kiss. There's something dark and twisted in the way I need her, in this compulsion I feel to claim her. My hunger for her emanates from the deepest, most savage part of me, one that I've done my best to hide from her and from the world at large… one that my sister saw that awful winter night, much to her detriment.

Chloe is right to be wary of me.

I'm not a normal, gentle man.

Civilization is just another suit I wear.

She stiffens under my assault at first, but after a moment, her body softens against mine, her arms wrapping around my neck as she gives in to the heated need consuming us. She embraces me as I fuck her with my tongue and eat at her soft, lush lips, holds on to me as I bear her down to the table, my hands roaming greedily over her hips, her ribcage, the small, plump mounds of her breasts.

Her dress is in the way, so I tear it open at the bodice, too impatient to figure out all the hooks and zippers. She's braless underneath, and her breasts spill into my hands, round and perfect, tipped by gorgeous brown nipples. My mouth waters at the sight, and I bend my head, sucking one into my mouth. It tastes like salt and berries, like everything I've never known I craved, and as she arches into me with a gasping cry, her small hands fisting in my hair, I know I'll never get enough of her.

It's utterly impossible.

My cock is so hard it hurts, my balls tight against my body as I switch my focus to the other nipple, sucking it in deep before biting down with calculated force. She cries out again, her nails digging into my skull, and I soothe the sting with gentle strokes of my tongue before delivering another bite of pain.

She's panting now, writhing underneath me, and I know I was right about her, about our compatibility in this regard. The beast in me calls to its mirror image in her, heightening the dark chemistry between us. Pain and pleasure, violence and lust—they've coexisted since the dawn of time, feeding on one another, forming a sensual symphony like no other.

A symphony that I intend to play with her.

Releasing her nipple, I move down her body, ripping her dress in half along the way. It was a fine, pretty dress, but I'll buy her another. I'll buy her everything, take care of her every need. She'll never go hungry, will never know want again. Because she's mine now, her body and her mind, her secrets and her fears and her desires.

I want it all from her.

Gripping her hands, I pin them at her sides as I trail burning kisses over her heaving ribcage, her flat belly, the vulnerable V under her navel. She's wearing a white thong, and I rip it off as well, then pin her hands again as I continue my oral exploration of her body. It's beautiful, all slim and toned, her bronze skin like warm silk under my lips. The hair on her pussy is delicate and fine, as if it's just growing out after a waxing, and jealousy sears me like hellbroth as I imagine her grooming herself for an ex-boyfriend… for some man who isn't me.

Never again.

No one else will ever touch her.

I will eviscerate any man who tries.

Her breaths speed up as my lips approach her sex, the muscles in her thighs tightening even as her legs part and her hips rise off the table. She wants this, badly, and though I'm dying to taste her fully, I prolong her torment by nuzzling just the outside of her tender folds, breathing in her scent and letting the anticipation build.

"Nikolai, please…" Her voice quivers, her hands flexing in my grasp as I kiss and lick at the seam of her slit, giving her just a fraction more. "Oh God, please, just—" She gasps as my tongue finally delves between her folds, and I lap at the creamy evidence of her desire, tasting her sweet, rich essence. She's everything I've imagined, everything I've ever wanted, and my cock throbs violently with the need to be inside her, to slide deep into her tight, wet heat. Instead, I find her clit and greedily attack it, alternately sucking and licking, and as she comes with a choked cry, I push two fingers into her spasming flesh, intensifying her orgasm and preparing her for what's to come.

Because I won't be gentle when I take her.

I can't be.

Not this time.

44

CHLOE

AFTERSHOCKS ARE STILL RIPPLING THROUGH MY BODY when I open my eyes to find Nikolai leaning over me, one hand propped on the table next to me and the other possessively cupping my sex, two long, thick fingers buried inside me. His eyes are narrowed fiercely, his jaw taut. "I'm going to fuck you now." His voice is hard and guttural, dangerously savage. "Do you understand?"

I do. It's a warning as much as a statement of fact.

This is happening, and there's no going back.

The sane part of me wants to run, to shrink back from the dark intensity in his stare, even as something twisted in me revels in his loss of control, in the raw, unvarnished hunger on his face. His smooth black hair is disheveled from my fingers, his lips glistening with my wetness, and the top buttons on his shirt are missing, as if he's ripped them off.

This is not the elegant, sophisticated man who mandates rigid meal times.

It's the feral being I've sensed lurking underneath.

"I…" I wet my lips, my body clenching on his fingers. "I understand."

His jaw flexes violently, and then he's on me, his lips and tongue consuming me as his fingers thrust deeper, finding a spot that makes sparks dance at the edges of my vision. He tastes like the forest, primal and wild, his cedar-and-bergamot scent mixing with the musky undertone of my arousal. Gasping into his mouth, I arch against him, clutching at his sides as he starts to fuck me with those fingers, driving them into me with a hard, relentless rhythm that makes tension skyrocket in my core. I can feel the orgasm barreling at me with the speed of a runaway locomotive, and then it's crashing over me, blasting me with white-hot, dizzying pleasure.

Panting, I sprawl bonelessly on the hard surface of the table, but Nikolai's not done with me. Before I can recover, he pulls out his fingers and pushes away from me. Forcing open my heavy eyelids, I watch as he pulls down his zipper and rolls a condom onto his erection.

A very large erection.

I was right about his size. He's bigger than any guy I've known.

A frisson of purely feminine alarm snakes through me, but he's already over me, gripping my wrists to pin them above my head as he claims my lips in another scorching kiss. The broad, thick head of his cock prods at my entrance, and finding it, presses in.

I'm wet and soft from the two orgasms, but the stretch still burns, my body struggling to accommodate his size as he slides deeper. A sound of distress escapes my throat, and he stills, lifting his head.

Breathing heavily, we stare at each other, and unbidden, his words come to me. Crazy words, about predestination and threads of fate… about the inevitability of us. I still don't know if I believe it, but I can't deny the powerful connection that thrums between us, can't refute that this feels more like bonding than mere sex.

He must feel it too, because the savage fire in his eyes intensifies and his grip on my wrists tightens. "Yes, zaychik…" His voice is a deep, dark rasp. "You're mine now."

And with a heavy push, he thrusts in all the way.

The shock of the invasion is still reverberating through my body as he begins to move, his eyes locked on mine. His strokes are ruthless, so hard and deep they hurt, but the pain is soon edged out by a darker kind of pleasure, one that's only partially related to the fresh tension coiling in my core. Each merciless thrust slams his pelvis against mine, pressing on my clit, but it's the look in his eyes that drives my arousal higher and sends another orgasm blasting through me.

It's a look of possessiveness, complete and total, mixed with something dangerously tender and intense.

He comes a few moments after I do, still holding my

gaze, and my heart pounds wildly as I watch his gorgeous face contort with the pleasure-pain of his release as he grinds into me, emptying himself deep inside my body.

It's the most intimate thing I've ever experienced, and the most beautiful.

Our bodies are still joined, my wrists held captive in his grasp, when he lowers his head and presses the softest, sweetest kiss to my lips, then lays his cheek against mine, his warm breath washing over my bare shoulder. I want my hands free so I can hold him, but this feels right too, comforting in some strange way. The table is cold and hard under my back, my inner flesh throbbing from his rough possession, but I feel utterly at peace, my rapid breathing slowing as every remnant of tension drains from my body.

I could lie like that for hours, days, weeks, but after a few long moments, he stirs, raising his head to look at me with a tender smile. Releasing my wrists, he carefully withdraws from me and pushes up to stand. "You okay, zaychik?" he murmurs, running a warm, callused palm over my arm, and I nod, blushing as I sit up.

"More than okay," I admit, pulling together the edges of my torn dress as he disposes of the condom in a trashcan by the desk.

"Good," he says softly, zipping up his pants. "Because we're far from done."

And scooping me up against his chest, he carries me out of the office.

45

CHLOE

I HALF EXPECT TO RUN INTO ALINA OR LYUDMILA, BUT we make it to Nikolai's bedroom without encountering anyone. It's a huge relief, given the state of my dress—and, I realize as I catch a glimpse of us in a mirror, my face and hair.

With my lips swollen from his kisses and my hair wild, I don't just look freshly fucked.

I look ravished.

And that's pretty much how I feel as he lays me down on his king-sized bed and begins to strip, volcanic heat kindling anew in his golden eyes. I don't know if I'm up for more so soon, especially with the questions raised by the video hanging over us, but when he's fully naked, his magnificent body bared to my gaze, I can't find the will to protest as he climbs over me and takes my lips in a deep, tenderly erotic kiss.

It's a lovemaking this time, not a fucking. He

worships every inch of my body, bringing me to another orgasm with his lips and tongue before carefully sheathing himself in my sore flesh. Somehow, I manage to come again alongside him, and then, exhausted, I lie in his arms like a ragdoll before drifting off to sleep.

I wake up to the feel of being submerged in warm water. Blinking my eyes open, I realize we're both half-lying in a bubble bath, with Nikolai spooning me from underneath so I don't slip in and drown.

"Relax, zaychik," he murmurs in my ear, running a soapy sponge over my breasts and stomach. "Close your eyes, let me take care of you."

He doesn't need to ask twice. After the sleepless night I've had and with my body jellified by all those orgasms, I'm already drifting off to dreamland. Vaguely, I'm aware of him washing me all over, then lifting me out of the tub and wrapping a big, fluffy towel around me. At that point, I wake up enough to ask for privacy to use the bathroom, and then I stumble off to bed, where he's waiting for me with a tray of food.

Sleepily, I let him feed me grapes, cheese, and various spreads on crackers—since we missed dinner in favor of sex and all—and then I pass out in his embrace, feeling safe, secure, and cared for.

Feeling like I've found my new home.

46

CHLOE

We make love twice more throughout the night, with Nikolai giving me two orgasms each time, and by morning, I'm so sore I can't move, yet so satisfied it's worth it. Of course it's possible I can't move because his heavy arm is slung across my ribcage, securing me to him as he sleeps—almost like a child with a teddy bear.

Grinning at the incongruous thought, I carefully wriggle out of his embrace and tiptoe into the adjoining bathroom, where I find a brand-new toothbrush considerately laid out for me. Trying to be as quiet as possible, I brush my teeth and take care of business, then put on a huge, soft robe I find hanging on the door. It's obviously his, but hopefully, he won't mind if I wear it long enough to get back to my room.

He did destroy my dress, after all.

The thought is both disturbing and exhilarating, my

pulse speeding up when I think about how he reacted when I proposed leaving. I don't know what I'd thought his reaction would be when he learned of my predicament, but it wasn't that.

Nothing is resolved between us, but there's one thing I now know for sure, and it fills me with immense gratitude and hope.

Despite the danger I've brought with me, Nikolai doesn't want me gone.

I'm not surprised to find him still asleep when I return to the bedroom. Between the jet lag and the long flight—plus all that sex—he must be exhausted. Holding up the sides of the robe to prevent it from dragging on the floor, I pad quietly toward the door, but as I'm passing by the bed, I can't resist the urge to stop and stare at my new lover.

Because that's what my gorgeous, mysterious Russian employer is now.

My lover.

Covered by a blanket up to his waist, he's lying half on his side, half on his back, face turned partially toward me and one muscled arm folded above his head. Some men look younger in repose, softer, but not Nikolai. Sleep only enhances that dangerous, animalistic quality I've sensed in him—even as it heightens his striking male beauty. With those intense eyes closed, I can see just how long and thick his jet-black lashes are, how sharply carved his cheekbones. His lips are slightly parted, but even in this relaxed state, there's something cynical in their curve, a wicked sensuality in the way their softness contrasts with the hint of stubble darkening the hard, molded lines of his jaw.

I could stand and stare at him for a solid hour, but that would be creepy, and in any case, I need to get back to my room and get dressed before the rest of the household wakes up. I don't know what time it is, but judging by the soft light seeping through the blinds, it's not long after sunrise—which makes sense, given how early I fell asleep last night.

With one last look at sleeping Nikolai, I tiptoe out of the room. As I hoped, nobody's around, the house completely silent as I make my way to my bedroom. I'm not particularly embarrassed by what happened—sooner or later, everyone will know we're dating—but Nikolai and I need to talk about it first, along with everything else.

I still feel terrible about endangering him and his family, and it's only the knowledge that they have all those guards and security measures that's preventing me from jumping into my car and fleeing anyway. Well, that and the fact that I still don't have my car keys.

I'm going to seriously insist they get a locksmith here ASAP.

Stepping into my room, I close the door behind me and am about to take off the robe when I spot the figure on my bed.

My heart leaps into my throat, even as I recognize who it is.

"Did you and Kolya have a nice fuck?" Alina asks,

rising to her feet—and as she comes unsteadily toward me, barefoot and wearing only a sheer peignoir, I see the overly bright glitter of her eyes and realize she's on something.

Something way stronger than pot.

47

CHLOE

"What are you doing here?" I demand, my heart rate kicking higher as she stops in front of me, swaying. If I had any doubts about her state, they dissolve as I take in her huge black pupils and smell the sickly sweet odor of her breath. For the first time since I've known Nikolai's sister, she's not wearing makeup, and her beautiful face is pale and puffy, her green eyes red-rimmed and underlined by shadows.

"I was waiting for you." Her pretty lips are bloodless as they stretch into an uneven smile. "My brother wanted you to get paid for the first week by noon yesterday, but I didn't feel well enough to get out of bed until later in the evening, so that's when I came by to drop that off." She waves a careless hand at the thick envelope sitting on the nightstand.

"You've been here *all night?*"

She laughs, a too-bright peal of a sound. "Don't be silly. I dropped off the envelope and left. But I couldn't sleep, so I swung by to check on you again this morning—and you still weren't here. So…" Her gaze falls to my robe. "Did you have a nice time fucking my brother? Rumor has it, he's got mad skills."

Heat invades my face. "I think you better leave."

"I will. Just tell me, Chloe… Have you already fallen for him? Did that handsome face of his fool you into thinking he's your knight in shining armor, after all?"

I take a deep breath. "Alina, listen… I don't know what beef you have with your brother, but I think it's best if we talk when you're feeling better. Nikolai and I *have* started dating, but that doesn't mean—"

She sways toward me. "Poor child. He did fool you, didn't he?"

"Uh-huh." I grip her shoulders, steadying her; then I turn her around and march her toward the door. "We'll talk more about this later."

She twists out of my hold. "You don't understand. I'm trying to help you." Her glassy eyes are wide, imploring. "You need to listen to me. He's just like *him*."

I shouldn't listen to anything she says in this state, but I can't help myself. "Him?"

"Our father. Kolya is his carbon copy, in *all* ways." She grips the lapels of my robe. "Do you understand? He's a monster, a killer. He—" She stops, her face turning even paler as she realizes what she's said.

Releasing my robe, she backs away as I stare at her, my stomach churning as every suspicion I've ever entertained about the Molotovs surfaces like a poisoned cork in a well. Alina is clearly out of her mind, but to call her brother a killer?

That's not an accusation one throws around for no reason, even when drunk or high.

She's already reaching for the door handle when I shake off my shock-induced paralysis and dash after her. "What are you talking about?" Grabbing her arm, I spin her around to face me. "What the fuck are you talking about?"

She's shaking her head, tears leaking out of the corners of her eyes. "Nothing. It's nothing. Forget it. I just… didn't want you to end up like her."

"Her?"

"Just leave, Chloe. Go before it's too late."

I grit my teeth. "I can't. Pavel lost my car keys. But even if I had them, there's no way I'd just—"

"I found them. In Kolya's nightstand drawer."

I step back, reeling. "What? When?"

"Yesterday morning, when I went into Kolya's room to get the cash for you." Her jade-green eyes look haunted. "That's when I knew."

A chill wraps around my spine. "Knew what?"

Ignoring my question, she steps around me and unsteadily makes her way to the bed, where she starts digging through the folds of the blanket. "Here." She holds up a pair of keys on a pink, furry keychain. "That's another reason I came here—to give this to you."

The sick churning in my stomach intensifies. She's lying. She must be lying. She could've found the keys anywhere, wherever it was that Pavel had lost them. Because if she's not lying, if they were in Nikolai's nightstand yesterday morning, then they were never lost. That or Nikolai found them before leaving for his trip—before our video chat in which he claimed Pavel couldn't locate them.

As if reading my mind, Alina says unevenly, "Pavel doesn't lose things, by the way. I've known him all my life, and he's never misplaced so much as a holey sock —at least not by accident. He's like my brother in that regard. Whatever he does is planned."

My heart pounds at my ribcage like a mallet. "Give me the keys." Stepping toward her, I snatch them from her hand and stuff them into the robe's pocket. My mind is racing, my thoughts tumbling over each other like pieces of colored glass in a kaleidoscope. I don't know what to think, what to believe.

Why would Nikolai lie about my keys?

Why would Alina?

"What did you mean when you called your brother a killer?" I ask, staring into her drug-clouded eyes. "Who is this *her*?"

Her face crumples. "You don't want this. Believe me, you don't."

"I do. Tell me."

She shakes her head, more tears leaking from her eyes.

"Alina, please… I have to know. I have to know because—because you're right. I—" I suck in a breath, my chest tightening as the truth sinks its fangs into me. "I *am* falling for him, and fast."

Her shoulders shake with silent sobs as she sinks to the floor, her back against the bed and her long hair falling forward to hide her face as she hugs her knees.

Desperate, I kneel in front of her. "Please, Alina. I have to know. How's he like your father? How's he a monster? What happened? Who is he supposed to have killed?"

For several long moments, there's no response. Finally, she lifts her head, and through the black veil of her hair, I see the screaming agony in her eyes. "Our father." The words come out in a broken, ragged whisper. "He killed her. And then Kolya killed him. Sliced him open, right there—" Her voice cracks. "Right in front of me."

And as I stare at her, mute with horror, she buries her face against her knees and cries.

48

CHLOE

My stomach is a pit of ice and churning acid, my fingers numb and clumsy as I stuff my old clothes into my suitcase. Alina is on my bed, passed out, the drugs and the sleepless night having finally taken their toll.

I don't know where I'm going or what I'm doing; I just know I have to leave. Right now. Before Nikolai wakes up. Truth or lies, reality or madness, I stand no chance of sorting it all out while I'm here, under his roof and at his mercy, with that overpowering chemistry simmering between us, dragging me deeper under his lethal spell.

I'm not sure what I'd thought I'd hear from Alina. An admission that they're mafia, after all? And maybe they are. At this point, nothing would surprise me. From the beginning, my instincts have been warning me about Nikolai, and I should've heeded them.

I should've listened to that voice inside my head.

You're not leaving.

Yesterday, his fervently uttered statement seemed romantic, if somewhat autocratic, his possessiveness a turn-on rather than reason for alarm. But now, with Alina's revelations ringing in my ears and my no-longer-lost keys jabbing my leg through the pocket of my jeans, I can't help but view his words in a different, infinitely more sinister light.

Was he never going to return the keys to me?

Have I been a de facto prisoner all along?

Frantically, I throw in the last of my clothes and zip the suitcase, then slip on my old sneakers and grab the envelope with the cash from the nightstand, stuffing it into my pocket. My heart is pounding so hard I'm sick from it, or maybe I'm just plain heartsick.

I just... didn't want you to end up like her.

I still have no idea to whom Alina was referring; after the slicing-open bit, she became incoherent, sobbing until she passed out from exhaustion—and no wonder. It sounds as if she's witnessed Nikolai murdering their father, and maybe this mysterious "her" as well. An ex-girlfriend of his? Or worse, their mother? Or was the "he killed her" part referring to their father, who's allegedly also a monster?

I strain my memory to recall any mention of how Nikolai and Alina's parents died, but there was nothing in the Russian articles I came across. Nikolai did react strongly when I asked about his parents that one time, but I attributed it to grief. But what if there's more to it? What if there's guilt and anger, the self-loathing of a man who's done the unforgivable, committed the most heinous of crimes?

I don't know if I believe it of Nikolai. I don't want to believe it. Despite the darkness I've sensed in him, despite his savage hunger for me, I felt safe in his embrace last night. His roughness had been tempered with tenderness, his strength carefully leashed. And the way he cared for me afterward, washing me, feeding me, holding me so tenderly …

Is a monster capable of caring?

Can a psychopath fake emotion so well?

Maybe nothing Alina said is true. Maybe it's a ploy to make me leave, to break up a relationship she's disapproved of from the beginning. Maybe if I talk to Nikolai, he'll explain everything, prove to me that Alina is simply ill, out of her mind with all those drugs.

It's a tempting thought, so tempting that as I'm stepping out of my room, I stop and glance longingly down the hallway, where the door to Nikolai's bedroom is still firmly shut. I want to trust him so badly, and under different circumstances, I would. If we were a regular couple hooking up in an apartment in a city, I would march down that hallway and demand an explanation, hear his side of the story before deciding what to do. But I can't take that risk, not when I'm so completely in his power on this remote, highly secure estate.

Nobody knows I'm here.

Nobody will know or care if I disappear for good.

The only reasonable thing to do is to go now, to

leave and assess the situation from a distance. Once I'm in a motel somewhere, I can reach out to Nikolai, let him know what happened and why I left. We can talk it out over email or on the phone, and I can do some more online digging, see if I can find out anything about his parents' deaths.

This doesn't have to be forever, just for now.

Just until I know the truth.

Still, my heart feels agonizingly heavy as I carry my suitcase down the stairs and to the garage entrance in the back. Not only will I miss Slava, but the mere possibility that I might never see Nikolai again fills me with cold, hollow dread. So does the knowledge that I'm going out there, where my mom's killers are still hunting me. But I've evaded them before, and I have to believe that I'll be able to do so again—especially with all that cash on hand. When I fled Boston, all I had were a couple of twenties in my wallet, plus the five hundred I withdrew from an ATM before ditching my debit card along with everything else that could be tracked.

It's going to be fine.

I'll make it.

I have to believe that.

Swallowing the growing knot in my throat, I approach my car and throw my suitcase into the trunk. Then I press the button to open the garage door and watch it lift silently. No slow, noisy mechanisms here, thank God. As quietly as I can, I start the car and back out of the garage, then steer around the house to the driveway.

It takes everything I have to drive down the mountain calmly, sedately, like I'm in no rush. If the guards are watching the road, I can't have them getting suspicious. As is, icy sweat trickles down my back, and my knuckles whiten on the steering wheel as I pull up to the tall metal gate.

What if Nikolai gave them instructions not to let me out?

What if I'm a prisoner here for real?

But the gate slides apart at my approach, and nobody stops me as I drive through. Shaking with relief, I maintain my slow, steady speed for another thirty seconds or so, until I'm out of view, and then I floor the gas, speeding away from the safe haven that just might be the devil's lair.

From the man I yearn for with every fiber of my heart.

49

NIKOLAI

I WAKE UP WITH MY BODY HUMMING WITH CONTENTMENT and my mind filled with greater peace than I've ever known. Last night was everything I thought it would be, and more. I can still feel her, smell her, taste her on my lips. Smiling, I roll over, patting the sheets for her small, warm body, and when my hand encounters nothing but a bunched-up blanket, I open my eyes and survey the room.

Chloe is not here, which is disappointing but not surprising, given the bright sunlight. She's probably already had breakfast and is teaching Slava; maybe they're even out on a hike. Normally, I would've heard her get up—I'm a light sleeper—but I was coming off thirty-plus hours with no sleep and the jet lag kicked my ass hard.

My mood darkens a fraction, my adrenaline levels rising as I think of the video that dominated my thoughts on the flight over, keeping me from getting any shut-eye, and of everything else Chloe told me. The idea that someone out there wants to hurt her, kill her, fills me with incandescent rage, one tempered only by the knowledge that they can't get to her in my compound.

The precautions that keep my family safe from our enemies will keep Chloe safe from hers while I work to figure out who they are.

Eager to get started on that, I get up and fire off an email to Konstantin, detailing everything I learned last night. Then I hop into the shower for a swift rinse, get dressed, and go in search of Chloe.

I start with my son's room. Nobody's there, so I go downstairs. The dining room is empty, but I hear voices from the kitchen, and when I walk in, I'm surprised to find Lyudmila feeding breakfast to Slava all by herself.

He smiles at me shyly, and my chest fills with uncharacteristic warmth as I recall how he greeted me last evening. Even as laser-focused as I'd been on getting answers from Chloe, I couldn't help reacting to that small, sweet voice calling me *Daddy*.

I didn't know how badly I'd yearned to hear it until it happened.

Until *she* made it happen.

"Good morning, Slavochka," I murmur, going down on my haunches in front of his chair. Switching to Russian, I ask, "Did you have a good night?"

He nods, eyes big and wary, and my ribcage tightens with a familiar squeezing pain. I want to step away, end the conversation so I can be rid of the discomfort, but instead, I lean into it, letting myself feel it as I smile gently at my son.

He's so much—too much—like me, but maybe with Chloe in his life, he won't follow in my footsteps.

Maybe he won't grow up hating me the way I hated my old man.

"Where is Chloe?" I ask, and my smile broadens as his eyes brighten at the mention of her name.

"I don't know," he says shyly and glances up at Lyudmila, who's putting berries into his bowl of cream of wheat.

"I haven't seen her this morning," she says. "Maybe she's still sleeping?"

My smile fades, an unpleasant feeling stirring low in my gut. I haven't checked in Chloe's room, but I assumed she left my bed to start her day, not sleep in hers. Rising to my feet, I tell Slava, "I'm going to go find your teacher. You're eager for your English lessons, right?"

He nods vigorously, and I grin at him. On impulse, I ruffle his hair the way I've seen Chloe do it, and ignoring the surprised look on Lyudmila's face, I go back upstairs.

The door to Chloe's room is shut, so I knock and wait a few seconds. When no response comes, I open it and walk in.

The blinds are still closed, blocking most of the daylight, but I can see a small mound on the bed under the covers.

She *is* sleeping, after all.

A tender smile tugs at my lips as I approach the bed and sit down on the edge. She's lying turned away from me, the blanket covering her up to her neck, leaving only her hair spread out on the pillow. For some reason, it looks much darker in this light, the golden streaks missing.

Leaning over her, I lift my hand to gently brush the hair off her face—only to jerk my fingers back as my heart launches into a furious gallop.

"What the fuck are you doing here?" I growl at my sister as she rolls over onto her back and blinks open her eyes. "Where is Chloe?"

She blinks a few more times, then slowly sits up. "What?" she says hoarsely, pushing her hair off her face with an unsteady hand. She smells like a drug cocktail, I realize, my fury growing as she asks dazedly, "What are you doing in my room?"

I jackknife to my feet. "*Your* fucking room?"

She stares up at me. "I don't…" Her eyes sweep the bedroom, and the confusion on her face slowly morphs into horrified comprehension. "Oh, shit. Chloe."

My stomach tightens with an awful premonition, and it takes every shred of restraint I possess not to grab and shake her. "Where the fuck is she? What did you do?"

My sister's spine straightens, her eyes narrowing on my face. "Me? What are *you* doing in her bedroom?"

"Alina," I warn through clenched teeth, and whatever she sees on my face convinces her that she can't fuck with me right now.

"Look, I may have..." She dampens her lips. "I may have told her some things."

"What things?"

"About you and... and our father."

Fuck. "What exactly did you tell her?"

"Probably more than I should've," Alina admits, even as her chin lifts defiantly. "But she deserves to know what she's getting herself into, don't you think?"

My hands flex at my sides, rage pulsing through every cell in my body. If it were anyone but my sister, they'd already be bleeding out. "So you told her... what? That I killed him? Gutted him like a fucking fish?"

She whitens but doesn't look away. "I don't remember, exactly."

Of course she doesn't. She was fucking high—still is, probably.

Leaning over the bed, I yank the blanket off her. This is my fault for babying her, letting her wallow in her weakness. "Get up and get dressed," I bite out as she scrambles back, eyes wide. "We're going to search this place top to bottom, and when we find her, you'll tell her that you made it all up. Every last word, understand?"

"Kolya..." There's a strange note in her voice. "Have you looked in the garage?"

My blood ices over. "What?"

"I found the keys in your bedside drawer," she says defiantly. "And I gave them back to her. She's a person, not a thing, and if she wants to leave, you have no right—"

"You fucking idiot," I whisper, so overcome by rage and terror I can hardly speak. "She's got assassins after her. If she left here and they get to her..."

And as my sister blanches, I pivot on my heel and sprint to the garage.

Sure enough, the Toyota is gone, the garage door raised.

Cursing violently, I run back into the house—only to nearly mow down Lyudmila, who's stepped out of the kitchen to see what the ruckus is about.

"Tell Pavel I need him. Now," I bark into her startled face and race upstairs to my office.

Grabbing my computer, I pull up the footage from the gate cameras and rewind the recording until I see Chloe's car pulling up to the gate. The time stamp reads 7:05 a.m.—well over two hours ago.

By now, she could be anywhere.

She could be dead.

The thought is so unbearable, so paralyzing, that I cease breathing for a moment. Then logic kicks in.

Unless Chloe's enemies were camped out right outside my compound, there's no way they've found her so quickly. And with our infrared drones patrolling the area, my guards would've known it if they were there.

The most likely scenario is that Chloe is fine, albeit freaked out by Alina's revelations. I still have time to find her and get her back here, where she'll be safe.

A fraction calmer, I videocall Konstantin.

"I need you to scan the footage from every camera in a two-hundred-mile radius of my compound for any sighting of Chloe's car in the last two hours," I say as soon as my brother's face fills my screen. "Start with the gas stations—Pavel mentioned the car was low on fuel."

To Konstantin's credit, he doesn't ask any questions. "I'll get my guys right on it."

"Call my phone when you have it. I'll be in the car."

He nods and disconnects.

I call my guards next. "Get Kirilov and come up to the house," I order when Arkash picks up. "Full gear. We're going on a road trip."

I don't expect to run into trouble retrieving Chloe, but only an idiot doesn't prepare for the worst.

"Be there in ten," Arkash replies.

As I hang up, a knock sounds at my door and Pavel comes in.

"The girl?" he asks tersely, and I nod, already striding toward the wall in the back.

I press my palm to a hidden panel, and a section of

the wall slides away, revealing a small room full of weapons and battle gear—the main armory in the house.

"Gear up," I tell him, stripping off my shirt. "We're going to get her back."

I put on a bulletproof vest and button my shirt over it to avoid looking conspicuous. Pavel does the same, and we each strap on several weapons.

If we do run into trouble, we'll be ready.

Kirilov and Arkash are already pulling up to the house in an armored SUV when we step outside. Pavel and I jump into the backseat, and we tear down the driveway, gravel flying. I don't have a concrete destination in mind, but there's only one road leading down the mountain, and wherever Chloe is by the time Konstantin calls me, we'll be closer to her than if we stay here and wait. Besides, we can start with the nearby gas stations as well, see if someone might've spotted Chloe at one of them.

"What happened?" Pavel asks quietly as we clear the gate. "Why did she leave?"

My upper lip curls. "Alina."

"Ah." He falls silent then, staring out the window, and I do the same, trying to ignore the heavy thudding in my chest—and the growing pain of betrayal spreading through it.

My zaychik ran.

She left me.

Just like that, without so much as a goodbye.

It's unreasonable to feel this way, I know. I *am* the

kind of man she should fear and despise. Whatever my sister told her in her drugged-out state must've painted me in the worst possible light, but that doesn't mean Alina's story is untrue.

I did kill our father in front of her.

Still, Chloe's desertion hurts. She gave herself to me. She came willingly into my arms. Last night was so much more than sex, our connection so deep I feel it in my bones. But she must not. Because if she did, she would've known I'd never harm her; she would've trusted me to protect her. The fact that she'd rather be out there, facing mortal danger, speaks volumes about her opinion of me.

She's afraid of me.

She thinks I'm a monster.

My jaw hardens, a dark resolve settling in as the car picks up speed. I should've kept those keys in a safe, not my nightstand—and I definitely should've warned the guards not to open the gate for her car. It didn't occur to me that she'd run after last night, but it should've—and I won't make that mistake again.

When I get her back, she's not leaving.

I won't let her.

I'll do whatever it takes to keep her safe.

The first gas station we stop at is manned by a pale, pimply twenty-something with a hint of a beer belly.

"Nope, haven't seen her," he says after peering at

Chloe's picture. "Cute chick, though. What's her deal? She part-Asian? Latina?"

"What about a blue Toyota Corolla circa late nineties?" I ask softly, and whatever the guy sees on my face causes him to lose what little color he possesses. "Any car like that stop by?"

"No, sorry, man." He gulps. "I would've seen it. I've only had two other customers today."

I glance at Pavel, and he jerks his chin toward the exit.

Like me, he doesn't think the guy is lying.

The next closest gas station is the one by the town. A white-haired cashier looks up from a newspaper as Pavel and I walk in, her rheumy gaze sharpening as she takes in our appearance.

I approach the counter and pull out Chloe's photo. "Have you seen this girl? Or a blue Corolla circa late nineties?"

The old woman puts on a pair of glasses and carefully examines the photo before looking up at me. "You two cops or something?" she asks in a croaky voice.

I rein in my impatience with effort. "Or something. Have you seen her this morning or not?"

"Not this morning, no." She squints up at me through her glasses. "Would you look at that pretty face… just like one of them magazines. And so nicely dressed, too. You her boyfriend, dearie?"

My hand tightens on the edge of the counter. "When did you see her?"

"Oh, about a week ago. She stopped by to get gas, asked about a job listing in the paper. I haven't seen her since, and I told them that."

Ice fills my chest. "Them?"

"Two fellas, about your height. Came by yesterday, late in the day. Showed me her picture and all. I told them I only saw her that one time, and I have no idea where she went—"

"What did they look like, exactly?" Pavel cuts in as I stand frozen, my mind racing a mile a second.

They're here.

They know she was here.

Worse yet, they know she was looking at my job listing.

"The two fellas? Well, tall, like I said. One's got dark hair, a little lighter than his"—she waves at me—"the other's more like you. You know, salt and pepper, except kind of balding."

Pavel's jaw tightens. "Age? Race? Body build?"

"Caucasian. Thirties—forties for the older one, maybe. Kind of big and muscular." She looks me up and down. "Not as pretty as him, that's for sure."

"Anything else?" Pavel demands. "Tattoos, scars? What were they wearing?"

"Jeans, I think. Or khakis? I don't remember for sure. Black or gray shirts, maybe navy blue. Something dark. No scars, I don't think. Oh, but"—she brightens—"the older one had a tattoo on the inside of his wrist. I saw the edge of it under his sleeve."

"Did they ask about the job listing?" I ask, keeping

my voice even despite the rage and fear pounding through me.

I have to know how bad the situation is, how close they are to finding her.

The woman nods. "Sure did. Wanted to know all about it, who and what and where. I told them I don't know for sure, but it was probably that old Jamieson property up in the mountains, the one that was bought out by that rich Russian. Say"—she squints up at Pavel—"where's that accent of yours from? You boys wouldn't happen to be from—"

"Thank you," I say tersely and pull out my phone to call Konstantin as we hurry back to the car.

As soon as my brother picks up, I rattle off the description we've gotten and demand an update on the search.

It's infinitely more urgent that we find Chloe now, before the assassins do.

"Nothing yet," Konstantin says. "In fact— Wait a minute. Let me call you back. I think we just got a hit."

I was about to jump into the SUV, but now I pace in front of it, my adrenaline levels climbing with each passing second.

We may already be too late.

They know about my compound and Chloe's interest in it.

Maybe they weren't camped out by the gate when she drove out, but they couldn't have been far.

Spinning around, I rap on the window next to

Pavel. "Get a medical team over to the compound," I tell him tersely. "We might need it."

My phone vibrates in my pocket, and I snatch it up. "Yeah?"

"No sightings, but we got a partially erased tape," Konstantin reports. "Same digital signature as the others. Two hours wiped out—and it looks like it was done about a half hour ago. If I had to guess, I'd say they've caught her scent and don't want anyone to know that."

I'm already halfway inside the car. "Where's the tape from?"

"A gas station some forty miles west of you. I'll send you the coordinates."

I hang up and order Kirilov to hit the gas.

50

CHLOE

The road blurs in front of my eyes for the umpteenth time, and I jerkily wipe at the wetness on my cheeks. I don't know why I can't stop the tears from coming, why my chest aches like I've just lost Mom all over again. The banana I picked up at a gas station is lying on the passenger seat, half-eaten, and though it's the only food I've had today, the thought of taking another bite makes me want to vomit.

I'm driving blindly again, heading nowhere. I must've been in shock for the first couple of hours because I can barely recall how I got here. I know I filled up the car somewhere, because the fuel gauge shows the tank is full, but I have only a vague recollection of walking into a dingy store and paying. The banana came from there, I'm sure—I grabbed it on autopilot—but I don't remember eating it, though I must have.

I'm pretty sure they don't sell half-eaten fruit, even at the dingiest of gas stations.

The road ahead of me slopes up and curves sharply, and I force myself to concentrate. The last thing I need is to drive off a cliff. As is, I feel like that's more or less what I'm doing with every mile of distance I'm putting between myself and Nikolai.

I did the right thing, the smart thing.

I keep telling myself that, but it doesn't help, doesn't lessen the feeling that I've made a terrible mistake. It's only been a few hours since I left, yet I miss him so acutely it's as if we've been apart for months. When he was away on the business trip, I knew I'd see him again, knew we'd speak each evening, but there's no such certainty now.

He may refuse to talk to me when I call him.

He may be so angry that I left he won't want me to return.

Now that I'm out here, away from the compound, Alina's revelations seem even more like the ramblings of an ill, drugged-out mind, and though I can't dismiss them entirely, I shudder at the thought of confronting Nikolai and asking whether he did, in fact, kill his father.

What innocent man wouldn't be insulted by that query?

What boyfriend wouldn't be furious that his girlfriend believed such monstrous lies?

I should've stayed. Fuck, I should've stayed. Even if it felt risky at the time, I should've given Nikolai a fair hearing. The keys prove nothing. Alina could've had them all along; she could've even stolen them from Pavel. If Nikolai wanted to deprive me of my freedom, there are all kinds of other actions he could've taken—like telling the guards not to let me out.

And that's the thing, I realize with a start. That's why what seemed so rational when I was packing feels like such an awful error now. It's because the moment I drove through the gate, I got proof that I *could* leave, that Nikolai didn't plan to keep me there with some sinister intentions. I'd been too panicky to realize it at first, but the farther I drove, the deeper that knowledge settled, the consequences of my impulsive actions weighing on me more with every passing mile.

I should've turned back hours ago.

In fact, I should've done it the moment I cleared the gate.

I cast a frantic glance around me. Trees and cliffs everywhere. I'm deep in the mountains again, the road in front of me so narrow it's barely two lanes. I can't do a U-turn here; it would be suicide to try.

Clutching the wheel tighter, I keep driving—and finally, I see it.

A little extra space to the left of where the road curves.

I look in the mirror, then straight ahead and back.

Nothing. No cars. I'm all alone.

Braking hard, I make an illegal U-turn and head back.

I'm twenty minutes into my return trip and desperately trying to remember if I need to turn right or left at the upcoming intersection when a black pickup truck turns onto the road, coming toward me.

A chill ripples down my spine, the fine hair on the back of my neck rising.

It could be my paranoia working overtime again, but those tinted windows look familiar.

There's no time to second-guess myself; in another thirty seconds, we'll be passing next to each other. With a sharp tug on the wheel, I swing the car onto a small dirt road leading up the mountain to my right, and slam on the gas, ignoring the complaining whine from the Corolla's ancient motor.

If it's not them, they won't follow me.

I'll feel like an idiot, but better that than dead.

My heart thumps violently against my ribcage, each second marked by half a dozen beats as my gaze flits between the rearview mirror and the steep, pothole-filled road ahead. *Please don't let it be them. Please don't let it—*

The pickup truck appears in the mirror, its dark shape gaining on me swiftly.

I push the gas pedal to the floor, my breath coming in jagged gasps as my car bounces over a series of potholes. Adrenaline sloshes in my veins, ratcheting up my pulse until all I can hear is its roar in my ears.

Pop!

My right side mirror explodes, and my terror doubles as I catch sight of a man leaning out the truck's passenger-side window, gun in hand. Instinctively, I jerk the wheel left, and the next bullet shatters the back window and punches a hole in the windshield, barely a foot from my head.

The third bullet whines past my shoulder, and I taste death. I feel its icy, scaly fingers. It's everything left undone, unsaid, all the things that won't come to pass. It's Nikolai whispering into my ear how much he wants me, loves me, and Slava giggling as he hugs me tight. It's the bitter knowledge that these men will get away with this, like they did with Mom's murder, and regret that no one will ever know how I died.

A fourth bullet pierces the seat an inch from my right side, and I jerk on the wheel again, desperate to avoid the inevitable, to live at least a second longer. The pickup is right behind me now, looming over my Corolla like a black mountain, and as I try to swerve out of the next bullet's path, its bumper rams into mine, hard, making my head whip forward.

Pop!

Fire punches through my upper arm, the sensation so sharp and sudden it doesn't hurt at first. Instead, I feel something hot and wet slide down my arm as the truck slams into my car again, making it shudder from the massive jolt. The pain hits me then, a nauseating wave of it, and with the desperation of a dying animal, I jerk off my seat belt and push open my door.

Pop!

What remains of the windshield shatters as I hit the dirt so hard air whooshes out of my lungs. Stunned, I roll twice before landing on my back and watching in dazed horror as the truck rams one last time into my Corolla, forcing it off the road and squashing it against a thick tree. With an earsplitting screech of metal crushing metal, the old car crumples, and then, just like in the movies, catches fire. The truck immediately backs up, and some remnant of strength propels me to my feet.

Run, Chloe.

Dragging in a wheezing breath, I lurch toward the trees on legs that feel like broken matches, my knees threatening to buckle with each step I take. My foot catches on a root, and pain shoots through my left ankle—the same ankle I twisted hiding in Mom's closet—but I just clench my teeth and force my strides to lengthen, ignoring the hot blood dripping down my arm and the dizziness washing over me in waves. I can't give up, not if I want to live, so I keep going, keep limping forward at a zombie-like half-jog, half-run.

A male voice yells something behind me, and I force myself to pick up speed, ragged sobs sawing between my lips as another bullet whizzes past my ear, splintering a branch in front of me.

"Fucking bitch!"

Some sixth sense makes me duck, and a bullet slams into a tree instead of me as I lurch sideways.

Run, Chloe.

Mom's voice is clearer than ever, and with a surge

of strength I didn't know I possessed, I launch into a full-scale run. My ankle screams each time my foot strikes the ground, my vision blurring from nausea and waves of pain, but I run with everything I've got.

Only it's not enough.

Not nearly enough.

A truck-like force rams into me, knocking me off my feet, and a massive weight crushes me into the leaf-strewn dirt. I can't even wheeze as my ribcage flattens out—and then, miraculously, the weight is gone and I'm flipped over onto my back.

When my vision clears, I see a huge dark-haired man straddling me, gun pointed at my face and mouth twisted in a triumphant snarl.

"Gotcha, little bitch," he says, panting. "And since you made us work for it, you owe us some fun."

51

CHLOE

AIR RUSHES INTO MY OXYGEN-STARVED LUNGS, AND I swing my fist blindly, aiming at that smug face. He intercepts it with ease, brutal fingers catching my wrist and pinning it to the ground as he jams the barrel of the gun under my chin.

"Move again, and I blow your fucking head off," he growls, and I believe him.

I see my death in his flat, dark eyes.

"What the fuck, Arnold?" a second voice exclaims, and another man appears above us. Also armed with a gun, he looks to be some dozen years older than my captor, with receding salt-and-pepper hair and ruddy skin flushed from the exertion of the run. Breathing heavily, he orders, "Put a bullet in her and be done."

"Not yet," Arnold mutters, eyes glued to my mouth. "She's pretty. You ever notice that?"

The other man's voice turns gruff. "That's not the way we do things."

"Who gives a fuck? She's dead meat anyway. Who cares if we enjoy a bite before we bury it?"

My stomach heaves with a fresh surge of nausea, and only the cold barrel jammed under my chin keeps me from clawing the asshole's eyes out as he lets go of my wrist and presses a thick, dirty thumb to my tightly clamped lips.

"Just finish the fucking job already."

The older man's tone is sharper, more impatient, and for a moment, I'm half-afraid, half-hopeful that Arnold will obey. But he just leans in and drags a wet, jerky-scented tongue over my cheek, like a dog—and as an involuntary cry of disgust escapes my throat, he jams his thumb into my mouth, pushing it so far in I gag.

"That's nice, bitch," he whispers, eyes gleaming with lust and feral excitement. "That's real—"

A sharp *crack* shatters the silence, and he yanks his hand back. A millisecond later, he's on his feet above me, gun coming up as he spins around lightning fast—yet still not fast enough.

The second bullet slams him into the tree behind me, and as I scramble backward on my hands and ass, I see the older man already on the ground, mouth slack and skull blown open, brains spilling out like moldy cottage cheese.

52

NIKOLAI

I'M MOVING BEFORE THE SOUND OF MY LAST SHOT FADES, leaping out from behind the cover of the trees to close the distance between me and Chloe. Her gaze jerks up from the dead man at her side, her face streaked with dirt and blood, her brown eyes uncomprehending as she backs away, mouth opening in a silent scream at my approach.

"Shh, it's okay. It's me." Dropping to my knees, I gather her against me, feeling the convulsive trembling of her body—and of mine. I'm shaking with relief and rage and the aftermath of bone-chilling terror, the awful fear that we were too late.

We were almost at the gas station when Konstantin called me again with the news that his team had accomplished the nearly impossible feat of hacking into an NSA satellite, and that he was able to pinpoint the exact location of Chloe's car—and the black pickup truck that was less than a half hour behind her.

To say that we broke every speed limit in existence would be an understatement. Arkash is still recovering from the half-dozen times we nearly flew off a cliff. And we almost didn't make it anyway. The terror that assaulted me when I saw her car in a crumpled, burning heap… If it hadn't been for the empty pickup next to it and the sound of gunfire nearby, I would've lost my fucking mind.

Actually, I did lose it when I saw her on the ground with the dark-haired assassin straddling her, twisted lust painted on his face.

The motherfucker was going to rape her before killing her.

It was the only reason she wasn't already dead.

My arms tighten around her reflexively, and she makes a faint sound of distress.

I immediately pull back. "Are you hurt, zaychik? Injured in any way?"

She doesn't reply, just stares at me with huge, blank eyes, her pupils blown so wide her irises look black. She's in shock, and no wonder. Even a trained soldier would be traumatized.

Gently, I lay her down and begin inspecting her for injuries, starting with her ribs and stomach. I'm relieved to find only scrapes and bruises on her torso, but as my hand brushes over her right arm, she jerks with a pained cry, her face turning gray. I snatch my hand back, my pulse doubling at the sight of the red smear on my fingers as she squeezes her eyes shut, her breathing painfully shallow.

Fuck. She *is* hurt.

Steadying my hands, I rip open her sleeve.

"Gunshot?" Pavel asks in Russian, appearing at my side, and I nod grimly, ripping off a piece of my shirt to fashion a makeshift bandage.

"Looks like it went clean through, but she's losing a good amount of blood."

"So is he," Pavel says, and I tear my gaze from Chloe to glance at her assailant. He's sitting slumped against a tree trunk a few feet away, with Kirilov putting pressure on his chest wound and Arkash standing guard over them.

"I don't think he'll last long enough to get him back to the compound," Pavel says as I swiftly finish tying the bandage and resume my inspection of Chloe. Her color is a little better, but her eyes are still closed and her breaths are too shallow for my liking. "If you want to interrogate him, it has to be now."

Fuck. I deliberately tried to only wound the motherfucker so we'd be able to question him. If he dies, so does our chance to get answers.

I quickly finish patting down Chloe and leap to my feet. As much as I want to get my zaychik to a doctor right away, her injuries aren't life-threatening—but not knowing who her enemies are could be.

These men are pros, which means someone hired them, someone powerful, and I need to know who it is.

"Watch over her," I tell Pavel and step over to our captive.

He's breathing in jerky gasps, his face starkly pale and the entire front of his body soaked with blood.

Pavel's right. He doesn't have much longer. I meant to shoot him in the shoulder, but he spun around too fast, alerted to my presence by the bullet I had to put through his colleague's skull. With Pavel and the rest of the team unable to keep up with my terror-fueled sprint, I had no choice but to take out both assassins quickly, before they could do anything to Chloe.

In hindsight, I should've wounded them both.

As I crouch in front of the dying man, his lids lift, revealing baleful dark eyes.

"Who the fuck are you people?" he rasps, only to close his eyes, exhausted by the effort.

"Don't worry about that." Despite the volcanic rage boiling in my veins, my voice is lethally calm, controlled. "Who hired you? Why are you after her?"

His upper lip twists in a snarl. "Fuck you."

"You're dying, you know. I can let you fade away in peace or"—I take out my switchblade and flip it open—"I can mince you into pieces and make you feel every last slice."

His eyes open heavily. "Fuck off."

I throw a glance over my shoulder. Chloe is lying perfectly still, her eyes closed. Hopefully, she's passed out, or at least is so deeply in shock she won't register this next part.

Either way, there's no choice.

I need to get answers, fast.

I catch Arkash's gaze. "Do it."

The guard pulls out a syringe and stabs the dying assassin in the neck, injecting him with our pharmaceutical division's patented drug—the one the Russian military pays millions for.

The man barely reacts at first, only swatting at the site of the injection with a feeble hand. A moment later, however, his eyes go wide and he sits upright, his breathing speeding up as color rushes into his pallid cheeks.

"Epinephrine mixed with a few other fun substances," I tell him cruelly. "It'll keep you wide awake until the moment you croak. Which will be either a few neutral or a few terrible minutes from now. Your choice."

He's panting now, sweat running down his face. "Who the fuck *are* you?"

"If you don't start talking, the man who makes your last moments hell." I nod at Arkash and Kirilov, and they seize the man's arms, easily lifting them above his head despite his struggles.

"Last chance," I prompt, but the motherfucker just glares at me.

I smile darkly. I was hoping he'd prove difficult. As much as I prefer to play nice, this is the one time I'm looking forward to applying the skills Pavel taught me.

With the speed of a striking rattler, I stab my knife into the man's kidney and twist the blade.

The scream that rips from his throat is barely

human. The drug not only keeps him conscious, it enhances all sensations, magnifying pain a thousandfold.

Before he can recover, I yank out the blade and slice at his stomach twice, slashing through skin, fat, and muscle in a big X.

His eyes bulge, another inhuman scream tearing through his throat as I peel back the triangular flaps of flesh, revealing his insides.

"Have you ever wondered what it feels like to have your intestines cut out without anesthesia?" I ask conversationally. "No? Because you're about to find out. Actually, wait—I think that might kill you too quickly. We'll start lower." With another swift motion, I slash through the groin of his jeans, exposing his limp cock and balls.

"Wait!" His eyes are wild as my blade descends again. "I'll—I'll tell you."

I stop an inch from his shriveled dick. "Go ahead."

"I don't know why, okay? He never told us." He coughs, spitting up blood. "Just said we had to take them out."

"Them?"

"The woman and… the girl."

Fuck. "You were supposed to kill them both that day?"

"Yeah." His face is paler with each moment. "Only the girl was late. And then somehow she saw us and…" He coughs again, weakly, and I know the drug is losing the battle against his dying body.

"Who was it?" I demand urgently as his lids drift down. "Who hired you?" I press the sharp point of the knife against his balls. "Give me a fucking name!"

His eyes open blearily, and he croaks out three syllables—a name that nearly makes me drop my knife. My stunned gaze meets Arkash's and Kirilov's; written on their faces is the same slack-jawed look of disbelief.

"Did you just say—" I begin, returning my attention to the assassin, only to fall silent in frustration.

His eyes are vacant, his chest unmoving as his head lolls bonelessly to one side.

It's over. The motherfucker's gone.

I leap to my feet, my mind furiously sifting through what I know.

The man he named would definitely have the resources to do this, but what's the motivation? The connection? How would his and Chloe's paths have even crossed?

Unless… they didn't.

Chloe wasn't the only person on his hit list; her mother was on it too.

And then, like an avalanche, it hits me.

California. Young mother, still underage at the time of Chloe's birth. A father she never knew. A full-ride scholarship that came out of nowhere.

A different man, one with a normal, loving family, would never leap to a conclusion so twisted, so dark. But I'm a Molotov, and I know shared blood doesn't buy loyalty or safety.

I know love can be more violent than hate.

Heart thudding heavily, I turn to look at Chloe.

If I'm right, her very existence is a career-ending scandal—and another so-called father deserves my knife.

53

CHLOE

I'M IN HELL. EITHER THAT OR TRAPPED IN A NIGHTMARE. My arm is on fire, my insides are roiling, and each time the dark haze in my mind clears and I crack open my eyelids, I see Nikolai doing something ever more terrible as his deep, smooth voice utters threats that make bile churn in my throat. And the screaming that follows… My stomach lurches, and it's all I can do not to roll over and vomit.

This isn't real.

It can't be.

The dark haze threatens to swamp me again, and I focus on taking small, shallow breaths and keeping my eyes closed. It has to be a dream, a horrible, graphic dream, or a hallucination brought on by extreme terror. How else would Nikolai be here? How would he have found me?

Then again, how did my mom's killers?

My consciousness must cut out again, because

when I open my eyes next, I'm in the backseat of a moving SUV, comfortably ensconced on a man's lap. Nikolai's lap—I'd recognize that cedar-and-bergamot scent anywhere. His powerful arms are around me, holding me tight, and my pulse leaps with joyous relief as I realize this isn't a dream.

Nikolai is here.

He came for me.

I must make some kind of noise because he pulls back, eyes fiercely golden in his taut face. "Almost there," he promises, voice rougher than I've ever heard it. "The doctor is already waiting."

As he speaks, I become aware of a throbbing pain in my right arm and the general feeling of lightheadedness and extreme weakness, along with the sensation that I've been beaten all over with a club. The latter must be from jumping out of the car—and also from being tackled to the ground by the younger killer. My heart rate triples as I recall his face above me, the twisted hunger in those flat, dark eyes.

How did I go from there to here?

How is it that Nikolai—

Abruptly, my mind clears and the memories rush in, each more nauseating than the next. The older man with his skull blown off... Nikolai leaping toward me, gun held like an extension of his hand... His interrogation of the man who planned to rape me; the threats Nikolai made and the brutal, skilled way he wielded that switchblade... And the screams, those raw, blood-curdling screams...

I begin to shake as my gaze sweeps the car, taking in Pavel's stone-faced presence next to us and the two dangerous-looking men up front. I've never seen them before, but they must be guards from the compound. My eyes snap back to Nikolai's face, that perfectly sculpted face that can look alternately savage and tender, and I notice a reddish-brown streak over one high cheekbone.

Blood. Dried blood.

My shaking intensifies. Misinterpreting the cause, Nikolai strokes my jaw, his fierce expression softening. "It's okay, zaychik, you're safe. They can't hurt you."

But *he* can. I'm painfully, acutely aware that I'm at the mercy of this beautiful, terrifying man. Being held on his lap only highlights the size and strength differences between us; his large, powerful body surrounds me completely, the muscular band of his arm at my back as inescapable as any iron chain. Not that I'd be able to escape in any case—not with his men here, not while the SUV is driving at full speed.

I'm better off not knowing, but I can't hold back the question. "It was you, wasn't it?" My voice emerges as a strained whisper. "You shot him in the head."

It's as if a veil drops over Nikolai's face, all hint of expression disappearing. "I had no choice. If I'd only injured him, he could've killed you while I dealt with his partner. With the two of them there, I had to eliminate one, fast."

"And the other man..." I swallow down a surge of nausea at the recollection of the screams. "Is he...?"

"Dead from his injuries, yes." There's no remorse in Nikolai's voice, no sign of guilt in his level gaze, and shards of ice form in my veins as I realize he's done this before.

He's killed and tortured others.

Including, most likely, his own father.

"Stop the car!" The words fly out of my mouth before I can consider their wisdom. Ignoring the dizzying flare of pain in my arm, I wedge my hands between us and push against his chest—which, for some reason, feels like it's plated with steel. Desperate, I resort to begging. "Please, Nikolai, let me out. I need… I just need a minute."

He doesn't budge, and neither do any of his men as he says quietly, "We're almost home, zaychik. Just a few minutes longer."

Home? My panicked gaze jumps to the window, and fear squeezes my chest as I recognize the road leading up to the compound, the steep curves of which I navigated just this morning as I fled from the man holding me… the man I didn't truly believe was a killer.

"Don't worry. I had the doctor and his team come out here," Nikolai says, addressing a question that's just started forming in my mind. "They brought everything they need to treat you."

I take in his implacable expression, my fear growing with each passing second. "I would prefer a hospital. Please, Nikolai… just take me to a hospital."

"I can't." His chiseled features might as well be made of granite. "It's not safe."

"Safe? But—"

"Those two were just hired guns. There's plenty more where they came from."

My throat goes dry. In my panic, I almost forgot about the mystery of the killers' motivations. "Is that what he told you? The man you… questioned?" Is my theory right, after all? Did my mom witness something she shouldn't have?

"Yes, and Chloe…" He frames my cheek with his large, warm palm, the tender gesture belying the hard set of his features. "They were there to kill you both."

"What?" I jerk back. "No, that's not poss—"

"That's what the assassin said. If you hadn't been late coming home…" He drops his hand, a muscle flexing violently in his jaw.

"But that doesn't—" I stop short as fragments of the conversation I overheard that day surface in my mind.

Supposed to be here… Maybe there's traffic…

I heard the killers say that, but for some reason, I didn't put two and two together, didn't realize they were talking about *me,* waiting for *me*.

"I don't understand." I'm shaking again, trembling with a chill that has nothing to do with the AC inside the car. "Why would anyone want me dead? I haven't done anything, I don't know anyone, I'm just—just me."

Nikolai's expression shifts, a strange pity entering his gaze. "No, zaychik, I don't think you are."

"What?" I push against his bizarrely hard chest again—and nearly faint from the fresh explosion of pain in my arm. His face swims in front of my eyes, and I'm still fighting not to pass out when a startling realization filters in.

That hardness is a bulletproof vest.

In the next moment, however, I forget all about it because Nikolai asks, "Does the name *Tom Bransford* mean anything to you?"

The syllables don't make sense at first. "You mean… the presidential candidate?" As soon as the question leaves my lips, I realize how absurd it is. He can't possibly be talking about the California senator who's all over the news these days, the one they're comparing to JFK. I must've misheard or—

"That's the one." His eyes gleam like antique gold. "Unless there's another Tom Bransford with the resources to hire professional assassins, erase security tapes, and alter police records."

"Police records? What—"

"I've gone through all the files relating to your case," he says gently, "and there's nothing about the masked men at your mom's apartment—nor the black pickup that nearly ran you over. In fact, according to the official record, it was a neighbor who discovered your mother; you never even showed up to identify the body."

"That's not true! I went to the station and—"

"I know." His gaze darkens. "And there's more. Your emails to the journalists never reached their destination. Someone with a very specific set of skills made sure they'd be blocked or marked as spam—and they also got rid of whatever proof there was of your story, like traffic cam recordings and security tapes that would've shown you getting attacked."

I feel like a sinkhole is opening underneath me. "How do you know all this?" My voice shakes, my thoughts spinning like twigs in a tornado. I don't know what to think, what to believe, and the throbbing pain in my arm isn't helping. "How did you—"

"Because I also have resources. Including some that Bransford doesn't."

Of course. That's how he found me so fast today—and why I'm completely screwed if he intends to harm me. My heart thuds painfully, a cold sweat drenching my shirt as another wave of dizziness attacks me, making black dots dance at the corners of my vision. Blood loss, I realize dimly; that must be what's causing this. Desperately, I suck in air, but it only helps a little, and my voice sounds like it's coming from far away as I ask shakily, "Why did you come after me today? Why —" I drag in another breath. "Why are you bringing me back?"

His eyes return to their bright, savage tiger hue. "Why wouldn't I?"

Because I ran, I think woozily. *Because you're most likely a psychopath incapable of real feelings. Because none of this, especially you and me, makes any sense.*

I end up giving the only reason I can, one that weighs on me heaviest of all. "Because if you're right about Bransford, you and your family are in even greater danger." My voice wavers as another wave of lightheadedness crashes into me. Still, I persevere. "You have to let me go. Now. Before it's too late."

A dark curve touches his sensuous lips, a glimmer of wry amusement kindling in his gaze as he gently cups my cheek. "I don't know if you've picked up on it, zaychik," he says softly, "but my family and I aren't exactly strangers to danger. In fact, we're well acquainted with it."

He kisses me then, softly at first, then with increasing urgency, and despite everything, familiar heat sparks low in my core. He deepens the kiss, his tongue mating with mine in a primal dance that makes no allowance for our lack of privacy, and my head spins, my dizziness increasing until he's the only solid anchor in my world. Overwhelmed, I cling to him, clutching fistfuls of his shirt, and with my thoughts dissolving under the dark pull of desire, it doesn't matter that I've seen him take two lives today, that he may be the very definition of a monster.

Nothing matters except the two of us, and by the time he lets me come up for breath, we're already past the gate, back in his domain.

"Don't worry, zaychik," he murmurs, his thumb stroking my lower lip as a shiver racks my battered body. "We'll get to the bottom of this, I promise. I'll keep you safe." And in his eyes, I read the unspoken:

Even if you object.

ANGEL'S CAGE

BOOK 2

1

CHLOE

I'M BACK. BACK IN THE DEVIL'S LAIR.

The thought loops through my pain-dazed mind as the car rolls to a stop in front of Nikolai's ultra-modern mountain mansion. A man and two women in hospital scrubs—presumably the medical team Nikolai mentioned—are waiting for us on the driveway with a gurney. Behind them is Alina, Nikolai's sister, her beautiful face pale and worried.

I register all this only in passing. All my senses are consumed by the man holding me possessively on his lap.

Nikolai Molotov.

The devil himself.

His powerful arms are wrapped around me, securing me against his large body, and even though I've just seen him kill two men, I can't help but derive comfort from his touch, his warmth, his familiar cedar-and-bergamot scent. His taste lingers on my tongue, my lips throbbing from his kiss, and as much as I want to deny it, dread isn't the only emotion filling the pit of my stomach at the thought of him keeping me here against my will.

"Just a few seconds longer, zaychik," he murmurs, smoothing back my hair, and a shudder ripples through me as my eyes meet his tiger-bright gaze.

I can see the monster underneath his beautiful façade. It's now clear as day.

Pavel jumps out of the car first, opening the door for us, and a wave of dizziness crashes into me as Nikolai climbs out, holding me clasped against his chest. Though he's careful, the movement sends a stab of nauseating pain through my arm, and the distant mountain peaks spin in a sickening circle in my vision as he gently places me on the gurney.

Squeezing my eyes shut, I focus on breathing and not passing out as I'm wheeled inside the house, with Nikolai barking orders to the medical team in between speaking Russian to Alina and Lyudmila. I presume he's explaining what happened, but I'm in too much pain to care either way.

I've never been shot before, and it's not fun.

When I open my eyes next, I'm in my bedroom, with the doctor and his team bustling around my gurney. Within seconds, an IV is taped to my left arm, and I'm hooked up to several monitors. I have no idea where all this medical equipment came from, but my bedroom appears to have been transformed into a hospital room.

The doctor, already in scrubs and a surgical mask, asks if I'm allergic to latex or any medication as he pulls on a pair of gloves.

"No," I croak out, and one of the nurses attaches a bag of liquid to the top of the IV stand. Immediately, a pleasant lassitude spreads through me, making my lids heavy.

The last thing I see before the world fades away is Nikolai standing in the corner of the room, his golden eyes trained on me with fierce intensity. There's still a dark smear on his cheekbone—blood from the man he tortured to get answers—but with the sweet relief of anesthesia spreading through my veins, I can't help the loopy smile that curves my lips.

I'll keep you safe, he said, and as the darkness claims me, I believe him.

He'll keep me safe from everyone except himself.

2

NIKOLAI

My sister intercepts me as soon as I step out of Chloe's room. She must've been standing in the hallway the entire time.

"How is she?"

"She'll live, no thanks to you." My tone is harsh, but I don't give a fuck.

It's Alina's fault we're in this mess. She told Chloe I killed our father. She gave her the car keys, enabling her to flee.

At my words, Alina flinches but stands her ground. Her face is still pale and puffy, but her green eyes are clear and she no longer smells like a drug cocktail. "I mean, what's her condition? What did the doctor say?"

I sigh, raking a hand through my hair. "She got lucky. The bullet went straight through her arm, just barely grazing the bone. She's lost a good amount of blood, but not enough to require a transfusion. She also has a sprained ankle. Other than that, she's just bruised and scraped all over."

"Kolya..." My sister looks as miserable as I've ever seen her. "I'm really sorry. I didn't know about the—"

"Stop." I'm not in the mood to listen to her apologies and justifications. She might not have known about the killers hunting Chloe, but that doesn't excuse what she did. Nor does the fact that she was high on her meds. Before I say something I'll regret, I ask, "Where's Slava?"

"Lyudmila took him to visit the guards. I asked her to keep him out of the way for now, given... you know." She waves toward Chloe's door.

"Good thinking." I know I shouldn't mollycoddle my son, but I'm oddly reluctant to expose him to the brutal realities of our life, the way our father did with me. Hunting and fishing is one thing—I'm happy to have Pavel teach Slava that, along with other key life skills—but I'd rather not have him see his tutor covered in blood.

He'll learn what it means to be a Molotov eventually, but not yet.

Alina looks relieved at my praise. "So what happened?" she asks, following me as I head to my room. "Who sent the assassins after her?"

"It's a long story." One I'm still digesting myself. "Suffice it to say, she's still in danger."

Alina grabs my sleeve, bringing me to a halt. "So you didn't...?"

"I did." I put a bullet in the brain of one of the

assassins and wounded the other badly enough that he died shortly after—but not before I got a name out of him.

A name I'm still trying to come to grips with.

My sister peers at me with a frown etched into her forehead. "But you think there are more coming."

"I'm sure of it."

"Why? Who is she, Kolya?"

"That's what I intend to find out."

Pulling out of her hold, I step into my room and close the door.

Though Chloe is still under, I'm anxious to get back to her, so I quickly shower and change. Then I fire off a message to Konstantin, updating him on what I've learned and asking his team of hackers to look into the man the assassin named as their employer.

Tom Bransford.

The presidential candidate who may be Chloe's father.

She doesn't know that last part yet, and I don't know if I should say anything regarding my suspicions until I have more concrete proof. Right now, the evidence is circumstantial at best, and if I'm wrong, Chloe will have even more reason to think I'm a twisted monster.

Which I am. I just don't want her thinking that way about me.

My chest tightens as I picture the sweet, radiant smile she gave me before the drugs in the IV took hold. I want more of that, not the blank, terrified look she'd worn in the woods when I came toward her, gun in hand, having killed one of her assailants and wounded the other.

I never want to see that look on her face again.

Alina is gone when I emerge into the hallway and hurry back to Chloe's room. I know she's fine with the doctor and the nurses watching her, but I can't help the anxiety that gnaws at me each moment she's out of my sight. She came so fucking close to dying. If I'd shown up a few minutes later, if Konstantin's team hadn't been able to hack into the NSA satellite to pinpoint her exact location, if the bullet had pierced her body a few inches to the left—there's an infinite number of ways this could've turned out differently.

An infinite number of ways I could've lost her.

"She should be coming to in a few minutes," the doctor informs me when I step into her room. He's one of the best trauma surgeons in the state; Pavel had him and his team flown in on a chopper from Boise for an exorbitant fee that buys both their services and their discretion.

"Good. Thanks." Ignoring the stares from the two female nurses, I approach Chloe, a painful ache squeezing my ribcage as I note the grayish tinge of her bronzed skin. They've washed the blood and dirt off her face and arms and dressed her in a hospital gown, but her hair is still matted, with a couple of twigs and leaves caught in the golden-brown strands.

I remove the debris, dropping it onto the small table next to her gurney. I hate seeing her like this, so small and fragile and wounded. I'd give anything to have been able to take that bullet for her, or better yet, to have woken up a few hours earlier, so I could've stopped her from leaving.

Reaching over, I tenderly stroke my knuckles over her finely shaped jaw. Her skin is soft and warm. Unable to help myself, I rub my thumb over her slightly parted lips. Plush, doll-like lips, the upper slightly fuller than the lower. Sinful lips that could seduce a saint—not that I am or ever have been one.

Pulling my hand away before my body can react inappropriately, I go to a chair in the corner of the room and settle in to wait as the doctor disappears into the bathroom. The nurses pack up the supplies; as soon as Chloe regains consciousness and is stable, they'll be leaving.

True to the doctor's promise, only a few minutes pass before Chloe stirs, a faint noise escaping her lips as her eyelids flutter open. I'm immediately on my feet, crossing the room toward her.

"Hi," she murmurs sleepily, blinking up at me. "Did they already—"

"Yes, zaychik." I gently clasp her left hand, being careful not to dislodge the IV in her arm. Her delicate fingers are cold in my grip despite the sheet covering her up to her chest. "How are you feeling? You want something to drink?"

She blinks again, still clearly dazed, so I press a button to lift the head of her gurney to a half-sitting position, and then I bring a cup of water with a straw to her lips. She sucks on it greedily, making me smile.

The doctor bustles over and I step back, letting him and his team do their thing. The nurses put Chloe's right arm in a sling while he asks her a few questions and takes her vitals; then they remove the IV and all the monitoring equipment.

She's been deemed awake and stable.

"Take this for pain as needed," the doctor tells her, setting a bottle of pills on the table. "And take care not to get the bandage wet. It'll need to be changed every twenty-four hours." He glances toward me, and I nod.

I have a fair amount of experience with gunshot wounds and would be more than happy to play the role of Chloe's nurse. What I'm not happy about are the painkillers, but I know she'll need them.

Her injury may not be life-threatening, but it'll still hurt like hell.

"Here, I got this," I say as the nurses move to lift Chloe, presumably to transfer her to her bed. Shooing them away, I carefully pick her up and carry her over there myself—not a difficult task, as she's barely heavier than Slava. Though she's been eating like a lumberjack during the week she's been here, my zaychik is still much too thin from her month on the run.

She winces as I lay her down, and I feel it like a stab to my stomach. I've never been so viscerally attuned to another person before, to the point that I experience her pain as my own. If there'd been any doubt in my mind about what she means to me, it disappeared the moment I saw her Toyota gone from the garage.

I'd never known such rage and terror as when I learned the assassins were in the area—when I thought I might not find her in time.

My guts twist, and I shove the thought away before I'm tempted to strangle Alina. The important thing now is that Chloe is safe here with me. I've already told Pavel to beef up our security, in case the assassins had figured out who hired Chloe and conveyed that information to their employer before I found them. I doubt it—the one I tortured seemed to have no idea who I was—but I'm not taking any chances.

Besides, there's always the threat of the Leonovs. Alexei will be even more pissed now that we've stolen the lucrative Tajik nuclear reactor contract from his family's Atomprom.

Pushing that thought away as well, I focus on propping up Chloe on a couple of pillows and covering her with a blanket while the doctor and his team wheel the gurney and all their equipment out of the room.

A minute later, we're finally alone.

I sit on the edge of her bed and pick up her small hand. "Are you comfortable, zaychik?" I ask, rubbing her chilly palm. "Can I get you anything? Something to drink, to eat? I imagine you must be hungry."

She swallows and nods. "Some food would be great." She looks more alert now, her big brown eyes distinctly wary. Her fear has a double-edged effect on me, making my chest ache even as it arouses that primitive, twisted part of me that wants to chase her down and mark her, to claim her in the most brutal way possible.

Suppressing the dark instinct, I lift her hand to my lips and kiss her knuckles. "I'll bring it to you. Do you want something to entertain you while you wait? A book or—"

"I'll just watch some TV."

I smile and hand her the remote. "Okay. I'll be right back."

Leaning over, I drop a quick kiss on her forehead and hurry out of the room.

3

CHLOE

Heart beating unevenly, I watch the door close behind Nikolai's tall, broad-shouldered figure. My forehead still tingles where his lips touched my skin, even as my mind replays the raw, agony-filled screams of the man he tortured.

How can a ruthless killer act so caring and tender?

Is any of that real, or is it just a mask he wears to hide the psychopath within?

I'm not actually hungry—the anesthesia has made me somewhat nauseated—but I need a few minutes alone. Everything happened so fast I haven't had a chance to formulate my questions, much less attempt to come up with any answers. One moment, one of my mom's killers was straddling me, lust gleaming in his flat, dark eyes, and the next, his partner's brains were all over the forest floor and Nikolai was slicing open my attacker and threatening to remove his intestines.

Swallowing a surge of nausea, I push aside the

recollection. As brutal as Nikolai's interrogation methods were, they did yield some results, and with the worst of the shock wearing off and my mind clearing from the haze of anesthesia, I can finally think about the implications of what I've learned.

They were there to kill you both, Nikolai had told me in the car before asking if the name *Tom Bransford* means anything to me.

Which it does.

Because it's been all over the news lately.

With an unsteady hand, I lift the remote and power on the TV, tuning in to a news channel.

Sure enough, they're covering the primary debates, which Bransford appears to be winning, putting him ahead in all the polls.

My insides roil as I study his image on the screen. If Nikolai is telling me the truth, this is the man responsible for my mom's murder.

Youthful and trim at fifty-five years of age, the California senator oozes charm and charisma. His thick, golden-blond hair is barely touched with gray, his eyes are a brilliant blue, and his smile is bright enough to light a warehouse.

No wonder they're comparing him to JFK; he could be the dead president's even more handsome brother.

I search for signs of evil on his evenly featured face and find none. But then again, why would I? However good-looking Bransford is, he can't hold a candle to Nikolai's darkly magnetic appeal, and I know what *he's* capable of. I'm not the only one dazzled by Nikolai, either.

Even woozy from anesthesia, I couldn't miss the covetous looks the nurses surreptitiously cast toward him.

I've never been out in public with my employer, but I imagine panties drop left and right when he walks down the street.

A bizarre pang of jealousy strikes me at the thought, and I realize I'm getting distracted from the key question.

Why?

Why would a leading presidential candidate want to kill me and my mom?

It makes no sense. None whatsoever. Mom couldn't have been further removed from politics if she'd lived in the Amazon jungle, and God knows I don't follow the stuff. As embarrassing as it is to admit, I didn't even vote in the last election, being too busy with starting college and all. Nor have I ever met Bransford in any capacity; I have a good memory for faces, and his is more memorable than most.

Maybe Mom had encountered him somehow? At the restaurant she'd worked at, perhaps?

It's possible, theoretically. The upscale hotel the restaurant is attached to is frequented by all sorts of VIPs. Maybe Bransford had stayed there during a visit to Boston, and Mom witnessed him doing something he shouldn't have.

But then why would he want to kill me as well? Unless… was he afraid Mom had told me whatever it was she knew about him?

Holy crap. Maybe she hid some kind of evidence at her apartment, and he thinks I know where it is.

Excited, I sit up, only to fall back onto the mound of pillows with a groan. The anesthesia is definitely wearing off because that movement *hurt*. A lot. It felt like hot knives plunging into my arm, and the rest of my body isn't doing much better.

It's as if I've been knocked off my feet by an actual truck, instead of an assassin the size of one.

Before I can catch my breath and refocus, the door opens and Nikolai walks in, holding a tray of covered dishes.

My heart launches into a sprint, and what little breath I did recover evacuates my lungs.

Without the veil of shock dulling my senses and the distraction of the medical staff bustling around me, his effect on me is devastatingly, terrifyingly potent. I've never known a man who could make my body react by merely walking into a room. And it's not just his looks; it's everything about him, from the raw animal intensity in his striking amber-green gaze to the aura of power he wears as comfortably as one of his custom-made suits.

Right now, he's dressed more casually in a pair of dark jeans and a light-blue button-up shirt with the sleeves rolled up to his elbows. He must've changed and showered while I was under, I realize; not only are his clothes different from what he'd worn in the car, but the smear on his cheekbone is gone and his raven's wing hair is slicked back wetly, exposing the sharp symmetry of his striking features.

Greedily, my eyes trace over his face, from the thick black slashes of his eyebrows to the full, sensuous shape of his mouth. For once, it's not curved in that dark, cynical way of his; instead, the smile on his lips is warm, tinged with unsettling tenderness.

"I had Pavel warm up some leftovers and prepare a selection of different snacks," he says, crossing the room toward me as I reflexively power off the TV. His deep, rough-silk voice is like a caress to my ears, so much more pleasant than the newscaster's strident tones. Placing the tray on my nightstand, he takes a seat next to me and begins uncovering the dishes one by one. "I figured you might be dealing with some nausea, so I have some plain toast here as well."

Wow. Could he be any more considerate? If I hadn't seen him kill and torture with my own eyes, I would've never believed him capable of such cruelty—even with that dark, dangerous vibe I kept getting from him.

"Thank you," I murmur, trying not to think of his hands wielding a blade that sliced open a man as he extends the tray toward me, letting me pick what I want. There's everything from cut-up fruit to stuffed blintzes to cold cuts and various cheeses, but I *am* still nauseated, especially with the gruesome images refusing to leave my mind, so I just grab the plain toast and a handful of grapes.

He watches me eat with an approving half-smile, and I try not to think about how warm that smile makes me feel—and not just in a sexual way. It's an illusion, this feeling of safety and comfort he gives me, a leftover from when I thought he was a good man who just had trouble connecting with his young son.

I was beginning to fall for that man.

No. I'm lying to myself. I *did* fall for him, so much so that even with Alina's terrifying revelations ringing in my ears, I had turned my car around and was heading back here when the assassins ambushed me.

His own sister told me he was a monster, and I didn't believe her. I didn't *want* to believe her.

I still don't.

"Where's Slava? How is he?" I ask, choosing the most innocuous topic I can think of. There are so many things we need to discuss, from Bransford's motivations to whether or not I'm a prisoner here, but I'm not ready to go there yet.

That last question, in particular, is too disturbing to contemplate at the moment.

"He's just returned from a walk with Lyudmila," Nikolai replies. "Alina had her take him away before our arrival."

"Ah, good." I was worried the child might've seen us from his window. "What will you tell him about… you know?" I wave at my sling with my left hand.

"We'll just say you fell on a branch." His jaw tightens. "I'd rather he didn't know you left him."

"I didn't—" I stop, because I did. I was coming back, but Nikolai doesn't know that. Nor am I planning to tell him.

I don't want him to know how easily he'd fooled me, how even now, a part of me refuses to believe that he's a killer as ruthless as the men who'd murdered my mom.

His tiger eyes narrow with speculative interest. "You didn't what?"

"Nothing." The word comes out unconvincingly fast. I scramble to cover it up. "I just meant, I didn't leave *him*."

It's as if a thundercloud passes over Nikolai's face, blocking out all light and warmth. His gaze turns shuttered, his magnificent features taking on a statue-like hardness. "Right. You left *me*. Because of what Alina told you."

I swallow hard. I'm not sure I'm ready to go there either, but it looks like I have no choice. Ignoring the throbbing pain in my arm, I push up to a more upright position. "Did she lie?" My voice wavers slightly. "Did she make it all up?"

He stares at me, the silence stretching into painfully long seconds. "No," he finally says. "She didn't."

Something inside me withers. Up until this moment, I'd still held out hope that his sister was wrong, that despite what I saw him do to the two assassins, he's not guilty of the horrific crime of patricide. But there's no room for doubt now.

By his own admission, the man in front of me killed his father.

"What happened? Why—" My voice cracks. "Why did you do it?"

He doesn't respond for another long, nerve-racking moment. His face is that of a stranger, dark and closed-off. "Because he deserved it." His words fall like a hammer, heavy and brutal. "Because he was a Molotov. Like me."

I dampen my dry lips. "I don't understand." My heart pounds against my ribcage, each beat echoing in my ears. A part of me wants to shut this down and run away screaming, while another, infinitely more foolish part longs to curve my palm over the harsh, uncompromising line of his jaw, offering comfort with my touch.

Because hidden underneath that hard, emotionless façade is pain.

There has to be.

He opens his mouth to reply when someone knocks on the door. The sound is quiet, tentative, but it kills the moment as surely as a gunshot.

Springing to his feet, Nikolai strides over to the door to open it.

"Konstantin is on the phone," Alina says from the doorway. "His team has found something."

4

CHLOE

My stomach is in knots by the time Nikolai returns, the toast I've eaten sitting inside like a rock. I know Konstantin is his older brother, the tech genius of the family, and I strongly suspect that the "something" his team has found relates to my situation.

Now that I've had a chance to think about it, Konstantin is probably how Nikolai had known all those things about me from the beginning—like the fact that I hadn't posted on my highly private social media during my month on the run. And he's also how Nikolai got access to the police files and discovered that they'd been altered to make my mom's murder look even more like a suicide.

Konstantin and his team must be the "resources" Nikolai mentioned during the car ride here, the advantage he has over Bransford.

Sure enough, Nikolai's face is grim as he takes a seat on the edge of my bed and clasps my left hand in his strong palm. His touch both warms and chills me. "Chloe, zaychik..." His tone is worrisomely gentle. "There's something you should know."

My heart, which was already galloping in my chest, does a backflip. His gaze is no longer that of a stranger; instead, there's pity in his golden tiger stare.

Whatever he's about to say is awful, I can tell.

"How much do you know about the circumstances of your conception?" he asks in that same gentle tone. "Did your mother ever talk about it?"

It's as if an icy wind sweeps through my insides, freezing every cell on the way. "My conception?" My voice sounds like it's coming from some other part of the room, some other person.

He can't mean what I think he's saying. There's no way Bransford is—

"Twenty-four years ago, your mother lived in California," Nikolai says quietly. "In San Diego."

I nod on autopilot. Mom had told me that much. She'd lived all over southern California, in fact. After the missionary couple who'd adopted her from Cambodia were killed in a car accident, she'd gone from one foster home to another until she emancipated herself at seventeen—the same year she'd given birth to me.

"She wasn't the only one who lived in San Diego at the time," Nikolai continues. "So did a certain brilliant young politician whose local campaign she volunteered at to get extra credit for her American History class."

The icy wind inside me turns into a winter gale.

"Bransford." My voice is barely a whisper, but Nikolai hears it and nods, squeezing my hand gently.

"The one and only."

I stare at him, simultaneously boiling over with emotions and numb. "What are you saying?"

"Your mother tried to commit suicide when she was sixteen. Did you know about that?"

My head nods of its accord. When I was a child, Mom had always worn bracelets and bangles around her wrists, even at home, even while cooking and cleaning and bathing me. It wasn't until I was almost ten that I walked in on her changing and discovered the faint white lines on her wrists. She sat me down then and explained that when she'd been a teenager, she'd gone through a difficult time that had culminated in her trying to take her own life.

"She said it had been a mistake." My throat is so tight each word scrapes it on the way out. "She told me she was glad she'd failed because soon after, she learned she was pregnant. With me."

His eyes turn opaque. "I see."

He sees? Sees what? Suddenly enraged, I yank my hand out of his grasp and sit up all the way, ignoring the accompanying wave of dizziness and pain. "What exactly are you trying to tell me? What does her suicide attempt have to do with Bransford? Did he try to kill her that time too? Is that his freaking MO?"

"No, zaychik." Nikolai's gaze fills with that disconcerting pity again. "I'm afraid that attempt wasn't staged. But there's reason to believe that Bransford *was* responsible. According to the hospital records my brother's team dug up, your mother had been to the ER twice that year: once for the suicide attempt, and two months earlier as a rape victim."

A rape victim? I stare at him, black flecks dotting the edges of my vision. "Are you saying Bransford *raped* her?"

"She never filed any charges nor named her attacker, so we can't know for sure, but her first ER visit coincided with the last day of her volunteering at the campaign. She never went back after that—and nine months later, almost to the day, she gave birth to a baby girl. You."

The black dots multiply, taking over more of my vision. "No. No, that's not… No." I sway as the room blurs in my vision.

Nikolai's strong arms are already around me. "Here, lean back." I'm guided back onto the mound of pillows. "Take a few deep breaths." His warm palm smooths my hair back from my clammy forehead. "That's right, just like that," he murmurs as I attempt to obey, dragging shallow inhales into my unnaturally stiff lungs. "It's okay, zaychik. Just breathe…"

The dizziness recedes, slowly but surely, and by the time Nikolai pulls back, my brain is functioning again —and beginning to process what he's told me.

Mom had been raped.

Nine months later, I was born.

I want to throw up.

I want to scrub my skin raw and boil my DNA in bleach.

"She never..." My voice falters. "She never talked about my father. Not even once. And I asked, repeatedly."

Nikolai nods, watching me with that same unsettling pity.

The words keep coming out of my mouth, like water leaking from a faulty pipe. "She told me it had been a difficult time in her life. She dropped out of high school. Got a job as a waitress and applied for legal emancipation, on account of the pregnancy and all."

He nods again, letting me work it out on my own—and I do. Because for the first time, so much about my mom makes sense. It had always puzzled me how she'd gotten pregnant because as far as I knew, she'd been the polar opposite of a wild teen. Though Mom had rarely talked about herself, I'd gleaned enough to know she'd been a straight-A student prior to dropping out, too quiet and introverted to go out to parties and flirt with boys. Nor had she displayed any interest in dating as an adult; she'd never brought home a single boyfriend, never left me with a babysitter to go out and have fun. As a kid, I thought that was normal, but as I got older, I realized just how strange it was for a beautiful young woman to close herself off like that.

It was as if she'd taken a vow of chastity... *or never recovered from the trauma of rape.*

"Do you think..." I swallow the sour bile in my throat. "Do you think he knew? About her pregnancy? About... me?"

I always thought my father had simply walked away from the responsibility, though Mom had never said that outright, only implied it. I figured he'd been a teenager himself, someone who just wasn't ready to be a parent. But this—this changes everything. Mom might not have even told him of my existence. Why would she have, if he'd raped her?

Except... he has to know now.

Because he killed her and tried to do the same to me.

Oh God.

I barely hold back a surge of vomit.

My biological father is not only a rapist—he's a murderer.

Nikolai takes my hand in his again, his touch shockingly warm on my icy skin. "I think he had to know," he says, echoing my thoughts. "Maybe not from the beginning, but later on, for sure."

"Because he tried to kill us."

"Yes—and because of the scholarship you got."

I blink, not comprehending at first. Then his words filter through. "You mean... *he* paid for my college?"

"Konstantin is tracing the exact source of those funds, but I'm almost certain about what he's going to uncover." Nikolai's eyes are somber on my face. "It was a private scholarship, zaychik, intended for only one recipient: you. Remember how you told me that your friend applied for it and didn't get it, despite being even more qualified than you? That's because it was never meant for her. That money was yours all along."

Fuck. He's right. My friend Tanisha had been our class valedictorian with perfect SAT scores, but she didn't get this full-ride scholarship to Middlebury—I did. I even told Nikolai how strange that was. Except…

"I don't understand. Why would he do that? Why would he pay for my education if he hated me and my mom? If he… planned to kill us?" I can barely utter the last words.

Nikolai squeezes my hand. "I don't know for sure, but I have a theory. I think your mother contacted him at some point and told him about you. And I think she threatened him. It was likely something along the lines of 'if you don't provide the funds for our daughter's education, I'll go public with my story.'"

"You think she blackmailed him?"

At Nikolai's nod, I sink deeper into the pillows, shaking my head. "No. No, you're wrong. Mom wouldn't have done that. She's not—she wasn't…" To my shame, my eyes flood with tears, my throat closing as a wave of crushing grief catches me off-guard.

"A criminal? A blackmailer?" Nikolai's deep voice is gentle as his thumb massages my palm in soothing circles. Tactfully, he waits until I get myself under control, then says quietly, "You have to remember, zaychik, she was a mother first and foremost. A single mother who worked as a waitress, whose earnings couldn't have covered even a fraction of the exorbitant costs of college education in this country. What would *you* have done to ensure your child's future?"

I would've done whatever I had to—and most likely, it had been the same for Mom.

"If that's true, why did he wait?" I ask in desperation. Some childish part of me is still hoping that this is all a huge misunderstanding, that my biological father isn't a total monster. "Why pay for all four years of my schooling and then try to kill us? If he'd already spent the money—"

"It wasn't about the money. He's rich enough to have paid for ten illegitimate daughters." Nikolai's tone hardens. "It's about his career. His run for president."

Of course. The stakes are infinitely higher now, and while some politicians thrive on scandal, Bransford is an all-American icon of middle-class morals and values, with a squeaky-clean reputation that won't survive this kind of hit.

Still, assuming all of this is true, there's something that doesn't fully make sense. I can see how Mom was a threat to him, since she could go public with her story at any point. But why try to kill me?

How villainous do you have to be to send assassins after your own child? Especially if she knows nothing about you?

Then, in a burst, it comes to me.

"I'm walking proof of his crime, aren't I?" I say, staring at Nikolai. "A single DNA test, and he's toast.

Even if he tries to claim it was consensual, Mom was still underage at the time of my conception. Sixteen to his thirty-plus."

Nikolai nods. "At the very least, he's guilty of statutory rape. It's the rare case where it's not his word against hers. No matter how he tries to spin it, what he did is a criminal offense."

"And he probably doesn't know that Mom never told me about him. As far as he's concerned, I can pop up at any moment, publicly claiming him as my father."

"Afraid so, zaychik." He tilts his head, studying me intently. "Are you okay?"

I start to nod on autopilot, then shake my head. "No. No, I'm not. I need a minute." Or ten thousand minutes. Or the rest of my life.

My biological father is a rapist and a murderer who's trying to kill me.

I don't know how to even begin processing that.

Gaze filled with understanding, Nikolai squeezes my hand again, then curves his palm over my jaw and leans in, stroking my cheek with the edge of his thumb. "I'll let you rest, zaychik," he murmurs, his breath warm and subtly sweet against my lips. "We'll talk more when you're feeling better."

Closing the small distance between us, he kisses me. His lips are gentle on mine, tender, yet I can sense the hungry possessiveness underneath the restraint. It terrifies me nearly as much as my body's instinctive response.

I may evade Bransford with his help, but there will be no evading *him*.

There's no escape from the devil.

5

NIKOLAI

Closing the door behind myself, I make a mental note to install some cameras in Chloe's room, the way I have in Slava's. Not because I feel compelled to watch her every moment of every day—though that need is definitely there—but because I'm worried about her.

I've had my entire life to come to terms with my fucked-up heritage, and there are days when I'm still tempted to slit my own throat. That or get a vasectomy, so the mistake I'd made that night with Ksenia can never be repeated. I wasn't even aware that the condom was faulty, but it must've been.

That's the only explanation for the existence of my son.

I was planning to go to my office, but my feet carry me to his room instead, propelled by the same compulsion I'm experiencing with Chloe.

Daddy, he called me when I returned home last night. I'd been too distracted by everything related to

Chloe to take it in fully, but now I can't help thinking about that word and the way my ribcage had filled with a strange, piercingly sweet ache. And it's all because of her.

Chloe Emmons had not only discerned my deepest, most secret wish regarding my son; she'd made it come true.

Quietly, I push open the door to Slava's bedroom and step in. As usual, he's on the floor, diligently working on his LEGO castle. Lyudmila told me once that my son has a remarkably long attention span for a child who's not yet five, and I suppose that must be true. From what I can recall of my younger brother, Valery, at this age, he was always running around and getting into trouble. Slava, on the other hand, is quiet and focused, much more the way Konstantin was as a child. I wonder if Slava has inherited my older brother's aptitude for math and programming as well. I should probably introduce him to these subjects and find out.

At my entrance, his eyes—my eyes in miniature—shoot up to my face, the look in them equal parts quizzical and wary. My chest tightens with the usual discomfort, but I ignore the urge to back away, distancing myself from the unsettling feeling. Instead, I crouch in front of my son, giving his LEGO creation my full attention, the way I've seen Chloe do.

"That's a very nice castle," I say in Russian, studying the carefully assembled building blocks in front of me. Though Slava's English skills are rapidly improving under Chloe's tutelage, he's far from fluent in the language of our adopted country. "Did it take you long to build it?"

He blinks at me for a couple of moments before a shy smile blooms on his face. "You like it?"

"I do." I mean it, too. The castle displays admirable symmetry and complexity, especially given the fact that it was put together by such tiny hands. Even if math and computers turn out not to be Slava's strengths, he might have a future in architecture and structural design.

That is, if he doesn't take after me and Valery—and every other Molotov before us.

My mood darkens, but I force myself to maintain a calm, inquisitive expression as I ask again how long it'd taken him to build the castle.

"I worked on it in the morning and again after I came back from the woods," Slava says, visibly more comfortable with me now. He's still nowhere near as chatty and animated as he is with Chloe, but I consider this progress. Before, he'd reply to most of my questions with just a word or two, or stay completely silent.

For the next few minutes, he shows me all the ins and outs of the castle—there are turrets and towers and big windows, the latter similar to the ones in our house—and then he shyly asks where Chloe is and why he hasn't seen her all day.

"She's resting," I tell him. "A branch injured her arm, so we had to have some doctors come out here and fix it. She's all better now, but she'll be staying in bed for a couple of days while it heals."

As I speak, his eyes grow wide with worry. "Chloe is hurt?"

"Only a little bit. She'll be better soon."

He still looks concerned. "She won't die, like Mama?"

It's like a shard of glass goes through my chest. "No, Slavochka. I won't let that happen." Alina told me he occasionally asks her about Ksenia, but this is the first time I've heard him talk about his mother—and I hate it.

I hate her for hiding him from me all those years, and I hate even more that she got herself killed in a car crash, leaving him with her vile family.

At my words, Slava brightens. "Can Chloe stay with us forever?"

Now this is a question I'm happy to answer. "Yes." I look my son square in the face. "She can, and she will."

No force on earth is powerful enough to take Chloe away from me now that I have her back. I will do whatever it takes to keep her—both for Slava and for myself.

She's asleep when I stop by her room on the way to my office, so I let her rest. That's what she needs now. Her physical injuries will heal in a matter of weeks, but the emotional wounds are a different matter. I contemplated not telling her what Konstantin uncovered about Bransford and his relationship with her mother, but I decided it was important that she know—that she understand the full extent of the danger she's in.

I didn't tell her everything, though—like the fact that her teenage mother slit her wrists *after* she'd learned she was pregnant. Or that after that unsuccessful suicide attempt, she visited an abortion clinic twice, only to chicken out both times. None of that is important. What matters is that after Chloe was born, Marianna was able to power through her trauma and become the caring mother Chloe had known and loved.

The first thing I do upon stepping into my office is call Pavel and tell him to come up. The second is videocall Valery.

"I need you to send a dozen of your best men here," I tell my younger brother in lieu of a hello. "I need them right away."

"On it," Valery says, as coolly emotionless as always. Konstantin must've already briefed him on my situation. "Anything else? Weapons? Explosives?"

"Yes. Everything." I already have a large stash here at the compound, but more won't hurt. "Also, send over some pharmaceuticals."

"You got it."

He hangs up just as a knock sounds on my door.

I walk over to let Pavel in.

My right-hand man's gunmetal eyes are unblinking. "War?"

"War," I confirm grimly.

I'm not waiting for Bransford to send more assassins after Chloe.

Now that we know who her enemy is, we're taking the fight to him.

6

CHLOE

My eyes pop open as I wake with a gasp, my heart racing and my hospital gown soaked with sweat. Only the throbbing pain in my arm and the paralyzing soreness throughout my body keep me from reflexively sitting up. Instead, I force myself to lie still and take in the stunning view of the sun descending behind the distant mountain peaks outside my floor-to-ceiling window.

Slowly, I begin to calm.

A nightmare.

It was just another nightmare.

Unlike the vivid, horror-movie-style dreams that have been tormenting me since Mom's death, this one was more of a jumble of images and impressions. The whine of a bullet past my ear, branches hitting me in the face as I run through the woods from some kind of beastly creature, a heavy weight knocking me down—it doesn't take a psych degree to know that my mind was replaying my encounter with the assassins in an attempt to deal with the lingering terror.

A quiet knock distracts me from the gorgeous view. Before I can say anything, the door swings open and Nikolai steps in, a warm smile curving his sensual lips as he sees me awake.

My heart rate kicks up again, but with an emotion far more complex than fear. He's changed yet again, this time into one of the perfectly tailored suits he favors at dinnertime. A crisp white shirt and a skinny black tie complete the formal outfit, setting off his masculine beauty in a way that should be illegal—not that he'd care about something as trivial as legality.

Given what I saw him do earlier today, my captor is not exactly big on the rule of law.

At least I suspect he's my captor. We still need to have *that* conversation.

"How are you feeling?" he asks softly, stopping next to my bed. Before I can reply, he feels my forehead with the back of his hand and frowns, then pulls out a thermometer from the inner pocket of his jacket.

Huh. I guess I do feel a bit feverish.

"Open," he instructs, bringing the thermometer to my lips, and I obey, feeling incongruously like a child as he sticks it in my mouth and orders me to hold it. A few seconds later, the thermometer beeps, and he glances at the small screen on the side.

"Ninety-nine point two," he says, looking relieved as he hides the device back in his pocket and sits on the edge of the bed. "The doctor warned you might run a low-grade fever before the antibiotics kick in."

"Really? Is that a thing? I've never been shot before."

His white teeth flash in a dazzling grin. "It is—I know from personal experience."

My unruly heart picks up pace again, and my skin warms in a way that has nothing to do with the low-grade fever. "Great. I guess we each have our war stories now."

"I guess we do." His smile fades. "How are you feeling, aside from the fever?"

"Like someone's used me as a tennis ball in a match with Serena Williams," I say without thinking, only to regret it as his expression darkens, his jaw going dangerously taut.

"Those motherfuckers. If only I'd gotten there sooner…" His fingers flex menacingly on his thigh.

"No, don't." Instinctively, I reach over to cover his hand with mine. "If it hadn't been for you, I wouldn't have—" I swallow, the jumbled images from the nightmare invading my mind. "I wouldn't have made it."

And it's one hundred percent true. I haven't had the chance to really think about it, but if he hadn't come after me, if he hadn't used his scary "resources" to track me down as quickly as he did, I would already be six feet under, after first suffering through a brutal rape.

Nikolai saved me.

However terrifying his methods, he saved my life.

His gaze drops to my hand for a second, and his

expression shifts again, the menace in his tiger eyes giving way to a dark heat that feels infinitely more dangerous. "Zaychik…" His voice grows softer, deeper. "I—"

"So thank you," I blurt, pulling my hand back. Savior or not, I can't let myself fall under his spell again, can't let myself forget what he is and what he's done. "I'm sorry I haven't said it before, but I'm so, so grateful. I know I owe you my life and more. You didn't have to come after me, but you did, and I hugely appreciate it. If you hadn't been there, I—"

He presses two fingers to my lips, stopping my rambling. "You don't need to thank me." He leans over me, propping one palm on the pillow beside me and curving the other over my cheek. His gaze is darkly intent, his tone grave. "I will always protect you, zaychik. Always."

I stare up at him, my chest ballooning with a contradictory mixture of emotions. Relief and worry, gratitude and fear, joy and pain—it's like a pendulum inside me, swinging back and forth between the two extremes, the two versions of Nikolai that exist in my mind.

The one before Alina's story and the one after.

The caring lover and the brutal killer.

Which one of them is real?

With effort, I curtail my spinning thoughts and blink to break the hypnotic pull of that golden gaze. The most important thing right now is to figure out where we stand.

"You don't have to protect me," I say, injecting my tone with a confidence I'm nowhere near feeling. "Mom's killers are dead, and even if Bransford sends others, there's no guarantee they'll find me. I can just leave the country, disappear and—"

"No." The word is filled with harsh finality as he straightens and pulls back his hand. His beautiful face is set in hard, uncompromising lines. "You're not going anywhere."

"But you're in danger with me here. Your family's in danger."

I've made this argument before, and it's as ineffective now as it was then. Nikolai's expression hardens further, a savage intensity entering his gaze. "You're not leaving. The guards will stop you if you try."

So it is true then. I didn't misinterpret his refusal to let me out of the car. I *am* his prisoner.

The knowledge fills me with equal parts dread and relief. It's out in the open now; we're done pretending. Of course he's not going to let me go. I know his family's awful secret. I've seen him kill with my own eyes. The crimes he's committed would land an ordinary man in an electric chair, but Nikolai Molotov is too rich, too powerful—and more importantly, too ruthless—to ever have to pay for what he's done.

Whatever his intentions had been toward me before Alina's revelations, there's only one thing he can do now.

Detain me. Keep me where I can never reveal what I

know.

At least I hope that's the only course of action he's considering. Because there's a much more efficient way to ensure my silence, the one my biological father appears to have chosen.

But no. It might be naïve of me, but I can't bring myself to believe that Nikolai would kill me. Not with the potent, emotionally charged connection that sizzles between us. Not when he's gone to so much trouble to save my life.

And that's the thing, I realize, staring at his implacable expression. That's why, in a twisted way, it's a relief to know I can't leave. I should want to leave. I should want to run as far as possible from this dangerous man and the fixation he seems to have on me. But I don't want to. Not deep down, where it matters—and it's not just because of the stupid crush I've developed on him.

The truth is, I'm not brave and strong. I learned that today when I came face to face with death, when I felt the bullet tear through my flesh and looked into the assassin's empty eyes. I'd come close to dying before—the time I'd hidden in Mom's coat closet after finding her body, the night I'd woken up to scratching sounds at the door of my Airbnb, the couple of times the assassins had nearly run me over with their car, and the time they'd shot at me in Boise—but I had never known such prolonged, nauseating terror as when I was driving my rickety Toyota on that pothole-ridden dirt road with the bullets whining past my ears.

I don't want to die. I'm nowhere near ready to die—and I know that however ruthless of a killer Nikolai is, he doesn't wish me dead. The opposite, in fact.

He's promising to protect me.

To keep me captive and protect me.

I swallow to moisten my dry throat. "May I please have a sip of water? I'm thirsty."

The fierce expression on Nikolai's face eases. "Of course, zaychik. And you must be hungry, too. I'll get you dinner in a moment." Leaning over me, he arranges the pillows in a mound and gently props me up against it.

My breath catches at his nearness, even as my arm throbs harder at the movement, making me glad I didn't attempt this on my own.

I must've grimaced anyway, because he smooths my hair off my face, looking concerned. "Do you want a painkiller?" he asks, and I shake my head as he brings a cup of water with a straw to my lips.

The pain is not unbearable, and I want to keep my wits about me for now.

I suck down the entire cup, and when I finish, I become aware of another pressing need. "Um…" My face burns as I force myself to sit up, ignoring the spike of pain accompanying the movement. "I actually need…"

"The bathroom? Of course." He scoops me up and carries me to the adjoining bathroom, where he carefully sets me on my feet in front of the toilet. "Do you want some help here?"

"I've got it, thank you." I could've walked here on my own too—or at least limped—but it's probably best that I rest my injured ankle. Besides, some weak, needy part of me is enjoying his tender care, reveling in his nearness, his strength, his obvious worry for me.

He can't be a complete psychopath if he cares for me like this, can he?

"All right," he says, though his gaze is still filled with concern. "Don't lock the door and call me if you need anything, okay?"

At my murmured agreement, he drops a light kiss on my forehead and walks out, closing the door behind him.

I do my business as quickly as I can—which isn't quick at all, as I only have one arm to work with—then I limp over to the sink to wash my hands. The reflection in the mirror makes me wince. I can't believe Nikolai wanted to kiss me earlier. I look like a hot mess, all scratched up and bruised, my hair limp and matted. And… is that a *twig* by my ear?

I look at the shower stall, then at the sling holding my right arm immobilized against my side. Could I manage a shower? Maybe not a full-blown hair washing, but at least a quick rinse…

A rapping on the door ends my musings. "Zaychik, you done? Can I come in?"

"Yeah, okay." I try not to cringe in embarrassment as he approaches me, all clean and well-dressed and stunningly handsome. In comparison, I'm in a hospital gown that I've sweated through during the nightmare, looking—and probably smelling—like I haven't showered in weeks.

I must glance longingly at the stall again because Nikolai asks, "Would you like a bath?"

A bath? That sounds even more heavenly than a shower. Just the thought of submerging my bruises and aching muscles in hot water makes me want to moan out loud.

Nikolai reads the answer on my face. "I'll prep it for you while you eat," he says with a smile and scoops me up to carry me back to bed, where a tray of covered dishes is already sitting on the nightstand.

Carefully depositing me on the mattress, he arranges me against the mound of pillows and uncovers one of the dishes. A rich, savory aroma fills the room, making me salivate. It's Russian-style garlic potatoes with mushrooms, the ones I'd happily stuff my face with every day if I could.

While I'm drooling in anticipation, he uncovers the rest of the offerings on the tray, including a Greek salad with crispy lettuce and plump black olives, a platter of roast duck with poached pears, and buttered baguette slices with black caviar.

It's official: Pavel is back in the kitchen. His wife's cooking is nowhere near as fancy or good.

What amazes me is that Nikolai managed to assemble everything and get it up here while I was in the bathroom. He must've flown downstairs and back, Superman style.

"Pavel brought this up," he says, once again picking

up on my thoughts. It's uncanny how he does that—how he's always been able to do it. From the moment we met, I've had the unsettling sensation that he can see straight into my brain, viewing my most private fears and desires.

It's as if we really are joined by those threads of fate he's talked about, connected on a level that's far deeper than the short length of our relationship should allow.

But no. I'm not buying that—especially not now that I know what kind of man he is. It's bad enough I can't extinguish the sexual chemistry that burns between us like wildfire, nor forget the crush I'd developed on him before I learned the truth. To believe that we're somehow meant for each other, that this can be something lasting and real, would be beyond foolish.

There's no such thing as fate, and even if there were, I can't be fated to love a monster.

"Here, zaychik," the monster in question says, setting a plate filled with a little bit of everything on my lap and handing me a fork. His gorgeous mouth curves in a warm smile. "Start eating while I run you a bath."

My chest squeezes tight as he gently brushes his fingers over my ear, extracting the twig I'd noticed earlier, and walks out of the room—presumably to draw me a bath in his bathroom, where there's an enormous tub. We took a bubble bath there last night after he'd worn me out with the hottest, most intense sex of my life.

A wave of scorching heat moves through me at the memory, adding to the aching tightness in my chest. I close my eyes, willing the feeling away, but it's futile.

The arousal that electrifies my body is nothing compared to the desperate craving in my heart.

By the time Nikolai returns a few minutes later, I've gotten myself under control and am working on devouring all the food on my plate. It's a little awkward, eating with my left hand, but I'm so hungry I'd eat with my feet if I had to.

"Here, zaychik, let me help you," Nikolai says, taking the fork from me after I drop a piece of mushroom onto my chest. Ignoring my objections, he feeds me as if I were a clumsy toddler—which, to be fair, I might as well be right now—and when I'm so stuffed I can't swallow another bite, he pats my lips with a napkin, carries the tray away, and returns a couple of minutes later with the announcement that the bath is ready.

To my surprise, Lyudmila comes into my room behind him, her face carefully neutral as Nikolai picks me up and carries me out past her. "She'll change the sheets while you're bathing," he explains, walking down the hallway with long, easy strides, as if my weight in his arms were nothing.

He's strong, this captor of mine.

So strong I should be far more terrified than I am.

Pushing open the door to his bedroom with his back, he carries me past the king-sized bed where he'd taken me so many times last night. At least some of the soreness in my body must be from that, I realize with a flush. Nikolai was insatiable, and so was I.

I lost count of how many orgasms he'd given me.

The memories are still playing in my mind in an X-rated reel when he sets me on my feet in front of the tub and reaches for the tie of my hospital gown. Those memories must be why I stand there like an obedient child, letting him pull the gown off me, baring my body to his hooded gaze—and why I don't voice a single objection as he picks me up again and deposits me into the hot, bubble-covered water, being careful to drape my bandaged arm over the side of the tub to keep it dry.

I can feel the tension in him as his hands brush over my naked skin, the same tension that coils inside me, making my skin burn and my pulse thunder in my ears.

Killer. Torturer. Monster. The damning words float through my mind, but they do nothing to cool the fire raging in my blood. Having experienced the devastating, addicting pleasure of his possession, my body craves more, needs more. It doesn't care that the hands running the soapy sponge over my chest and shoulders had taken two lives mere hours ago, that I'm not his lover but his captive.

"Sink in a little deeper," he murmurs, his voice a low, sensual rasp, and I mindlessly obey, reveling in the feel of his strong fingers on my skull as he cradles the back of my head, keeping my face above the water while soaking my hair.

I must still be under the influence of whatever drugs were used for the anesthesia because this doesn't feel entirely real, especially when I close my eyes to protect them from stray drops of water. It's as if I'm in a dream, one in which nothing matters but the warm pleasure of his touch, the soothing comfort of his tenderness. Everything about this should feel wrong, repellent, but instead, I feel like a pampered pet as he lifts my head out of the water and applies shampoo to my wet strands, then rubs the lather into the roots, his fingers exerting just the right amount of pressure as his short fingernails gently scratch my skull.

It's the best head rub I've ever gotten, and it's all I can do not to beg for more when, after a few blissful minutes, he deems my hair sufficiently lathered and guides my head back into the water.

Thankfully, it's not over. He applies conditioner to my hair next and rubs it into the roots as well. I'd tell him that's the wrong way to do it, but I'm enjoying the experience too much to care that my hair will lie flat tomorrow and will get greasy faster. The latter might even be a plus if it incentivizes him to do this again soon.

"Dip your head back in," he orders huskily, and I oblige as he runs his fingers through my strands, rinsing off the conditioner and detangling them in the process.

He's good at this, so good he's either a natural or he's had some practice.

A sharp stab of jealousy catches me off-guard. I open my eyes, the warm lassitude engulfing me fading as I glare up at him, my head still half-submerged in the water.

How many women has he done this with?

How many have known the bone-melting pleasure of his ministrations?

"What's wrong, zaychik?" His dark eyebrows pull together as he helps me sit up. "Did I hurt you?"

"No." I know I shouldn't say anything, but I can't help it. "You've done this for a lot of women, haven't you?"

He looks taken aback for a second. Then a wickedly sensual smile spreads across his face. "Not a lot, no. You're the only one, in fact."

"Oh." Now I feel like an idiot. "Never mind then. I just..."

I'm about to close my eyes and slide back into the water to hide my mortification when he gently grasps my chin, forcing me to meet his gaze.

"But even if that weren't the case," he says softly, "every other woman is in the past. You're the only one for me going forward. Just keep in mind, zaychik"—he leans in so close I can see the forest-green flecks in the rich amber of his irises—"I'm the only one for you now as well. No other man will ever touch you. You're mine as much as I'm yours."

I stare into those hypnotic eyes, enthralled and

terrified by the possessive intensity in them. He means it, I can tell. For whatever reason, he's decided we belong together, and there's nothing I can say or do that will alter that conviction—a conviction that would be dangerous even if the man himself weren't the embodiment of darkness.

It's as if he's obsessed with me… and not in an entirely healthy way.

He holds my gaze for a few beats longer, then leans in and presses a kiss to my forehead. The gesture should feel tender, paternal even, but instead, it's an imprint, a brand. His lips linger on my skin for a couple of seconds too long, his grip on my chin tightening to hold me in place. *You're mine,* that kiss says, and when he finally pulls back, the same message is repeated in his eyes, then echoed in his touch as he picks up the sponge and resumes washing me, his hands traveling over my body with a platonic restraint that only emphasizes the hunger he's keeping so carefully leashed.

He thinks that hunger is dangerous, I realize. Too dangerous to give in to while I'm weak and hurt.

With effort, I push the thought away and close my eyes, letting myself simply enjoy the moment. Tomorrow, I'll worry about the future and what Nikolai's obsession with me means—what the cost of his care and protection may turn out to be. Tonight, I'll just revel in the fact that I'm his prized possession.

That I'm as safe in the devil's arms as anyone can be.

7

NIKOLAI

It's two o'clock in the morning and I'm still wide awake, staring at the dark ceiling above my bed. Partially, it's because my body is still on Dushanbe time, but mostly, I'm just too wired, my thoughts cycling between my plans for Bransford and the adrenaline-spiking recollections of yesterday. The latter are especially intrusive, filling my chest with all sorts of violent emotions.

Chloe ran from me. I almost lost her. Another few minutes and—

Fuck. Enough is enough.

I jackknife off the bed and stride to the closet to pull on my running shorts. I already ran this evening. As soon as I finished bathing Chloe and tucked her in for the night, I laced up my sneakers and headed out. But I need another run. That or a nice, hard sparring with Pavel or the guards. Or better yet, a run *and* a sparring, since I need to work off some serious sexual frustration as well.

Touching Chloe's wet, naked body without fucking her had required all of my willpower and then some.

Before exiting the room, I pull up a video feed of Chloe on my phone. I had Pavel install a small camera on the TV above her bed while I was bathing her, so I'd be able to keep an eye on her without coming into her bedroom and disturbing her sleep.

As expected, my phone screen shows her tucked under the covers in the darkness, with only the sound of her even breathing filling the silence. Unlike me, she's sleeping peacefully, and I'm glad. She needs good rest in order to recover—which is why I have to keep my hands off her, no matter how much it kills me.

I'm stronger than the savage beast inside me.

At least I hope I am.

Leaving the phone in my room, I head downstairs, and my chest expands as soon as I step outside. The night is dark and cool, the mountain air crisp and pure.

I set off for the woods, running down the mountain and into the forest, as is my custom. But this time, instead of returning to the house after I've worked off most of my restless energy, I head to the north side of the compound, to the guards' bunker.

I'm not surprised to find Pavel there, playing cards with Arkash and Burev by a campfire. Like me, he must be wound too tight to sleep, even with Lyudmila by his side.

Seeing me, he jumps to his feet, and so do the

others. "All good," I say, motioning for them to relax. "Just need a workout is all."

"You got it," Pavel says, eyes gleaming with eagerness. "Knives or not?"

"Knives, of course."

The guards provide the weapons, and for the next forty minutes, my mind is blissfully free of all except the primitive goal of survival, of avoiding getting sliced into pieces by Pavel's ruthlessly wielded blade. Twice, I'm nearly disemboweled; three times, I narrowly miss having my jugular sliced through. Pavel pulls no punches, and by the time I finally get the sharp edge of my blade against his throat, we're both covered in stinging nicks and cuts.

Panting, I step back and return the knife to Arkash, who claps me on the shoulder in congratulations. None of the guards are good enough to go up against Pavel with a blade and win, but then again, none of them have been trained by him since they were my son's age.

Leaving them to their duties, Pavel and I head back to the house together. At first, we're both too tired to talk much—the fight was as draining as I hoped it would be—but when the house appears within view, Pavel says quietly, "You really should forgive her, you know."

I glance at him in surprise. "Chloe? I already have." As much as it upsets me that she ran, I understand why she did it. What my sister told her would've frightened anyone, not just a vulnerable young woman who'd already seen the worst of humanity.

"No. Alina." Pavel shoots me a sidelong look. "She's upset. Lyudmila caught her crying."

Fuck. I should've known he'd take my sister's side in this. "She should be upset. She fucked up, big time." My words come out harsher than I intended. I've been trying not to dwell on Alina's role in all of this, but the fact of the matter is, Chloe almost *died*.

I don't know if I'll ever be able to forgive Alina for that.

"She knows she fucked up," Pavel says evenly. "But she's still your sister."

"And blood is thicker than water, right?"

He ignores my sarcasm. "It's not good for her, to be so upset. The headaches—"

"I know all about her fucking headaches." I take a steadying breath. "Look, I'm not sending her away or punishing her in any way. We'll still do her birthday celebration Friday, as planned. But you can't expect me to just forgive and forget. High or not, Alina knew what she was doing when she opened her big mouth and handed Chloe those car keys."

"But she didn't know." Pavel's expression is grim as he steps in front of me, blocking my way. "You hadn't told her Chloe was in mortal danger. And don't forget *why* she was high last night."

My molars grind together. "Get out of my fucking way. Now." He might be my friend and mentor, but if I had my knife to his throat right now, I wouldn't care—

not with the dark memories surfacing in my mind, filling my stomach with a toxic brew of rage, horror, grief, and guilt.

Alina's need for medication *is* my fault, I know.

However big her fuckup, it can't hold a candle to mine.

Pavel must realize he's gone too far, because he wisely steps out of my way and drops the topic. We cover the remaining distance to the house in tense silence, all the benefits of our sparring undone by this short exchange.

There's no way I'm falling asleep now.

Not when I can once again feel my blade sinking into my father's stomach and see the monster that is me in his dying eyes.

8

CHLOE

I'M ABOUT TO CONSUME THE FORKFUL OF SCRAMBLED eggs Nikolai is holding to my mouth when I hear voices in the hallway, followed by a knock on the door. My gaze jumps to Nikolai's face, and my cheeks flame at the amused gleam in his eyes.

We both know I'm not incapacitated enough for him to be spoon-feeding me; it's just a peculiar, slightly kinky dynamic we've fallen into. I didn't even try to eat with my left hand this morning when he brought me breakfast—he just started feeding me and I let him.

Even his four-year-old eats without help, yet here I am, with one arm completely functional, acting as if I can't hold a fork on my own.

My embarrassment deepening, I snatch the fork from Nikolai and set it down on the tray sitting on the nightstand. "Come in!"

I was expecting Pavel or Lyudmila, but it's Alina

who steps into my room, Slava's tiny hand clasped in hers.

The child's eyes brighten when he sees me. "Chloe!" Letting go of Alina, he dashes toward me, babbling excitedly in Russian.

"He's been worried about you," Nikolai translates, smiling wryly as Slava jumps onto my bed with the boundless energy of a puppy. "Even though I told him you won't die like his mother, he feared you might, so he's been asking to see you ever since he woke up this morning. Which was forever ago because—and I quote —you slept *so, so late*."

"Oh, no, darling, I'm totally fine." I pat his back with my left hand as he wraps his arms around me in as fierce a hug as his childish strength allows. "It's just my arm that's hurt, see?" I show him the sling when he pulls back.

He frowns and rattles out a question.

"He's asking why you're in bed if it's just your arm," Alina says, and I look up to find her standing next to the nightstand. Her strikingly beautiful face is again fully made up, her slender figure clad in a sleeveless yellow dress that looks like it came off the runway. No trace remains of the tormented, broken woman who'd confronted me yesterday morning with terrifying warnings about the man sitting at my side.

I give her a cautious smile before shifting my attention back to Slava. "It's because my ankle hurts a little too," I tell him, and Nikolai translates my words. I notice he's avoiding looking at Alina; he hasn't acknowledged her presence at all, in fact.

Slava peers at my blanket-covered feet and asks another question.

"He wants to know how you hurt your ankle," Nikolai says. "I'm going to tell him you twisted it when you fell on the branch."

"Makes sense."

While he speaks to the boy, I glance up at Alina and give her a bigger smile. She's probably worried that I'm mad at her, but I'm not. I'm grateful, in fact. I don't know what would've happened if I hadn't run, but I'm guessing that, at best, it would've delayed the clusterfuck I now find myself in. The assassins would've located me eventually, and either then or at some point later, I would've learned what Nikolai is capable of. By then, though, I might've been several weeks or months into an intense relationship with him, and it would've been that much more devastating to have my illusions shattered.

Or maybe, just maybe, he would've succeeded at keeping me in the dark, and I would've never found out that he kills and tortures as easily as other men cut grass. I would've slept in his arms and taken him into my body all the while convincing myself that my instincts are wrong, that the thread of darkness I've sensed in him is nothing more than my overactive imagination.

Ugh. Maybe I *should* be upset with Alina. That kind of ignorance does sound like bliss.

Visibly relieved, Alina returns my smile, and I push aside silly notions about how nice it would've been never to face the truth about Nikolai—or about Bransford and all the rest of it. If I were to indulge in that kind of thinking, I might as well wish for my mom to be alive, or better yet, for her to have never encountered my biological father in the first place.

I wouldn't exist in the latter case, but it would be worth it to have her alive and happy in a life that hadn't been derailed when she was a teen.

Realizing I'm again spiraling into useless what-ifs, I look up at Nikolai and say brightly, "How about Slava and Alina stay with me for a while? I don't want to monopolize your time. I'm sure you have work to do, and I can teach Slava from my bed as well as from anywhere."

Nikolai's face tightens at my clear hint that I want him gone, but he rises to his feet and says calmly, "All right. I'll see you in a bit. Don't forget to eat, okay?"

"On it." I grab the fork and bring the eggs to my mouth with exaggerated clumsiness. My goal is to make Slava giggle, and I succeed.

By the time I look over, Nikolai is gone.

Alina's face is somber as she sits on the edge of the bed, taking Nikolai's spot. "How are you feeling?" she asks quietly as Slava runs over to the window, apparently curious about the view from my room.

"I'm good. Already on the mend." I stuff a big forkful of eggs into my mouth to showcase how quickly I'm healing. I'm not lying, either. My arm still hurts, but with the painkiller I swallowed upon waking, it's manageable, and I'm able to put some pressure on the ankle without it protesting too much.

Alina smiles hesitantly. "That's good." She takes an audible breath. "Listen, Chloe… I was in bad shape yesterday morning. Really bad shape. I might've said things that didn't make sense. Things that weren't… necessarily true."

I put down my fork, my appetite having vanished without a trace. I understand what she's trying to do, and I hate it. "You don't have to lie. He's admitted it. And I saw what he did to the men who attacked me."

A myriad of expressions flashes across Alina's face before it turns carefully neutral. "I see. And you're… okay?"

Okay? Does *not* jumping out of the window or running out the door screaming constitute okay? If so, I'm totally fine, or at least as fine as you can be after discovering that your biological father is a rapist and a murderer who's trying to kill you, and that you're being held captive by a man who might be even more ruthless than said father.

"I'm handling it," I say, and to my surprise, it's not a total lie. Maybe it's the month of living on the run, or the horror of finding Mom's body and hiding from her killers in the coat closet, but I'm not freaking out nearly as much as I would've expected. About any of it—but especially the fact that I'm Nikolai's prisoner. It's as if my mind has erected a wall between the present and the recent past, between what I'm experiencing and what I know.

Right now, I'm cozy and well fed, my safety ensured by the same security measures that would prevent me from leaving if I tried. And it's possible to focus on just that first aspect of it. Just as it's possible to forget Nikolai's true nature when he's being so caring and tender… when my blood turns to warm molasses at his touch.

Somehow, I'm able to put all the horror in a little box and pack it away, to pretend it isn't there.

"Good," Alina says. "I'm glad. But if you're ever having trouble dealing, or just need someone to talk to, I want you to know that you can always come to me." Jade eyes gleaming softly, she adds, "No matter what you're going through, I'd understand."

And she would, I know. My throat tightens as I take in the genuine sympathy in her gaze. I didn't know until this moment how much I'd longed for this: not an offer of friendship, precisely, but something that feels an awful lot like it. "Thank you," I say thickly. "I appreciate it—just as I appreciate what you tried to do before, what with warning me and all."

Maybe it's another illusion that's bound to be shattered, but it feels like I have an ally in Nikolai's sister. Like I'm not completely alone in this mess.

She smiles wryly and rises to her feet. "Yeah, well, that didn't exactly turn out how I'd hoped. I—" She stops as Slava exclaims something from his spot by the window and runs back to us, chattering excitedly in Russian.

"He says there's a family of raccoons on our driveway," Alina translates with a grin. "Apparently, they've just come out of the forest."

"Really? I want to see." I sit up straighter and, ignoring the pang of pain in my arm, swing my feet to the floor. Carefully, I stand up, mindful not to place too much of my weight on the sprained ankle.

So far, so good.

"Here, lean on me." Alina lends me her elbow, and with her help, I limp over to the window, where the raccoons—a mama and two babies—are indeed frolicking in plain sight.

Slava laughs in excitement as one of the babies playfully jumps on the other, and I ruffle his silky hair, my chest expanding as he gives me a beaming smile.

"Raccoons," I say, recalling my role as his English tutor. "Those are called *raccoons*."

He obediently repeats the word after me, and the three of us watch the animals until they disappear back into the woods. Then Alina helps me limp back to the bed, and I ask her to bring me a book that I can read with Slava.

"No problem," she says, already heading for the door. She returns a few minutes later with a stack of children's books that she sets on the blanket next to me. "Do you want me to take that away?" she asks, gesturing at the tray on the nightstand, and I nod as Slava gets comfortable at my uninjured side.

It'll be lunchtime soon, and I've eaten enough to tide me over until then.

She picks up the tray and heads out again. It's only when she's almost by the door that I realize I haven't asked her something important.

"Alina, wait," I call as she opens the door with one stiletto-clad foot.

She turns around, a quizzical look on her face.

"Will you come back in a bit? I'd like to know more about what happened." My voice turns unsteady. "With Nikolai and… and your father."

She stiffens, her face wiped of all expression.

"Please, Alina. I need to know."

I need to find out just how much of a monster I've fallen for.

She closes her eyes and takes a deep breath, then opens them again. "It's not my story to tell." Her voice is low and strained. "It never was. Nikolai's the one you should talk to."

And before I can plead with her further, she steps out and closes the door.

9

NIKOLAI

Unclenching my tightly balled fist, I click away from the camera feed of Chloe's room and open my inbox. I don't know what I would've done to Alina if she'd agreed to Chloe's request. Fortunately, my sister has recovered enough of her wits to realize she needs to keep her mouth shut.

It *is* my story to tell—and I'm not sure I want to tell it.

Yesterday, when Chloe asked me if what Alina had told her was true, I was tempted to lie, to tell her that Alina had made it all up—that she'd been delusional because of all that medication. But for some reason, as I looked into Chloe's soft brown eyes, the words refused to form in my throat. As much as I hate it that my zaychik sees me as evil, something deep inside me wants her to know the real me.

To know me and love me regardless.

Fuck. This is a problem—but not as big of one as the email from Valery that's just popped into my inbox.

LEONOV IN AMERICA, the subject line states in all-caps, and when I open the message, it informs me that my younger brother's US contacts have gotten word of Alexei Leonov's presence in New York City. What he's doing there is anyone's guess, but just the fact that he's on the same continent as my sister and my son is bad news. I haven't forgotten what he said to me in the restroom of that Tajik restaurant, the threat he made about holding Alina to their archaic betrothal contract. At the time, I figured he was just trying to piss me off—and I still suspect that's the case—but there's a chance he meant it.

Tell Alina it's time. I'm done being patient.

I grit my teeth, shutting out the memory of those softly uttered words. Whatever Alexei's agenda is, he's not getting anywhere near Alina. It's bad enough that my son spent almost two months in the tender care of the elder Leonov before I was able to get him out; the last thing I want is for my emotionally fragile sister to be pulled into that nest of vipers.

Alina and I may have our differences, but she's my responsibility, my cross to bear, and I will protect her from anyone who wishes her harm—especially her so-called intended.

Tamping down on the rage burning in my stomach, I reread the email. New York City—that's about as far from Idaho as it gets. Could Alexei's presence in the US so soon after our run-in in Dushanbe be a coincidence after all? I flew to Tajikistan on our private jet, and I know Konstantin's team put safeguards in place to prevent anyone from learning my flight plan, so it's possible Alexei is in New York for a reason totally unrelated to my family.

And it's also possible he's learned I'm in America, but he doesn't know where, so he's starting his search with the most logical place: the Big Apple.

Either way, it's a headache I don't need, especially with the *Mission Impossible*-level task of assassinating a presidential candidate already on my plate.

Switching my focus to that, I pull up the email that details Bransford's upcoming travel and public appearance schedule. Step one is to verify that he is indeed Chloe's father. For that, we need his DNA.

There are a dozen ways to go about doing this, but the most straightforward would be for me to attend one of his fundraisers under the guise of a potential donor and discreetly acquire a sample—say, by stealing his wine glass. The problem with that strategy is those events are far more public than I'm comfortable with, especially given Alexei's unexpected arrival in the States. Now, more than ever, I have to stay under the radar to avoid exposing our location—which rules out another simple solution: getting a one-on-one meeting with Bransford.

Given his status as the frontrunner in his party's primary race, I'd be thoroughly vetted, and my information would end up in some database that the Leonovs' hackers might access. Additionally, it wouldn't be wise to get on Bransford's radar. Even if the assassins hadn't made the connection between me and Chloe before I took them out, Bransford might know that she'd last been spotted in this area of Idaho, and if he somehow learns that this is where I'm residing, he'll get suspicious.

No, as convenient and satisfying as it would be, I can't get his DNA—or carry out the assassination—personally. Not without putting my family and Chloe in greater danger. As is, the clock is ticking. If the assassins told their employer that Chloe had inquired about my job posting at the local gas station, it's only a matter of time before some other hired guns of his show up at my door.

I have to eliminate Bransford as a threat, and fast.

Reaching a decision, I fire off an email directing one of Valery's new arrivals to pose as a waiter at the next event, so he can get Bransford's DNA from a used glass or a utensil. It's a formality at this point; I know I'm right about him—I can feel it in my gut. However, given the magnitude of what I'm planning, I need ironclad proof, and this is the best way to go about it. The only stronger evidence would be an outright confession of his guilt, and I don't see a way to get that short of kidnapping the man—a task even more difficult than killing him outright.

For now, I will proceed as if he's guilty, and plan out the hit. That way, as soon as the DNA test confirms his relationship with Chloe, I can pull the trigger—figuratively, if not literally. A sniper bullet would generate too much heat, so our best bet is to use one of our carefully crafted pharmaceuticals, or to stage some sort of accident.

Either way, he'll pay for killing Chloe's mother and trying to kill her.

Tom Bransford might not know it yet, but he's already dead.

I spend the next two hours working out various logistics, and then I check the camera feed from Chloe's room again.

She's still with Slava; he's camped out on her bed, his books and LEGO pieces scattered all over her blanket. They appear to be playing a game where she shows him something in a book, and he acts it out for her. As I watch, he jumps off the bed and hops around the room, imitating a rabbit.

"That's a *zaychik*, right?" she says, smiling, and Slava's eyes go wide before a huge smile takes over his little face.

"*Da!*"

"Yes," she corrects, her own smile widening. "We say *yes* in English."

My son vigorously bobs his head. "Yes, yes, yes!" He's jumping up and down now, too excited to stand still, and I make a mental note to teach Chloe some more words in Russian. That way, she can surprise him randomly like that again, and I'll enjoy listening to her cute, American-accented Russian.

Come to think of it, I should teach her some sex words as well, so I can hear her soft, husky voice crooning them to me when we're in bed.

My body hardens at the image, and I have to take a deep breath to control myself. I've already had her once—or rather, several times in one night—and it's nowhere near enough. I feel like a starving man who was allowed a single lick of ice cream.

I want more. I want to fuck her every night, to take her every hole and pleasure her in every way possible. I want to go to sleep holding her and wake up buried deep inside her. I want to do all sorts of dark, depraved things to her, and I want to cuddle her afterward as she comes down from the pleasure-pain high.

I want to possess her so completely she'll forget all about wanting to leave me.

Soon, I promise myself, shutting the laptop as I get up. She'll be better soon, and then I'll have her.

In the meantime, I have to do whatever it takes to keep her safe.

10

CHLOE

A FEW MINUTES BEFORE THE OFFICIAL LUNCHTIME OF twelve-thirty, Lyudmila comes to take Slava downstairs.

"Nikolai come with food soon," she says in her thickly accented English, correctly surmising that the growling sounds from my stomach indicate hunger. I smile at her bashfully, but she's already hustling Slava out the door while speaking to him in rapid-fire Russian.

Sure enough, Nikolai appears with a tray at twelve-thirty on the dot.

"What's with the military-style adherence to specific meal times?" I ask as he sits next to me and places the tray on the nightstand before uncovering the delicious-smelling dishes.

It's something I've been wondering about for days but haven't had a chance to ask—and I figure this question is a lot easier to answer than the other ones I have prepared.

A wry smile lifts one corner of Nikolai's sensuous lips. "You said it: It's a leftover from the military. More specifically, Pavel's time in the military. He's been running our household ever since he got out of the army some thirty years ago, and this is one of his rules. I don't mind. I grew up this way, so I find it a comforting ritual."

"What about the formal wear at dinner? Is that also Pavel's thing?" That would be odd, given that I've never seen the bear-like Russian in anything resembling a suit or a tux, but there's a lot of weirdness in this household.

The tiny muscles around Nikolai's eyes tighten, though the smile remains on his lips. "Not exactly. That's something my mother insisted on. She said we needed something beautiful in our lives to cover up all the ugliness."

"Oh, I see." My pulse speeds up with anticipation. This is the first time he's spoken of his mother to me—of either of his parents, really. All I'd known before Alina's terrifying revelations was that both of their parents were dead.

"Here," Nikolai says, bringing a piece of French bread slathered with butter and caviar to my lips. "Open up."

I obediently bite into the gourmet offering like the invalid we're both pretending I am. My mind isn't on our strange little game, though; it's churning with all the questions. There's still so much I don't know about my dangerous protector, and I need to know.

I need to know everything, because some small, irrational part of me is still hoping that the darkness in him is not as pitch-black as it seems.

I let him feed me some of the other appetizers on the tray, as well as the flaky white fish with lemon sauce and scalloped potatoes that is the main dish, and when he switches over to dessert—poached pears with black currants and honeyed walnuts—I steel my spine and launch into my planned interrogation.

"So," I say in as casual of a manner as I can, "are you guys mafia?"

I'm pretty sure I already know the answer to this, but might as well hear it from the horse's gorgeous mouth.

To my surprise, instead of flattening in offense or anger, said mouth twitches with amusement. "No, zaychik. At least not the way you imagine it. We don't do illegal drugs or weapons or anything along those lines—that's more of the Leonovs' province. The vast majority of our businesses are legal and above board, and the small portion that are not fall within Konstantin's domain—dark web, hacking, social media bots, all that high-tech jazz."

I blink at him in disbelief, the image of the gun in his hand crisp and clear in my mind. There's no way a regular wealthy businessman, even one with military training, would be able to kill and torture as casually as he had. "But I saw you… And your men… And—"

"I didn't say we were angels. Open up." He brings a forkful of currant-dotted pear to my lips and waits for me to start chewing before he continues. "In Russia, to gain and retain power, you have to be ruthless. You have to be willing to do whatever it takes. It's always been that way, since time immemorial."

I open my mouth to speak, but he just feeds me another bite of the pear and continues in a light, even tone, as if reading a bedtime story.

"My family has always understood that," he says, "which is why we've prospered since the times of the Mongols' rule. In fact, our first known ancestor was one of Genghis Khan's right-hand men—a nice, kind guy who looted, burned, and raped his way all across Siberia and into the Moscow region back in the thirteenth century. His children followed in his footsteps, and by the time Peter the Great was building his city, the Molotovs—or Nebelevskys, as we were known back then—were a fixture at the tsarist court, guiding and directing national policy from behind the scenes. We were also filthy rich and owned thousands upon thousands of serfs—which makes it extra ironic that during the Revolution, my great-grandfather was one of the ones putting the 'despicable nobles' and 'evil bourgeoisie' on trial for crimes against the common people. He even changed his name to Molotov, the root of which means "hammer" in Russian—a much more Communist-friendly last name than Nebelevsky. But that's how we roll." A hint of bitterness twists Nikolai's lips. "We do whatever it takes to stay on top: whether it's running the gulag labor camps during Stalin's era, or spearheading the propaganda machine of the Communist Party in the fifties and sixties—or jumping on the oil and gas vouchers during the Perestroika and then diversifying to retain the resulting billions in wealth. We're like cockroaches—except the kind that know not just how to survive but how to rule their corner of the world."

I'm both disturbed and fascinated, so much so I forget to chew the next bite of dessert before asking, "So you're not actual mafia?"

My mouth is so full the words come out jumbled, but Nikolai understands and smiles. "No—but that doesn't mean we shy away from getting our hands dirty. Staying on top in Russia is like building a house on a sandy ocean beach: The ground underneath washes away with every tide, and a storm is always brewing on the horizon. My late grandfather, for example—my father's father—was nearly executed back in the fifties when a high-ranking Party rival falsely accused him of disloyalty to the Communist regime. He spent two years in one of the Siberian gulags he'd been overseeing, and when he made his way out, the first thing he did was plant evidence on his rival and get *him* sent away to the gulags while having the government transfer all of his property to himself. Then, later on, my father—" He stops, his expression darkening.

I sit up straighter. "Your father what?"

Nikolai's face turns impassive. "Nothing. The nineties in Russia were just a particularly corrupt and volatile time, so my family had to be extra vigilant and ruthless."

"Specifically, your father." I'm not about to let him drop this topic, not when I'm finally getting some answers.

"And his brother, Vyacheslav—my uncle. His son, Roman, is now nearly as rich as we are."

"Uh-huh." At any other time, I'd jump at a chance to learn more about Nikolai's extended family, but right now, I'm solely focused on his father. I let him feed me a couple more forkfuls of dessert, and after I swallow, I ask cautiously, "So what kind of things did your father have to do to stay on top in the nineties?"

Nikolai's eyes turn a greener shade of amber. "Nothing worse than any other oligarch of his generation: a lot of bribery, some blackmail and racketeering, a little physical coercion, and—when required—forceful elimination of obstacles. Tactics you might think of as falling into the organized crime domain, except they were standard business strategies in Russia at the time. And it wasn't just the oligarchs—the government used the same toolbox. That's still the case to some extent; lawfulness and criminality are highly flexible, constantly evolving concepts in my country, each with a lot of room for interpretation."

I do my best to keep my expression neutral, even as my arms prickle with a chill. *Physical coercion* and *forceful elimination*—those are obviously euphemisms for torture and murder. And this is what he's been raised to view as standard business strategies?

The Molotovs might not be mafia in the formal sense of the word, but in some ways, they're even more dangerous.

"Is that why you brought Slava here? Because Russia is such a lawless place?" I ask, unable to help myself. This is another mystery that's been gnawing at me, and though I intended to keep this interrogation focused on his father, I can't pass up a chance to get some answers on this front.

After what he's just told me about his home, I can't blame him for wanting to raise his son as far away from Russia as possible.

"No, zaychik." His beautiful mouth takes on the cynical curve it wears so often. "I'm not that good of a father, I'm afraid."

"So why *are* you here? You promised you'd tell me." Actually, he promised no such thing. All he said on the videocall where I'd questioned him about this was that it was a long story.

He must remember that too because his eyes gleam with amusement. "Nice try." He glances at the now mostly empty tray. "Are you full, or would you like anything else?"

I'm so full my stomach is on the verge of exploding, but I don't want him to go yet. Not when we're just getting to the things I'm dying to know about. "I'd love some fruit," I say hopefully. "Maybe some berries if you have them? And coffee. I'd love some coffee."

He looks even more amused but rises to his feet without arguing. "All right. I'll be right back."

Dropping a kiss on my forehead, he picks up the tray and walks out.

11

NIKOLAI

I'M STILL SMILING WHEN I STEP INTO THE KITCHEN. MY zaychik is so wonderfully transparent in her attempts at manipulation. *You promised me.* It was all I could do not to grab and kiss her on the spot—especially since as she said it, she pushed out her bottom lip in a small pout, like a wheedling child.

I love that she's less afraid of me now, that instead of horror, there's curiosity in her pretty brown eyes. I've been doing my best to keep the beast inside me leashed in her presence, to make her feel comfortable and secure, and it looks like I'm succeeding—which makes all the restraint worth it. So what if my hands all but shake with the need to touch her, to press her to me tightly as I drive myself deep into her slick, warm body?

I can be patient.

I can be gentle.

I can care for her like a fucking eunuch if that's

what it takes to wipe the memory of my sister's tale from her mind.

Not that it's likely to happen. I know where Chloe was leading with all her questions. She wants to know the full story, and I can't blame her. The coffee, the berries—that's just a pretext. What she wants is more time with me, more time to probe, and I have to decide how much of the truth I'm willing to give her, if any.

"How is she?" Lyudmila asks as I place the tray on the counter, and I fill her in on Chloe's condition—namely, that she's doing better. I changed her bandages this morning, and the wound looked like it was healing nicely. I also surreptitiously counted the pills on her nightstand, and it seems she's only taken a couple so far—another good sign.

Rationally, I know Chloe isn't likely to spiral into addiction from a few painkillers, but after witnessing Alina's struggles, I can't help but worry.

"It's good that she has such an appetite," Lyudmila says after I convey Chloe's requests to her. "Better if she were to drink tea, though."

"Agreed. But let's give her the coffee she wants."

Lyudmila grunts in agreement and prepares a tray of artfully arranged strawberries, raspberries, and blueberries, along with a cup of steaming-hot coffee. I thank her and hurry back upstairs, where my zaychik is waiting.

I've decided there *is* a question of hers I can answer today, a portion of the truth I can give her.

Her eyes are brightly inquisitive as I walk into her

room and take my seat on the edge of the bed, placing the tray on its spot on the nightstand.

"So," she begins, "about the—

"Open," I order softly, picking up a strawberry by its stem, and when her plump lips part obediently, I push the juicy berry in and watch her white teeth sink into its flesh—the way I want to sink my teeth into hers.

The jolt of lust is so sudden, so strong, I have to tense every muscle in my body to prevent myself from acting on the urge. There's something almost cannibalistic in the way I want her, the way my mouth waters at the thought of tasting her smooth, bronzed skin and licking the droplets of sweat off her naked body after I fuck her to exhaustion once again. I remember how her nipples felt on my tongue, the salt-and-berry essence of her, and the control I was just priding myself on suddenly feels as thin and frayed as an ancient rope.

She tenses too, her eyes locked on mine, her slender body stiff with the primal awareness of prey. A trickle of strawberry juice escapes her mouth, and I instinctively catch it with my thumb, my heart hammering violently at the feel of her warm skin, the plushness of her bottom lip, all glossy red and sticky from the juice. Holding her gaze, I bring my thumb to my mouth and suck it clean, the way I'd suck on those sweet, berry-sticky lips of hers if I could trust myself to stop there.

Her eyes widen, her breath hitching at my action as her gaze drops to my lips for a beat before meeting my eyes again. She's as turned on as I am, I can see it, and the scorching tension simmers in the air between us, heating the room until my very bones feel like they're on fire, my cock so hard the zipper is going to leave an imprint on its length. I can all but feel her supple flesh under my palms, can all but taste those glistening, red-tinted lips—

A distant peal of childish laughter brings me to my senses, and I realize I was leaning toward her, my hand already fisting in her blanket. *Fuck.* Unclenching my fist, I jackknife to my feet and stride over to the window. Dragging in deep, cleansing breaths, I take in the sight of my son running around the driveway with Arkash chasing him. He's laughing so hard I can hear him even through the bulletproof glass, and the sound further clears the fog of lust enveloping my brain.

Fucking fuck. I thought I had a handle on myself—I was sure of it after I bathed her yesterday while maintaining rigid self-control. I wanted her, yes, but I could distance myself from that want and focus solely on her well-being, on the fact that she was just out of surgery and needed me to be her caretaker. Today, though, she's better—and my self-control is a thousand times worse.

"Um, Nikolai…" Chloe's tone is uncertain, her voice soft and slightly husky. Hearing it makes me shudder with hunger once again. This time, though, she's not right there, and it's easier to pull myself together, reining in the savage need.

Smoothing out my expression, I lock my hands

together behind my back and turn to face her. "Yes, zaychik?"

Her delicate throat ripples with a swallow. "What's Slava doing out there?"

"Playing a game of tag with one of my guards." I walk back to the bed and sit at the foot of it, about as far away from her as I can be while still occupying the same piece of furniture. "Pavel must've asked him to watch Slava while he cleans up after lunch."

Her small white teeth worry her bottom lip. "Right. Right." Watching me intently, she picks up the coffee mug and blows on the hot liquid. I can guess what's going through her mind—she's debating the best way to approach the topic of greatest interest to her—so I decide to help her out.

I'm not ready to talk about my father, but I can tell her the truth about my son.

Holding her gaze, I say evenly, "Five years ago, my brother Valery celebrated his twenty-second birthday at a nightclub in Moscow. It was the party of the year; everyone who's anyone in our part of the world was there—including, as I learned later, Ksenia Leonova, the reclusive daughter of our family's long-time enemy and rival."

Chloe frowns in confusion. "Leonova? As in, the Leonovs you mentioned earlier? The actual Russian mafia family?"

"They would reject that label also, but yes. They fish in a much dirtier pond. In any case, unlike her brother Alexei, Ksenia had always stayed out of the public eye, so I had no idea who she was when she approached me." I take a breath to control the familiar rage kindling inside me. "I thought she was just another socialite or model wannabe, so we danced, downed a few shots, and then went to a hotel to fuck."

Chloe flinches slightly, the coffee mug wobbling in her hand. I move swiftly, grabbing it from her and placing it back on the tray before any of the dark liquid can spill. Then I sit closer to her.

The good thing about remembering Ksenia is that it kills my libido dead.

"I wore a condom, as I always do," I continue, and Chloe's eyes widen. She must realize where the story is heading. "Yes," I say before she can ask, "it broke. Either that or she tampered with it somehow—I still don't know which it is. I didn't notice anything at the time. I'd had a few drinks, and the night wasn't especially memorable. In fact, I'd forgotten all about it until a little over eight months ago, when I got a call from a friend of Ksenia's telling me that Ksenia had died in a car crash, leaving behind a son—*my* son, according to her diary."

"Oh my God," Chloe breathes, looking horrified. "So Slava's mother was—"

"Someone I wouldn't have touched in a hazmat suit if I'd known who she was, yes. The relations between our families had been strained for decades, to say the least."

"Decades? Why?"

"Remember the story I just told you, about my grandfather being sent away to the gulag?"

Chloe nods and cautiously picks up her coffee again.

"The man who accused him of disloyalty to the Party was Matvey Leonov, Ksenia's grandfather."

She freezes, the mug midway to her mouth. "Oh. Wow."

"Yes. He was a poisonous snake, like all the Leonovs—but especially Ksenia." Despite myself, my voice drips with bitter hatred. "To this day, I don't know if she'd planned to fuck me over all along, or if it was an accident that she'd gotten pregnant. Either way, she didn't tell me that I had a son. Was probably never going to tell me. If she hadn't died, I might not have ever learned of Slava's existence—at least not until he was old enough to appear in our circles. At that point, the resemblance would've clued everyone in to his Molotov heritage, if not necessarily his actual paternity." My mouth twists. "You haven't seen my brothers or my cousin, but we all look very much alike."

Chloe puts the coffee back on the nightstand without so much as taking a sip. "Why do you think she approached you that night? She must've known who *you* were, right?"

"Of course she did." Unlike her, I was well known among Moscow's high society. "As to why, I still have no clue. Maybe she planned the whole thing, right down to the broken condom, or maybe she was just young and stupid and wanted to flirt with danger. I don't even know why she was at the party or how she got in—certainly, none of the Leonovs had been invited. Either way, the end result is the same: I have a son I didn't know about until eight months ago. A son who's half Leonov."

Chloe sucks in a breath. "Wait a sec. Is that why you're—"

"Here?" At her nod, I smile humorlessly. "You guessed it, zaychik. His mother's family didn't exactly hand him over to me. I learned about Slava's existence a week after Ksenia's death, and by then, he was already living with Boris Leonov, Ksenia's father—a man known for his cruel and violent proclivities. I never wanted children, never planned to have them, but I couldn't leave my son in his clutches, couldn't abandon him to grow up in that vipers' nest."

"So you what? Stole him from them?"

I nod. "It took my brothers and me almost two months to figure out a way to breach their security, but we got him out and I brought him here, where nobody knows who we are and can't report to the Leonovs that I suddenly have a child."

Her smooth forehead knits in confusion. "I don't understand. Why didn't you just go through the legal channels? You're Slava's father. Couldn't you have gotten custody with a simple paternity test?"

"I could've—and would've—if it had been anyone but the Leonovs. They hate our family as much as we hate theirs, and they'd do anything to thwart us… to thwart *me*. The moment I filed for custody—the moment they realized I knew of Slava's existence—he would've been spirited away, hidden someplace we would've never found him. Maybe his death would've been faked for the sake of the courts—or maybe they would've actually killed him. Anything to deprive me of a chance to raise my son."

Chloe gasps in horror. "You think they would've…?"

"I wouldn't put anything past the elder Leonov." Or Alexei and Ruslan, Ksenia's equally ruthless brothers.

Chloe looks horrified. "That's terrible." Then her eyes widen, and she gasps again. "Grandpa Duck! Oh God… do you think Ksenia's father hurt Slava while he was living with him?"

"I wouldn't be surprised." I try to keep a level tone, but dark rage seeps into my voice, making it hard and guttural. "Slava has never talked about his time with his grandfather, but the way he'd acted around me and Pavel at first… the way he still acts around me, to a certain extent…" I stop, my throat closing on a surge of fury.

The vague suspicions I'd harbored about Boris Leonov's treatment of my son had crystallized into near certainty when Chloe told me about Slava's odd reaction to Grandpa Duck in the children's story. The only reason Ksenia's father is still alive is that Konstantin's team has uncovered the carefully concealed fact that he has late-stage pancreatic cancer and is not expected to last longer than a couple of agony-filled months.

Killing him would be a mercy I'm not willing to extend.

Chloe places her hand on my knee. "I'm so sorry, Nikolai." Her soft brown eyes are filled with sympathy, and an echo of the same rage that burns inside me.

She, too, would like to tear apart anyone who's hurt Slava, I can tell.

With effort, I tamp down on my fury. Nature has already devised the most exquisite torture for Boris Leonov, and I have to be content with that. The only thing ordering a hit on Ksenia's father would achieve is shortening his suffering and triggering an outright war between our families. Right now, we have, if not precisely a truce, then at least a détente: No blood has been spilled in a number of years, despite constant friction on both business and personal levels.

That will change if I kill Boris—or if they learn that I'm behind Slava's kidnapping. They may harbor some suspicions on that front now—Alexei certainly dropped some hints during our encounter in Dushanbe—but they won't act on those suspicions unless they're sure. Not only because doing so would mean starting that war, but because if they're wrong and I don't know about Slava, their attack might clue me in, opening up the entire ugly, wriggling can of worms.

On my end, I've done my best to ensure that doubts are all they have. I left Russia three weeks before we extracted Slava from their compound, so the timelines wouldn't match too closely, and Ksenia's friend, the one who called me after finding the diary, has been relocated to New Zealand with a million dollars and a new identity—and a promise that should she contact any of the Leonovs to relay our conversation, her family in Russia would pay the price.

I don't go into all those details with Chloe now. There's no need; she can draw her own conclusions from what I've told her. Instead, I cover her hand with mine and say gravely, "Thank you, zaychik." Her sympathy and her anger on Slava's behalf cool my rage, the warmth from her small palm seeping into my skin despite the thick material of my jeans.

She swallows and pulls her hand back, averting her gaze. She's afraid of this, I realize with a pang—afraid of emotional intimacy with me. It's both disheartening and encouraging. Disheartening because I want us to be past this, to go back to the way things were before Alina's revelations. And encouraging because it tells me there's hope for us… that no matter how much she'd like to be repulsed and terrified by me, her feelings are more complex than that.

Reining in my frustration, I wait for her to look back at me, and when she does, I pick up the coffee and hand it to her. "Here, zaychik." My tone is calm and bland. "You should drink this before it gets cold."

I'll let her hide from the truth for now, allow her to put up her shields and defenses. They won't save her from me. Nothing will.

Whether she likes it or not, I will own her.

Heart, mind, body, and soul.

12

CHLOE

DESPITE DOWNING THE FULL CUP OF COFFEE, I FALL asleep right after lunch and nap until Nikolai brings me dinner. I think it's the painkillers that make me so drowsy—that or my brain is using sleep as a way to process the most recent revelations while hiding from the anxiety-inducing unanswered questions.

They kidnapped Slava, stole him from his mother's family. I suppose I should be shocked, but I'm not. I think I suspected something like that on some level; it was part of the wrongness I was picking up on, that unsettling vibe I kept getting from this family—especially my darkly mesmerizing captor.

I want to condemn his actions, but instead, I can't help but applaud them. To extricate his son from a potentially abusive situation, Nikolai has completely upended his life, leaving his home country and giving up his role as the head of the Molotov conglomerate.

Not every father would do that for his child, especially a child he didn't know about.

A child he claims never to have wanted.

My chest squeezes as I recall that admission, thrown out so casually, so offhandedly, as if it doesn't matter. He didn't explain, didn't go into details, but I could read between the lines.

It wasn't a desire to live for himself, or travel, or prevent overpopulation—or any other reason people typically give for choosing not to have children. In Nikolai's case, he didn't want to be a father because he didn't think he'd be a good one… and because he didn't want his line to continue. There's a part of my captor that despises himself, either because of what he's done or what he is.

A Molotov.

I've been thinking about the story he told me, about his family's history and the way he was raised. He didn't say much about the latter, but his omissions were as telling as the details he did include. It was obvious that he was taught to view life as a never-ending battle for survival and dominance, a fight that only the most ruthless can win.

I'd bet anything that his upbringing at his father's hands wasn't far from the way his Mongol ancestor might've raised *his* son back in the thirteenth century, torture skills and all.

I try to probe deeper during dinner, but Nikolai is no longer in the mood to talk about himself. Instead, as he feeds me wine-poached venison with mushroom gravy and sweet potato mash, he keeps the conversation focused on me: my food likes and dislikes, my favorite movies, my friends in college. And he does it so skillfully that I find myself talking to him without reservations, smiling and laughing as I describe the time my roommate's cat peed on my bed and how one of my guy friends mistook my mom for one of the students and hit on her during our freshman-year orientation.

It's as if we're back to our video chats, as if everything that's transpired since his return has been nothing but a terrible fever dream.

It's not until dinner is done and he kisses me goodnight, his lips soft and cool on my forehead, that I realize I've missed the opportunity to get the answers for the rest of my burning questions.

The pattern repeats the next morning, when Nikolai brings me breakfast. He skillfully avoids my attempts to bring the conversation around to his father—or *my* father. Instead, as he feeds me *grechka*—the roasted buckwheat kasha Alina likes in place of oatmeal—we discuss Slava's progress and the next lessons I have planned. Then he helps me shower, changes my bandage, and, at my insistence, dresses me in a pair of yoga pants and a soft T-shirt.

My ankle is feeling better, as is my arm, so I intend to be up and about.

"Don't overdo it," he warns me as I determinedly limp over to Slava's room instead of letting him carry me there. "You still need time to heal."

"I'll take it easy, don't worry," I say, plopping on Slava's bed—much to the boy's delight. "We're going to read some books, build some castles… Nothing strenuous, I promise."

Nikolai still looks concerned, so I give him a bright smile. "I'm all better, I really am. Didn't even need a painkiller this morning." The latter is not entirely true —I could definitely use a painkiller for the dull, nagging ache in my arm—but I decided against taking one, to see if I can tough it out on my own.

Either way, my reassurance works as intended. Nikolai's face clears. "All right then," he says, and with a few words in Russian to his son, he leaves us to our lessons.

By mid-morning, my arm is aching harder—Slava accidentally bumped against the sling while climbing onto my lap—so I limp back to my room to take the painkiller after all.

In the hallway, I run into Lyudmila, who's carrying a huge bouquet of flowers, everything from lush roses to sunflowers and tulips. "Alina birthday," she informs me when I ask what it's for. "Big one. Twenty-five today."

Oh, shoot. Alina did mention that her birthday is

this week when we smoked pot together. I had no idea it was today, though.

Thinking fast, I ask Lyudmila, "Where's Nikolai?"

I need some kind of gift, and the only thing I can come up with is a bouquet of my own—wildflowers gathered in the forest nearby. During my hikes, I spotted a few places where they grow in abundance.

The trick will be getting to one of those places with my ankle misbehaving, but that's where Nikolai hopefully comes in.

Lyudmila nods toward his office. "He working."

Brushing past me, she continues on to Alina's room, and I bite my lip, eyeing Nikolai's closed office door. Do I dare interrupt?

A trill of feminine laughter and animated Russian chatter coming from Alina's room decides it for me.

I can't not get at least *something* for Nikolai's sister.

I limp over to Nikolai's office and quietly knock.

"*Da*," his deep voice replies—*yes* in Russian.

I take a deep breath. "It's Chloe. I was just wondering if—"

The door swings open, and the words die on my lips as stunning green-gold eyes meet mine, stealing my breath and spiking my heart rate.

Dammit.

Will my body ever stop responding to him so strongly? At this point, we've fucked and he's bathed me several times, yet his masculine beauty still blindsides me each time we've spent a couple of hours apart.

"What is it, zaychik?" he asks, dark eyebrows pulling together as he gives me a swift, concerned once-over. Before I can reply, he grips my hands. "Is everything okay?"

"Yeah, everything's fine. I just…" I throw a quick glance over my shoulder. The hallway is empty, but I still lower my voice, just in case. "I need a gift for Alina."

"Ah. Come in." He shepherds me into his office and guides me to a chair, which I gratefully sink into. I might've overdone it with all the walking today—my ankle is better, but it's definitely not completely well. Neither is my arm.

That painkiller is becoming more necessary by the minute.

"Here," Nikolai says, pulling open a drawer in his desk. He takes out a small black box and hands it to me. "You can give this to her."

Confused, I open it—and gape at the diamond-studded bracelet inside.

What the hell?

My gaze jumps to his face. "What do you mean, give it to her?"

"It can be your gift," Nikolai says matter-of-factly. "I'll give her another piece of jewelry."

Is he serious?

"Of course it can't be my gift," I say when I've recovered my powers of speech. "*You* got it for her, not me. I can't afford a single stone in that bracelet, and Alina knows that."

He shrugs. "So what? She'll enjoy it regardless."

Oh my God. I take a breath and count to three. "No, she won't. Because I'm going to give her something else —something that's actually from me."

"Such as?"

"Flowers. I'd like to put together a bouquet for her. I saw some really pretty ones blooming not far from here."

His eyebrows draw together again. "There's no way you're going for a hike with that ankle."

"It's not far. I can make it. Especially if you come with me and help."

A peculiar gleam appears in his tiger eyes. "You want me to take you flower-picking?"

Now that he's said it, I realize how ridiculous it sounds—and how big of an ask it is. What the fuck was I thinking? He's not my boyfriend; he's my captor, a powerful, dangerous man who has far more important—

"All right," he says before I can backpedal. "Give me a minute to finish up here, and we'll go."

13

NIKOLAI

Ignoring Chloe's claims that she can walk "just fine," I carry her to her room and return to finish the message I was writing, instructing Valery's newest arrival on how and where I want the DNA sample collected. It's not a man my brother is sending for this job, but a woman—which is even better.

It opens up some interesting possibilities in regard to getting close to Bransford.

I then answer a few more urgent messages and go get Chloe for our flower-gathering expedition.

My heart pounds with anticipation as I approach her room. Maybe I'm reading too much into this, but I feel encouraged that she's actively sought me out, that she wants to spend time with me, even if it's under this bullshit pretext.

My strategy of being nothing more than her patient, platonic caretaker is working. Slowly but surely, my zaychik is losing her fear of me, letting down her shields. And that's good—because I don't know how much longer I can remain patient.

The better she feels, the harder it is to control the beast inside me, to stop myself from claiming her as my instincts demand.

She's watching the news as I walk into her room. Seeing me, she powers off the TV and stands up, a radiant smile on her face. "I'm ready."

Something deep inside my chest simultaneously expands and contracts. "Let's go get those flowers, then."

I let her walk toward me on her own, just to see how well her ankle is healing. As soon as she reaches me, though, I pick her up, once again ignoring her objections. I can't watch her limp—it hurts me too much—so the only way this hike is happening is with her in my arms.

"You're not seriously planning to carry me all the way there," she says as we exit the house.

I smile down at her. "Why not, zaychik?"

I love holding her, feeling her pressed against me. Until her ankle is healed, I intend to carry her around as much as possible—and maybe afterward as well.

"For starters, it's at least half a mile to the spot I have in mind," she says with utmost seriousness, as if half a mile is any sort of real distance. "If you just lend me your elbow, I could walk there at a slow pace."

"That's not happening."

"But I'm heavy. There's no way—"

"You're kidding, right?" I grin into her small,

indignant face. "Zaychik, I've carried backpacks heavier than you for a day straight."

She blinks. "You mean… when you were in the army?"

"And now. Pavel and I frequently train with the guards to keep fit."

"Uh-huh. But still—"

"How about this? I promise I'll let you walk if I get tired." Or rather, if I drop dead. That's the only way she's hiking through these woods on that ankle of hers.

She huffs. "Fine. Be all macho, see if I care when your arms fall off. The flowers are that way." She points to a small dirt path leading into the woods to the east of us, then lays her head on my shoulder, as if planning to take a nap.

I laugh and head down the path she indicated, being careful to protect her from low-hanging branches and shrubs. I can't remember the last time I felt so light, both physically and mentally. Instead of tiring me, her slight weight in my arms buoys me, the feel of her body against mine evoking not only the usual carnal hunger but also something warm and pure… something almost like joy.

It's as if the dark clouds that have hung over me for the past several years have lifted for a moment, revealing a sliver of sunlit sky.

The sensation persists the entire way to our destination, aided by her occasional grumbling about foolish macho men and their egos. I'm sure she means to be insulting, but all I feel is amusement mixed with relief. I like her snarky and grumpy; it means she's feeling safe with me, forgetting the things she's heard and seen me do.

Forgetting that I'm a monster.

When we get to a small, wildflower-dotted meadow, I put her down to let her gather the flowers. Despite the sling, she's quick and efficient in her task, her nimble fingers plucking the straggly plants and arranging them into something beautiful. By the time she's done, I have to admit that it *was* a good gift idea—my sister will love this unusual, forest-scented bouquet.

"I'm ready for my ride home," she says with faux haughtiness, and I laugh as I pick her up, careful not to crush the flowers she's holding. Their aroma mingles with the fresh, intoxicating scent of her hair, and my body ignites with a surge of arousal, my cock hardening as she lays her head on my shoulder, her nose brushing my neck.

"Harder uphill, isn't it?" she says gleefully as I start up the path leading back to the house. Raising her head, she places her palm over my chest and grins. "Your heart is beating faster already."

So it is—but not for the reason she thinks. It's all I can do not to pin her against the nearest tree and drive deep into her tight little body. The feel of her, the smell of her, that mischievous sparkle in her eyes—it all adds fuel to the fire burning inside me, to the violent hunger I've been trying so hard to suppress.

My pace slows as my gaze falls to her lips, so pretty

and plush, so temptingly curved in that bright, teasing smile.

Don't do it.

My thudding heartbeats intensify to a roar in my ears.

Don't fucking do it.

My vision turns tunnel-like, the world around us blurring out of focus. All I can see is her smile, as brilliant and warm as the sun; all I can feel is the carnal heat scorching my veins.

Do not fucking do it.

Her smile fades, a wary look entering her soft brown eyes as I stop completely, staring at her. "Nikolai, I didn't mean—"

My lips cover hers, swallowing the rest of her words. *Fuck, she tastes good.* Like apples and berries and flowers, something wholesome and wild and fresh. The heady flavor feeds the dark hunger inside me, adding to the ferocious need thrumming under my skin.

Her lips part under the pressure of mine, and my tongue invades the slick, warm depths of her mouth, seeking every bit of that flavor, of the sweet, clean essence of her. Greedily, I breathe in her panting exhales, reveling in the moan that vibrates her throat as I tug on her lower lip with my teeth, nearly breaking the fragile skin in the process.

Mine. She's fucking mine. I want to consume her, devour her, brand her… take her, savage her, destroy her. No, not destroy—possess, though with my being a Molotov, it's basically one and the same. My need for her is obsessive and dark, dangerous to her and to me. But I refuse to think of that now, refuse to remember my parents' fights and my grandmother's warnings. Fate has brought Chloe to me, and fate will determine our path. For now, she's mine to claim, mine to own.

Ravenously, I deepen the kiss, and she responds with equal ardor, her tongue dueling with mine as her left arm loops around my neck. My arms tighten around her, crushing her against my chest—and wrenching a pained cry from her throat.

Fuck. Her sling.

What am I doing?

With superhuman effort, I tear my mouth away and set her down on her feet. Breathing hard, I back away as she stares at me, eyes wide and kiss-swollen lips parted.

Shocked. She's shocked by what happened, and so am I. Shocked that I let her go, that I found the strength to release her when the beast inside me is howling and raging, demanding that I take her here and now, no matter how hurt and fragile she is.

"Nikolai, I..." She swallows hard, bringing her left hand to her chest. The bouquet she's holding is damaged, some flowers torn and bent in half. "I don't think it's a good idea. I mean, you and me—"

"I know what you mean." My tone is as sharp as the blade-like hunger twisting inside me, whittling away at my self-control.

I came so close to fucking her. Another minute, and

I would've been plunging deep inside her tight, wet heat, having forgotten all about her injuries.

It's official. I'm a fucking savage.

There's no longer any doubt in my mind.

She chews on her plump lower lip, making me want to do the same. "I'm not—"

"You should fix that." At her blank look, I growl, "The flowers. They're crushed."

She blinks and glances down, as if only now realizing they're still in her hand. "Right." She steps back unsteadily. "Let me do that."

She kneels to gather the few straggly flowers that grow along this path, and I turn away, taking deep breaths. By the time she calls my name again, I have myself under control. *Mostly.*

Turning back to face her, I smooth out my expression. "Let's go."

She starts toward me with a limp, and I grit my teeth as I swoop in, lifting her off her feet. Self-control issues or not, I'm not letting her hike back on her own.

Holding her tightly against my chest, I lengthen my stride until I'm almost running. She stays silent, though she must hear my breathing pick up from exertion. There's no more teasing about macho men, no more protests about how she can walk by herself. She doesn't want to draw attention to herself, and it's just as well.

My restraint is hanging on by a thread.

It's only when we're approaching the house that she speaks. "Thank you," she says quietly, forcing me to meet her gaze—something I've avoided the entire trip back. "I really do appreciate it."

"Of course. Happy to help." My tone is casual, calm, as if we're discussing taking her to gather the flowers. But we both know we're not.

What she's grateful for is the fact that I didn't fuck her—that for now, she gets to keep her walls up and pretend.

14

CHLOE

As soon as Nikolai deposits me in my room, I go looking for Alina. I find her in the kitchen, chatting with Lyudmila, and I give her the flowers, along with the birthday congratulations.

"Thank you." She accepts the bouquet with a beaming smile. "Where on earth did you get these? They're so pretty."

I smile back. "Oh, just around here."

"Really? With your ankle this way?"

My cheeks heat at the memory of what almost happened in the forest. "Nikolai might've helped."

Her smile dims slightly, but she doesn't say anything to me. Instead, she turns to Lyudmila, who's chopping up some veggies by the sink, and speaks a few words of Russian to her. The blond woman bustles off to fill a pretty vase with water, and Alina arranges the flowers in it before taking it out to the dining room, where it joins the other bouquet decorating the table.

"How are you feeling?" I ask, following her there. The table is already set with a variety of appetizers; it looks like it's going to be an extra-fancy lunch today. "Any more headaches?"

"I should be asking you that." She faces me, her jade eyes gleaming. "How's your arm? Your ankle?"

"All better." The ankle not so much right now—I've definitely overdone it today—but I keep quiet about that.

"I'm glad." She hesitates, then asks quietly, "Have you spoken to Nikolai?"

My pulse quickens. "He's told me about Slava and the Leonovs." Is she about to tell me more? Has she decided to reveal the full story after all?

Her face takes on a sphinxlike expression. "I see."

I guess the answer is no. I'm tempted to press her, but I don't want to bring up a traumatic topic on her birthday—though it could be argued she's just brought it up herself.

"Do you want to hang out tonight after dinner?" I ask impulsively. "Maybe play some board games, grab a couple of beers? Obviously, Lyudmila's welcome too."

My offer is only partially motivated by my desire to probe for more information. Mostly, I just want to get to know Alina better, as I'm starting to really like her.

She looks startled but quickly recovers. Flashing me a warm smile, she says, "That sounds great. Let's see how long the dinner lasts, and then we'll decide what to do."

Since I'm already downstairs, I join everyone for lunch instead of having Nikolai feed me in my room. Not only am I feeling well enough to resume being a functional adult, but after what nearly happened in the forest, being alone with Nikolai feels like a dangerous undertaking—especially next to a bed.

I'm certain he only stopped because he was worried about hurting my arm, something that would be way less of a concern if it were comfortably arranged on a pillow.

My heart hammers faster at the thought, and I sneak a glance at him from under my lashes. I can still feel his lips devouring mine, can still taste his warm, minty breath. My nipples feel overly sensitive, and my lower lip throbs where he'd bitten it, the pulsations echoing deep into my core.

I want him. And not in a casual, would-be-nice-to-have way. Even knowing what he is, I crave him so desperately it's like a sickness, an addiction as unhealthy and dangerous as a heroin user's dependence. I have no willpower around him, no ability to resist his touch. By all rights, he should terrify and repulse me, but instead, I'm drawn to him as much as, if not more than, before.

It's twisted. It's wrong. I know that, but I can't help it.

My body and heart refuse to sync with my head.

He catches my gaze on him, and his tiger eyes grow hooded, filled with unmistakable dark heat. My pulse spikes further, my breath hitching as I look away. However much I want him, he wants me even more. And his desire is not of the soft and sweet variety. I felt the savage urgency in him today, the need to dominate and conquer. If not for my injuries, he would've taken me right then and there, on the leaf-strewn dirt. And he wouldn't have been gentle, either.

When we have sex again, it will be devastating for me, both physically and mentally, and the only way to prevent it from happening is to stay out of his reach—an impossibility in my current situation. Even if I were willing to risk an encounter with a new set of Bransford's goons, Nikolai won't let me leave.

For the first time, I allow myself to think about the future and what it holds. Will Nikolai ever let me go? And if he does, will I ever be safe? If Tom Bransford does indeed want me dead, what's to stop him from coming after me again and again? Judging by the polls, he's most likely going to be his party's nominee. If he then wins the general election, there will be almost no limits to his power—not that there are many limits now.

Raised voices pull me out of my dark ruminations. It's Alina and Nikolai, having what sounds like an argument in Russian. I was so lost in my thoughts I didn't notice the strained atmosphere at the table, but there's no missing it now.

Brother and sister are clearly at loggerheads, and Slava is watching them, his golden eyes wide with curiosity—and more than a hint of worry.

I tug on his sleeve. "Hey. What do we call this in English?" I point at the tomato on his plate.

He blinks up at me.

"We just learned it this morning, remember?" He still looks clueless, so I decide to give him a hint. "It's a vegetable that we call the to—"

"Tomato!" he exclaims, beaming up at me.

"That's right." Grinning, I fluff his silky hair. My goal was to distract him from the adults' argument, but it looks like my interference has ended the argument altogether, with Alina and Nikolai turning their attention to us instead.

"He's learning so fast," I say, and Slava proudly puffs out his chest as Alina gives him a warm smile and says something that sounds like praise in Russian.

"We should speak English to him." Nikolai's tone still holds a bite. "At least when Chloe is around. He'll learn even faster that way."

Alina's lips tighten, but she nods. "As you wish. He's your son."

I'm beyond curious to know what their argument was about, but I don't think it's a good idea to go there. Instead, I ask Alina how she normally celebrates her birthday, and she entertains me with descriptions of trips to exotic locales and lavish parties in Moscow, the latter attended by all sorts of glitterati.

"Wait, back up," I say when she casually mentions how one movie star passed out on her yacht during a birthday bash in Mykonos. "You know Hollywood celebs?"

She laughs. "Not all of them, obviously, but some. They're people too, you know. Nothing special in the grand scheme of things."

Not special to *her*, maybe, but I'm fascinated. I make her tell me all about her famous friends and acquaintances, and before I know it, we're wrapping up the meal. Which is good—because even *TMZ*-worthy stories about misbehaving celebs haven't lessened my awareness of Nikolai and his intent, unwavering focus on me.

Throughout the entire meal, he's been watching me with the lethal patience of a predator, one who knows it's only a matter of time before he consumes his prey.

Our eyes meet as we get up from the table, and I look away again, my skin tingling as my pulse jumps uncontrollably.

This is bad. I've been counting on at least a few more days of Nikolai restraining himself, but I don't think I'll get nearly that much time. Another day, maybe, if I'm lucky.

If not, I'll end up in his bed tonight.

"Let's go to your room," I tell Slava, trying to ignore

the flush heating my entire body. "We can play Batman and Robin—or Batman and Superman."

The child eagerly grabs my hand, and we walk out of the dining room together as Nikolai and Alina start what sounds like another argument in Russian.

15

NIKOLAI

"I'M TELLING YOU, YOU CANNOT KEEP HER IN THE DARK," Alina says again as Chloe and my son disappear from view. "It's her father. She deserves to know what you're planning."

Fucking Pavel. He's told Lyudmila about Bransford, and she, naturally, couldn't resist spilling the beans to my sister—who's again determined to have a say in a matter that doesn't concern her.

I glare down at her. "You need to stay the fuck out of it. This is between me and Chloe, understand?"

Alina's green eyes blink up at me, all wounded innocence. "I wasn't going to interfere. I'm just saying that if you want a chance at a real relationship with her, you have to—"

I scoff. "What do you know about real relationships?"

She takes a breath and squares her shoulders. "Look, I was wrong to interfere before. I can't apologize enough for that. But the fact remains: Chloe is not like us. No matter what Bransford's done, he's still her biological fa—"

"He's her mother's rapist, nothing more." I can't even bring myself to call him a sperm donor. That's what *I* was to Slava for the first four years of his life, but as soon as I learned of his existence, I couldn't imagine harming a hair on his head, much less ordering a hit on him… not even if he one day orders one on me.

Alina flinches at my sharp tone. "I know. I'm not saying she views him as family or anything. But she still deserves to be consulted."

"Why? So she can have his death on her conscience?"

"What if she doesn't want him dead?"

"That's not her decision." There's no way I'm letting the fucker live, not even if Chloe begs for it.

"But it should be," Alina says in frustration. "If it were me—"

"I wouldn't place that burden on you either." I'd carry it myself, the way I'm doing now.

Her eyes darken. "Kolya…"

"Don't." Our father's death is not a topic I want to discuss with her. Ever. "Just stay the fuck out of my relationship with Chloe, understand?"

And before she can aggravate me further, I stride away.

I spend the afternoon catching up on business—even with my brothers assuming most of the responsibility for our family's conglomerate, there's plenty for me to do—and then I turn on the video feed from Chloe's room, where she should be getting ready for dinner.

Sure enough, I catch her emerging from her closet, already dressed in an evening gown. For a second, I wonder how she managed to change without assistance —I was planning to go help her in a minute—but then my sister steps into the camera's view.

"Stand here," she tells Chloe, guiding her to the window. "Since your arm is out of commission, I'll do your makeup."

I lean back in my chair, watching with amusement as she begins to paint Chloe's face with the various tubes and brushes she takes out of a small bag. I remember her painting her dolls much the same way when she was little; I guess she's never outgrown it. I don't mind. Chloe doesn't need any makeup—she's beautiful without it—but this is something women do when they dress up, and I like my zaychik dressed up. Or dressed down. Or better yet, completely naked.

My body hardens at the thought, and I have to take a few deep breaths to control my accelerating pulse. I can't have her. Not yet. No matter how much it physically hurts to deny myself.

For now, I can only watch and plan what I'll do to her once she's completely well.

16

CHLOE

To my relief, the atmosphere at dinner isn't strained in the least, partially because Pavel and Lyudmila join us instead of staying in the kitchen. Their presence adds to the festive feel of the meal nearly as much as all the exotic, colorful dishes populating the table.

Pavel has outdone himself today; it's more like a gourmet wedding celebration than an at-home birthday.

Aside from the gorgeously arranged, delicious food, there's plenty of alcohol, everything from wine to vodka and cognac. Every few minutes, either Pavel, Lyudmila, or Nikolai proposes a toast to the birthday girl, and we drink—or in my case, take a sip of wine. There's no way I can keep up with the copious amounts of hard liquor the Russians are consuming. Well, everyone except Slava. He's guzzling orange soda —a treat for special occasions, I'm guessing, as it's the first time I'm seeing the child drink anything but water.

As the meat course comes out, the volume and frequency of toasts go up until it feels like someone is raising a glass to Alina's health, beauty, smarts, or future success nonstop. The conversation is a boisterous mix of Russian and English, the latter likely solely for my sake. There's plenty of laughter too, along with jokes that don't always make sense when translated from Russian—"anecdotes," Nikolai calls them. They're something along the lines of "a donkey and a horse walk into a bar," but way more creative and elaborate. He explains that telling these funny anecdotes at social gatherings is a tradition in his country, and that just about every self-respecting Russian has a repertoire that they constantly replenish by scouring the internet and buying special books.

By the time Pavel disappears into the kitchen and emerges with a tea tray and a three-tier, candle-studded cake, I'm laughing so hard I'm convinced I've managed to get drunk despite my precautions. Nikolai out to amuse is not something I've seen before, and I have no defense against his dry, witty charm. Neither does anyone else at the table, it seems. Slava, hopped up on sugar and adult merriment, forgets all about keeping his distance from his father and climbs on his lap, while Alina drunkenly loops her arm around Nikolai's neck and gives him a big smooch, leaving a lipstick imprint on his cheek—the first time I've seen her act like a playful younger sister.

It makes me realize how reserved she and everyone else in this household usually are, how little of a normal family dynamic I've seen between them.

The realization brings me back to my senses, reawakening my caution, but then Alina blows out the candles among loud cheers and I forget that I'm not at a typical birthday celebration, that the gorgeous, sharply dressed man laughing with his family is as much my captor as my protector.

Nikolai is dangerous, and not just because I've seen him kill with my own eyes.

It's because he's so much more complex than a man without a conscience should be.

As I observe him closer, I realize that unlike everyone else, he doesn't seem drunk. There's a certain calculated quality to his laughter and jokes, to the charming, light-hearted façade he's assumed. It makes me recall Alina's assertion that her brother does nothing by accident, that all his actions are planned.

Still, even this can't keep my heart from squeezing with tenderness when I notice the genuine softness in his eyes as he carefully embraces his son—who's now giggling and bouncing on his lap while chattering away in Russian. I catch the word "Papa" in the rapid stream of words, and my chest swells with an emotion so intense tears prickle behind my eyelids.

Daddy, Slava called him in Russian, unprompted.

They're finally bonding as father and son.

Blinking back the burning moisture, I look down at my half-eaten dessert—only to feel the back of my neck tingle with familiar awareness. Sure enough, when I glance up, Nikolai's gaze is trained on me, his tiger eyes filled with unnerving intensity.

I was right. He's not drunk in the least. If anything, the alcohol has made him sharper, more focused.

"You don't like the cake, zaychik?" he murmurs, his voice too low to carry to the rest of the table, where Pavel and Lyudmila are loudly toasting Alina yet again. "Or are you simply too full?"

My face warms. Why does that simple question feel like a sexual innuendo? It shouldn't, not even with that seductive, intimate edge to his tone.

He's holding his son, for fuck's sake.

"I'm stuffed," I say, only to immediately want to take the words back as his mouth curls in a wicked half-smile.

It's Slava who comes to my rescue. "Daddy," he says loudly in English, twisting his little body to wrap his arms around Nikolai's neck. "*My* daddy."

Nikolai's gaze shifts to his son, and the wicked gleam in his eyes disappears, replaced by an expression so achingly tender my heart all but dissolves in my chest. This is so much more than the child casually dropping a "Papa."

Slava is officially claiming Nikolai as his father, embracing him with all the possessiveness in his little Molotov heart.

I force the words out through the growing lump in my throat. "Yes, darling. That's *your* daddy. Good job." The stupid tears are back to burning my eyelids, and I realize my joy at witnessing this is bittersweet, tinged with envy.

As a child, I dreamed of meeting my father—and embracing him exactly this way.

Fortunately, Nikolai is not looking at me. All his attention is on his son. Murmuring something in Russian, he gently smooths back Slava's hair… and my throat threatens to close completely as I catch a tiny tremor in his strong, callused hand.

What I'm seeing on Nikolai's face is just the tip of the emotional iceberg. The powerful, ruthless man in front of me is completely undone by his son.

Swallowing thickly, I force myself to look away before I also come undone. It's bad enough my body melts for him; now my heart is joining in as well. There's no way I can label him a psychopath going forward, no way for me to pretend that the ruthless killer I've fallen for is incapable of genuine emotions.

Whatever Nikolai might or might not feel for me, he's deeply in love with his young son.

17

CHLOE

THE DINNER PARTY LASTS LATE INTO THE EVENING, SO I don't get a chance to hang out with Alina afterward. By the time Nikolai carries me up to my room and helps me shower and change, I'm so drunk and exhausted I all but pass out in his arms.

It's not until the next morning that I realize that, contrary to my fears, I didn't end up in Nikolai's bed. Once more, he'd been the perfect nursemaid, taking care of me without demanding anything in return. Even the copious amount of alcohol hadn't undermined his self-control—though I'm guessing the fact that I was more or less comatose when he brought me upstairs helped his resolve.

After that scene with his son, I turned to wine to manage my unruly emotions, and between that, the painkiller I took earlier in the day, and my still-healing body, I was basically a humanoid log.

Fortunately, I don't have much of a hangover, so I

make it to breakfast on time. To my relief—and more than slight disappointment—Nikolai isn't there.

"On a call with Russia," Alina explains. Like me, she doesn't seem to be overly affected by the late-night festivities, and after breakfast, she joins me and Slava in our play lessons, even going so far as to chase her nephew in a game of tag despite wearing her usual uniform of a fancy dress and high heels.

"I have no idea how your toes don't fall off," I say, eyeing her stilettos, and she laughs, explaining that she's so used to wearing such shoes that sneakers feel weird to her.

"Russian women pride themselves on being able to tolerate all sorts of discomfort in the name of beauty," she tells me wryly. "It's our long-suffering, masochistic nature. So while leggings and such have made inroads in my home country, you'll have to pry our high-heeled shoes from our cold, dead feet."

I laugh and drop the topic. I really do like Alina. Her beauty was so intimidating at first that it took me a while to see past it. Now that I have, I realize that a lot of her initial reserve was a form of self-protection. With her family the way it is, she needs her glossy, prickly façade to conceal her vulnerability—and the trauma she's still recovering from.

Over the next few days, my wish of getting to know Alina better is fulfilled, partially because Nikolai has delegated much of my care to her. It's now she who helps me get dressed and shower, though he's still the one who changes the bandage on my arm when necessary.

I suspect it's because as I'm getting better, he doesn't trust his restraint to hold.

I don't mind. Not only does this enable me to maintain some semblance of emotional equilibrium when I do see him, but Alina and I are developing a real rapport. With my ankle quickly improving and my arm finally out of the sling, we go on short hikes near the house—during which she does swap her stilettos for stylish boots—and we spend a lot of time with Slava, whose English is progressing with lightning speed.

I think it helps him to listen to me talk with Alina; he's starting to pick up words and phrases I haven't formally taught him.

The only fly in the ointment is Alina's refusal to talk about what happened with her father—or in general expound on her family and her past. No matter how much I probe and pry, she discloses nothing, and with Nikolai avoiding me except during bandage changes and mealtimes, I'm no closer to getting answers.

In a way, I don't mind this either. As much as I'm dying to understand how a man who's becoming so openly affectionate with his son could've committed the terrible crime of patricide, not knowing all the details forces me to put it out of my mind. Same goes for the situation with Bransford; without any updates coming my way, I can go for hours, even days, without dwelling on the danger my biological father poses and what my future may hold.

These calm, easy days feel like an interlude out of time, a respite from the terrifying reality that is my life.

A respite that ends when the mystery girl arrives.

18

CHLOE

SLAVA AND I ARE IN FRONT OF THE HOUSE, OBSERVING three squirrels chasing one another from tree to tree, when the black pickup truck rolls up the driveway. The windows aren't as darkly tinted as those of the deceased assassins' vehicle, but I still freeze in place, ambushed by a flashback so intense I break out in a cold sweat.

"Chloe? Chloe, who is it? Who is it, Chloe?"

I blink at Slava, who's tugging insistently at my sleeve, and force down the gruesome recollections of my Toyota getting smashed against the tree. I thought I was getting over what happened—even my nightmares have eased during these halcyon days—but I guess I was fooling myself.

I'm no more recovered from my trauma than Alina is from hers.

"Who is it?" Slava demands again, rocking back and forth on his heels as the truck comes to a stop some dozen feet from us. As both his English skills and his relationship with Nikolai have improved, he's become much more of an assertive—and occasionally annoying—little boy, much to my delight.

I manage a warm smile in his direction. "I don't know, darling. Let's see."

The two of us stare intently at the car as the driver's side opens and a petite young woman dressed in a pair of jeans, a tight-fitting white T-shirt, and scuffed hiking boots bounces out of the seat. Small-boned yet subtly curvy, with delicate, symmetrical features and thick blond hair piled up high in a messy bun, she looks to be seventeen or eighteen, and reminds me of a cross between Saoirse Ronan and Marilyn Monroe—if either were hopped up on speed.

Like a whirlwind, she descends on us. "Hey there! You must be Chloe." Before I can reply, she grabs my hand and pumps it enthusiastically. Then she drops down to her knees and beams at Slava. *"A ti Slavochka, da?"*

Her sudden switch to Russian catches me off-guard; she'd spoken to me in pure American English. Slava seems taken aback as well. None of the adults around him are usually this bubbly and energetic.

"Hi," I say as she jumps back up to her feet. Literally jumps, like a child. Maybe she's even younger than I thought? "I *am* Chloe. And you are?"

Her wide grin is dimpled, her gray eyes sparkling appealingly. "You can call me Masha."

"Nice to meet you, Masha. Are you—"

"Where's Nikolai?" she interrupts. "I'm here to see him."

Something pinches deep inside me, an ugly suspicion stirring in my mind. "He should be in his office. Do you want me to take you there?"

"No need," she says breezily and runs up to the house.

The pinching sensation transforms into an outright churning in my stomach. This girl is pretty—more than pretty. She's dazzling, even in her casual clothes. Put her in one of Alina's dresses, and she could strut her stuff down the runway—or at least on the red carpet, since she's not even my height. And while she's young, she's far from childlike; in fact, her self-assured manner makes me think she might not be a teenager at all. As I watch her disappear into the house, I can't help recalling that prior to meeting me, Nikolai was in the habit of flying in all sorts of beautiful women—which, for all I know, included this Masha.

How else does she seem to know where to go? Or has heard about Slava?

Or me?

That last bit doesn't fit this theory, I have to admit. If she's Nikolai's hookup, present or past, why would he tell her about me? Unless, of course, they have some weird friends-with-benefits situation going on, and, unlike me, she doesn't have a jealous bone in her body.

"Have you ever seen her before?" I ask Slava, doing my best to keep my tone casual. "I mean, prior to today?"

Slava blinks up at me. He understands some of what I say now, but not everything.

Heaving a sigh, I grab his hand and lead him to the house. I don't understand why I'm so anxious to find out who this young woman is—if Nikolai is losing interest in me, it can only be for the best. Yet no matter what my rational mind says, the mere thought of him with Masha makes me want to break every bone in her tiny, Marylin Monroe-like body.

19

CHLOE

LEAVING SLAVA WITH LYUDMILA IN THE KITCHEN, I HEAD over to Nikolai's office, my ribcage tight as I go up the stairs.

It's stupid to be jealous. Irrational. But I can't help the green monster clawing at my chest. What if I have completely misinterpreted Nikolai's avoidance of me over the past two weeks? Maybe instead of fighting his desire for me, he's simply stopped wanting me. After all, taking care of my injuries could've made him view my body in a different light.

I've never been particularly insecure about said body, but I've also never been in a relationship with a man as wickedly gorgeous as Nikolai.

Wait, no, we're not in a relationship. That might've been happening before, when I thought he was a normal, law-abiding—albeit obscenely rich—man. I don't know what to call it now. If the person you've slept with is holding you captive while also protecting you from someone who wants to kill you, does that constitute a relationship? At least of the non-Stockholm syndrome variety? Not to mention, he's still technically my employer—the cash envelopes have been arriving in my room every Tuesday like clockwork.

Shelving those ruminations for now, I approach his office door. It's closed, and when I press my ear to it, I can hear voices speaking Russian. As I listen, I can discern the new arrival's bright, feminine tones, along with Nikolai's deep, smooth, dangerously seductive ones.

"What are you doing?"

Startled, I whip around to face Alina, who's standing in the hallway, head cocked inquisitively. "Um…"

Amusement glimmers in her eyes. "Are you spying on my brother?"

"No, of course not." I can feel my face burning as I scramble for a good explanation. "I was just—"

"Come." She grabs my elbow and tugs me down the hallway to her room, where she all but pushes me inside before turning to face me. "Okay, now tell me. What's going on?"

"Nothing."

She arches an eyebrow, looking disconcertingly like her brother.

I cave. "Okay, fine. There's this young woman who's just arrived, and—"

"You mean Masha?"

My heart sinks. "You know her?"

"She's Valery's newest find." At my uncomprehending look, she says, "My youngest brother collects people with various useful skills. I have no idea what hers are, but I ran into her briefly at his place before we left Moscow, and unlike his other pets, she introduced herself."

"His pets?"

She nods. "That's what I call them. He inspires almost pathological loyalty in these people."

Huh, okay. Maybe she's not Nikolai's hookup—or at least not only that.

"Has Nikolai met her also? Like back in Moscow? Or—"

"Chloe..." Alina hesitates, then says gently, "I don't think you have to worry about her in that way."

My face heats again. "I'm not—"

"You are, and I get it. She's unusually pretty. But she's not here to warm Nikolai's bed."

"So you know what she's here for?" My relief is quickly eclipsed by anxiety-tinged curiosity. For some reason, this Masha's arrival feels portentous, like a bad omen.

Alina hesitates again, then shakes her head. "Not really. You should talk to Nikolai about all this."

"All what? Is it connected to your father?"

Her flinch is nearly imperceptible, as is her quickly hidden surprise. "I can't say," she says, her expression carefully veiled. "My brother is the one with all the answers."

I stare at her, my mind churning. If this isn't about her father… "Does this have something to do with *me*?"

She sighs. "Just talk to Nikolai, Chloe. Please."

And before I can press her further, she shepherds me out of her room.

I don't get a chance to talk to Nikolai until later that evening. He spends the entire afternoon in his office with Masha—I know because I walk past his door dozens of times. At some point, Pavel joins them, and the murmur of two voices becomes three, with the bear-man's growl easily identifiable.

By dinnertime, Masha leaves—Slava and I watch her pickup truck depart through his bedroom window—but a family meal is not a good time to drill Nikolai about a potentially combustible issue, so I swallow my burning questions and wait.

My moment arrives after dinner, when Lyudmila clears the table and everyone gets up to go to their rooms. All dinner long, I have felt Nikolai's intense tiger gaze on me, have sensed the speculation in his stare.

Whatever's going on does concern me. I'm almost certain of it now.

As if wise to my plan, Alina grabs Slava and disappears up the stairs with record speed, leaving me and Nikolai alone in the dining room.

"Can we grab a nightcap?" I ask as he turns to leave

as well. My voice is steady, even as my heart beats unevenly. This is dangerous in more ways than one. Not only am I risking an end to the peace and calm that's reigned in my life over the past two weeks, but my gunshot wound is almost fully healed.

If Nikolai is still interested in me in that way, there's little to stop him from acting on that desire.

He turns back to face me. His jaw is taut, his eyes gleaming like ancient amber. "A nightcap? I thought you weren't big on digestifs, zaychik."

I swallow against the dryness in my throat. "I'm in the mood for a little cognac."

If nothing else, I could use it to bolster my courage.

Nikolai's voice roughens. "All right. Give me a minute." He disappears into the kitchen and emerges with a tray of crystal decanters surrounded by drinking glasses. Pavel must be off server duty tonight —that or Nikolai also wants privacy.

As he pours us each a drink, I sit back down, surreptitiously wiping my damp palms on the skirt of my evening gown. It's made of a silk material in a coral-peach hue that, according to Alina, makes my complexion look "all golden and glowy." I wonder if Nikolai thinks that too, or if all he sees when he looks at me now is his son's tutor.

Which would be fine. Amazing, really. I shouldn't want such a dangerous man fixated on me, making all sorts of unnerving claims about threads of fate and—

"What did you want to discuss, zaychik?" Nikolai's voice is once again brushed velvet as he sinks into the seat across from me. Swirling the cognac inside his glass, he regards me over the rim, lids at half-mast. "I'm assuming you're not here because you're suddenly craving my company."

My skin flushes all over. I actually am craving his company, as reluctant as I am to admit it. Ever since our flower-picking expedition, we haven't spent much time together—at least not by ourselves. At mealtimes, Alina and Slava serve as a buffer, and Lyudmila and Pavel are always around in the background. Even the bandage changes, the one time he'd enter my room by himself, stopped once my wound scabbed over and no longer needed to be covered.

The truth is, I've barely interacted with him in recent days, and I've missed it. I've missed our conversations, his unwavering focus on me… even the way he makes me feel like a mouse being toyed with by a scary-hot cat. Of course, I can't have him know this. Not when I still have a shred of hope that someday my life will go back to normal—a normal that won't involve dangerous men who torture and kill.

Taking a breath, I launch right into it. "Why was she here? Who is she?"

He's silent for a few moments, studying me in that intense way of his while the cognac goes untouched in his hand. "She's an asset," he finally says. "My brother Valery sent her over when I explained your situation."

My heart leaps, and my mouth goes dry. After my conversation with Alina, I wondered if this might be the case, but to hear it confirmed so bluntly… Shakily, I reach for my cognac and take a sip, letting it light a path of fire down my esophagus. "What kind of asset?" I ask when the urge to cough subsides.

"Originally, the government kind. Now ours."

A spy then, or some other kind of operative—and not nearly as young as I thought if she has this kind of background. I suppose I can see it. If I'd met Masha on the street, I would've never suspected her of being any sort of "asset," but that's probably the point. That bubbly, youthful exterior makes for an effective mask.

Before I can ask what exactly her role is in my situation, Nikolai speaks again. "Zaychik…" His tone is once more disconcertingly gentle. "It's confirmed. Bransford is your biological father."

My heart rate spikes further, a chill prickling the skin on my arms. "You mean…"

"Masha obtained a DNA sample from Bransford. It matches yours."

Matches mine. My stomach twists nauseatingly, the chill spreading to engulf the rest of my body. I've known this had to be the case ever since Nikolai told me what his older brother had uncovered, but a part of me must've been still holding out a sliver of hope.

A hope that's now crushed and ground to dust.

"Why did you—" I stop to clear the hoarseness in my throat. "Why did you want to confirm it?"

I don't want to think about how this Masha obtained Bransford's sample, or mine. Actually, the latter must've been easy: my toothbrush, a few loose hairs on my pillow, a cup I drank from… A presidential candidate with all the accompanying security, though—

"Because I needed to be certain."

I blink, realizing I've let my thoughts wander away from the key question. "But why? I mean, don't get me wrong, I'm grateful." At least I think I am. Is it better to know you're the offspring of a murdering rapist, or to just suspect it strongly?

Nikolai sets his glass down, the liquid inside still untouched. "I promised to protect you, zaychik."

The chill ripples over me again, my mind venturing down a path I wish it wouldn't go. "You did. You have. I'm safe here, aren't I?" At least from Bransford.

He leans forward, his big, warm palms covering my frozen hands. "You are. And you'll be even safer once he's no longer a threat to you."

I stare into his hypnotic irises, that rich, deep gold speckled with green. "Not a threat how?" I've avoided thinking about the future for this very reason: because I can't imagine one where Bransford *won't* be a threat. Like a turtle, I've been content to hide inside my shell, taking it one day, one hour, at a time, all the while telling myself that eventually, I'll get it figured out and bring Mom's murderer to justice.

Not Nikolai, though. He hasn't been hiding from reality—he's been planning. And it's the nature of those plans that makes icy fingers dance down my spine.

I have a feeling Nikolai's idea of justice differs drastically from mine.

He smiles as if I were a naïve child. "You don't need to worry, zaychik. I'm handling it."

For a brief, cowardly moment, I'm tempted to do just that: not worry, leave the matter in his capable, ruthless hands… the ones holding mine so possessively, so gently.

The same hands that had taken two lives in front of me without hesitation.

It's that memory, that vivid recollection of the tortured assassin's screams, that decides it for me. I may have developed a knack for avoiding reality, but even I can't close my eyes and pretend to be blind.

"What are you going to do to him?" My voice is as unsteady as my pulse. "Nikolai, please, I have to know. What are you going to do?"

The tiny muscles around his eyes tighten—the only change in his expression. "Nothing he doesn't deserve."

I draw back, pulling my hands out of his grasp. "You can't kill him."

"Why not?" His voice is even, his tone as bland as if we were speaking of going to a party. Leaning back, he picks up his cognac again, and this time, he takes a leisurely sip before setting it down.

I stare at him incredulously. "Because he's a *person*." How is this not self-evident? "An evil person, sure, but you can't just go about killing anyone who—"

"Who tries to kill you? I can, and I will."

My heart misses a beat. He means it, I can see it, and the realization fills me with all kinds of fucked-up emotions: gratitude overlaid with terror, hope edged with dread, and most disturbing, a vengeful sort of glee.

I want Bransford dead for what he did to my mom. I want it so badly I can taste it. And I want it for myself as well. I want my life back, my freedom, my peace of mind. I want to sleep through the night without nightmares and walk down the street without fear. I want to stop seeing danger in every pickup truck, every unfamiliar face.

I want Bransford six feet under, and if Nikolai makes it happen, I'll be free… and as much of a murderer as he is.

It's that last thought that squashes my dark longing. As much as I want freedom and vengeance, we're talking about murder—cold-blooded, premeditated murder. It was one thing for Nikolai to dispatch the two armed assassins in the woods; as disturbing as it had been to witness, what he did is ultimately no different than what a cop in his situation might've done, minus the torture bit. What we're discussing now is a whole other level of fucked up, and though some part of me can't help but rejoice in Nikolai's willingness to protect me to this extent, I can't stand by and let it happen.

Since appealing to common-sense morality didn't work, I try a different tack. "Nikolai, please. Be reasonable. He's a prominent political figure. You can't just kill him. It would be an assassination, one with major global ramifications. The FBI, the CIA, the media—"

"I know. Which is why I had to be certain of his guilt."

Another chill runs down my spine. His face is implacable, his voice still disturbingly even. He's thought this through; this isn't some impulse on his part.

To protect me, he's going to take out a presidential candidate, and there's nothing I can do to change his mind.

I try anyway, if for no other reason than to protect *him*. "What about your family? The life you're building here with Slava? If they find out you're behind it—"

"They won't."

"How can you be so sure? There will be a global manhunt, the kind not seen since—"

"Zaychik…" Leaning forward, he covers my hands again, making me realize I've been wringing them on the table. His voice is soft, his tone eerily calm as his gaze holds mine. "I know what I'm doing. Bransford will die, and it will be of natural causes. His party will mourn, the nation will mourn, and then they'll move on to another shiny new thing, some other silver-tongued politician."

"Natural causes? At fifty-five?"

"A heart defect, hitherto undiagnosed. It will be properly tragic." He sits back, picking up his glass. "Where there's a will, there's a way—and us Molotovs excel at finding those ways."

20

NIKOLAI

SHE STANDS UP SHAKILY, STARING AT ME, AND I FIGHT the urge to gather her into my arms. I fight it because underneath the need to comfort are darker, more dangerous urges, ones born of a hunger so deep and savage it scares even me.

Once I give in to it, once I unleash the beast snarling inside me, there will be no going back.

Two weeks I've given her. For two century-long weeks, I've done the impossible and stayed away. Well, not entirely. I've spent dozens of hours watching her through the cameras in Slava's room and in her bedroom, but that and our brief interactions at mealtimes have only added to my torment.

I've never thought of myself as a masochist, but I must be, because I've willingly embraced the exquisite torture of having her within arm's reach yet not allowing myself to possess her.

And tonight, it seems, is the ultimate test of my self-control. Because she's finally sought me out, though not for the reasons I wished. A part of me hoped that she'd miss me, that she'd come to me because she wants me with the same desperation I want her.

Because she's ready to be mine, with all that it implies.

"I should go to bed," she says, her voice unsteady, and I have to quell a surge of disappointment. What did I expect? She's shocked, and for a good reason. Few ordinary citizens realize how easy it is to make a murder look like something else—if that's the desired outcome. All the high-profile assassinations and radiation poisonings that make the news are meant to be newsworthy. They're a message, a warning to others who may try to go against the establishment.

For every exotic poison that screams of secret government involvement, there are dozens of health failures and routine accidents that clear away the obstacles in the paths of powerful, ruthless people... people like my family.

This isn't the first covert assassination I've had to plan.

Originally, I wasn't going to tell Chloe any of it. She would've learned about Bransford's death on the news, same as everyone else, and whatever suspicions she'd have harbored at that point would've been nowhere near as burdensome as the knowledge she's now carrying. But she came to me tonight demanding answers, and I couldn't bring myself to lie to her. In a way, my sister is to blame for that, too. Though Alina has kept her mouth shut around Chloe, she's been coming to me almost daily, insisting that Chloe has a right to know what I'm planning, that it should be her decision.

I strongly disagree about the latter, but I've come to see some merit in the former. I don't want my zaychik stressing about her situation, worrying that at any moment more assassins might show up on our doorstep. Not that they'd get through, but still, it has to weigh on her, the knowledge that someone out there wants her dead.

That her biological father wants her dead.

No, it's for the best that I've told her. Masha needs at least a few weeks to complete her mission, and this way, Chloe knows that I'm taking care of it and she doesn't need to worry.

Having lodged her objections, she can relax with a clear conscience. It's my decision, my sin, not hers.

Getting up, I smile at her, hoping she can't see the twisted hunger in my eyes, the dark need that bubbles in my veins like fresh lava. "Of course. If you're tired, go to bed, zaychik."

As much as I want to claim her, tonight is not the night. I'm too hungry, too close to the edge, and though her injuries are all but healed, she's still nowhere near where she needs to be to handle me.

She backs away, as if she's read my mind, but then

her shoulders pull back and her delicate chin comes up. "No," she says firmly, stepping around the table toward me. "I'm not leaving until you promise to find another one of those 'ways.'"

21

CHLOE

I KNOW THIS IS A BAD IDEA. I ALSO KNOW THAT I CAN'T be a coward and slink away like he hasn't just admitted to me that he plans to assassinate a man on my behalf. A terrible, awful man, but still a man… who happens to be my biological father.

Something dark flickers in Nikolai's eyes as he gazes down at me, and belatedly, I notice the dangerous tautness of his jaw.

"Zaychik…" His voice is a soft growl. "You should go. Now. While you still can."

My breath stutters to a halt as the realization of what he means crashes into me, ratcheting up my pulse and paralyzing my muscles.

He still wants me, badly, yet for whatever reason, he's restraining himself.

I should listen to him. I should back off and back away while he's giving me this chance. If I don't, it'll change everything, put an end to this interlude out of time, bridge the distance between us that's kept me so safe.

Because the biggest danger to me is not out there.

It's here.

It's always been him.

I will my muscles to move, to obey the frantic commands of my brain, but I might as well be wishing to bench-press a car. All I can do is stare up at him, mouth dry and heart pounding as pulsing tension gathers low in my belly, peaking my nipples and painting my skin with swirls of heat.

I can see the savage storm brewing in his eyes, can feel the crackle of that electric charge in the air, yet I remain still, frozen and mute, the perfect prey for the taking.

"Chloe..." The hoarsely uttered word is equal parts warning and capitulation. Slowly, with exaggerated gentleness, he cups my face with both hands, the heat of his broad palms burning my chilled skin. His eyes are a hypnotic alchemist's gold as he whispers, "My sweet zaychik, it's over. You've lost your last chance to escape."

22

CHLOE

I'M STILL FROZEN IN PLACE WHEN HIS LIPS DESCEND ON mine, as inevitably and violently as lightning striking a tree on a plain. The shock of it jolts my whole body, scalding every cell on the way.

There's no finesse to his kiss, no gentleness. He doesn't ask, he takes. With my head immobilized between his palms, he plunders every inch of my mouth, sucking me into a vortex of savage desire, a lust so dark and volcanic it scorches me from deep within.

He tastes like cognac and danger, like every twisted, secretive yearning of mine. The heady flavor intoxicates me, the sensual notes of his cedar-and-bergamot cologne making my head spin. Whatever thoughts of resistance I still entertained evaporate, my willpower dissolving like a grain of sugar in hot tea. With a helpless moan, I arch against him, my belly pressing against his groin as my hands clutch his sides.

He's fully hard, the thick bulge in his pants jutting

against my softness, reminding me of what it felt like to have him inside. The memory evokes both arousal and trepidation—it hadn't been easy, taking in something that size. But even that thought soon disappears, burned away by the fierce heat of desire, destroyed by the brutal seduction of his merciless kiss.

I forget where we are. I forget everything, so much so that I'm startled when he pulls away to scoop me up against his chest. It's only when he starts up the stairs, taking them two at a time, that my head clears enough for a sliver of rational thought.

What on earth am I doing? This isn't what I intended. It's the polar opposite, in fact. My goal was to talk to him, to convince him not to—

With a low growl, he pins me against the wall in the upstairs hallway and reclaims my mouth, as if he can't bear not to taste me all the way to his room, and I forget all about my goals. I forget that I exist outside of this moment, that there's anything out there but him.

We merge, or at least that's what it feels like. His mouth is fused to mine, his breath is in my lungs, his scent is in my nostrils. His powerful body surrounds me, all heat and hardness and raw, primal maleness. I'm vertical now, standing on tiptoes as he devours my lips, and his hands roam over my back, my sides, my ass, squeezing and kneading the latter, working the long dress up my thighs. Breathless, I grip the cool, silken strands of his hair as he lifts me up until my legs are wrapped around his hips and my pelvis is riding on his, my aching sex grinding against his erection.

We kiss, our tongues dueling, until we're completely out of air. Then his mouth trails over to my neck, raining hot, biting kisses over the tender hollow near my ear. Moaning, I arch my head back and grind harder against him, lost to everything but the dark, scorching pleasure. The tension inside me is coiling and building, my nerve endings so sensitized the movement of air feels like a touch on my skin.

I'm going to come from dry-humping him, I realize with distant surprise.

It's going to happen again.

And then it does, the release as startling as it is welcome. My fingers convulsively clench in his hair and my inner muscles spasm as ecstasy rips through my body, curling my toes and wrenching a cry from my throat. Only he doesn't stop; he keeps going, rocking his hips into my pelvis, intensifying the aftershocks blasting my core. Eyes squeezing shut, I cry out again, and like an animal claiming his mate, he bites down on my neck as his big, callused hand delves into my bodice, squeezing my naked breast as his thumb grazes over my—

"Chloe? Nikolai, what are you—oh fuck. Never mind."

Alina's voice wrenches me out of the heated delirium, and I stiffen, my eyes flying open. Sure enough, over Nikolai's shoulder, I see her backing away, her pale face uncharacteristically pink. Before I can say anything, or process the fact that this is the second time she's caught us nearly fucking, she spins on her heel and disappears back into her room.

Which is just down the hallway.

The public hallway where anyone could've seen us —and heard me coming.

My face, my body, even the roots of my hair feel as if they're on fire as Nikolai pulls back to stare at me. His golden eyes are heavy-lidded; his hair, with my hands still clenched in it, is mussed; his sensual lips are wet and swollen, parted in an expression of pure lust.

It's the way a fallen angel might look after committing his first sin—except this angel has never known an innocent existence.

He's been the devil all along.

I dampen my lips. "Your sister—"

"Fuck my sister."

Before I can address that furiously growled sentiment, he sweeps me up in his powerful arms and carries me to his room with long, impatient strides.

23

NIKOLAI

I SHOULD STOP, OR AT THE VERY LEAST SLOW DOWN, BUT I can't. Now that I've tasted her again, the hunger inside me is too strong, too feral. Like an alcoholic who's downed his first drink of the night, I can't even imagine moderation. The dark need pulses in my veins, a drumbeat of sexual desire and a deeper, less defined yearning, a craving that seems to emanate from my very soul.

With the fraying remnants of my self-control, I lay her down on the bed, careful not to hurt her arm. There's a scab there now, marring her silken, golden-hued skin. The sight of it feeds the savage beast inside me, filling my chest with equal parts possessiveness and rage.

She's mine, and I'll annihilate anyone who's ever hurt her.

No one will ever lay a finger on her… except me.

Already, without my willing it, my hands are on her

dress, ripping at the pretty, flimsy fabric, tearing it off her body in a furious campaign to bare it to my gaze. Her breasts pop out of her bodice first, two small, delicious globes tipped with erect brown nipples, followed by her narrow ribcage and flat belly, all covered by that glowing, bronzed skin that makes me think of captured sunshine, of warmth, light, and purity—all the things I hunger for, everything I want.

Her lower body is next, her barely-there thong all but disintegrating in my hands to expose a pussy that's as delicate and soft as I remember. My mouth waters at the recollection of her sweet, rich flavor, of how those tender folds felt on my lips, under my tongue, clenched on my fingers... fingers that can't help but grip her thighs, pulling them wide apart.

Her soft brown eyes meet mine, slumberous with desire, edged with that provoking wariness, and the last shreds of my self-control unravel. Like a starving animal, I fall upon her, burying my face between her thighs, lapping at her slickness, gorging on her salt-and-berry essence, on the warmth and sunlight that is her.

She gasps and grips my head, her fingers clenching in my hair as she arches underneath me, writhing at each greedy stroke of my tongue. Soon, my fingers join in as well, toying with her clit while I lick her opening, reveling in the wetness I find there. She's as delicious as I remembered, all silk and heat and molten honey, and though my cock is on the verge of bursting, I can't tear myself away from what I'm doing, can't stop until I feel her come again.

And come she does. With a choked cry, she bucks underneath me, her back bowing off the bed as her fingers tighten in my hair, all but tearing it out by the roots as more delicious slickness coats my lips and tongue.

The surge of satisfaction is as intense as it is brief, my lust having only sharpened with her orgasm. Hot blood pounds in my temples, my balls drawn tight and every muscle in my body tense with need. There's no gentleness left inside me, no patience, just raw, primal hunger to possess and claim, to bury my throbbing cock inside her heat.

Driven by a purely animalistic instinct, I flip her over and loop my arm under her hips, raising her shapely little ass toward me until she's standing on all fours. Her smooth cheeks are a little fuller, a little rounder than the last time I saw her naked, the rosebud of her sphincter a tiny, tempting dot, and my hunger intensifies to a knife's edge sharpness, my body tightening to an unbearable degree. I'm barely cognizant of my actions as I rip open my fly and free my cock, then line it up against her gleaming slit.

I have to have her. Now.

The drumbeat of desire grows deafening, drowning out everything, blurring the world around us. I'm no longer man; I'm nothing more than primal hunger, a savage, atavistic need.

Gripping her slim hips, I plunge inside, reveling in

the slick grip of her inner walls, in the delicious tightness of her narrow passage. She cries out, a sound of pain, but I can't stop, can't do anything but thrust even deeper, taking her, claiming her, satisfying the feral lust scorching me inside.

Mine. All fucking mine. My hips pump savagely, my heart pounding like a fist against my chest. Distantly, I'm aware that I'm being far too rough, but I can no more slow down than I can let her go. She's all silky tightness and wet heat, the closest thing to heaven a man can know. Her pleading gasps and cries only spur me on, heightening my lust, fueling the beast inside me.

I fuck her like there's no tomorrow, like nothing outside this moment matters. Maintaining my grip on her with one hand, I wind the other in her hair and pull, making her arch her back as I thrust in harder, deeper, imprinting my brand on her tender flesh. I can feel the orgasm boiling up inside me, my balls tightening until they're nearly as hard as my throbbing cock, and as she screams my name and spasms around me, the release crashes over me like a tsunami, sending ecstasy exploding through my nerve endings and painting the world around me bright white.

24

CHLOE

Dazed, I flop onto my belly as soon as Nikolai lets go of my hair and pulls out of my swollen, twitching flesh. Even with the orgasmic aftershocks still rippling through me, my sex feels battered, my insides sore. My thoughts are scrambled too, my mind as sluggish as if I were emerging from a deep sleep.

Despite that, when he gathers me against his side and begins murmuring sweet nothings, I again experience that unusual sense of peace, the one I've known only in his arms. My eyes drift shut, a floating sensation coming over me as he strokes and pets me, raining light, soothing kisses over my face and neck, massaging away the aches and bruises from his rough handling. Eventually, my disjointed thoughts coalesce into something coherent, and I force open my eyelids to find his mesmerizing eyes peering into mine, the gold-hued amber of his irises streaked with the darkest green.

"Zaychik…" His voice is soft, his expression hard to read as he curves his large palm over my cheek. "I didn't use a condom."

For a moment, the words don't make sense to me. Then, with a jolt of adrenaline, I become aware of a warm wetness between my legs and on my thighs.

A lot of wetness. Way more than I've ever felt.

My heartbeat spikes, the floaty feeling disappearing. Pulling back sharply, I sit up. "What do you mean? I'm not on anything. I ran out of pills weeks ago. I thought —I thought you always wore a condom." I dart a glance at the thick white liquid on my naked thighs, trying not to panic as I frantically count the days.

When was my period? Was it this week or last week? Why haven't I bothered to keep track? I know it's been several days since I've stopped bleeding, but maybe—

"I do." Nikolai sits up as well, the powerful muscles in his chest and arm flexing as he rakes his hand through his hair, mussing the black locks further. "At least I always have until today."

I finally recall when my period started: early last week, almost twelve days ago. Last Monday was when I had to ask Alina for supplies.

I'm roughly in the middle of my cycle.

I must look as panicked as I feel because Nikolai tilts his head, regarding me with that same indecipherable expression. "The timing is just right, isn't it? Or more precisely, wrong?"

I nod, my hand instinctively moving to my stomach.

"Why—" I stop to steady my shaking voice. "Why didn't you use a condom?"

The enigmatic gleam in his eyes deepens as he moves toward me. "Why don't we get cleaned up and then talk more?"

I must still be in shock because I don't voice any objections as he scoops me up and carries me to the bathroom. Instead, I let him take care of me in the shower the way he'd done when I was hurt. His touch is again gentle, soothing and tender, even as his cock grows harder with each stroke of his callus-roughened hands over my wet, naked body.

By the time he's done washing away the evidence of our mistake, he's fully erect, and his hands are moving over me with growing intent, cupping my breasts and playing with my nipples, venturing between my thighs to find my clit. It should be too much, too soon, but my body responds as if it hasn't just survived a cataclysmic upheaval of its senses, as if the savage fucking that's left me so overwhelmed had been nothing but a preview of the main event.

My breathing picks up, a tension gathering low in my stomach as his lips slant over mine in a deep, searching kiss, then venture over to my ear, my neck, my shoulder. Panting, I clutch at his shoulders as he wraps my wet hair around his fist and arches me backward over his powerfully muscled arm, lifting my breasts toward him like a sacrificial offering. His broad back shields me from the water spray as he bends over me, latching on to one nipple, then another, the hot, powerful suction of his mouth sending tugs of sensation straight down to my core, heightening my growing arousal.

Still, I'm sore inside, way too sore to feel pleasure as two of his fingers push into me, forcing apart the swollen, tender tissues. That is, until those fingers curve inside me, finding a spot that makes sparks detonate behind my closed eyelids and taking me over the edge so swiftly I can barely gasp out his name.

The spasms are still rippling through my body when he releases my nipple with a wet *pop* and guides me down to my knees while still shielding me from the shower spray with his body. Dazedly, I blink up at him, only to realize what he wants as he slaps the hard, massive column of his cock against my cheek, then drags the tip over to my mouth.

On instinct, I brace my hands on his muscled thighs and part my lips, taking him in as far as he'll go. I've given blow jobs before, but this feels different, nothing like those casual, playful times with my ex-boyfriends. I'm not in control—he is—and there's nothing playful in the merciless way he fucks my mouth. His hands grip my skull, holding me still for his deep, slow thrusts, and it's all I can do not to gag as he goes farther down my throat with each stroke.

It shouldn't be hot—he's using me solely for his pleasure—but something about being treated like a fuck doll sends pulses of heat directly to my clit. He's taking what he wants from my body, and it's both degrading and perversely liberating. There's nothing complicated in this exchange; I please him simply by existing, by being nothing more than a warm, wet mouth for his use. My eyes scrunch shut, tears leaking out the sides as he picks up pace, forcing his big cock down my aching throat, yet the urge to gag remains quiescent, even as my mouth floods with enough saliva to fill a lake. It drips down my chin, my neck, my chest, but none of that matters because I can sense the tension building in his body, can feel his thick shaft swelling in my mouth even more. With a groan, he thrusts in so deep I lose the ability to breathe, and warm liquid spurts down my throat as his fingers clench tightly in my hair, tugging on the roots hard enough to make me wince.

By the time he pulls out of my throat, I'm so desperate for air my nails are digging frantically into his thighs. Yet when I open my watering eyes and look up to meet his gaze, I shiver with pleasure at the warm possessiveness reflected there.

"Zaychik…" His voice is a dark, velvety rasp as he hooks his hands under my arms and lifts me to my feet, then steadies me until I regain my balance. Holding my shoulder gently with one hand, he rinses the cum and saliva off me with the other, then cups my chin, staring down at me with a peculiarly intent expression.

My pulse kicks up anew, a strange premonition tightening my stomach as he says softly, "You are everything to me, the source of my greatest happiness and pleasure. I want you with me for the rest of our lives, for as long as breath remains in our bodies. Fate brought you to my door, delivered you to me like the gift you are, and I couldn't be more grateful."

My heart is now in my throat, my breath coming so fast my vision is going gray. This can't possibly be heading where I think it's heading. There's no way he's—

"Chloe Emmons..." He frames my face with his broad palms, his tiger eyes filled with a fiercely tender light. "I want you to marry me. I want you to be my wife."

25

CHLOE

For a moment, I'm convinced I misheard him. Because there's no way he's proposing, not when we've known each other less than a month. Except there's no mistaking the intensity in his hypnotic stare, no hiding from the fact that he's just used the words "marry" and "wife."

My mind spins frantically as I clasp his powerful wrists, instinctively tugging his hands down from my face. The shower behind him is still running, filling the spacious stall with steam, but I'm all of a sudden freezing, goosebumps rippling over my wet skin.

"Nikolai, I…" I have no idea what to say, how to approach something so insane. Finally, I blurt, "You're joking, right?"

His gaze darkens. "Why would I joke about this?"

"Because… because we hardly know each other!"

He lays his hands on my shoulders and squeezes lightly, his tone remaining soft even as his jaw hardens dangerously. "I know everything I need to know about you."

"Well, I don't. Know about you, I mean." I back out of his hold and wipe a shaking hand over my face to rid it of the water droplets. My heart hammers unevenly, my stomach knotting at his rapidly darkening expression as I grope for the shower stall door. "Nikolai, please, don't get me wrong—I'm super flattered. It's just… this isn't a good idea right now." Or ever.

I may have fallen for this lethally gorgeous man, but I haven't forgotten who and what he is—or what he's about to do for me.

I'm not cut out to be a mafia wife, even if that's not the formal label.

He watches my retreat with narrowed eyes, steam billowing in the air behind his powerful body, and it's all I can do not to trip over the bathroom mat as I step out and grab a towel.

There's no need for me to be so freaked out.

He asked and I refused.

End of story.

"What do you need to know about me?" He steps out after me, his movements soft and deliberate. A predator following his prey. "What will it take for you to say yes?"

"Well…" I wrap the towel around myself, frantically searching for the least offensive answer. There isn't one, so I'm forced to opt for the truth. "Nikolai, I just can't marry you. We're too different. Our values, the way we approach things… The truth is, I don't think—" My heart jumps at the storm gathering in his eyes, but I'm committed, so I plow ahead. "I don't think this can work long term."

He stills, his hand halfway to his own towel. Then, slowly and deliberately, he pulls it off the rack and dries himself, his eyes trained on me the whole time, his face now darker than a moonless night.

I swallow hard as the tense silence grows. "I should go to bed. We can talk more in the morning."

He moves like the big feline he reminds me of. A blur of explosive motion, and he's between me and the bathroom door, chiseled muscles flexing as he stares down at me, golden eyes in slits.

"No, zaychik," he says softly. "*We* should go to bed. And tomorrow, you will marry me. No matter how you feel."

26

CHLOE

I WAKE UP BLEARY-EYED, MY HEAD POUNDING AND MY body aching all over. Suppressing a groan, I attempt to roll over onto my side, only to find that I'm pinned in place by a heavy arm slung over my torso.

Adrenaline floods my veins, clearing away the fog of sleep, and I realize where I am.

In bed with Nikolai.

My breath catches, and I carefully turn my head to look at him. I've only seen him asleep once before, the one other time we spent the night together, and I'm again struck by how beautiful and dangerously animalistic he looks in repose, with jet-black lashes fanning over his sharp cheekbones and dark stubble shadowing the hard lines of his jaw. Sleep doesn't soften his starkly molded features; instead, it lends them a savage kind of sensuality, a darkly primitive appeal.

Even now, there's something predatory, something

wicked in the way his sensuous lips are curved, the way they're slightly parted.

Realizing I'm wasting a precious opportunity by staring at him like a star-struck groupie, I carefully wriggle out from under his arm and creep naked to the door, my heart pounding against my ribcage.

I need to escape, if only to my own room.

I need to put some distance between us.

Last night, at least the portion after the shower, is a blur in my mind, a jumble of darkly sexual sensations and wild emotions. I think I was so stunned by his declaration that I went into a kind of shock, and by the time I recovered, I was already in his bed, with my wrists pinned above my head and him driving into my sore yet perversely eager body.

I don't remember saying no, but I must have. I don't want to believe that I let him fuck me after what he said... or that I came several more times as he took me with unbridled ferocity over and over again.

At least he'd used a condom those other times; I'd be hyperventilating now if it had been bareback.

Reaching the door, I cast a glance behind my shoulder. Thank God he's still asleep. I don't know how I'm going to face him—or what I'm going to do about his marriage threat. And it is a threat. I have no idea how he can force me to say yes against my will, but I know it's within his capabilities. That darkness I've always sensed in him is now directed at me.

As he told me yesterday, he excels at doing whatever it takes to get his way.

Holding my breath, I reach for the door handle and turn it, wincing internally at the faint click it makes. To my relief, he continues sleeping, so I stick my head out in the hallway, making sure it's clear, and then I sprint down to my room, ignoring the twinge of pain in my barely healed ankle.

I get inside without incident and beeline for my bathroom, where I jump in the shower and scrub myself with soap in an attempt to wash away the memory of his rough touch. It's futile—marks of his possession are all over my body, my skin scraped in a dozen places by his stubble, my nipples aching where he'd sucked on them and grazed them with his teeth. The worst, though, is the soreness deep inside me, a reminder of his insatiable hunger for me—and my complete inability to resist him, even in light of the madness he intends.

I turn off the water and step out of the stall, taking deep breaths to control my growing panic. Maybe he didn't mean it. He could've just been upset that I turned down his proposal, and when he wakes up this morning, he'll realize how premature it was.

He hired me just over three weeks ago, and we've spent a grand total of two nights together. How can he be so sure that he wants me for a lifetime, that I'm indeed the one?

Yet no matter what I tell myself, my panic refuses to abate. Despite what I said last night, I know Nikolai. Deep down, I know him—and I know he doesn't say things he doesn't mean. He decided we were fated when I'd been here barely a week, and nothing that's happened since has convinced him otherwise.

What's scarier is he doesn't claim to love me—and I don't think he does. What he feels for me is more of an obsession. With a jolt, I remember Alina warning me about this the night we smoked weed together, telling me her brother isn't my white knight.

"Molotov men don't love, they possess," she said. "And Nikolai is no exception."

Wrapping a towel around my wet hair, I stare at my reflection in the mirror, noting the puffy redness of my lips, still bruised and swollen from his kisses. Near my collarbone is a hickey, and on my hips are faint dark marks in the shape of male fingers.

No, this isn't love. Not even close.

At best, it's a mutual fixation—because even now, as I stand here looking like I've been assaulted, the memories of how each mark got on my body make me throb deep inside.

It's as I'm getting dressed that I decide on the best course of action.

Alina.

She helped me once; maybe she can do so again.

I don't even know what kind of help I have in mind—after my near miss with the assassins, the idea of another escape attempt holds little appeal. Nonetheless, I feel a spark of hope as I knock on the door of her bedroom, and she opens it for me, dressed in her peignoir. Before I have a chance to apologize for waking her up, she glances around the hallway and swiftly ushers me inside.

"Are you okay?" she demands, stepping back to give me a thorough once-over. Her gaze zeroes in on my puffy lips, and her dark eyebrows pull together. "Did Kolya—"

"No, no, I'm fine." My face burns hot, making me grateful my bronzed skin conceals my flush—and my high-necked T-shirt hides the hickey. "He wouldn't— It was all consensual, believe me."

She blows out a breath. "Okay, good. I figured that was the case. It's just... my brother is not entirely sane when it comes to you."

"You can say that again," I mutter under my breath.

She hears me anyway, and her frown returns. "What happened?" Grabbing my hand, she leads me over to her unmade bed and makes me sit next to her. Since she's just woken up, her face is bare, like that fateful time she ambushed me in my bedroom, but her jade-green eyes are clear, clouded only by concern. "What happened? Tell me, Chloe. Please."

I take in a deep breath and brace myself for her reaction. "Nikolai proposed."

Zero response. Not so much as an eyelash flicker.

Did she not hear me?

"He asked me to marry him," I enunciate, in case it wasn't clear. "Last night, he asked me to be his wife."

Now her long lashes sweep over her eyes. "I see."

"Why aren't you more surprised?" I demand, stunned and more than a little disquieted by her calm acceptance. "Did you know he would do this?"

"Know? No. Suspect? Yes." She sighs, pushing back her hair with one hand. "From the moment I saw your keys in his drawer, I figured this is where it might be heading. But of course, Kolya doesn't talk to me about these matters, so I can't say I knew for sure."

My disquiet increases. "I don't understand."

"Chloe..." Facing me fully, she clasps my hands in both of hers. "My brother is obsessed with you. I saw signs of it from the first day we hired you, but I thought—I hoped—it was just a passing attraction on his part, that you'd just be another girl he'd fuck and forget."

"Gee, thanks."

"It's nothing against you. It would've been a good thing, believe me." She squeezes my hands. "Look, Nikolai is... He's a lot like our father. And our grandfather. And from the stories I've heard, other Molotov men before them. Konstantin and Valery—they're a little different, but Nikolai... he's a Molotov male through and through."

"What does that mean?" I ask, frustrated. "He's what? Prone to proposing after knowing a woman for a month?"

She shakes her head. "To the best of my knowledge, he's never proposed to anyone else—or become this obsessed with a woman." She takes a breath. "You're the first, and if I had to guess, the last. Which is how it often happens with the men in our family. Our father saw our mother at a party, swept her off her feet by showering her family with presents, and married her two weeks later. And his father—our paternal grandfather—literally kidnapped our grandmother when she was sixteen, stole her from her village when he happened upon her tending a field with other schoolgirls."

"You're kidding me."

"I wish." Her face is somber. "Our grandmother passed away when I was ten, but I remember the stories she told me about her life with my grandfather, the way he'd control her every move and demand absolute obedience. She was deeply unhappy with him, but she was just a poor peasant girl and he was a powerful, well-connected man, so there was nothing she could do. He wouldn't let her leave him."

I stare at her, my stomach roiling. "And your mother? Was she unhappy also?"

She pulls back her hands, her face turning shuttered. "Not at first. She didn't know what kind of man she'd married, not until much later. It was when she found out that things started to unravel and—" She stops and takes another deep breath. "In any case, that's neither here nor there. My point is, Nikolai possesses that same intense, passionate personality, an obsessive tendency that seeks, and eventually finds, something—someone—to latch on to. Like our father and our grandfather before him, he's single-minded when it comes to getting the woman he wants, and he wants you, Chloe. And he'll have you, at any cost."

I don't know what to say. Struck dumb, I simply stare at her as she says softly, "Also, I don't know if you've noticed, but there's a streak of mysticism within Nikolai, this belief in fate and destiny that he's inherited from our grandmother. Having grown up in a small rural village, she was both religious and deeply superstitious, and she spent a lot of time with Nikolai when he was a little boy. He'd probably deny it—he doesn't consider himself religious in the least—but he's absorbed a lot of her beliefs, including her attitudes about our family and how our very blood carries evil within it… how it was inevitable that our father, her son, would turn out the way he had."

I swallow hard. "Which is how?" And more importantly, has Nikolai turned out the same way?

Alina's lips flatten. "Never mind that. We're talking about Nikolai right now."

"And me. Alina…" It's my turn to grip her hands. "What do I do? I told him I can't marry him, but he's not listening to reason. He insists we're getting married today."

Her face finally displays a flicker of surprise. "Today?"

"Yes, today!" Releasing her hands, I modulate my tone. "Look, I might be freaking out for nothing. I don't know how he can force me into marriage—it's not the Middle Ages. But just in case, can you maybe talk some sense into him? Or help me figure out how to do so?"

She tilts her head, her jade eyes gleaming. "So just to be clear, you don't want to marry him?"

I blink. "Of course not. I mean… I've known him less than a month."

"But you want him, right? Last night and that other time—"

"That's different." My face turns hot again. "That's just biological. He's a very attractive man and—"

"So it's just sex for you?"

I open my mouth to say yes, but the word refuses to come out.

"I see." The gleam in her eyes intensifies. "Do you love him?"

"I…" I swallow against the sudden dryness in my throat. "I don't know. Does it matter? I still can't marry him. He's—that is, he's not…"

"What you imagined as a husband?" she says as I trail off. A wry smile curves her lips. "You know, most women would jump at the chance to marry a rich, handsome man who's crazy about them."

"Would you? Jump at a chance to marry someone like your brother?"

Her features tighten, the smile falling off her face. "We're not talking about me." Standing up sharply, she strides over to the window, her back ramrod stiff as she stares out at the distant peaks.

Confused, I walk over to join her there. I have no

idea what's upset her, but clearly, something has. Cautiously, I touch her shoulder. "Hey, I—"

She turns to face me, her features composed once more. "Listen to me, Chloe. You're right to freak out. If my brother says you're marrying him today, that's going to happen. I don't exactly know how, but he's resourceful. If you really don't want this, your best bet is to delay the wedding."

"Delay? But—"

"Delay," she says firmly. "Outright refusal won't work—it'll only make him more determined—so you have to say yes and then figure out a way to impose some conditions. Maybe you've always dreamed of a particular wedding venue, or a special dress, or having your college friends as bridesmaids. He may honor that, or he may not. Either way, it's worth a shot."

I stare at her, my pulse racing. She's right: I've gone about this all wrong. Last night, until I told Nikolai the truth—that I didn't think it could work between us long term—he seemed amenable to reason, more interested in persuading me than bending me to his will.

Maybe if I agree to marry him at some point in the future, we can go back to a saner dynamic, restore the way things were.

"I'm sorry I can't be more helpful," Alina says, and I can tell that she's sincere. "Anything I say to him will only backfire. It's better if you approach him yourself."

"No, this was very helpful, thank you." I turn to leave when a thought occurs to me. Hopeful, I spin around. "You wouldn't happen to have the morning-after pill, would you? There was a bit of a… memory lapse on our part last night."

She stills, blinking. When she speaks, her voice is strange. "No, I'm afraid I don't have anything like that. And Chloe… you might want to think of a really, really good delaying tactic. Remember what I told you about my brother and accidents? Same thing goes for memory lapses."

I stare at her, my stomach dropping. "You mean…"

"It sounds to me like he's dead set on binding you to him—and is already pulling out all the stops."

27

NIKOLAI

I WAKE UP WITH AN UNSETTLING SENSE OF DÉJÀ VU. EVEN before I roll over and feel the cool, empty sheets next to me, I know Chloe is not there.

I can feel her absence deep inside.

Logic tells me she couldn't have run away again—the guards are under strict orders not to let her leave the compound—but my heart still thuds heavily against my ribcage as I jump off the bed and get dressed with military speed.

I have to find her. Now.

Before I can exit the room, a flicker of movement outside catches my eye. I step over to the window, and a wave of relief washes over me.

It's Chloe and Slava, standing together on the edge of the driveway, peering into the cluster of trees on the side. As I look closer, I notice a gray-brown ball of fur in front of them—a wild rabbit. I also catch a glimpse of a long, skinny carrot in my son's hand.

The relief merges with a new, purely incandescent sensation, a glowing sort of warmth that fills every crevice of my chest. My son and my wife to be—it feels so right, so perfect.

So utterly fucked up.

I don't deserve this. Deep down, I know that. A man like me doesn't get to experience this kind of happiness, to bask for any length of time in real joy. And Chloe certainly doesn't deserve me. The blood that runs through my veins is pure poison, my nature ruthless through and through. A better man would've let her go long ago, protecting her from the darkest parts of himself instead of seizing this mirage of happiness with both hands.

But I am seizing it. Because I'm a selfish monster. Because when I finally had her in my arms last night, I knew that was where she belonged. And I knew it wasn't enough to simply have her there.

I need the world to know that she's mine, that she belongs solely to me.

I let myself watch her and Slava for a while longer, enjoying the unearned happiness, these stolen moments of uncomplicated joy. I don't know how I'd been able to restrain myself all that time, how I'd managed to hold back and give her the two-week reprieve. Now that I've had her again, I can't imagine spending another night without her, can't even attempt to put the beast back on its leash.

She doesn't want to marry me. So be it. The scorching burn of rage and hurt at her refusal is still there, but it's cooled slightly, hardening into a grim resolve.

It's time Chloe understood with whom she's dealing. One way or another, she's going to wear my ring on her finger.

Tonight, she's going to become my wife.

28

CHLOE

I GET THROUGH THE MORNING BY SHEER WILLPOWER, going about my lessons with Slava with a smile despite the anxiety shredding my nerves. It helps that Nikolai doesn't show up at breakfast, locking himself in his office with Pavel instead. In fact, I don't see him at all except briefly in the hallway, when he strides past me with nothing more than a heated once-over and a murmured "excuse me, zaychik."

It's as if last night never happened, as if my body doesn't bear the imprint of his possession and my stomach isn't in knots as I try to work up the courage to confront him.

It's not until eleven that the first sign of the changes to come appears. By then, I've grown hopeful that Nikolai has changed his mind, and his threat was empty after all. But no. I walk into my room to find Lyudmila in my closet, grabbing dozens of dresses together with their hangers and carrying them past me without a single word.

"Hey!" I hurry after her as she walks briskly down the hallway. "What's going on?"

She casts a sidelong glance at me as I catch up. "You move today. To Nikolai's room, no?"

"What? No! Give me those." I try to grab the clothes from her, but she proves to be surprisingly agile. Sidestepping my move, she darts into Nikolai's bedroom, then emerges thirty seconds later and beelines for my room.

Fuck.

I run after her. "Don't. Just leave them."

She doesn't listen, snatching another batch of clothes and pushing past me, her matryoshka-doll face devoid of all expression. "If you in my way, I get Pavel to help."

Dammit.

Brimming with anger, I step back and let her do her thing. The alternative—physically fighting her and her mountain of a husband—would be both pointless and stupid. Who cares where my clothes reside? It's what this move signifies that matters.

Nikolai is taking away my room, my private space… my only refuge from him.

I can't hold off on the confrontation any longer. If I don't want to become his wife today, I have to act.

Leaving Lyudmila to do as she will with my closet, I stride to Nikolai's office and knock decisively on the door.

"Yes?"

"It's Chloe." My voice is low and furious, my anger burning away all caution.

The door swings open, revealing Nikolai's large, broad-shouldered frame. Propping a muscular forearm on the doorframe above his head, he rakes his gaze over my body. When his eyes return to my face, they're a bright, predatory gold. "What is it, zaychik?"

"We need to talk."

He takes a half-step back, his sensuous lips curving with dark amusement. "Come in, then."

He's still partially in the doorway, so I have no choice but to push past him. My shoulder brushes against his hard-muscled chest, and I catch a faint whiff of bergamot and cedar, mixed with the enticing musk of warm male skin. A familiar heat scorches my veins, my insides turning soft and liquid despite the fury burning in my chest.

Fucking biology. This is the last thing I need.

Clenching my teeth, I head over to the round table, where I plop down in a chair, my eyes locked challengingly on his face. I refuse to let my body dictate my actions, to have sexual needs decide my fate.

I'm not marrying this beautiful, amoral man if I can help it. No matter how I respond to him in bed.

"So..." He leans back, lacing his long fingers over his ribcage. His voice is brushed silk as he says softly, "You wanted to talk."

I've had all morning to think of the best way to approach him, yet I still find myself tongue-tied, my thoughts in a chaotic jumble. Partially, it's the way he's watching me, with that cynical, mocking half-smile, like he's already looked into the future and knows exactly what I'm going to do and say. But mostly, it's the cool resolve I sense in him. The arguments I've rehearsed suddenly seem inadequate, the very premise of bargaining with him deeply flawed.

"How are you planning to do it?" I blurt finally. It's not what I was going to lead with, but I have to know what's in store for me if I fail. "How can you make me marry you against my will?"

The muscles around his eyes tighten minutely, even as the smile remains on his lips. "Against your will? Is that the lie you're feeding yourself, zaychik? That you are being forced?"

Blood rushes to my face, anger mixing with illogical embarrassment. "What are you saying?"

"I'm saying that I'm doing you a favor." His smile sharpens. "Decisions can be a heavy burden, especially when your ideas of what's right conflict with your actual wants."

My nails bite into my palms. "I don't *want* to marry you. You asked and I said no, remember?"

"Oh, I do." He sits forward sharply, the smile dropping from his face. "Some things are meant to be. One day, you'll see it and be thankful, zaychik. For now, I'll do what I must."

"Which is what? Get some kind of officiant here? And then what? How will you get me to say yes?"

He doesn't reply, just leans back with an inscrutable expression, and my imagination makes the leap.

Staring at him in horror, I choke out, "You're going to drug me, aren't you? That's your plan."

29

NIKOLAI

My clever zaychik. She does know me, no matter what she claims.

The little vial is already in my desk, the liquid inside ready to be sucked into a syringe and pumped into her veins. It's the mildest, gentlest form of one of our special drugs, the dosage just barely enough to blur the edges of reality and lower a person's inhibitions.

When I use it on Chloe, she'll be aware of what's happening, but she won't object… because deep inside, she also wants this.

I know her by now as well.

Which is why I'm not surprised when she takes a breath and squares her slender shoulders instead of pleading or crying. "Fine," she says, her voice shaking only slightly. "You win. But just so you know, I won't forgive you if you go through with this. It will poison everything between us… just like your grandfather's actions ruined whatever chance his marriage ever stood."

Fucking Alina. I should've expected this, yet Chloe's words still spear me like a fishhook, penetrating deep and snagging directly on my heart.

I lean forward, my tone sharpening. "You're leaving me no choice."

"No. You're trying to leave *me* no choice." She leans forward as well, glaring at me from across the table. "The no-condom thing—that was on purpose, wasn't it? You didn't actually forget."

I hold her gaze, the flare of anger cooling as a peculiar ache bands around my chest. Is she right? At the time, it didn't seem like a conscious decision, more like a primordial directive, an overpowering urge to be inside her with no barriers of any kind. The condom wasn't even a consideration; it's as if my mind had blocked out the existence of such protective measures, much less the need for them.

I don't want more children—or at least I thought I didn't. Then I saw my seed on Chloe's thighs, and all sorts of tempting images flooded my mind: of Chloe growing round with our child, of her nursing a chubby infant… of us playing with a brown-eyed toddler whose radiant smile lights a room.

It was like a montage from some fucking Hallmark movie, except it made me ache deep inside.

With effort, I shut down that line of thinking. Whether or not I acted consciously doesn't matter. The outcome is the same either way.

Forcing my shoulders to relax, I sit back and study Chloe's tightly drawn features. "Tell me something, zaychik… what will it take for you to accept our marriage and be happy? For the two of us to avoid my grandparents' fate?"

She's too smart, too cautious to come in here just to castigate me. There's something she's after, some kind of goal she's hoping to achieve, and I suspect I know what it is.

She stares at me for a couple of long seconds, and I sense the battle playing out in her mind. Continue pressing me on the condom question or move on to her actual agenda?

She must decide on the combination of the two because she sits up straighter and says, "Well, for one thing, unless and until I agree to have a baby, I want us to always use protection. In fact, I want you to get me back on birth control pills right away and get me a morning-after pill today."

"Done," I say, suppressing an irrational surge of disappointment.

It's really for the best; another Molotov is the last thing this world needs. I don't know what came over me last night, but I intend to control myself better in the future. In fact, I did use condoms throughout the rest of the night, so I will chalk up what happened to a momentary lapse of reason.

Chloe blinks, clearly surprised by my easy acquiescence. "Okay. Good. Then how about we discuss the timing of the wedding? I think next summer or fall should be—"

"No." I didn't intend to rush her into marriage, but now that we've gone down this path, I can't imagine waiting a day longer. As impatient as I've been to have her in my bed, it's nothing compared to my burning urge to tie her to me. I wasn't planning to propose until some weeks from now, after I'd dealt with Bransford, but everything changed the moment I saw my seed on her and knew I could've made her pregnant. At that moment, putting my ring on her finger became my top priority—and it still is, regardless of whether or not there's going to be a child.

The mere possibility of it made me realize that nothing less than having her as my wife will do.

She sucks in a breath. "But—"

"No. The timing is nonnegotiable." I know I'm being unreasonable, but I can't—I won't—relent on this. Something irrational in me is convinced that if I don't make this happen now, I will lose her… that I must seize this chance at happiness, illusory though it might be.

She balls her hands as spots of darker color appear on her cheeks. "I thought you wanted this to work, for us to actually be happy in this marriage."

"I do… and we will be. But first, there has to be a marriage. And for that, there has to be a wedding—which is what's happening at five o'clock today."

"This afternoon?" Her voice jumps in pitch. "You realize how insane that sounds?"

I smile grimly. "Sanity is overrated, zaychik. What sane person is ever happy? In any case, you don't need to stress about the logistics. Everything's already been arranged."

For a few beats, she just stares at me, breathing shakily; then she pushes back her chair and launches to her feet. "What about what I want? What I need to accept this marriage?"

"Tell me what it is, and I'll do my best to make it happen—as long as it doesn't result in a delay." Rising to my feet as well, I step around the table and cup her delicately carved chin, tilting her face up to take in her mutinous expression. "Tell me, zaychik. What can I do to make you happy? What is it you need?"

She grips my wrist, her eyes dark with turbulent emotions. "I need you to not make me do this."

I smile and bend my head to kiss the fragile shell of her ear, my body tightening as I breathe in her wildflower scent. "No, zaychik," I murmur when I feel her shiver. "That is precisely what you need."

Someone as innocent as her will never embrace a man like me without worrying about how it compromises her society-imposed morals and feeling at least some form of guilt.

I meant what I said. In my own selfish way, I *am* doing her a favor. This way, she can pretend she doesn't want this, that she's embracing me against her will.

The delicate line of her throat ripples with a swallow, and she inhales raggedly, backing out of my hold. Her eyes are even darker as they meet mine, her delicate features tightly drawn.

"In that case," she says unsteadily, "I have two more conditions. If you can meet them, I will marry you at five o'clock today, no drug required."

Intrigued, I cock my head. "Go on."

"First, I want you to tell me what exactly happened with your father. And second..." Her voice wavers. "I need you to promise not to kill mine. I want Bransford to pay, but not that way."

30

CHLOE

Nikolai's jaw turns to stone, volcanic clouds gathering in his eyes. In a dangerously level voice, he says, "I can do the first, but not the second. Bransford is a threat to you for as long as he's alive."

"Not if he's been exposed and people know what he is. I can go public with my DNA results; with that kind of proof, the media will have to listen."

I don't know when the idea of this Faustian bargain with Nikolai came to me, at which point I decided that since there's no way to avoid losing the marriage battle, I will at least surrender on my own terms. These two matters—finding out the truth about Nikolai's past and getting him to leave Bransford alive—are equally important to me, and I need to use what little leverage I have.

Bransford has to pay for his crimes, but I don't want his blood on Nikolai's hands and, by extension, on my conscience.

"The media?" Nikolai's lips twist. "You do understand what that would entail, don't you, zaychik? They'll be on you like a flock of hungry seagulls. Every bit of your life will be dissected, your mother's death and everything about her past analyzed in nauseating detail. You'll never have a moment of peace again. And while the scandal will likely tank Bransford's political career, there's no guarantee he'll go to jail for your mother's rape; the statute of limitations might prevent that."

"He's also guilty of ordering her murder."

"Yes, but good luck proving that with the assassins out of the picture."

Dammit. He's right. In my haste to come up with an alternative to killing Bransford, I didn't consider that last part. I have no idea what Nikolai did with the assassins' bodies, but either way, dead men can't testify as to the identity of their employer. Worse yet, pointing the authorities to the assassins' graves—or even just disclosing the incident in the woods—could create all sorts of problems for Nikolai. The last thing I want is for him to be arrested for protecting me… or to have the media flock all over him, which they're bound to do if we are married.

With Slava needing to stay hidden from his mother's family, I can't go public with my relationship to Bransford. The very idea is a nonstarter.

Still, I'm not ready to give up. "What if it's not me? I bet there are women besides my mom he's done this to, other girls he's assaulted at some point. Men like that tend to have a certain MO, so maybe we can find his other victims and—"

"Find them how?" Nikolai's tone gentles. "I understand what you're trying to do, zaychik, believe me, but even if some victims were conveniently lurking in the wings, it could take us months or years to find them and persuade them to come forward. By that point, he might be President of the United States, and taking him down will require infinitely greater effort. In the meantime, he'll continue hunting you... and also potentially creating other victims. Have you considered that? If he does indeed have a taste for unwilling teenage girls, then every minute he's alive, he doesn't only pose a threat to *you*. By taking him out, I'll be doing the world a favor."

Ugh. I turn away, rubbing my forehead. He's right again, but I can't accept that assassination is the only answer. There has to be something else we can do. I'd even be down with something shady, like blackmail or—

I spin around. "What if we didn't need to find them, the victims? What if we created them ourselves?"

Nikolai's dark eyebrows arch, his gaze lighting with a hint of amusement. "Are you suggesting paying some women to accuse him? Manufacturing false evidence? You don't find that unethical and wrong?"

"Not when the alternative is killing him. Besides, it's not like he's innocent."

"No," Nikolai says flatly, all humor gone. "He's not."

"So is that a yes?" Stepping closer, I gaze up at him hopefully. "Can we try this, see if it works out?"

He brushes a strand of hair off my face. "No, zaychik. False accusations won't work."

"But—"

"If we're going to create victims, they have to be real... or at least the evidence needs to be."

I blink up at him. "What do you mean?"

"I have one idea, but I need to run it by Valery."

A lightbulb goes off in my head. "Are you talking about Masha?" Whatever age his brother's "asset" really is, she could easily pass for a teenager, so if we got her close to Bransford—

"Exactly." Nikolai walks over to his desk and opens his laptop. I watch with bated breath as his long fingers dance over the keyboard, firing off some message.

Maybe I'm counting the chickens before they've hatched, but it seems like he's on board. He thinks this idea has merit.

"All right," he says after a minute, closing the laptop. "Let's see what Valery thinks, and if Masha would be open to altering the current plan."

"Which is what?"

The curve of his lips holds a hint of irony. "Let's just say the first part of it isn't too different."

I blink. "She was going to seduce him?"

"Just enough to get him to have a meal with her."

Where she'd give him whatever is supposed to result in that fatal "heart defect."

I do my best to keep my tone even. "Okay, so then it

should be easy, right? Maybe she could seduce him just a bit further and take some compromising pictures. Or—"

"Don't worry about the specifics, zaychik." He walks around his desk and stops in front of me, his eyes the darkest shade of amber as he tucks another strand of hair behind my ear. "Your only job today is to choose the dress."

31

CHLOE

Nikolai was wrong. It's not just the dress. After lunch, a pack of fashionably dressed people invades the house, bringing with them everything from a department store's worth of shoes to hair styling tools. Alina directs them all with brisk efficiency, and before I know it, I'm washed, waxed, plucked, perfumed, styled, and made up to the nth degree.

By the time we actually get to the dress selection, I feel like I've been through a mild form of torture, and everything takes on a surreal vibe. My wedding day—just those words are like something out of a book or movie, a fictional tale featuring a girl who can't possibly be me.

Marriage was never my dream. Not the way it is for some women. It was just something I figured would happen in the future if I met the right person and all the stars aligned. Say, if we were both doing well in our careers, liked each other's families and friends, and had tons of interests in common. Also, if we were of a proper age, which to me is late twenties at the earliest.

I never imagined myself getting married at twenty-three—and certainly not to a Russian mobster. Because that's what Nikolai is, whether or not he accepts that label. The Molotovs cloak themselves in high-society trappings, but at the core, Nikolai and his brothers are savages, as violent and amoral as any cartel leaders.

The thought of joining my life to such a man should terrify me, but I feel numb instead, so overwhelmed that everything feels like white noise. Less than two months ago, my only worry was finding a job post-graduation, and then my life went so far off the rails that none of what's happening today seems all that scary or strange.

Or maybe that's a lie I'm telling myself to get through this day. Maybe the enormity of this will hit me later, when I'm better equipped to process it.

The dresses presented to me are stunning, each one a work of art. There are fourteen total, and Alina makes me try all of them on before declaring that number seven—an ivory mermaid-tail number with an off-the-shoulders neckline—is the one.

I don't know if I agree with her—to me, all the dresses are straight out of a fairy tale—but I'm grateful to have her guidance. Whatever she may think of today's proceedings, she's taken charge, running interference with the invading pack on my behalf.

Thanks to her, I don't have to make any tricky decisions, such as what color eyeshadow to apply; she tells them what to do with me and how, and I just have to sit there like a zombie doll while they do all the things, including dabbing some concealer on my neck to hide the hickey and other marks of Nikolai's lovemaking.

It's almost five by the time I'm fully ready, and as the pack leaves, two new cars arrive. One contains two people with fancy-looking camera equipment, while the other belongs to a slim middle-aged man dressed in a black suit with a white collar.

"Nondenominational priest," Alina explains, coming to stand next to me by the window. "He'll conduct the ceremony."

Ceremony, right. My heart gives a panicked thump, some of my numbness fading. This *is* real. It's happening. An actual wedding, with a fancy dress, a priest, and a photographer/videographer team. I have no idea how Nikolai managed to pull this off on such short notice, but I guess when you have enough cash to throw around, you don't need to worry about such plebeian concerns as booking highly sought-after professionals in advance.

"Where's Slava?" I ask, belatedly realizing I haven't seen the boy since our lessons in the morning. "Will he be at the ceremony as well?"

Alina nods. "Lyudmila's been keeping him out of sight, since the fewer people who know of his presence here, the better. But Nikolai does want him at the wedding and in the pictures, so he's taken the appropriate precautions with the priest and the photographer team."

"Precautions? As in, some kind of non-disclosure agreement? Wait, on second thought, I don't want to know."

She flashes me a dazzling grin. "Smart of you. But yes, an NDA is part of it, I believe. Along with some stronger measures."

My heart gives another thump, then launches into an all-out gallop. The reality is descending on me, fast, and with it, a sense of panic.

What am I doing? Why did I agree to this? How do I know Nikolai will hold up his side of the bargain? He still hasn't told me what happened with his father—though to be fair, with all the wedding preparations, we haven't had much time to talk. Which is a problem in and of itself. Everything is happening way too fast, all the decisions out of my hands, all the implications huge. For one thing, it's dawning on me that by marrying Nikolai, I'm not just gaining a husband, but also a son.

I'm going to be a stepmom to a four-year-old.

I must look a little wild-eyed because Alina reaches over to squeeze my hands. "Breathe. It's going to be okay. Just take it one minute at a time."

That's good advice. That's what Mom always told me: just focus on the next step, the next thing that needs to happen. Nobody has a crystal ball when it comes to the distant future, so it's pointless to think too far ahead. In any case, becoming Slava's stepmom is the least scary part of this venture, as I already love the boy and can't imagine not having him in my life.

I take a deep breath to settle my frantic heartbeat. "Thanks. We should probably head down before Nikolai comes looking for us." Stepping back, I give her sea-colored gown a swift once-over. "You look amazing, by the way."

Alina's grin returns. "Me? You're the gorgeous bride."

That may be the case, but she outshines me, as always. On a regular day, Nikolai's sister could pass for a starlet walking the red carpet, but when she puts in extra effort with her hair and makeup, as she has today, her beauty is almost unreal. If I saw a picture of her like this, I'd be sure it was Photoshopped to death, perfected with all sorts of filters. Yet here she is, standing next to me, as real as can be.

"Do you have anyone back in Russia?" I ask on impulse. "A boyfriend or anything like that?"

Despite our growing friendship, Alina's been as closemouthed on that topic as on the subject of her family, and I can't help but wonder why. I've told her all about my ex-boyfriends, but she's never reciprocated with such stories of her own.

If I didn't know better, I'd think she hasn't dated much.

"A boyfriend?" Her peal of laughter sounds forced. "No. There's no one like that."

And we're back to square one.

"Why not?" I ask, unable to leave it alone. Focusing on Alina's love life is vastly preferable to dwelling on where mine is heading. "Surely—"

"We should go downstairs," she says, turning away. "Let's go before we're late."

32

NIKOLAI

"SLAVOCHKA..." I CROUCH IN FRONT OF MY SON. "I HAVE to talk to you about something."

He stares at me unblinkingly, unease evident in his expression. He couldn't have missed all the people going in and out of the house, and I know he's been wondering about what's going on. Lyudmila told me he's been peppering her with questions all afternoon—questions she's held off answering, figuring I should be the one to break the news to him.

"It's nothing bad," I say when he remains silent. "In fact, it's something really great. Remember when I promised you that Chloe is going to stay with us forever?"

He nods warily.

"Well, that's what today is all about." I smile broadly. "We're getting married. Chloe is going to be not just your tutor, but your new mom."

His eyes go wide, and his small chin quivers. "My mom?"

"Technically, stepmom, but I'm sure Chloe would like it if you came to think of her as your mom over time."

I expect Slava to react with joy, since he absolutely adores Chloe. Instead, his chin quivers harder, and shiny tears pool in his eyes. "Does that mean—" His childish voice cracks. "Does that mean she'll die?"

Fuck. This again. I feel like someone smashed my chest with a hammer.

If Ksenia weren't already dead, I'd kill her for dying in that car crash and instilling this fear in our son.

I grip his arms tightly. "No, Slavochka. She won't. In fact, I'm marrying her to ensure nothing bad ever happens to her. She'll be safe here with us."

The chin quivering stops, even as drops of moisture cling to his lower eyelashes, making them sparkle. "You promise?"

"I promise."

"She'll always stay with us?"

"Always." Or at least as long as there's breath in my body—but I'm not going to say that, lest he starts worrying about me dying as well.

He rewards me with a beaming smile, and the hammer hits my chest again, the pain reverberating deep. Only it's a different pain this time, one I've learned to welcome. It's hard to verbalize the way my son makes me feel; all I know is I can no longer imagine a life without him, without these powerful emotions that oftentimes feel like they're tearing me apart.

Over the past two weeks, the tentative rapport we've established thanks to Chloe has deepened, our relationship changing to something I never thought I'd have… something that makes me wonder if another child, one with Chloe, would be so bad after all.

But no. I promised it would be her decision—and it has to be, if our child is to have any chance at overcoming the Molotov curse. I don't want him raised by a mother who resents his very existence and tells him that everything he is disgusts her, that evil is a part of him and always will be.

I don't want him to end up like my father.

Pushing that grim thought away, I smile back at Slava. "Let's get you dressed and ready. It's almost time for the wedding."

Standing up, I extend my hand to him, and as his small fingers close trustingly around my palm, I feel more certain than ever that I'm doing the right thing… for myself, for Chloe, and for my son.

33

CHLOE

We take our vows in the glass-walled terrace overlooking the ravine, where the mountain vistas provide an Instagram-worthy backdrop and the late-afternoon sun casts everything in a warm, golden light.

To an outsider, it would look like the most picture-perfect tiny wedding, right down to the music piping in through the ceiling speakers and the adorable tuxedo-clad child beaming in excitement to our right.

"Do you, Chloe Emmons, take Nikolai Molotov... your lawfully wedded husband... and to hold..." The priest's words fade in and out, like a faulty radio broadcast, the white noise effect returning to create a constant hum in my ears. I'm vaguely aware of Alina standing next to me, unofficially playing the maid of honor, and of Pavel's bear-like frame next to Nikolai. Is he his best man? Is that even a thing in Russia?

"I do," I say when I realize the priest is silent and has

been for a while. Nikolai has already said his part, so it's just down to me.

Lyudmila, who's holding Slava's hand, says something to the boy in Russian as the priest smiles and says, "Now exchange the rings."

We have rings?

Sure enough, Nikolai's strong fingers are already gripping my right wrist. Turning my hand palm up, he places a plain gold band in the middle of it, then picks up my left hand and slides a delicate, diamond-encrusted gold circle onto my ring finger.

Huh. I guess we have rings.

Clumsily, I work the plain band onto Nikolai's ring finger and look up. His eyes match the color of the precious metal on his hand, the scorching heat in them chasing away the white noise in my ears and bringing the proceedings into stark relief.

Holy fuck.

We just got married.

The man in front of me is now *my husband.*

"Congratulations. You may kiss the bride," the priest says, and my heart lurches into overdrive as Nikolai tilts my face up and bends his head, a darkly satisfied smile playing on his lips as they descend on mine.

It's a brief, almost platonic kiss, but there's no mistaking the raw possessiveness in it, or in the way he clasps my hand afterward as he turns to face the flood of applause and congratulations coming our way. Even as everybody hugs us, he holds on to me, refusing to let go.

Finally, the adults back off, and Nikolai kneels in front of Slava, my hand still firmly in his grasp.

"Slavochka…" His tone is solemn, his English words carefully enunciated. "We're a family now. Chloe is my wife—and your new mom."

Okay, whoa. I was not expecting this. Shouldn't we be easing into this? I don't want Slava to resent me for taking his dead mother's place. Sure, I'm technically his stepmom, but that doesn't mean he can't continue to think of me as Chloe for now, and later, when the timing's right, we can—

My thoughts come to a screeching halt as Slava gives me the biggest, brightest grin and throws his short arms around my skirt, hugging my legs with all his strength.

"Mama Chloe," he exclaims, looking up at me with an even bigger grin, and it's all I can do to hide my shock at his easy acceptance of this change in our dynamic. Where's the resentment? The wariness at the sudden change in his life? Not that I'm not happy he's so on board. Nikolai must've talked to him at some point today, warned him about what's going to happen. Still, I would've expected at least a short adjustment period. Unless of course—

I stop myself. None of that is important right now. Framing Slava's upturned face with my palm, I give him the brightest smile I can muster. "Yes, darling.

We're a family now. You can call me Mama or anything else you want."

As jarring as it is to suddenly find myself in the role of a parent, I have a feeling Slava is going to be the least complicated part of this marriage, and not just because I feel zero shame in admitting that the child already has my heart.

When I glance over at Nikolai, his expression is warmly approving. Smiling, he brings the hand he's holding to his lips and kisses my knuckles one by one, sending tingles down my spine and making Slava giggle.

"Mama Chloe," he repeats excitedly and bounces over to Alina, chattering at her in Russian.

"Congratulations again," she says as I catch her gaze. Quietly, she adds, "I'm glad to have you as my sister."

Sister. Right. Because that's what it means, to marry. One gains not just a husband, but a family. Like a son, a sister, two brothers, and however many cousins… all the siblings and relatives I never had.

For the first time, I comprehend just how much my life is changing.

I'm no longer an orphan, making my way alone in the world.

The realization is still reverberating through me as the photographer shepherds us outside to take a million pictures on the cliffside, where the summer breeze kisses our faces with pine-scented coolness.

Not an orphan.

Not an only child of a single mother who had no family of her own.

How long have I secretly wished for something like this? In my imagination, it was my father who would come into my life and introduce me to all the cousins, aunts, and uncles I never knew I had, but who turn out to be wonderful. Now, knowing what I know about Bransford, I can't imagine it. Just the thought of meeting someone related to the man who's trying to kill me is revolting. Thank God he has no other biological children—at least none the media is aware of. From what little I've allowed myself to read about him, I know he's a widower who recently remarried. His first wife battled some rare form of cancer for a decade before passing away a few years back, and his new wife has two young children from her prior marriage—a girl and a boy he regularly parades in front of the cameras, playing the role of a wholesome, all-American husband and father to perfection.

If only they knew.

Lost in thought, I obey the photographer's instructions on autopilot, and the next time I look around, the sun is setting behind the mountain peaks, bathing everything in a reddish-orange glow.

"That should be enough," Nikolai says, and we return to the house, where the gourmet spread on the dining table puts Alina's birthday celebration to shame.

There's everything from seafood to traditional Russian dishes to a huge variety of sushi and international delicacies like escargot.

They must've had most of this flown in; there's no way Pavel had time to make even a fraction of what's in front of us.

My stomach emits a growl, and I suddenly realize I'm ravenous. All that picture-taking must've been more energy intensive than it seemed. Or maybe it's the stress. Either way, as soon as we sit down and Pavel makes the first toast to our health, I load my plate with five different types of caviar sandwiches, followed by blintzes, puff pastries, an enormous variety of pickled fruits and vegetables, lobster tails, cured meats, gourmet cheeses, and salads of every kind. Everything is as delicious as it looks, and my dress is bursting at the seams by the time I finally pause to take a breath.

Looking up from my plate, I catch Nikolai watching me with an indulgent smile.

"What?" I ask self-consciously, putting down my fork.

"Nothing. I just enjoy seeing you eat."

More like seeing me pig out. My ears burn, but I grab another lobster tail. This food is just too freaking good, and if there's anything I've learned during my month on the run, it's not to take good food—or any food—for granted.

Two toasts later, however, I have to admit defeat. There's no way I can eat anything else, and the main course isn't even out yet. To distract myself from the overstuffed feeling, I look over at Nikolai, who's explaining something to Pavel in Russian.

I wait for him to finish, and when he glances at me, I say, "Your brothers… Have you told them about the wedding?" It's just occurred to me that I haven't yet met my new brothers-in-law, and they may have no clue that I'm now part of the family.

Nikolai gestures toward the videographer, who's discreetly circling around the table with his camera. "Valery and Konstantin are getting the live feed, and they'll videocall in a bit to congratulate us."

Of course. He's thought of everything. Why am I even surprised? Organizing a wedding in a matter of hours must be child's play compared to planning a high-profile assassination. Not that the latter is happening any longer—at least if Nikolai keeps his word.

With effort, I refocus on the celebration, which reminds me a lot of Alina's birthday, only with all the toasts directed at me and Nikolai. The majority of them are given by Pavel and Lyudmila, who seem determined to outdo each other with well wishes, but Alina raises her glass a couple of times too, first to wish us a long and happy marriage and then to toast to me as "the sister she's always wished to have."

She's had at least four shots of vodka by this point, I know, but her words still touch me, tugging at that small, secret part of me that's always wanted a sister too.

Maybe being a Molotov won't be so bad. Gaining a family—even a mafia family—might be worth it.

My tentative enthusiasm lasts through the main course and dessert, fueled by several glasses of wine and two shots of vodka. Everyone around me is happily buzzed as well, with the exception of Slava and Nikolai.

Like at Alina's birthday, I get the sense that alcohol only sharpens my new husband's faculties, that vodka is more like Red Bull or coffee for him. Or maybe it's simply that it strips away some of his polished, elegant façade, the one he uses to veil the potent force of his personality, that dark intensity that simmers within him and seeks to bend everything and everyone to his will.

To bend *me,* molding me into what he wants me to be.

His wife. His possession. His in every way… because the ring on my finger is a cage, one from which there'll be no escape.

The realization should frighten me—and normally it would—but alcohol doesn't act like Red Bull for me. Instead, it paints my world in warm, blurry shades, like the watercolor of a sunset—which is why I don't object when Nikolai pulls me onto his lap, where he feeds me chocolate-covered strawberries by hand while we talk to his brothers on a laptop Pavel brings to the table.

Konstantin calls in first, his lean face so reminiscent of Nikolai's my heart skips a beat when it first appears on the screen. Upon closer examination, however, the differences become apparent. Konstantin's nose is slightly larger and more hooked, his strong chin boasts a cleft, and his eyes are set deeper within their sockets, their striking color hidden behind his black-rimmed glasses. More importantly, his lips lack the cynical, wicked curve of Nikolai's, though they're just as beautiful in their own austere way.

For some reason, it's easy to picture Nikolai's older brother as a warrior monk, transcribing ancient scrolls by hand in between decimating hordes of invading barbarians.

"Congratulations on your wedding," he tells us. His voice is deep, like Nikolai's, his accent perfectly American. I wonder if he also studied here in the States. "I'm happy for you both." His gaze homes in on me. "Welcome to the family, Chloe."

"Thank you. It's so nice to meet you."

We exchange a few more pleasantries as Nikolai feeds me the strawberries, his arm looped possessively around my ribcage, and it's not until Konstantin hangs up that I realize he didn't react in any way to the sight of me being held on his brother's lap and fed like a child. There was no teasing smile, nothing to indicate he'd even been aware of it.

It's as if we've just spoken to an AI instead of a human being—which, given what I've heard about Konstantin's IQ and tech genius, is not out of the realm of possibilities.

Valery is up next, and the vibe I get from him is completely different. If possible, Nikolai's younger brother looks even more like his twin—or rather, his clone, given the four-year age gap between them. But that's where the similarities end. There's something cold and calculated about Valery. The smile on his sensual lips doesn't quite reach his eyes, which scan my face with an unsettling lack of emotion.

A puppet master—that's what he reminds me of, I realize as he congratulates us in a cool, even tone, his deep voice as unaccented as his brothers'.

As with Konstantin, our call with him is short, just a simple meet-and-greet. At the end of it, I have no idea what he thinks of me or our hasty wedding—or anything else for that matter.

"Your brothers are... interesting," I tell Nikolai when we disconnect. "Were you close growing up?"

He brings another strawberry to my lips. "Not exactly." Before I can ask him to elaborate, he pushes the sweet berry into my mouth, then picks up a glass of champagne and hands it to me.

I swallow the berry and take a sip of the fizzy, slightly sweet drink as Nikolai picks up another glass of champagne and waits until everyone's eyes are on us.

"To my beautiful bride," he says, pinning me with his intense tiger stare. "Zaychik... I couldn't be happier to have you in my life, and I will do everything in my power to ensure *your* happiness."

And again, I hear the unspoken "even if you object."

34

NIKOLAI

Two more toasts from Pavel and Lyudmila, and the dinner is over. Sweeping Chloe into my arms, I carry her upstairs to my bedroom.

No, *our* bedroom. Now that she's my wife, she's going to be sleeping in my arms every night.

My heart thuds heavily as I push open the door with my shoulder and carry her inside, where I carefully set her on her feet in front of the bed. She sways slightly and giggles; clearly, all that wine and champagne has gone to her head.

My head is clouded as well, but not from alcohol. It's lust that tangles my thoughts and fills my veins with slow-moving lava. The lengthy celebration was another test of my self-control, one I barely passed.

I wanted to grab Chloe and carry her off to bed right after we said our vows, to seal our bond in the most basic way possible. The only reason I resisted was for the memories.

When we're old and gray, I want to look back at the pictures and videos and recall every detail of this day.

Chloe sways again, blinking up at me owlishly, and I grip her shoulders to prevent her from falling. Then, ignoring the hunger coiling inside me, I look at her, imprinting every feature, every eyelash on my mind. Because the pictures and videos won't be enough. I want to remember all the sensations, from the silky warmth of her skin to the champagne-and-strawberries sweetness of her breath.

My bride.

My wife.

No two words have ever felt so right, so satisfying.

She's especially beautiful today, in this white, ethereal gown that makes my hands itch to rip it off her, baring more of her gorgeous, glowing skin. Her gold-streaked hair is arranged in an artful updo, her plump lips tinted with a rich berry color, her brown eyes made even bigger and softer with smoky makeup. Yet all I can think about is how much I want to see her with her face bare and puffy from sleep, her hair tangled from my fingers.

I want to watch her wake up in my embrace tomorrow morning, and every morning for the rest of our lives.

Ignoring the desire scorching my insides, I cup her cheek and bend my head, dragging her fresh, crisp scent into my lungs as I kiss the tender shell of her ear. As hungry as I am for her, tonight I will be gentle, making up for my ferocity last night.

No matter what it costs me, I will make our wedding night everything my zaychik's ever dreamed of.

35

CHLOE

I EXPECT NIKOLAI TO FALL UPON ME AS SAVAGELY AS usual, but he's excruciatingly tender, slowly unbuttoning the dress and pressing soft, warm kisses to my neck and throat until all the anticipatory tension drains out of my body, leaving warm lassitude in its wake. By the time I'm naked, my very bones feel as if they've melted, even as a different type of tension gathers low in my core, my body heating from the inside out.

Laying me down on the mattress, he steps back to disrobe himself, and I watch with a quickening heartbeat as he removes his black tuxedo jacket and bow tie. Underneath, he's wearing a silver vest over a crisp white shirt, both hugging his muscular, broad-shouldered torso in a way that leaves no doubt they were custom made for him.

Swiftly, he divests himself of both items, followed by his pants and briefs. Unlike with my dress, there's a jerky, impatient quality to his movements that makes me realize he's not nearly as in control as he seems. His erection, hard and massive, curves up toward his ridged stomach, betraying his hunger for me.

Nonetheless, when he climbs onto the bed, he's just as careful and tender, picking up one foot of mine to press small kisses to the top of the arch before moving higher up my leg. My breath hitches as his mouth approaches the V between my thighs, but he skips over it, instead kissing and caressing my lower belly, then my heaving ribcage and my breasts.

The softly lit room spins around me, the ceiling turning blurry in my vision as he latches onto my left nipple, laving it lovingly with his tongue before switching his attention to the other breast as I moan, my hands falling onto the cool silk of his hair. It's the alcohol, I know, but I feel like I'm floating in space, anchored only by the wet warmth of his mouth on my breasts and the gentle stroking of his callused hands over my burning skin.

Our wedding night.

It feels as surreal as it sounds.

My eyes drift shut as Nikolai's lips move higher, kissing my collarbone and my neck before claiming my lips in a deep, sweetly cajoling kiss. It's like a drug, that kiss, an aphrodisiac of the most potent kind. His sensual scent fills my nostrils, mixing with the faint aroma of vodka on his breath, and my arousal grows as his tongue strokes and caresses the recesses of my mouth, feasting on me with tender skill.

Still kissing me, he slips his hand between our bodies to find my aching clit, and I moan into his mouth as his fingers press on just the right spot, the one that intensifies the ache, adding to the tension growing inside me. A tension that swiftly turns unbearable as his fingers embark on a maddeningly uneven rubbing rhythm while his lips return to my neck, where the damp warmth of his breath sends pleasure chills down my arm.

I'm so turned on I may explode, yet the orgasm is still somehow out of reach.

Panting, I buck against his hand, desperate for a smoother, harder rhythm, and his teeth graze over my earlobe in warning. "No, zaychik," he whispers, and I feel the wicked curve of his mouth against my throat. "You're not ready yet."

Not ready? I'm ready to beg, plead, and sell my firstborn. With each light, circling stroke of his fingers, I get ever closer to the edge, but I can't go over it, no matter how hard I try.

"Please…" I shimmy my hips in desperation, my hands fisting in his hair. "Please, I need…"

He leisurely licks the underside of my ear. "What? What do you need?"

"To come," I gasp, bucking against his hand again. "Please, Nikolai, I need to come."

"Wrong answer." His fingers stop moving altogether. Lightly, he bites my earlobe and lifts his head, his eyes gleaming darkly. "Tell me the truth, zaychik. What do you need?"

"You," I whisper, staring up at him. "I need you."

And it's true. I can't imagine being anywhere else, with anyone else, ever. I need him not just for this orgasm but for him, for everything he is, good and bad, sublime and terrifying.

It must be the right answer because he kisses me again and his fingers return to my clit, bringing me back to the edge, to that elusive, maddening cusp of ecstasy. But sadist that he is, he keeps me at that peak, prolonging the exquisite torment until I'm panting and clawing at his back. Then and only then, when I'm ready to scream in frustration, he lets me go over.

The surge of pleasure is so intense it's like an endorphin bomb exploding in my brain. Every nerve ending in my body lights up with the potent force of it, my vision cutting in and out as my inner muscles spasm. The sensations are so overwhelming I lose myself in them, and by the time I come down to earth, he's already pushing into me, his thick cock forcing apart my tender tissues. His face is taut, his jaw clenched from the strain of holding back, and though he's still being careful and gentle, I'm so sore from last night I can't help wincing.

He stops, letting me adjust, distracting me with more of those deep, sweetly drugging kisses, and when I'm a quivering heap of need, my body wet and pliant, he begins thrusting. His pace is slow at first, controlled, but when I wrap my legs around his muscled ass, pulling him deeper into me, his control snaps and he takes me with all the driving power of his hard body.

I come again, screaming his name as he shudders over me, and it's not until he withdraws some minutes later that I realize he's kept his word and worn a condom. A condom he disposes of before carrying me off to the bathroom, where he deposits me into an already-prepared bath.

"Thank you," I murmur, meeting his gaze as he joins me in the warm, bubble-covered water, and he smiles, the look in his tiger eyes so achingly tender my heart squeezes in my chest.

"For what, zaychik?"

For you. It takes everything to hold back those words, words that are far too close to an admission of my feelings. Instead, I lay my palm along the hard contour of his jaw and plant my lips on his, expressing with my body what I don't dare say out loud.

Not yet, at least.

36

CHLOE

I WAKE UP STILL FEELING THAT WARM GLOW, A HIGH THAT intensifies when I open my eyes and find him lying propped up on his elbow next to me, watching me with a tenderly possessive smile.

"Good morning," I murmur, pushing my hair off my face and fighting the urge to rub the sleep out of my eyes.

How long has he been awake and staring at me like this? More importantly, how much of a hot mess am I this morning? I did my best to remove my makeup in the bath last night, but I'm sure traces of eyeshadow and mascara are still smeared around my eyes, raccoon style, and my breath is not the freshest after all that alcohol.

He must not mind that because he leans forward and kisses me with such hunger I'm certain he's going to fuck me right then and there. But he pulls back and smiles at me instead, cradling my face in his big palm. "Good morning, zaychik. How are you feeling?"

Like this marriage thing might not be so bad. "I'm good," I say, smiling back. It's only been a day, but it's already hard to recall why I got so freaked out when he proposed. Like Alina said, this is pretty much the dream nurtured by every fairy tale: a gorgeous, wealthy husband who's crazy about you.

Granted, Nikolai is closer to the Prince of Darkness than Prince Charming, but pretty much all of the terrible things he's done—or planned to do—were to protect me.

Except the bit with his father.

The unsettling words whisper through my mind, but I push them away. I don't want to think about that this morning. I'm sure there's a reasonable explanation for everything, and soon, I'll learn what it is.

For now, I want to enjoy the first married morning of my life with the man who's looking at me like I'm made of chocolate and starlight.

And enjoy it I do. We shower together, an activity that results in a prolonged, steamy—literally, because the stall is steamed up—lovemaking session, during which Nikolai eats me out as if I were his breakfast and makes me come three times in a row before pinning me against the glass and fucking me so hard I scream his name.

I guess he's decided that taking me just once last night was enough to heal my soreness—and he's right. Of course I'm a little sore after *this* session but so satisfied it's worth it.

Afterward, Nikolai decides we need actual breakfast, so Lyudmila brings us a tray of fruit and leftovers from last night, along with tea and coffee, and we feed each other in bed. Or rather, Nikolai feeds me and I try to reciprocate—only he grabs the fork from me and kisses me until I forget all about what I was going to do. Some honey comes into play as well, and next thing I know, I need another shower and am decidedly more sore.

By the time we finally emerge from our bedroom, it's almost lunchtime, and as we head toward the stairs, Slava runs out of his room, Lyudmila on his heels.

"Mama Chloe!" His tiger-cub eyes are shining as he throws his short arms around my legs and squeezes tight before switching his attentions to Nikolai. Hugging his legs, he looks up at him. "Papa! I miss you and Chloe!"

At the look on Nikolai's face, I melt. There's no other word for it. Instead of a muscle with life-sustaining functions, my heart turns into a gooey puddle, and the rest of me follows suit.

Bending down, Nikolai picks up his son and perches him on his hip with natural-seeming ease. "Slavochka..." His voice is strained as he gazes into the child's face. "We've missed you too."

Lyudmila's eyes meet mine, and I see my feelings

reflected on her normally impassive face. Clearing her throat, she says with a thicker-than-usual accent, "I go help Pavel, okay?" and hurries downstairs.

We follow her at a leisurely pace, with Nikolai carrying Slava on his hip as if he were a toddler. The boy seems glad to be there, though, and I can't blame him.

He's missed out on this for the first four years of his life.

As we join Alina at the table, I can't stop smiling—and she notices.

"Fun night?" she whispers to me slyly while Nikolai is busy filling Slava's plate.

I nod, flushing, and she laughs, causing Slava and Nikolai to look at us askance.

My joyous mood must be infectious—that or everyone is still in a celebratory mode—because the lunch proceeds without any of the usual tension between the siblings. Instead, Nikolai and Alina team up to tell me amusing stories about Russia, everything from how Americans are viewed over there to their family's tradition of wintertime dips in frozen lakes.

"That's horrible," I exclaim when Alina describes how she almost lost a toe to frostbite by walking barefoot across the ice when she was seven. "What were your parents thinking?"

I realize my mistake as soon as the words are out—the last thing I want is to remind them about their father—but to my relief, Alina doesn't bat an eye. "Oh, that wasn't our parents' idea. Our grandmother was the one who believed that cold exposure is good for the body and the soul. And you know what? The latest science confirms it. Same goes for saunas, another Russian staple. They're apparently exercise mimetics, and heat shock proteins released during those sweating sessions do everything from improving heart health to preventing cancer. So if you want to live a long, healthy life, you should partake in both ice baths and saunas—and ideally, both together."

"No, thank you," I say with a shudder, but Nikolai laughs and says that he'll have me try out the extreme regimen this winter.

"We'll get you addicted to it, I promise," he adds with a smile as I process the startling realization that I'll be with him this winter—and every other winter in the foreseeable future.

Because that's what marriage means.

We're together for the rest of our lives.

An echo of my earlier panic returns, but I suppress it. I'm not letting my irrational fears cast a shadow over what promises to be a beautiful day together—hopefully, the first of many.

After all, happiness is a choice, and I'd much rather be happy in this forced marriage.

37

CHLOE

The next few days pass in a similarly idyllic manner. Though we haven't gone anywhere, it feels like we're on our honeymoon. We make love multiple times a night (and oftentimes day), sleep in late, eat breakfast in bed, and go on long walks and hikes, both by ourselves and with Slava. One time, Alina joins us as well, and the four of us end up swimming in a nearby lake, where all three Russians make fun of my reluctance to get into the chilly, spring-fed water.

It turns out Slava is as comfortable being cold as the adults, making me the only wimp.

I do end up swimming, though, and as I'm shivering afterward, Nikolai warms me by rubbing me all over with his big, rough palms. If we were alone, he would've undoubtedly done more, but alas, even he draws the line at making love in front of his young son and sister.

That's about the only act where he does draw the

line, though. We engage in PDA all the time. My husband has zero shame when it comes to kissing me, massaging my neck and shoulders, and pulling me onto his lap whenever the mood strikes. It's like I'm a pet he likes to cuddle. I can't say I hate it; in fact, I not-so-secretly revel in his attention.

It would be different if anyone in the household made fun of it or otherwise made me feel embarrassed. But no one does. Even Alina, with her occasional gentle teasing, takes it for granted that her brother can't keep his hands off me, so much so that I have to wonder if it's one of those legendary "Molotov men" traits.

I'd ask, but I'm afraid it might be too close to the topic I'm skirting, the answers I've been telling myself I want, yet can't bring myself to demand. It just feels so good not to think about the darkness in Nikolai and the terrifying things he's capable of. I haven't even inquired about Masha and the new plan to take down Bransford; each time I think about my biological father, my pulse shoots up and my stomach contracts into a hard, tight knot.

Tomorrow morning, I tell myself each evening. *I'll talk to Nikolai about this first thing in the morning.* But then in the morning, I wake up in his embrace, feeling warm and secure, worshipped and adored, and I can't bring myself to risk the peace, so I tell myself we'll talk in the evening.

I know something is bound to happen to puncture our happy bubble, but I'm reluctant for that something to be me.

We go on like that for three more weeks, during which I bask in the attention he lavishes on me, reveling in both his tenderness and his roughness. Both versions of Nikolai—the gentle lover and the fierce savage—thrill me, which is a good thing, because when it comes to my husband, I can never predict what I'm going to get. In the same night, he might worship my body as if I were made of crystal, and fuck me until I can barely walk the next day. At times, I get the sense that he wants even more, that one day, he might push me further, try to possess me even more completely, but that like me, he's reluctant to do anything to bring any strife and tension back into our life, ending this honeymoon of ours.

Instead, he showers me with gifts, everything from expensive jewelry to accessories and clothing. It seems as if a new dress, or pair of shoes, or scarf, or *something* appears in my closet daily. It's almost too much for me—many of the earrings and bracelets I now own cost more than some people's houses—but he insists that it gives him pleasure to buy me things, so I eventually stop objecting… because having those things gives me pleasure too.

I've never known true poverty, thanks to my mom working nonstop to support us, but I also can't recall a time in my life when I didn't have to count every penny and carefully budget for every expense. Most of my childhood clothes were bought second-hand,

and the only jewelry I owned was of the cheap costume kind. Now, my closet is like Saks Fifth Avenue on steroids, and though it may be shallow of me, I love it. Rich people know what they're doing when they buy all those luxuries—they really can enhance one's life.

Also enhancing my life are the Russian lessons Nikolai has started giving me—with Slava's help, of course. The child takes great delight in my inability to pronounce the Russian phrases he says so easily, while Nikolai delights in a completely different thing: making me say love and sex words to him in bed.

"Say, '*Ya hochu tebya*,'" he instructs me while keeping me on the edge of an orgasm. And when I obey, desperate for relief, he orders mercilessly, "Now say, '*Ya lyublyu tebya*.'"

So I do. I say whatever he wants me to, including phrases so dirty they make me flush all over when I later look them up. But dirty or clean, my knowledge of Russian is growing by the day, which greatly amuses Alina and Lyudmila—the latter of whom finds my pronunciations downright comical.

"You so American," Pavel's wife says, laughing, as I attempt to ask her for *zavtrak*—breakfast—in her native tongue. "Why you even try? Everyone here speak English, even me."

I'd take offense, but she's right. Even her English, imperfect as it is, is a thousand times better than my Russian. I've offered to give her some lessons to improve it further, but she hasn't taken me up on it so far—because she hopes to go back to Russia and not need it, according to Alina.

"She really misses Moscow," she tells me. "She's bored here, with nothing to do and no one to see."

I can sympathize with that. Despite all the modern luxury and natural beauty surrounding us, the compound is a prison of sorts, or to put a more positive spin on it, a retreat from the world. I, too, miss my friends, and often scour social media to catch glimpses of their post-graduation lives. I want to contact them so badly, to reply to all of their messages asking where I am, why I haven't posted on my profiles in months, but I don't dare do so in case that somehow leads Bransford to me, to this compound and my new family.

I can't put them in danger, not even to assuage my friends' worries about me.

I would especially feel terrible if I did anything to endanger Slava. With each passing day, my attachment to Nikolai's son grows, and I feel increasingly comfortable in the role of his mom. Instead of Alina or Lyudmila bathing him and putting him to bed, Nikolai and I frequently do so together nowadays, telling him stories about superheroes and reading from his favorite books until he falls asleep.

The three of us are becoming a real family, and the knowledge fills me with a gentle warmth, a contentment that shouldn't be possible with a dangerous, mercurial man like Nikolai.

Not that everything is perfect, of course. For one

thing, the two of us disagree when it comes to what a not-quite-five-year-old should be allowed to do. As it turns out, Nikolai and his brothers—and to a lesser extent, Alina—were latchkey kids, allowed and even encouraged to play outside on their own and overall be dangerously independent. So while I panic each time I see a steak knife in Slava's hand or find him climbing a tree higher than six feet, Nikolai is annoyingly calm about such things.

"Don't you care that he can fall and break every bone in his body?" I ask in frustration when we go on a hike and he lets Slava scamper up an old oak until his tiny figure is barely visible through the foliage. "Or worse, fall on his head and break his neck?"

"Of course I do." His golden eyes narrow at me dangerously. "You think I don't worry about all the terrible things that can befall him on any given day? The stairs he can tumble down, the illnesses he can catch, the poisonous berries he might find and eat? Sometimes it's all I can think about, so much so I'm convinced I'm going insane. But just as we can't be there to hold his hand each time he takes the stairs, we can't expect to be there for every tree he encounters or every knife that comes his way throughout his life. In fact, there's no guarantee we'll be there for him tomorrow. Life can be unpredictable and brutal, and the better prepared he is to face it, the higher the odds that he'll survive."

"But he's still a child. You have to teach him *how* to survive."

"I am teaching him—by letting him face as many of the dangers on his own as he can. Children his age aren't stupid; they've fallen enough to know that it hurts. He wouldn't climb that high if he didn't feel secure in his strength, and the only way to grow and test that strength is to challenge himself when it matters… when there is no rubber mat underneath. Besides," he adds when I'm about to start arguing, "I *am* keeping an eye on him. If he should start to fall, I'll catch him."

I shut up then, because odds are, he will. The man has the reflexes of a cat. The other day, I accidentally knocked a water glass off the table with my elbow, and Nikolai caught it in mid-air without pausing in the conversation. Another time, I tripped over one of Slava's LEGO pieces and would've faceplanted, but Nikolai had his arms around me before I hit the floor—though he was on the other side of the room a second earlier.

If I didn't know better, I'd think he was one of Slava's comic book superheroes—or more likely, supervillains.

That label fits him as well as anything.

Later that night, as we enter our bedroom, something occurs to me in regard to our earlier conversation.

"If you're so determined to nurture Slava's independence, why are you so determined to shield *me* from any and all danger?" I ask, sitting down on the bed to watch Nikolai remove his jacket and tie. We're still doing the formal attire at dinner, and I must admit I've grown to like it. Not only do I get to wear gorgeous dresses on a daily basis, but my husband is surreally handsome in those sharply tailored suits he favors.

It's like we alternate between two realms: the daytime one where we go hiking in the wilderness and get dirty, and the evening one where glamour and glitz reign supreme.

"Because you're not a child, and you weren't raised the way I'm raising Slava," Nikolai replies smoothly, undoing his cufflinks. "Your mom, as wonderful as she was, didn't equip you to face assassins, zaychik… or men like me."

I swallow hard, my blood heating up as he rakes his gaze over my still fully dressed body. Ever since our wedding, I've gotten better at reading Nikolai's sexual moods and understanding what kind of night I'm in for. And tonight promises to be one of our wilder ones, the ones when I'm never quite sure how far he'll go.

When I can sense the darkness in him, feel it rising close to the surface.

Not that I'm afraid of him. Not really. I know he won't hurt me, at least not in any damaging way. I just sometimes get the sense that what we have isn't quite enough for him, that his voracious hunger for me remains unsatisfied.

At times, it feels as if he wants to consume me, all of me, and nothing less will do.

He takes off his shirt, revealing beautifully defined muscles, and comes toward me, his movements once again reminding me of a big cat's smooth, lethally graceful prowl.

Maybe he *was* a tiger in another life.

Maybe I was his prey.

Instinctively, I scoot backward on the bed, and his lips take on a wicked curve. As always, he knows what I'm thinking and feeling—and he likes what I'm feeling now.

He likes making me just a bit nervous.

Moving with that same predatory deliberateness, he climbs onto the bed and over me, pushing me down flat before catching my wrists and pinning them above my head with one hand.

My mouth goes dry at the look in his eyes, at the dark intensity within them. I dampen my lips, and his gaze follows the path of my tongue, his face tightening. When his eyes meet mine again, they're filled with such scorching heat I feel like I could burn up on the spot. My heart hammers wildly, my skin flushing all over as he lowers his head and audibly inhales, as if hungry for the smell of my hair.

"Um, Nikolai..." I wriggle underneath him, my pulse surging higher as I feel the bulge pressing against my thighs. Even with the layers of his pants and my dress separating us, I can feel how hot and hard his erection is, how massive. I swallow again. "When you said 'men like me,' what did you mean, exactly?"

His lips brush my ear, the heat of his breath making me shiver as he whispers, "Oh, my sweet, curious zaychik… you're about to find out."

38

CHLOE

A shudder ripples through my body, and he lifts his head to look at me, a dark smile tilting up the corners of his lips. I can all but feel him drinking in my trepidation, sadistically prolonging the anticipation.

I try to move my hands, to twist out of his grip, but it's futile. His fingers are an iron shackle around my wrists, pinning them in place above my head. His smile deepens, the golden gleam in his eyes intensifying as I struggle, and I know that he enjoys this too, seeing me helpless in his grasp.

Dipping his head, he drags in another hungry inhale, then finally lets go of my wrists. Before I can let out a relieved breath, he flips me over onto my stomach and, holding me down with one big hand, pulls down the zipper of my dress. When it's open all the way to my tailbone, he runs a warm palm down my bare spine, the roughness of his calluses scratching my skin pleasantly.

"Have I ever told you how much I love your back?" The soft, dark timbre of his voice is soothing, yet unnerving. "So toned and graceful, like a ballerina's. My favorite part of you, though, is this ass." His palm curves over my cheek and squeezes lightly. "So tight and round and perfect… so fuckable."

My heart jumps again as he pulls me up to a sitting position and props my back against his chest, banding one powerful arm around my ribcage to hold me in place as he drags the dress down my torso. He's handling me like a human-sized doll, and there's something perversely erotic about that, something that appeals to a part of me that I try not to think about… the one that's not put off by the darkness in him but drawn to it.

I'm not wearing a bra, and as he pulls the dress down to my waist, my naked breasts pop free, spilling onto his forearm, my nipples already peaked and aching. A low growl rumbles in his chest, and he bends me back over his arm in that way he likes to do, the one that makes me feel like a human sacrifice, an offering to a fierce, primordial god.

His hot, wet mouth closes around my nipple, and I gasp, gripping his head as he bites down, sending fire streaking directly to my clit. My nerve endings riot in confusion, the pain and pleasure blending until I'm desperate for more. And he delivers more, repeating the treatment with my other breast, alternating between sucking on the nipple and using his teeth on it. By the time he lifts his head to meet my gaze, I'm panting, burning from arousal.

I need him. I need him so fucking much.

Forgetting all about my fears, I pull his head to mine, and our lips fuse in a hard, deeply carnal kiss, our tongues tangling as I respond to the violence of his need, matching him stroke for stroke, bite for bite. I don't care what he does to me tonight as long as I can have more of this dark, dizzying pleasure, more of what I crave.

We're both breathing raggedly by the time he breaks the kiss and lays me flat to work the dress down my hips. It refuses to come off easily, so he rips it at the seams, too impatient to care that he's ruining yet another pricey gown. And I don't care either, not with the tension building rapidly inside me, not when every part of me burns for him.

When I'm dressed in nothing but a thong, he flips me back onto my stomach and stuffs two pillows underneath my hips before working the scrap of fabric down my legs. Then he reaches over to the right, and I hear a drawer open.

My trepidation returns, briefly overruling my arousal. I strongly suspect I know what he intends to do, and I'm proven right when I glance over my shoulder and see the bottle of lube and a small butt plug in his hands. Still, my heart jackrabbits into my throat, my ribcage tightening around my lungs. "Nikolai, I…" I gulp in air. "I've never… that is—"

"Never been fucked in the ass?"

My face heats unbearably, his dirty words further knocking me off kilter. Somehow, I manage a small nod, and his lips curve with primal male satisfaction as he says softly, "Good," and drizzles cool lube between my ass cheeks.

I gasp, clenching instinctively as he presses the plug to my opening, and he pushes my head down on the bed. "Relax, zaychik." His voice is rough velvet and dark heat. "I promise you'll enjoy this."

I want to object—the one time my ex-boyfriend tried to put a finger in, I hated every second—but this is Nikolai, whose mastery over my body is frighteningly total. In his embrace, I lose all sense of self, much less what little sanity I still possess. So I keep quiet and do my best to breathe through my nose as the tapered, rubbery tip of the plug presses in, pushing past the tight ring of my sphincter.

Slowly, it slides in deeper, and I stifle my groan against the mattress, overwhelmed by the strange sensations. As that other time, there's an almost nauseating fullness, a feeling of being stretched and penetrated, invaded in an unnatural, uncomfortable way. But there's also something more, a peculiar type of pressure that makes my pulse soar and my insides tighten—a sensation that grows stronger as Nikolai leans over me, covering me with his big, hard body, enveloping me in his sensual male scent.

His breath warms my ear as he kisses the sensitive

crook of my neck, sending pleasure chills down my arm. At the same time, he wedges one hand underneath my stomach and finds my clit while beginning to slowly fuck me with the toy. Immediately, the pressure intensifies, transforming into an erotic tension, a dark, heated pleasure that collides with the discomfort and somehow grows from it. His fingers on my clit, the toy in my ass, his lips on my neck—it's sensory overload, a seesaw of pleasure and pain that rocks back and forth, each time cresting higher.

With a muffled cry, I come undone, shuddering and shaking, but he's not done with me. Pulling the toy out of my ass with a slick *pop,* he penetrates me first with one finger, then two together, the stinging stretch only bearable because of the evil magic his other hand is performing on my clit. It hurts, it burns, yet the pain once again alternates with potent pleasure, heightening it in some peculiar way. Panting, I orgasm again, my ass clamping down on his big, rough-edged fingers, my vision dappling with spots of black and white as a gasping cry escapes my throat.

Before I can recover, he pulls his fingers out of my still-spasming body, and I feel the broad, smooth head of his cock at my opening instead. I tense, my pulse skyrocketing anew, and he runs a reassuring hand down my spine.

"Breathe, zaychik. You can take me." The words are a soft, deep murmur, as comforting as the gentle petting of my back. Yet the moment he grips my hips and pushes against the tight ring of muscle, the seesaw tips all the way to pain, and I know he's wrong.

I can't do it.

He's way too big for me.

"Nikolai, please, st—" I gasp, the plea catching in my throat as my sphincter gives in under the pressure and the massive head of his cock pops in. All air whooshes out of my lungs, my vision going full black for a dizzying moment. He's so big and thick it feels as if I'm being split apart, and as he slowly works his cock deeper into me, I'm certain I'm going to faint.

But I don't. Instead, I feel every long, hard inch of him, experience every bit of the excruciatingly careful invasion. My stomach twists and churns, my skin turning clammy with cold sweat, yet I can't form the words to call a halt to this, my brain as overwhelmed as my body.

It doesn't help that he's leaning over me again, kissing my neck and murmuring soothing endearments into my ear, his smooth voice rough with need. Nor that his skilled fingers are once again toying with my clit, coaxing out sensations that can't—shouldn't—coexist with this type of pain. It's not pleasure, exactly, but something like it, a mix of agony and ecstasy that winds me up anew, wrenching a tortured climax from my body.

I do pass out then, at least for a moment, because the next thing I register is him gliding smoothly in and out of my ass, each thrust generating a sensation of its own, the seesaw once more rocking back and forth, building the powerfully erotic tension. My body floods with heat, my heart rampaging inside my ribcage, and as I come for the fourth time with a ragged scream, he groans and shudders over me, warm jets of cum bathing my sore insides.

Shaken and shattered, I lie there, too weak to move as he withdraws from me and leaves the bed, returning a minute later with a warm, wet towel. He cleans me off, then turns me over and scoops me up into his lap. I force open my heavy lids to find his tiger eyes on my face, studying me with his signature intensity.

Gently, reverently, he cups my cheek, his voice rough as he murmurs, "I'm never going to let you go, you know. Not even if you beg."

I hold his gaze. "I know."

"Do you hate me for that?"

I should. However nice this honeymoon has been, the truth is, he forced me into marriage, took away my freedom, my choices. In just about every way that matters, I'm his captive, at the mercy of his darker whims and passions. Yet the lie refuses to leave my lips. Instead, I tell him the truth. "I love you."

Because I do. As wrong as it is, I love this beautiful, terrifying, complicated man. I love him even as I fear his relentless obsession with me.

I know that in the bright light of tomorrow, I'll regret this confession, that I'll think it a mistake. Right now, though, in this softly lit room, with his strong arms around me and my body still pulsing with echoes of the agony and ecstasy he's put me through, it doesn't feel like a mistake—especially since the tender smile that blooms across his face is the most beautiful thing I've ever seen.

"And I love you, zaychik," he says softly. "I always will."

39

NIKOLAI

I WAKE UP WITH CHLOE'S SMALL BODY WRAPPED IN MY arms and my brain flush with happiness. The glowing, incandescent kind that feels as flickering and fleeting as the burning wick of a candle.

As I have for the past week since we admitted our feelings, I absorb the feel of her, the sensation of her warm skin pressing against mine, of her delicate curves molding against the hard planes of my body, of her breath fanning over my forearm. And as has been the case for the past week, I battle an urge to wake her and demand the words from her again, so I can hear her soft, husky voice telling me she loves me.

It's bad enough I force her to say it to me every night, each time I take her.

Burying my face in her hair, I breathe in her scent, the sweet freshness of flowers shaded with sleep-warmed feminine skin. And as I have for the past two months, I fight off a surge of gut-wrenching fear.

Fear that I'm going to lose her. That the wick will burn out, leaving nothing but ashes.

It's irrational, illogical, but I can't help it. I thought extracting the words from her would rein this fear in, letting me get through the day calm and secure in the knowledge that she's mine, but if anything, the worry has grown stronger, more pervasive. Sometimes it's all I can think about: how fragile this happiness is, how illusory.

After all, in the beginning, my mother also loved my father. Once upon a time, they'd known happiness as well.

I try not to think about that, about how everything went to pieces for them, but there are times when I look at Chloe and see my mother's face. Not bright and healthy, the way it'd been when I was a child, but drawn and pale, deeply unhappy—the look she'd worn in her final years.

Partially, it's that I still haven't told Chloe about what happened that winter night—and she hasn't asked. Despite imposing it as a condition for our wedding, she seems reluctant to hear the full story. I think it's because she's afraid of the truth, fearful of finding out just how horrible of a monster she married. So she skirts the topic, and so do I.

There's every chance she'll hate me for what I've done, that she'll look at me with terror and revulsion.

It doesn't help that I'm aware I'm keeping Chloe like a captive princess in a high tower, completely isolated from everyone and everything. We don't leave the compound; we don't go anywhere. We exist in our own little world, one where she has no choice but to be mine. It's for her safety, true, but it's also for my peace of mind.

If given the opportunity, would she flee again?

If the danger to her were eliminated, would she want to leave?

I don't know the answers, and the questions torment me, so much so I've become even more obsessive about keeping tabs on her. I know she can't leave—and with Bransford hunting her, probably doesn't want to leave—but I still feel compelled to know her whereabouts each and every moment we're apart. To that end, I've installed cameras in our bedroom and every corner of the house with the exception of my sister's room and Pavel and Lyudmila's private quarters, and I check the video feed on my phone with the mindless frequency of a social media addict.

"What are you always looking at?" Alina asks, walking in on me in the dining room one day as I wait for Chloe to wrap up her lesson with Slava and come down for lunch. "Is something going on?"

I put my phone away. "Something's always going on."

It's not a lie. Not only is Masha working on getting close to Bransford and sending me daily updates on her progress, but I've also got men keeping tabs on Alexei Leonov. He's still here in the States, the last few days in Chicago. It appears he's there for business meetings, but I can't help feeling uneasy.

Chicago is that much closer to Idaho, to my compound and my son.

Alina regards me thoughtfully. "Is it the Volkov thing? Konstantin mentioned he's been inquiring about investing in his nuclear venture."

"That too." I'm not surprised she's heard about that. A self-made oligarch, Alexander Volkov is one of the wealthiest—and most dangerous—men in Russia. An alliance with him would be both advantageous and risky, especially given his propensity for business practices as ruthless as our own.

If things go south for any reason, we'll have another powerful enemy, but if all goes well, he could help speed up the approval process for the new technology, accelerating its adoption worldwide.

Alina sighs. "I wish he wouldn't go there, but Konstantin rarely listens. Maybe you can talk to him—unless you think it's a good idea, getting involved with Volkov?"

I shrug and change the subject. The truth is, Volkov and the potential joint venture are low on my list of worries, so I'm content to let Konstantin run with it. Our genius brother may be too intellectual for his own good at times, but he's still a Molotov and thus perfectly capable of assessing the risks for himself.

My priorities these days are Slava and Chloe, and I intend to do whatever it takes to keep and protect them both.

That night, one of my worst fears comes true. Shortly after midnight, the door to our room bursts open and Lyudmila runs in, yelling my name.

I'm on my feet and armed with the gun I keep under the mattress before she can explain—and when she does, I set the gun down and bolt into our closet.

"What happened?" Chloe demands, running in after me as Lyudmila rushes out of the room. Seeing me getting dressed, she starts pulling on her clothes as well. "What did she say?"

Realizing that Lyudmila had spoken Russian, I swiftly explain that Slava has fallen ill. "He's vomiting uncontrollably and running a high fever," I say as I hurriedly throw on a shirt. "He needs to go to a hospital right away."

Chloe's eyes widen. "Oh, no. I'm coming with you."

"Fuck, no." My tone is much too harsh, but I don't care. Fear, sharp and metallic, coats my tongue. My son is sick. So sick I have no choice but to risk exposing his whereabouts. The last thing I need is Chloe also in danger. "You're staying here, where it's safe."

She blinks up at me. "But—"

"I'll call you on the way." Catching her chin, I steal a brief, hard kiss, and then I'm running to Slava's room, my mind solely on my son and the fastest way of getting him to a hospital.

40

CHLOE

"MORE COFFEE?" ALINA ASKS, AND I NOD, HOPPING OFF the bar stool to pace over to the kitchen window. It's pitch-black outside, without so much as a sliver of moonlight visible behind the thick clouds.

They're promising rainstorms tonight—not a good thing, given the speed with which Nikolai, Pavel, and four of the guards are driving down those winding mountain roads in their SUVs. Lyudmila went with them to help take care of Slava, so Alina and I are the only ones left in the house.

The only ones not *allowed* to leave the house.

According to Alina, Nikolai has placed all the remaining guards on high alert, so five of them are guarding the house itself, while the rest are patrolling the perimeter of the compound in case of an attack.

"What attack?" I asked when she told me this. "Slava is just sick."

She gave me a look suggesting I'm a naïve idiot. "There's sick, and there's sick—and we don't know which this is."

"You think he might've been *poisoned*?"

"We can't rule out anything," she replied, making me realize yet again just how different her and her brothers' upbringing had been from mine.

In my world, no one would deliberately hurt a child.

I turn away from the window and walk back to the kitchen counter. "Any more updates from Pavel or Lyudmila?"

"No." Alina hands me a fresh cup of coffee. Her eyes are as tired as mine, but her makeup and dress are impeccable—I guess on the off chance we might get invited to a gala in the middle of the night. "I don't think they've gotten to the hospital yet," she continues as I take a big gulp of my coffee. "Lyudmila said she'll text me when they do."

The hot liquid burns the roof of my mouth, but I drink the rest of the cup anyway, masochistically relishing the pain. It keeps me from dwelling on the most terrifying possibilities—such as Slava having been poisoned to lure him and Nikolai out of the safety of the compound, or their car going off a cliff on some dark, rain-slick road.

To make matters worse, I can't even call or text Nikolai for reassurance, as he's forgotten his phone here.

"This is so not like him," I mutter, glancing again at the device I brought with me after finding it in our bedroom. "He never forgets anything."

Alina nods somberly. "I know. I've never seen him this worried. Well, except for that one time with you."

Right. When I ran, and he had to save me from the assassins—an incident that now feels like a lifetime ago.

Setting down the empty cup, I return to the window, my chest tight and my stomach on fire from nerves and excess caffeine. I've never felt so useless and helpless—or so much like a prisoner. Though I've known all along that Nikolai won't let me leave the compound, it somehow didn't sink in fully until tonight, when he outright refused to take me with him.

Logically, I understand why—he doesn't need to worry about me as well as Slava—but that doesn't change the fact that I can't be with the two people I care about most... that I'm stuck here, no matter what.

"I'll be right back," Alina says and slips out of the kitchen—presumably to use the bathroom. I debate pouring myself another cup of coffee while I wait, but I decide that three cups should be enough for now. Instead, I pick up Nikolai's phone and swipe across the screen on the off chance it's unlocked.

It's not, of course. My security-obsessed husband would never be so careless as to leave an unlocked phone lying around. The device demands either a fingerprint or a passcode, and I have neither.

Sighing, I lay the phone on the counter and begin to

pace. This is torture in the very real sense of the word. I'm so worried about Slava and Nikolai I feel physically ill, a feeling compounded by the occasional distant flicker of lightning and clap of thunder.

The storm hasn't gotten here yet, but it might already be where they are.

God, what if they don't reach the hospital in time? An icy needle pierces my heart. *What if Slava is so sick he dies?* It's a thought I hadn't allowed myself before, but now that it's crept in, I can't banish it, and the sickening anxiety expands, crowding out the air in my lungs.

I should be there with them.

I should be in that car.

"Where you should be is your bedroom, trying to get some rest," Alina says quietly, and I spin around, startled to find her back on her bar stool.

When did she come back? Also, was I talking out loud?

I must've been, because she's regarding me with weary sympathy while cradling another cup of coffee in her hands. Even though she's normally a tea drinker, tonight she's mainlining the real stuff, same as me.

"Do you really think we're going to get attacked?" I ask, ignoring her nonsensical suggestion. "And if so, by whom? My father?"

Alina sighs and rests her chin in her hand. "Or one of our enemies. God knows there're plenty—not that Nikolai or Valery tell me anything."

"But Konstantin does?" From what I've gathered

over the past few weeks, she has a much closer relationship with their oldest brother, the tech genius. The two of them talk at least a couple of times a week.

"Sometimes. When he thinks it won't upset me." Her beautiful mouth twists. "He thinks I'm so fragile I'll fall apart at the slightest hint of bad news. Especially anything to do with—" She stops. "Never mind. The point is, I'm not exactly in the loop."

Neither am I—and I don't have the excuse of Alina's headaches, which Nikolai told me stem almost entirely from her mental state.

"Some people get stomachaches when stressed, she gets headaches. Bad ones," he explained when she didn't come down for dinner because of a migraine one day. "Sometimes they last for several days, and get so painful she has to knock herself out with a whole cocktail of addictive shit. Hopefully, this won't be one of those."

It wasn't, thankfully, and Alina was back to her normal self the next day. But I can see why Konstantin worries—I'll never forget the drugged-out mess she was that morning in my room.

If Alina doesn't already have a prescription painkiller problem, she's not far from it.

"Do you think she might benefit from something like rehab?" I had asked Nikolai later that day. "Or at least therapy?"

"She hates shrinks and refuses to talk to them," he told me. "As to rehab, we've considered it, but it's not clear that she's actually addicted. Her drug use is sporadic, centered around times of extra stress. It starts with more frequent headaches, and then it spirals until the headaches are no longer the main problem. She's always been able to stop the pills after a bit, though, which is why I allow her to continue using them. They're the only way she can escape the crippling pain when it strikes."

"What about pot?" I asked carefully, not wanting to rat Alina out in case Nikolai didn't know about her occasional smoke sessions with Lyudmila. "Maybe it could help as well?"

His mouth quirked. "Sure. Which is why I don't say anything when she comes in smelling like an Amsterdam coffee shop."

So he did know. I wasn't surprised. He sees everything that goes on around here—including the tangled contradictions in my head.

I love him. I have no problem admitting that now, to myself and to him. And he says he loves me. It should be enough, more than enough, yet it's not. Even when I lie in his arms in the afterglow of mind-blowing sex, there's an inexplicable distance between us, words unsaid and fears unvoiced.

It's mostly my fault, I think. For one thing, I still haven't been able to bring myself to ask about his father. Each time an opportunity arises, I chicken out. The darkness in Nikolai is like a two-sided magnet, drawing and repelling me at once. I want to know him fully, to understand his past as well as he understands mine, yet I'm afraid of delving deeper into the part of him I saw that day in the woods, when he dealt with the assassins.

Sometimes when I wake up in the middle of the night cuddled against him, I can hear the tortured assassin's screams, and I want to scream as well.

I also can't forget Nikolai's threat to drug me into marrying him. It didn't come to that, but I know it would've. Because for my husband, love and possession are the same.

He would do anything to have me.

Of course, contradictory mess that I am, I don't always mind his ruthlessness. There are times I'm glad he forced the issue, leapfrogging over the normal stages of a relationship in favor of marriage. And there are definitely times I enjoy his darker side in bed—pretty much all the times he brings it out, really. Our sex life is as blazing hot as it is varied, and as overwhelming as his hunger for me can be, I never go unsatisfied, to the point that I have to question if there's maybe something wrong with me… if it's healthy to lose myself in his embrace so completely.

In the embrace of a man who is, in many ways, still my captor.

Plopping onto a bar stool next to Alina, I grab Nikolai's phone and absentmindedly swipe across the screen again.

Yep, there it is, password requirement.

Whatever. I don't even know why I want to get into it. What I really need is to speak to Nikolai, but I'm sure he's got his hands full with Slava and navigating those tricky roads.

"Why do you keep doing that?" Alina asks as I swipe across the screen again. "Do you want to read his messages or something?"

I push the phone away. "No. Maybe. I don't know." What I want is Nikolai in bed next to me and Slava sleeping soundly down the hall, but neither is a possibility right now.

"Try 785418," Alina says. At my startled glance, she explains, "I have a good memory for numbers, and I saw Nikolai put it in a couple of weeks back. He might've changed it by now, though."

My fingers are already flying over the touchscreen. "I'm in!" I grin at her triumphantly. "*We're* in."

Then the implications hit me.

Alina has just helped me invade Nikolai's privacy in a major way.

All of a sudden, I don't feel right about this.

She must read it on my face. "He's been glued to that thing for the past week," she says, and I hear the frustration in her voice. "He hasn't told me why, but it might have something to do with all the guards being placed on code red—and I don't know about you, but if there's a specific threat out there, I want to know what it is. I'm tired of being kept in the dark."

Whereas I have willingly kept myself in the dark for

weeks, again not even inquiring about the progression of our plans for Bransford.

My discomfort transforms into shame at my cowardice. Steeling myself, I hand the phone to Alina. "Here. You'd know better where to look." I'll apologize to Nikolai for invading his privacy once this crisis is past.

She nods, and I scoot toward her as her red-tipped fingers fly over the screen. The first place she goes is the inbox, where she rapidly scrolls through the subject lines, many of which are in Russian. Opening one message, she skims it, a tiny frown bisecting the space between her dark brows as her eyes move over the Russian text.

"Well?" I prompt when she closes out of the email and resumes scrolling through the inbox. "Anything?"

She looks up from the screen and blinks, as if she's forgotten I'm there. "Not really." Her voice is strange, though, tight and a little choked. So is the smile she directs my way as she adds, "Just the usual bullshit."

"May I?" Not waiting for her reply, I snatch the phone back and skim the subject lines myself. My inability to read Russian is a serious hindrance, though, so I exit the inbox and check the texts instead. Nikolai uses an app I've never seen for that—encrypted, most likely—and most of those messages are in Russian as well.

So much for my grand hacking attempt.

I'm about to set the phone down when an icon in the upper left corner of the screen catches my attention. It's one of only a few apps on this phone, and its prime location tells me it must be something Nikolai uses a lot.

Intrigued, I click on the icon—a tiny house—and a series of images, or rather videos, fills the screen. Each one is too small to see anything in detail, so I click on the one where I spot some movement.

Alina peers at the screen over my shoulder. "Is that—"

"This kitchen, yes." In fact, I'm looking at the two of us sitting huddled over the phone. Frowning, I look up at the ceiling and over at the cabinets. The angle of the video suggests the cameras are high up and to the left of us, but no matter how hard I look, I don't see them.

I close out of the kitchen feed and zoom in on another image, then all the rest in turn.

Living room.

Dining room.

Glass-walled terrace.

Laundry room.

Upstairs hallway.

Staircase.

Slava's room.

My former room.

My heart hammers faster, an unpleasant tightness banding around my chest.

Sure enough, there it is, our bedroom.

"Is my room on there also?" Alina asks, her tone carefully level. She must not have known about the cameras either—and to think that just a moment ago, I felt bad for invading Nikolai's privacy.

I return to the app home screen and carefully examine the collection of tiny camera views. "I don't see it," I tell Alina. "Here, take a look."

She methodically goes through every feed. "None of my room," she concludes, sounding relieved. "Nor of Pavel and Lyudmila's. Which makes sense—it's probably Pavel who installed the cameras. He's good with security tech."

"Installed when?" My best guess is this is an advanced version of a nanny cam, something Nikolai implemented when he decided to place the ad for a tutor. If so, the cameras would've been installed either shortly before or shortly after my arrival, when I was still a stranger and thus not to be trusted with Slava. Although why our bedroom, originally Nikolai's bedroom, would be wired as well is a mys—

"Looks like the app was installed a few months back," Alina says, rooting through the settings. "But there were two updates since: one in July right after your arrival, and another, much bigger one more recently. A week ago, in fact." Her eyes meet mine. "Right around the time I started seeing Kolya glued to this screen."

Also right around the time I told him I loved him.

Maybe it's all a coincidence. Maybe it has nothing to do with me and everything to do with the email Alina reacted to so strangely, but my instincts tell me otherwise.

The cameras are there for me. To watch me.

My husband's obsession with me is growing, terrifyingly so—and because I've kept my head in the sand like an ostrich, I still don't know what he's truly capable of.

41

NIKOLAI

"THE TESTS JUST CAME BACK," THE DOCTOR INFORMS ME when I return to Slava's room after a brief bathroom break. "Salmonella poisoning."

My breath escapes my tightly clenched throat as a wave of relief crashes into me. They've already stopped Slava's vomiting and gotten him on IV fluids, but until this moment, we'd had no idea what's made him so sick.

Salmonella.

Not some exotic designer poison from which there may be no cure.

Fucking salmonella.

I round on Lyudmila, who has the misfortune of being the only other person in the room. "Did you let him touch raw meat or eggs?"

She blanches. "No, I swear! He didn't even eat eggs today, unless—" Her eyes widen, and she presses her hand to her mouth. "Oh, no."

"What? Spit it out."

"Cookie dough," she whispers, her round face pale. "I think he must've sampled raw cookie dough. Pavel was making those chocolate chip cookies for dinner, and Slava and I came in to get some fruit for a snack…"

Fuck. What awful luck. There must've been an egg that had the bacteria, and of course Slava had to eat that cookie dough. In hindsight, it had to be something like this; I've personally vetted each and every single guard, and with our security being as tight as it is, the odds of some assassin being able to sneak poison into the compound were near zero. Still, I couldn't rule it out entirely—not until these tests came in.

"These poisonings are way more common than you'd think, especially among the elderly and the young," the doctor interjects, discerning the gist of my conversation with Lyudmila despite it being in Russian. "Salmonella is notoriously hardy if it's inside the yolk. You'd have to boil the egg for over eight minutes to ensure that you kill it all, and hardly anyone does that." He sighs. "You wouldn't believe the number of people who land in the ER after your standard omelet or scramble—and I'm not even talking about sunny-side-up or hollandaise sauce and what-not. Those are pretty much a Russian roulette… no offense."

I'm too relieved to be annoyed. "What are the next steps?" I cast a concerned glance at the adult-sized bed where Slava is sleeping, his small face pale and drawn from all the vomiting and diarrhea. He's already looking better from all the fluids, but I still shudder at the recollection of our frantic drive here, during which all I could think about was whether or not he'd make it.

"Normally, we'd just let the illness run its course, but he's got a fever, so we're giving him some antibiotics just in case. Between that and the fluids, he should be feeling meaningfully better soon. I'd like to keep him for observation for another day or so, though."

"Of course." If I'd known it was salmonella, I would've arranged for a medical team to take care of Slava at home, the way I did for Chloe, but I was so terrified that my son had been poisoned or exposed to some exotic neurotoxin that I couldn't risk not having the right specialists or equipment on hand. And now that we're in the hospital, it doesn't make sense to unhook Slava from all the machines and drive back in the storm. For fastest healing, he needs to rest and let the antibiotics do their job.

I just have to hope the Leonovs won't catch wind of our presence here—or that by the time they do, we'll be long gone.

The doctor leaves, and a contrite-looking Lyudmila excuses herself for a bathroom break as well. The two of us have been waiting by Slava's bedside while Pavel and the guards patrol the hallway. Not that I'm expecting an attack in an American hospital—at least I'm not now that I know my son wasn't deliberately poisoned. The compound is probably not in any greater danger either, though I'm not telling the guards to shift down from code red until we're back.

I've forgotten my fucking phone, and though Lyudmila's been texting with Alina and I know everything is okay back home, not being able to watch Chloe through the cameras makes me deeply uneasy.

It's as if someone's blindfolded me—or cut out my eyes.

"Let me use your phone for a bit," I tell Lyudmila when she returns, and she hands it to me before discreetly disappearing from the room.

As soon as she's gone, I call my sister and ask her to get Chloe if she's still awake.

If I can't see my zaychik, at least I'll hear her voice.

"First tell me how Slava is," Alina says.

I swiftly fill her in on his condition—Lyudmila has already informed her about the salmonella diagnosis—and again ask to speak to Chloe.

"Give me a minute." Alina's voice holds a peculiar note. I hope she's not getting another migraine, though I wouldn't be surprised if she were, given the events of the night.

I'm not prone to headaches, yet my temples feel like they're getting pounded by hammers.

I wait impatiently for Chloe to get on the phone. I probably should've called earlier instead of letting Lyudmila keep them apprised of the situation, but I needed to know what was happening with Slava first. The fear was like a boulder on my chest, but now I can finally breathe—and talk like a rational human being.

An hour ago, I was on the verge of ripping out the medical staff's throats with my bare teeth over their attempts to make us wait our turn for admission.

Luckily, money speaks even in this neck of the woods, so as soon as I told the ER receptionist that I will make a million-dollar donation to their children's department if my son is treated *immediately*, things got much smoother, and I didn't have to resort to more extreme measures—like, say, planting bullets in a few of the denser heads.

"Nikolai, hi." Chloe's soft voice is like a warm blanket wrapping around me, lessening the pounding in my head and unlocking the tension in my neck and shoulders. I didn't realize until this moment how tightly bunched they'd gotten.

Turning away from Slava's bed, I walk over to the window to make sure I don't wake him. "Hi, zaychik. How are you?"

"Better now that I know you and Slava are safe," she says quietly, and I hear a small hitch in her breathing. "I was so worried, with the storm and all."

My chest squeezes with tenderness. "We're fine. We made it." Keeping my voice low, I tell her all about the awful trip—how sick Slava had been throughout, and how we had to stop a dozen times for him to throw up and go to the bathroom in the pouring rain. How I kept wishing I were the one whose insides were being wrung inside out, and how terrified I'd been that we'd get to the hospital too late.

"I knew children get sick," I say raggedly. "And I

knew Slava might catch something one day, even though he's strong and healthy. What I didn't know was that it would feel like this… like someone was sawing through my heart with a dull knife, cutting it open one cell at a time."

"Of course." Chloe's tone is soft, gently sympathetic. "Parents always feel that way when something's not right with their children. Mom once told me she didn't know what worry meant until she had me—and then she no longer knew what it was like to exist *without* worry."

I pinch the bridge of my nose. "Great. Just great."

"She also told me she wouldn't trade being my mom for the world." She pauses, then asks quietly, "Would you? Trade being Slava's father for peace of mind?"

"Fuck, no." I glance at the tiny figure on the bed, and the tight, uncomfortable feeling I sought to avoid in the beginning invades my chest again. This time, though, I recognize it as worry. Worry and deep, all-consuming love. A different kind of love from the obsessive passion Chloe awakens in me, but one that's no less potent.

I'd kill for them both.

I'd die for them both.

If I lost either one, I don't know how I'd go on.

"So when do you think you're coming home?" Chloe asks, and as with Alina, I catch a strange inflection in her voice. Not a tightness, precisely, but something slightly off.

"We should be back before the evening," I say,

glancing over at a clock. It's five a.m., almost morning, though it's still dark outside. "Zaychik… is everything okay?"

Chloe's tone is now noticeably strained. "Of course. Why wouldn't it be?"

"You tell me. Is something wrong?"

"No, nothing. Just… come home, and we'll talk."

"Talk? What about? Did something happen while I've been gone?"

"No, of course not." She takes a breath. "It's fine. Everything is fine. Just tired from being up all night, that's all."

She's lying. I'm certain she is lying, and I'm about to press her for answers when Pavel walks into the room.

"Masha's on the phone," he says curtly, handing me his device. "The operation is finally on. He's coming to her place in fifteen minutes."

Fuck. "Zaychik, I have to go. Get some sleep, and I'll call you later today, okay?"

Not waiting for Chloe's reply, I hang up and bring up Pavel's phone to my ear. "You got the cameras all set up? And the live feed?"

Masha's voice is as bright as ever. "Of course."

"Send the recording to Konstantin for edits, and for the live stream, direct it to this phone. I don't have mine on me."

"No problem. Now, about Plan B—"

"Just focus on Plan A." I need Bransford compromised, not dead, as per my bargain with Chloe.

Masha heaves an exasperated sigh. "I will,

obviously. But if something goes wrong and I can't contain him, you still want me to eliminate him today, right? I won't be able to get this close again."

I rub my left eyebrow, behind which the skull hammers are back at work. Valery's asset has been crystal clear as to what she will and won't do on this job, and while she's not averse to having Bransford rough her up a bit for the sake of a convincing video, she won't let him fuck her.

"Just do your best to ensure it doesn't come to that," I say finally. "And if you do have to go to Plan B, use the drug."

Though it will be hard to explain Bransford's death to Chloe, I'll do whatever it takes to protect her.

Even go back on my word to her.

42

CHLOE

I WAKE UP WITH MY MOUTH DRY AND MY EYES AS GRITTY as if they've been filled with sand. Blinking against the bright light filling the room, I peer at a clock—and bolt upright in bed.

Five in the afternoon.

What the fuck?

Before I can gather my thoughts, there's a quiet knock on the bedroom door, and Alina sticks her head in. "Ah, good. You're finally awake."

I grab a water bottle from the nightstand and chug it to ease the parched feeling in my throat. "What happened?" I croak when every precious drop of liquid is gone. I feel dazed and groggy, as though I've been drugged.

Alina strolls in, looking fresh and glamorous, as if she's just stepped out of a full-service salon spa. I, on the other hand, feel—and probably look—like something the raccoons wouldn't fish out of a garbage can.

"You couldn't sleep the rest of the night, so you went to take a nap mid-morning, remember?" she says, gracefully perching on the edge of the bed.

I look at the clock again, as if doing so would change the time displayed on it. "But it's already five. How can it be five if I went down for a nap in the morning?"

She grins. "What can I say? When you crash, you crash hard." She crosses her long legs. "My brother's called about ten times so far, demanding to speak to you. I told him I'm letting you sleep."

My heart rate kicks up. "Is something wrong? Has Slava—"

"No, no, everything's fine. They're actually driving home already, should get here in less than an hour."

"Oh. Is Slava—"

"Doing much better," she assures me. "The doctor was going to keep him for observation until tonight, but he hasn't vomited once since the morning and was able to eat some chicken soup and Jell-O for lunch, so they discharged him early."

"Oh, thank God." I can't wait to hug Slava and kiss him silly. I only caught a glimpse of him last night as Nikolai ran out of the house with the child in his arms, but his pale, wan appearance has haunted me, making me feel exactly how Nikolai described: as if a dull blade were sawing apart my heart.

I guess my husband is not the only one who gets to

feel like a parent these days. With each passing week, Nikolai's son has crept deeper into my heart, and I'm now at the point where I couldn't love him more if he'd come out of my own body—and would be devastated if anything happened to him.

"Do you have your phone?" I ask Alina. "I want to call Nikolai back."

I want to talk to Slava myself and make sure he's truly feeling better, and I'm also dying to hear Nikolai's voice.

No matter how chilling I find those cameras, I can't help missing him, craving him in the most visceral way possible—which is why the thought of our upcoming conversation kept me from falling asleep last night even after they'd safely reached the hospital and I knew Slava would be okay.

"I don't have it on me, but I can get it," Alina says, getting up. "I don't know if you should call him at this point, though. They'll be here soon enough, and then you can talk."

I hesitate, then nod. "Okay."

She's right. Now that they're almost here, I might as well wait. As brief as our conversation last night had been, Nikolai somehow sensed I was upset, and if it weren't for whatever had distracted him, I'm sure he would've pressured me for answers. That must be why he kept calling throughout the day, and why it's best if I just talk to him in person.

It's time I stopped being an ostrich and learned the truth—and we both laid our cards on the table.

It's forty minutes later and almost dinnertime when their SUV pulls up to the house. I've spent these forty minutes getting ready, both mentally and physically. My hair is brushed and coiled into an updo, my makeup is nearly as perfect as Alina's, and I'm wearing a shimmering white gown with two side slits that show off my legs and my golden strappy heels. In my ears are a pair of diamond stud earrings Nikolai gifted me, and around my neck is the heart-shaped necklace Alina lent me once before, for my first dressed-up dinner here. I was going to wear one of my own pieces, but she insisted that her necklace was what the outfit required.

"Trust me on this," she said mysteriously. "This is precisely what Nikolai needs to see tonight."

I decided to do exactly that and trust her for now, though I'm beyond curious what she meant. If I don't get all the answers from Nikolai tonight, I *will* get them out of her.

No more burying my head in the sand.

I'm done being a coward.

Despite my resolve, my heart pounds erratically as I hurry downstairs to greet my husband and our son.

Slava comes in first—or rather barrels in like the little ball of energy a boy his age can be.

"Mama Chloe!" He runs straight for me, and I catch him mid-leap, staggering back under the weight of his small yet sturdy body as my previously injured ankle wobbles in its strappy heel. He smells like medicine and baby shampoo, and I'm so happy to feel his short arms squeezing my neck that I don't care about the potential re-injury—or my makeup getting smeared as he places wet, loud smooches on my cheeks.

"I puke lots," he announces triumphantly after I finally set him down, and I can't help laughing as he launches into a tale about his hospital adventures in a tangled mix of English and Russian, with the gist of the story boiling down to how gross all the puking was.

"What is this? Shouldn't you be all weak and sickly?" Alina asks with amusement, and I realize she's come down to stand next to me. Grinning hugely, she goes down to her knees and grabs Slava in a big hug of her own while whispering to him conspiratorially in Russian.

"Yes, I am Superman," he declares when she's done, and I laugh again, overjoyed to see him doing so well.

"He slept most of the way here and woke up with all this energy," Nikolai says, his deep voice startling me so much I pivot sharply—and nearly fall as the stupid ankle buckles underneath me, sending a spike of pain shooting up my leg.

I say "nearly" because, as always, Nikolai catches me, his powerful arms closing around me before I hit the floor.

"Easy there, zaychik," he murmurs, his eyes a greener shade of gold as he steadies me against his big, warm body and looks me over, holding me by my upper arms. "One trip to the hospital is plenty."

My heart teleports into my throat as the full impact

of his nearness hits me like a wrecking ball. My knees join my ankle in buckling, and my skin ignites with sensations, each cell drinking in the heat emanating from his fingers, the delicious strength and roughness of his callused palms. Like Slava, he smells of the hospital, but underneath is a seductive hint of bergamot and an even fainter trace of cedar, mixed with that warm, masculine aroma that's all his.

"You're here." It's a dumb comment, but all my neurons appear to have gone out for a hike. All I can do is stare up at his face with its high, wide cheekbones and fierce jawline, transfixed by the juxtaposition of wildness and elegance that makes him such a dangerously alluring contradiction.

My husband.

My protector.

My secret watcher.

Is his love something to crave or fear?

He cups my cheek, his eyes darkening as his gaze drops down to my lips. "I'm here, zaychik." Ignoring our audience, he dips his head and slants his mouth across mine, claiming it in a deep, soul-scorching kiss.

My heart is racing in my chest, my skin overly warm by the time he pulls away. As usual, everyone is ignoring our outrageous PDA. Pavel and Lyudmila have come in as well, and they're talking to Alina in Russian while Slava interrupts with stories of his own.

I look back at Nikolai—only to freeze at the chilling look on his face. His gaze is glued to my throat, a muscle ticking violently in his jaw. What the—?

And then I realize what he's looking at.

Not my throat.

The necklace Alina gave me, the one she said he needed to see tonight.

With sudden clarity, I recall her drugged-out mumblings that awful morning when I fled. Like with so many other things relating to my situation, I haven't allowed myself to think about her actual words in recent weeks, to dwell on them for any length of time. But now they come to me, along with everything else I've heard about this family, about how Nikolai is so much like his father.

If I had any doubts left that my husband and I need to have this conversation, they evaporate in this very moment—because if the suspicion forming in my mind is right, Alina is not the only one dealing with a major trauma.

Pretending all is normal, I turn away from Nikolai and walk over to grab Slava's hand. "Come, darling, let's get you into bed before you crash. We'll feed you dinner there."

"I do it," Lyudmila offers, but I shake my head with a smile.

"Let me. I've missed him."

"I'll join you," Nikolai says, his gaze hooded, and my pulse speeds up further as he picks up Slava and carries him upstairs in front of me.

The two of us bathe Slava and tuck him into bed, where he eats some soup and promptly falls asleep, his burst of energy expiring quickly.

"Is it always like this with children?" Nikolai asks in a hushed tone, smoothing his broad palm over Slava's forehead. His puzzled gaze shifts to me. "When they get sick, I mean? Zero to sixty and then back again?"

I smile despite the turmoil in my chest. "No, not always. Slava's just Superman. Haven't you heard?"

His answering smile sets off an explosion of endorphins in my brain. "Oh, yeah, there *is* a rumor going around."

And for a couple of heartbeats, that's enough—this uncomplicated moment of shared joy, of relief that the child we love is going to be okay. But then Nikolai's smile fades, and my pulse shifts into high gear as the space between us fills with simmering awareness, with that scorching chemistry that feels like a charged wire dancing across my skin. We're sitting just a foot apart, but even that small distance suddenly feels like too much… too much and not enough at the same time.

I swallow as he lifts his hand and curves it around my cheek, his rough-edged thumb stroking over my lower lip, making it tingle.

"Zaychik…" His voice is dark velvet. "I've missed you."

And I've missed you too. So, so much. The words pirouette on the tip of my tongue, ready to take flight. It would be so easy to fall back into his embrace, to forget what I saw on his phone and not rock the boat.

To dive back into our faux-honeymoon routine and pretend there's nothing frightening about a husband who obsessively watches me when we're apart… a killer whose complicated past is still a terrifying mystery.

"Nikolai, I…" I draw in a breath and force out a different set of words, the ones I've been avoiding. "We need to talk. It's time you told me exactly what happened with your father."

43

CHLOE

It's as if a dark shutter falls over Nikolai's face, transforming it into that of a stranger. All warmth leaves his voice as he pulls back his hand and stands. "Let's go then. We'll talk in my office."

My heart hammers as I follow him out of Slava's room and down the hallway. As we walk, a chime sounds in his pocket, and he pulls out his phone and glances at the screen. He must've reclaimed the device immediately upon arrival.

Whatever he sees there makes his jaw go taut, and when his gaze returns to me, his eyes are filled with a peculiar light.

A terrible premonition tightens my stomach. "What happened? What's wrong?"

"There's something you should see," he says, and as soon as we enter his office, he goes straight for his laptop and opens it, bending over his desk. His fingers fly over the keyboard for a second, and then he turns the screen toward me.

My heart leaps, and my knees turn into rubber.

Displayed on the screen is a popular news site, where the major headline reads in all caps, "LEADING PRESIDENTIAL CANDIDATE ASSAULTS WOMAN IN SHOCKING VIDEO."

Icy needles dance over my skin as I grab the laptop and carry it to the small round table, where I sink into a chair and read the article in full.

The story is still developing, but it seems that just under an hour ago, a video of Bransford attacking a young woman appeared on Twitter and instantly went viral. According to the news site, the "graphic and disturbing" footage shows him hitting her in the face and ripping her shirt open while she desperately fights back. After a couple of minutes of violent struggle, she escapes by kneeing him in the groin and running out the door while he screams obscenities at her.

"You can watch the video if you want," Nikolai says quietly, and I realize he's come to stand next to me, his gaze glued to the screen from above. "Konstantin's team has worked wonders with what Masha sent him."

My voice is thin. "This was filmed today?"

He nods, his expression unreadable. "Early this morning, some twenty minutes after you and I talked. She had him swing by her 'dorm' before work to sign off on her internship papers so she could volunteer at his campaign and get credit for her AP American Government class."

"AP?" I feel a surge of nausea. "As in, an advanced placement course in high school?"

"Exactly. He thinks she's seventeen, a junior at a boarding school in the DC area." Nikolai pauses, then adds softly, "An orphan whose parents died in a car accident, leaving her in the care of an indifferent uncle who wants nothing to do with her."

"The perfect bait for a predator," I whisper, my eyes burning. "The most vulnerable type of victim… like my mother."

"Yes. That seems to be his MO. We've located two more women he's done this to over the years." Nikolai's jaw flexes. "He likes them smart, pretty, and way too young—and with no one to turn to."

I suck in a breath, the icy needles piercing deeper. "You found them? Will they come forward?"

"They will now."

I swallow to keep the contents of my stomach down as I return my attention to the screen. As sickening as this is going to be, I need to see this video with my own eyes, to know exactly what kind of monster hurt my mom when *she* was a vulnerable teen.

I'm done hiding from reality.

Finding the video, I click "play"—and my nausea intensifies, my stomach cramping with the knowledge that I share this man's genes.

The recording begins with a short but violent chase, with a tall, fit, handsome older man—unmistakably Tom Bransford—lunging at a petite blonde dressed in a pair of tiny shorts and a cropped top. The camera is at such an angle that only a portion of Masha's face shows, but there's no mistaking the youthful line of her jaw—nor the terror in her frantic movements.

She makes it most of the way across the narrow, cluttered room before he tackles her from the back, slamming her into a wall next to a BTS poster, then spinning her around to face him. Sobbing in panic, she attacks, clawing at him with small, slender fingers, but he slaps her brutally across the face and slams a fist into her stomach.

I tense, feeling the blow as if it landed on me, but the worst is just beginning. While Masha is bent over, wheezing for air, he rips at her shirt, tearing it open at the shoulder.

A delicate, softly rounded shoulder, one that could belong to a young teen or a child.

I know that's not the case—I know with her government background, Masha must be at least in her early twenties—but it's easy to forget that I'm not witnessing an actual assault on an innocent teenage victim.

Or rather, that the assault is likely real, but not the victim.

Either way, I can't help exhaling in relief when, after a few more moments of agonizing struggle, Masha makes a twisting motion that seems to accidentally bring her knee in contact with her assailant's groin. He staggers back with a high-pitched scream, his hands cupped over his crotch, and she makes a break for it again, this time reaching the door and disappearing as Bransford screams, "You fucking cunt! Get back here, you fucking tease, or I'll fucking kill you!"

The video cuts off then, but not before the camera zooms in on Bransford's face, on the handsome, even features twisted into a red mask of thwarted fury, a bulging-eyed visage as monstrous as the man himself.

Shaking, I shut down the laptop and gulp in small breaths in an effort to bring oxygen into my tightly banded ribcage—and stop myself from puking.

To paraphrase Nikolai, one person vomiting around here this week is plenty.

When I'm sure my stomach won't expel its contents, I turn to look up at Nikolai. "How did you do it?" My voice is only marginally unsteady. "How did Masha get him to... you know?"

"To attack her?" At my nod, he says, "I don't know all the particulars, but I suspect it was by doing exactly what he accused her of at the end."

"Being a tease?"

"Whatever you'd call strongly encouraging his attentions, then deliberately withdrawing—what men like that think all women do. Only in this case, Masha *was* actually doing it, just with a different goal than what he thought." Nikolai's upper lip curls. "He undoubtedly figured she'd be so eager to get school credit for volunteering at his campaign, she'd let him fuck her, and when she didn't, things escalated quickly... as we figured they might, given his history."

I swallow down another wave of nausea. "So

everything that happened in the video took place for real? None of the footage was fabricated?"

"It was heavily edited, but not fabricated, no."

"Edited for what?"

Nikolai takes a seat across from me. "To hide her face and highlight his, for one thing. Her anonymity is important to her."

I mentally replay the video and realize he's right: Masha's face never actually appears in it. The angle is always wrong. Even when Bransford has her pinned against the wall and the camera is looking directly at her face, his shoulder or something blocks it, allowing the viewer to catch only a glimpse of her cheek, ear, or jaw—enough to get an impression of youth and beauty but not to capture a printable photograph.

"So she's not going to come forward to testify?" I ask, and Nikolai shakes his head.

"Too risky. We created a false identity for her, but it's not one that'll stand up to any real scrutiny. The video was uploaded to the internet anonymously, from an untraceable server—but of course, they'll blame it on Russian hackers, like so many things these days."

"Only in this case, they'll be right."

His lips quirk sardonically. "They're right in most cases, zaychik. Konstantin and his ilk are a menace, especially for your hapless politicians. In any case, it doesn't matter what they say about the source of the video—or whether they call it fake. The damage to Bransford's career is done, his two real victims emboldened. Once they come forward... Well, let's just say daddy dearest is as good as finished."

Daddy dearest. My stomach heaves so violently I nearly upchuck after all. "He's not my daddy anything." I shoot up to my feet, suddenly blindingly angry. "He's just—"

"Your mother's rapist and killer, I know," Nikolai says quietly, standing up as well. "That's all he is, zaychik. Nothing more, nothing to do with you."

The anger drains away as quickly as it came, and I sink back into the chair, dropping my head into my hands. My skull feels inexplicably tight and heavy, as if my brain has been turned into lead.

Large, warm hands land on my nape and shoulders, strong fingers digging into my tight muscles with just the right amount of pressure. "I'm sorry, zaychik." Nikolai's voice is once again soft and warm. "I know it's a lot to process, but I figured you needed to see this video... to know your mom has been avenged."

I want to melt into the seductive comfort of those massaging fingers, to lose myself in their skillful, soothing touch. To once again postpone learning what I fear and instead let myself enjoy Bransford's misfortune, basking in the schadenfreude of it all. The damage we've inflicted on his career doesn't come close to what he did to my mom or those other women, but it's a start—and hopefully, now that the shine is off his golden image, the wheels of legal justice will turn toward him, their spokes nice and sharp.

Gathering every ounce of my strength, I lift my leaden head and cover Nikolai's hands with my own as I twist around to meet his gaze.

"What about your mom?" I ask softly. "Has *she* ever been avenged?"

44

NIKOLAI

My hands tighten on Chloe's shoulders, her question hitting me like a punch below the belt. The necklace gleaming on her throat should've clued me in as to the direction of her upcoming interrogation, but I still didn't expect her to take this exact tack… to know so much about what happened.

"I guess Alina spoke to you again." My voice roughens as I step back. My gaze falls to her pendant, the heart-shaped diamond taunting me, reminding me of things I've been trying to forget. With effort, I tear my eyes away from it and refocus on Chloe's face. "What exactly has she told you?"

Biting her lip, she stands up. "Not much. She hasn't spoken to me again—it was just that morning, right before I left. She said something like, 'He killed her. And then Kolya killed him.' I wasn't sure whom she meant at the time, but I've been pondering it recently, and I think… I think it has to be your mom." She lifts her hand to touch the pendant, her brown eyes soft and dark. "Did this belong to her? Is that why Alina wanted me to wear it tonight and that other night? As some kind of reminder to you about it all?"

My throat tightens and I turn away, abruptly awash in memories—and the burning rage and grief that come with them. And underneath it all lurks the most horrifying guilt, the knowledge that what I've done is ultimately unforgivable. The toxic cocktail is so close to boiling over that I'm not sure I'll be able to keep my word and tell Chloe the whole story, but then her small hand brushes against mine and her fingers curl around my palm, lending me silent support.

"Tell me," she murmurs, stepping around to stand in front of me. Looking up at me, she lifts our joined hands to press them to her chest. "Please, Nikolai. I need to know."

And so she does. I owe her the truth, no matter how ugly.

Looking into her upturned face, I take a breath and begin.

45

NIKOLAI

"When I was around Slava's age, I thought my mother was a princess," I say, my tone cool and steady despite the witch's brew boiling in my veins. "Tall, slim, always perfumed and made up, she wore pretty dresses, sparkling jewels, and high heels, even around the house, and she insisted that everything around her be as beautiful as we could make it—especially ourselves." The memories press down on me, making me feel like the air is disappearing from the room, but I continue. "Valery was just a baby at the time and Alina wasn't born yet, so Konstantin and I are the only ones who remember those years… the ones when our mother was still somewhat happy."

"Somewhat?" Chloe's upturned face reflects both sympathy and wary curiosity as she holds my palm pressed against her chest. "She was never fully happy?"

"Not in my memory." I extricate my hand from her

grasp and walk over to take a seat behind my desk. I feel marginally more in control this way, less likely to give in to the urge to grab Chloe and fuck her until neither one of us can think straight, much less dredge up the noxious sludge that is my past.

She follows me, perching on the corner of the desk, a vision of white and gold in her evening dress, a captured ray of sunshine that's all mine. "Why? Were they never in love? Or did something happen?"

I do my best to keep my gaze on her face and not her cleavage, where the pendant is winking tauntingly at me. "I don't know for sure, but I suspect it started with Konstantin. My father wanted a son like himself, someone to eventually take over the newly capitalist empire he was building, but even as a toddler, my older brother was different. Crazy smart but different. I don't think he even spoke until age three or four."

Chloe's eyes widen. "Oh. So he's—"

"On the spectrum? Maybe. He's never been officially diagnosed. In any case, that may have been the start of the rift between them… or maybe it was just my mother figuring out what kind of man my father was. Whatever the reason, I remember their marriage deteriorating year by year. Each time I'd come home from boarding school, the atmosphere between them would be several degrees icier, their fights more frequent… my father's mood ever darker."

A frown gathers between Chloe's brows. "Why didn't they just get a divorce?"

"He wouldn't allow it. He wanted her, no matter

what." I remember my mother screaming at him about it during one of those fights, begging and pleading to let her go. Clenching my teeth, I shove the recollection away—it hits too close to home.

"In any case," I continue in a level tone, "the more time passed, the worse it got. When I was twelve, he took several lovers and paraded them in front of her. A year later, he killed a man rumored to be her lover. And a few weeks after my seventeenth birthday, I spotted a bruise on her face." At Chloe's expression, I say, "She denied it, of course, said she fell or some such. I didn't believe her for a second. I went to my father and told him that if I ever saw her hurt again, he'd answer to my fist—and I'd take her away where he'd never find her."

Chloe sucks in a breath. "Did he believe you?"

"He did." My mouth twists. "I was his favorite child, the son who was most like him. He knew that even at that age, I'd find a way to keep my promise."

"So what happened then? How did you...?"

"End up killing him?" The words taste like poison on my tongue.

She nods warily, her gaze glued to my face. "When did it happen?"

"Six—no, six and a half years ago. I'd just returned to Moscow after being away for several years—first for service in the army, then my degree at Princeton. Through it all, I kept tabs on my mother, on her health and mental state." My jaw is clenched so hard it feels as if my teeth are wired together, each word more difficult to get out than the next. "There were no more bruises as far as I could tell, but she was miserable, utterly wrecked by their discord. Yet no matter how many times I offered to help her leave him, she wouldn't go. She said she was afraid."

Chloe swallows. "Of him?"

"Of him. Of being without him. Of all of it. By then, they'd spent almost thirty years together. They'd raised four children, such as we were." I catch my hand curling into a fist under the desk and force my fingers to relax. "Konstantin and Valery tried to get her to leave too, but she refused to listen. The excuses were endless: She didn't want to face the judgement of their mutual friends, didn't want to lose the life they'd built together, didn't want to tear the family apart. But in reality, it came down to fear. Fear of my father and what her life would be like without him… without his toxic obsession with her."

"Obsession?" Chloe's voice shakes slightly.

I nod, grimly aware of the parallels. "For better or worse, she'd been the center of his world for close to three decades, long after whatever love they'd shared morphed into this bitter hate. I think a part of her enjoyed it too, the knowledge that she had that kind of power over him, that ultimately, he *couldn't* let her go." I draw in a harsh breath. "In any case, I kept tabs on her, but what I should've been doing was keeping tabs on *him*. Because as her misery grew, so did his—they fed off each other. He started drinking heavily and, as I learned later, using coke. It helped him stay away from her. In a way, he replaced his addiction to her with a potentially less harmful one—and my mother hated that development. Love or hate, she *wanted* his attention."

"So she what? Did something to get it back?"

"She did. She took another lover—a prominent government official, someone who couldn't be dispatched without serious consequences—and told my father she was leaving. I don't think she meant it—it was supposed to be the equivalent of a red flag waved at a bull. But that's the thing about enraged bulls: They can gore you." My voice roughens. "And that's precisely what my father did."

Chloe's hands lock together in her lap, her knuckles turning white as I continue. "Valery was away for his service in the army and Konstantin was in Dubai for business, but Alina was home for winter holidays, having just finished her first semester at Columbia. She's the one who called me that night when our parents' last fight began." My throat tightens, the memories so suffocating I'm not sure I'll be able to say the next part. Yet I go on somehow, my voice reflecting only a fraction of the pain tearing me up inside. "By the time I got there, the living room was like a scene out of a horror movie, with blood splattered all over the gleaming wood floors and white furniture. Alina must've tried to intervene, to protect our mother, because she was knocked out by the wall, one of her forearms slashed open where she'd tried to stop his knife. And our mother—" I stop, then continue gutturally. “She was barely recognizable as human. He’d beaten her to a pulp before slashing her to pieces. To this day, it’s one of the most violent deaths I’ve ever seen.”

Chloe’s face is ashen, visible tremors running through her slender body, and I want to stop, to end this tale before the horror in her eyes morphs into terror and revulsion, but I promised her the truth, so I divorce myself from the words I’m saying and the suffocating agony they bring.

“He was crouched over her body, knife still in hand as I came toward him. He’d lost control, he told me. It’d been an accident, he said. I knew better, though. Pavel and Lyudmila were scheduled to be there that evening, but they weren’t. He’d sent them away for the night. Them and Alina—except my sister had forgotten something and unexpectedly came back.”

“So he—” Chloe’s voice cracks. “He’d planned it? It wasn’t the coke?”

“It was. He was sky high, his pupils blown wide. But he’d known full well what he was going to do while in that state—a clean-up crew had been notified earlier that evening to be on standby. I know that because…” I drag in air, my throat burning from the acid rising into my esophagus. “Because I called them afterward. After he came at me with the knife.”

Chloe’s sharp intake of air is audible. “He was going to kill you?”

“Maybe. I don’t know. He knew I didn’t believe him, knew I wouldn’t let her murder slide. So when he came at me, his pupils the size of dimes, I acted on instinct." Looking into my wife's stricken face, I say hoarsely, "We fought, and when I got a hold of the knife, I did what he had Pavel train me to do. I gutted him from groin to gullet."

46

CHLOE

He propels himself to his feet then and strides over to the window, where he stands with his back to me, his powerful shoulders tight with tension, his big body as still and hard as if it were one of the mountains outside.

I stare at him for a few beats, absorbing what he's told me, and then I force my frozen limbs to move. "Alina…"

"She regained consciousness in the last few moments of our fight," he says, staring straight ahead as I come to stand next to him. His jaw looks as if it's been turned into granite, his sensuous lips flattened into a harsh line. "I didn't realize it, didn't hear her scream for me to stop—not until after it was done."

"So she…?"

"Saw me kill him, yes. She watched me slice him open."

I drag in a strained breath, reliving those awful

moments when *I* saw him wield the knife. It was against my assailant, my mom's killer who'd been about to rape me and take my life, yet I still feel sick at the memory. What must it have been like for Alina, who'd been barely eighteen the night she saw her parents die so brutally, one at her father's hand and the other at her brother's?

More importantly, what must it have been like for Nikolai?

What kind of damage has that night inflicted on *his* psyche?

My hand shakes as I touch his sleeve, drawing his gaze toward me. His beautifully carved face is carefully blank, displaying nothing of his feelings. But I can sense the well of anguish behind his opaque mask, can feel the paralyzing torment of his guilt and shame.

"Does Alina know?" I ask unsteadily. "That it was self-defense? That you didn't do it just to avenge your mother?"

His black lashes lower, veiling his tiger eyes. "I don't know. We've never really talked about that night. What would it change? I was twenty-five to his fifty-seven, faster and stronger. I could've wrestled the knife away and pinned him down—I didn't have to murder him."

"Did you not?" I can see the scene as clearly as if it had happened in front of my eyes, can picture the older version of Nikolai I saw in newspaper photos, fit and strong despite his age… dangerous even without being hopped up on blood and coke. And I can see a twenty-five-year-old Nikolai, thrust into that nightmare of a scene, stunned by his mother's gruesome death and terrified for his unconscious, bleeding sister.

What would've happened if he hadn't gotten a hold of his father's lethal knife?

Would his blood have also stained that blade, his body joining his mother's and sister's in an unmarked grave in some Russian forest?

"What are you saying?" Nikolai's voice tightens, his eyes glittering fiercely as his mask slips, revealing the raw, festering wound underneath. "I killed him. My own father. Who cares whether it was in self-defense or not? I wanted him dead for what he did to her. I wanted his blood—*my* blood—on my hands, and I'm not sorry I have it. Because you see, zaychik, Alina's right: I *am* like him. In every way that counts, I am my father."

My heart feels like it's being ripped to pieces, his anguish slicing at me as brutally as any knife. How has he been able to contain all this pain inside him? How has it not torn him apart? "No," I say, my voice steadier with each word. "You're not your father. And I'm not your mother. Their fate won't be ours—not if we don't let it."

I don't know when it was during his tale that I understood what drives him, at what point I realized that Nikolai branded *himself* a monster six and a half years ago—and has since done his best to live up to what he thinks is his nature, to the Molotov blood he views as his curse. Not that there isn't some truth to his belief. My new family is dark and ruthless, a throwback to the times when violence and might made right. Their relationships merit their own chapter in a book on broken family dynamics, and my husband is a product of that upbringing, his character shaped as much by the tragedy of his parents' slowly unraveling relationship as its explosive, gruesome end.

Still, he's not his father. Far from it. And I'm not his mother. She didn't know her husband's nature when she married him, wasn't prepared for a life with a man so violent and ruthless. Whereas I, thanks to my biological father, have been through living hell, and while I can't say I wasn't fazed by seeing Nikolai kill the two assassins, finding out what he's capable of hasn't changed my feelings—much to my initial dismay.

Merciless killer or not, he is and always will be my lover and protector.

"No?" He grips my upper arms, his fingers like bands of steel. "How will we escape their fate? You already hate me on some level, don't you? For killing those men in front of you and bringing you back when you begged me to let you go? For forcing you to marry me?"

I hold his fiercely golden gaze, refusing to flinch at the volcanic turmoil I see there, at all the long-repressed emotions that threaten to spill out in a tsunami, wrecking everything in their way. "No, Nikolai." My voice is soft and steady despite the uneven pounding of my pulse. "I told you, I love you. I don't hate you. I never could, so I never did—and I never will."

His fingers tighten, biting deeper into my flesh. "How can you be so sure? You've seen what I'm capable of, what I'm like… how I am with you. How exactly am I different from him?"

I fight the urge to shrink away from the pain and rage bleeding into his words. Instead, I ask softly, "Did your father love you and your siblings the way you love Slava? Did he truly love anyone except himself? And I don't mean his violent fixation on your mother."

His expression doesn't change, but I can feel the answer in the subtle slackening of his grip on me, so I press on. "Maybe you are like him in some ways, but not all ways. Not the ones that count. For instance, would you ever hurt me? Really hurt me? I'm talking fists and knives, not being rough in bed."

He recoils, yanking his hands away. "I'd sooner gut myself."

"What about Slava? Would you ever come at him with a knife… say, while high or drunk?"

Fury flashes across his face. "Fuck, no."

"Exactly." I step even closer to him, my heart drumming up a storm. "Because you're not like your father. No matter what your sister thinks… no matter what I feared after you saved me."

His nostrils flare as he stares down at me. "Feared?" His voice is sandpaper rough, the words tinged for the first time with a hint of a Russian accent. "As in, past tense?" He grasps my arms again, his eyes a feral golden-green. "You think you're safe with me? Because... what? You now know the full ugly truth? Because you think you understand me?"

"I've always been safe with you." And deep down, I've always known it. That's why I've been able to bury my head in the sand all these weeks, why seeing him kill and torture hasn't made me recoil at his touch—and why being forced to marry him hasn't changed my feelings.

Even when I feel like prey under that intense tiger gaze of his, I know he'd never hurt me.

His jaw flexes violently. "How the fuck can you be so sure? How can you trust me, much less love me, given the poison flowing through my veins?"

"Do you love *me*? Trust *me,* given the poison flowing through *my* veins?" My voice rises as the words spill out, filled with all the anger I haven't had a chance to process, all the self-loathing I've been suppressing. It's as if a dam has broken, and I can't stop the bitter torrent, can't rebuild the mental block that's kept me sane all these weeks. "I'm a child of rape, the result of a two-faced, sociopathic scumbag assaulting my teenage mother. At least your parents wanted each other at some point—at least you were conceived in something resembling love."

He lets go of me, his gaze turning opaque again. "It's not the same."

"Is it not?" I wind my fists in his shirt, not letting him turn away. "Think about it. My blood is tainted, same as yours. My father also killed my mother—not out of twisted passion but cold calculation. And he most definitely would've killed me too. Still might try, in fact. So how exactly are our stories different? How am I in any way better than you? If anything, we're a perfect fit—or as you like to say, fated to be together."

He stares down at me, his broad chest moving in an uneven rhythm, and I can see I'm getting through to him, that he's absorbing this basic truth. A truth I didn't fully comprehend myself until this moment.

I may not believe in fate as such, but *something* brought me here, to this family with all its ugliness and beauty. To this wonderful, lethal, damaged man, who'll never flinch at doing what it takes to keep me safe and slay my demons… as long as I also slay his.

I let go of his shirt and lay my palms on each side of his face, feeling the hard strength of his bones under the warm, stubble-roughened skin. "I love you, Nikolai… I love you and I want to be with you, dark past, obsessiveness, and all. Whatever our fathers did, however fucked-up our parents' relationships, we are not them, and we don't have to follow in their footsteps. I'll never rape a teenage girl—and you will never hurt me, no matter how strong your feelings for me become… no matter what trials we go through in the future."

His chest heaves faster as I speak, his eyes darkening until they're the color of tarnished bronze. "Chloe…" His voice is hoarse as he cups his hands over mine. "Zaychik, you have no idea how strong my feelings for you already are, how all-consuming my obsession with you."

I dampen my lips. "I think I do." The cameras are a good indication. We'll need to talk about them at some point soon, but for now, I have more important things to focus on... such as the way his gaze falls to my mouth and ignites with familiar volcanic heat, the dark hunger that excites me and, on some level, scares me—but only because it evokes an equally potent response in me.

He's not the only one whose love now borders on obsession.

He stares at my mouth for another beat, his hands clenching over mine. Then, with a sharp inhale, he crushes his lips to mine, one hand fisting in my hair while the other grips my ass cheek, yanking my lower body flush against his.

He's already hard, the bulge of his erection pushing into me as he drags me over to his desk while devouring me with a brutal kiss, a kiss that I respond to with equal fervor. We fall onto the hard surface in a tangle of limbs and eagerly groping hands, coming together in a fury of lust and love, in the tender violence of passion.

In the most perfect way for two imperfect people.

47

NIKOLAI

As the last echoes of the ecstasy fade away, I become aware of the hard surface of the desk under my naked back and the slight weight of Chloe's body draped across my sweat-dampened chest. My brain is overflowing with endorphins, and my heart is thudding in a newly hopeful rhythm in my chest.

I told her everything, and instead of recoiling in revulsion, she embraced me.

I laid bare the worst parts of myself, and instead of running away in terror, she told me that we're fated.

Which we are. I've known it from the beginning, but at some point in the last couple of weeks, I've lost sight of it, begun to doubt whether our relationship can survive the poison festering inside me… whether we're destined to go down my parents' agonizing path.

"We're not," Chloe murmurs, lifting her head off my shoulder, and I realize I said the last part out loud. Smiling tenderly, she traces the edges of my lips with one slender finger, her eyes so soft and warm her gaze is like a physical caress on my face. "We decide our life, our future."

Sitting up, I pull her onto my lap, a surfeit of emotions filling my chest as I inhale her wildflower scent and feel her slender arms wrap trustingly around my neck. Tenderness and possessiveness, love and lust, fear and joy—they battle inside me until it feels as if my ribcage can't contain it all.

Is it possible?

Could Chloe's love for me be more than a sweet mirage?

Could this kind of happiness be real and lasting?

There's so much I want to talk to her about, so many things I want to tell her… another confession I want to make concerning her father's fate. But for now, this is enough. I don't want to spoil this perfect moment by bringing up any sort of contentious topics. So I just kiss the top of her head and hold her tight, content—truly content—for the first time in my life.

48

CHLOE

I WANT TO STAY LIKE THIS, CUDDLED ON NIKOLAI'S LAP, forever, but I know that we eventually have to move. Out of the corner of my eye, I spy my dress on the floor next to his shirt—along with the laptop we knocked off the desk in our passion. We should retrieve the computer, make sure it's okay… maybe talk about the cameras as well. Or better yet, about our future overall. But before we get there, there's something I have to tell him.

Lifting my head from his broad shoulder, I pull back to meet his warm amber gaze. "Thank you," I say softly. "Thank you for doing what you did to Bransford. I know it's not a perfect solution—I know that even dethroned, he might be dangerous—but I think—"

A loud banging on the door makes us both jump. "Nikolai!" Pavel's deep voice is tense, the stream of Russian that follows urgent.

"Fuck!" Nikolai shifts me off his lap and jackknifes to his feet, grabbing his clothes and yanking them on in a series of explosive movements.

It's such a sudden transition from the peace we were just enjoying that I'm too stunned to process it at first. But then adrenaline clears my mind, and I leap into motion as well.

"What's wrong? Is Slava sick again?" I scramble for my dress, my heart in my throat as I pull it on.

Nikolai is already by the back wall, pressing his palm against the smooth, white surface. "Slava is fine," he says grimly as a section of the wall slides away, revealing a room full of weapons to my startled gaze. "It's our guards. Arkash messaged Pavel about spotting something strange, and now Pavel can't get in touch with him—or any of our other men."

I gasp, my fist flying up to press against my lips. "You think—"

"We're being attacked? Yes." He grabs a terrifying-looking M16. "And if I had to bet, my money would be on the Leonovs."

49

NIKOLAI

Chloe's brown eyes are wide with fear and shock as I set my weapon down on the desk and shepherd her out into the hallway, where Pavel is waiting. My heart thuds furiously in my chest, adrenaline pumping through my veins as I order harshly, "Get her, Slava, and Alina to the safe room."

He nods, grabbing Chloe in a bear hug. "Lyudmila and the two of them are inside already."

"Wait!" Chloe cries out as he picks her up and carries her down the stairs. "Let me help. I can—"

I don't hear the rest of what she says because I'm already back inside my office. I can't take the time to calm my zaychik, not when every second brings Alexei Leonov closer to our door. And it has to be him. He has to be the one behind this. Our faces must've blipped on some security camera at the hospital, and his hackers tracked us here. It's the only explanation that makes any kind of sense, the only way they could've triangulated our location.

If it were just Pavel and myself, I wouldn't worry. We're trained for this, prepared to go into battle at a moment's notice. But Chloe and Slava are here too, as are my sister and Lyudmila. It's the thought of them in danger that chills my bones and fills my gut with acid.

I'll tear Alexei Leonov apart with my bare teeth before I let him take my son from me. And if he harms a single hair on Chloe or Alina's head, I will eviscerate each member of his family.

With effort, I rein in my rage and open my laptop to pull up the drone footage and the feeds from the perimeter cameras. What matters now is assessing the situation. Where are our attackers coming from? What are their numbers? My chest tightens as I think of Arkash and our other guards, many of them my friends, good men with families back home. How many of them have already been killed? How many wounded?

No matter what, I have to know.

I grab my laptop off the floor and flip it open.

The screen is dark and silent, unresponsive when I try to manually power it on.

Fuck. The fall must've damaged it.

I grab my phone instead—and feel my blood ice over.

It's the same story. The device is dead, the screen black no matter what I do to it.

I whirl around and hit the light switch on the wall.

It works.

My mind works furiously, leaping from one possibility to another. Could they have sent out some sort of EMP, frying our electronics? Is that why Pavel couldn't get in touch with the guards? Because their devices have also been disabled? But then what about Pavel's phone? Wouldn't he have noticed that it's dead?

Unless it wasn't at the time.

If the EMP was hyper-targeted, it might've hit our guards on the perimeter of the compound first, then struck the house.

I have no idea how Alexei could've gotten his paws on such an advanced weapon, but I do know one thing: Konstantin, paranoid techie that he is, thought an EMP attack wasn't completely out of the question. That's why our backup generator is analog and resides inside a Faraday cage deep underground, and why our key power lines are underground as well, hardened with metal casings.

The fuckers would've loved to cut our power, I'm sure, but they've had to settle for taking out our drones and cameras.

A distant *rat-tat-tat* of gunfire reaches my ears.

Thank fuck.

The guards must still be alive and doing their jobs.

I toss my dead phone aside and yank on a bulletproof vest, then strap on several guns and loop a dozen rounds of ammo over my shoulder. I also grab two functioning radios from the armory—like the metal-lined box with the generator, the hidden room is a Faraday cage.

By the time I'm done, Pavel bursts into my office, armed to the teeth as well. "The phones and radios, they're—"

"Dead, I know. Here." I thrust the second radio device into his hands. "Let's go. It's time the Leonovs learned who they're fucking with."

50

CHLOE

"Stop it, Chloe," Alina snaps, and I realize I've resumed tapping my foot—a physical manifestation of my anxiety that inexplicably annoys her. In general, she's more on edge than I've ever seen her, her own movements jerky and her spine so tense it's a wonder she can turn her neck.

"Sorry about that." I shift Slava so he's sitting more comfortably on my lap. "I'm just worried for them."

I'm holding the child as much to calm myself as to comfort him. In fact, out of the four of us, Slava is the least anxious—probably because he doesn't understand the magnitude of the threat we're facing. Lyudmila told him we're here as part of a security drill, and though I'm sure he's picking up on the adults' tension, he hasn't questioned the explanation.

I wish I could be calm as well, but I'm not. My chest is agonizingly tight, my insides churning like they're on a high-speed cycle in a washer. I'm acutely, terrifyingly aware of the fact that Nikolai is out there, facing down an unknown number of enemies—who may or may not be the Leonovs.

For all we know, Bransford has sent a whole army of assassins after me. It could very well be my fault we're in danger.

I catch my breathing speeding up again, and I force myself to inhale deeper to avoid hyperventilating. The safe room—a place I had no idea existed until Pavel tossed me in here—is carved into the mountain under the garage, and is large enough to be considered a studio apartment, complete with a king-sized bed, two futons, a fully stocked mini-kitchen, a small bathroom, and enough supplies in the pantry to survive a nuclear winter. Theoretically, there's plenty of oxygen here, but I keep feeling like we're running out of air, like the walls are inching closer to me with each passing second.

Nikolai is out there, and I'm stuck here, unable to do anything to help him.

"Can you just fucking stop?" Alina shoots up to her feet. Her face is vampire pale in the white light of the LED ceiling strip, her chest heaving as she glares at me, and I realize I've inadvertently resumed my foot tapping.

Before I can snap back—she's not the only one whose nerves are frayed—Lyudmila says something in Russian. Though her round face is pale as well, the tone of her voice is soothing, and Alina sinks back onto her futon, pushing back her hair with a shaking hand before smoothing it over her red evening gown.

I stare at her, struck by just how distressed she is, way more than when we had the incident with Slava. Does she know something that I don't?

Are we in even greater danger than I'm aware of?

I set Slava down on the bed and walk over to her, the cement floor cold on my bare feet—in the rush to get me down here, my strappy heels were left behind in Nikolai's office. Sitting next to her on the futon, I ask quietly, "Are you okay?"

She looks at me, her jade eyes glittering too brightly.

"Is something else going on?" I press. "You seem unusually agitated—not that you don't have good reason to be."

She opens her mouth to say something, then shakes her head. "It's nothing." Her voice is tight. "I'm getting a bad headache, that's all."

Of course. That's what happens when she's under stress. Poor thing. I cover her icy hand with mine, glad to focus on something other than my own debilitating fear. "Do you have your medication?"

"No."

I glance at the fold-out ladder leading up to the garage. What are the odds I could run upstairs and get it for her quickly?

"Don't even think about it," Alina snaps, reading my mind with her brother's uncanny skill. "If I want it, I'll get it myself. But neither one of us should—"

The ceiling light flickers as a loud *boom* shakes the room, making my stomach seize and sending plaster raining down on our heads.

As one, we jump to our feet, and I rush over to Slava, whose eyes are now wide with fear. "Mama Chloe." His voice is thin as I pick him up and settle his sturdy weight on my hip. "Where's Papa? I don't like this. I want him with me."

I tighten my arms around him. "Me too, darling. Me too. But don't worry. It'll be okay. Your daddy will be here soon. We just need to wait." I hope Slava can't feel me shaking—or see the expression on Alina's face.

She looks like she's been placed on death row, with the execution scheduled for today.

Lyudmila must notice because she steps up to Alina and wraps an arm around her slender shoulders, murmuring something in Russian. I catch the words "Alexei" and "braht"—the Russian word for "brother"—and I wish for the hundredth time that I knew more Russian.

I also desperately wish I knew what's happening up there, whether Nikolai and Pavel are okay. In addition to all the supplies, there's a panel of monitors on the other side of the room—presumably a window to the outside world—but the only thing we were able to see on the monitors when we turned them on was static.

"What do you think caused that?" I ask, unable to stay silent any longer. Despite my best efforts, my voice betrays my agitation, the awful terror gnawing at my insides at the thought of Nikolai getting hurt. Hugging

Slava to me tighter, I steady my tone. "The explosion, I mean. Do you think—"

"Could be an RPG." Alina's voice is flat now, oddly unemotional as she extricates herself from Lyudmila's supportive embrace, and even though her eyes are still glittering with that painful brightness, her features are composed once more. "They could've launched it at the garage to take out our vehicles and eliminate the option of escape. Either that, or they manually planted some explosives at the garage entrance—which would mean they're already here, at the house."

And Nikolai is badly injured or killed.

The nausea that twists my stomach is so severe I have to swallow to hold back vomit. It takes everything I have to keep my voice steady for Slava's sake. "Are there any guns down here? I've been to a shooting range a few times, so I can—"

Alina is already walking to the panel with the monitors, where she presses her palm against the wall the way Nikolai did in his office. And as in his office, the wall slides away, revealing a collection of weapons that would make an arms dealer proud.

"My brother has foreseen everything," she says, picking up a Glock. "They're unlikely to find this room anytime soon, but if they do, we're ready." She loads the gun with swift, sure movements that make me realize she's been to a gun range more than a few times.

In fact, she might be as dangerous with that weapon as her brother—and he is lethal. I've seen him in action. He can handle himself.

At least that's what I tell myself to keep from having a total freakout as I set Slava down so I can arm myself. He immediately grabs onto my legs and stares up at me, moisture pooling in his enormous eyes. "I want Daddy." His bottom lip quivers. "Where is he?"

I pat his silky hair, my chest contracting agonizingly. "I don't know, darling, but I'm sure we'll see him soon. For now, we just need to be prepared, okay? So your daddy knows we didn't fail this drill and that we can take care of ourselves—that we're all strong, like Superman."

Slava sniffles but lets go of my legs and steps back to let me pass.

"Good boy." I glance at Lyudmila to see if she can take him for now, but she's arming herself as well, handling the weapons with the same impressive skill as Alina. Which begs the question…

"What the fuck are we doing down here?" I burst out, forgetting myself for a moment. "We should be out there, helping them!" Realizing I'm scaring Slava, I lower my voice as I pick up a gun and begin to load it. "Maybe one of us can stay down here to watch over—"

Another *boom* rattles the dishes in the kitchen and sends more plaster raining down from the ceiling. The lights flicker several times, then wink out, plunging us into total darkness.

In the silence that follows, there's only my ragged breathing—and the sound of muffled gunfire overhead.

51

NIKOLAI

My radio crackles to life as I step out of the house. "Kirilov here. Do you read me?"

My stomach unknots slightly. "It's Nikolai. I read you." The guards must've realized what's happening and grabbed the emergency stash of radios from their own Faraday cage armory. "Status report, now."

"Twelve heavily armed attackers on the north side of the wall, fifteen by the gate. We've taken out half of them and are holding off the rest. No drones or cameras operational, and we've lost contact with Arkash and Ivanko by the east wall."

Fuck. That means there's most likely been a breach. "Take whichever men you can spare and get over there. Also send reinforcements to the house—Pavel and I might need them."

"On it."

The radio goes silent, and I pick up my pace. If our enemies are already here, inside the perimeter, there's very little time left to prepare an important line of defense—the bombs I've buried around the house.

The first one is on the driveway, precisely three-and-a-half meters from the front door. Stepping onto the subtly marked patch of gravel, I take out a remote activation fob and type in the pin required to sync it with the explosives underneath. It can only be done at a close distance, so no one can accidentally set off the bomb by grabbing the device from my office safe. Not that it's likely, with Pavel the only other person who knows the code to my safe, but with my son always playing around here, I couldn't risk it.

The second bomb is on the southeast corner of the house, the third by the garage. I sync the remote activators with them both and radio Pavel to check on his progress inside the house, part of which—the heavy-duty metal shutters covering the windows—I can see already.

"All set," he reports. "I'm heading up to the roof."

"I'll join you there in a minute."

With us positioned on two corners, no one will be able to approach the house unseen, and the sniper rifles and machine guns we have stationed there will hold off anything short of an army.

I'm about to instruct Pavel to grab extra ammunition when a flicker of movement to my right catches my attention. Swiftly, I step behind a thick tree—and watch with rage and disbelief as figures in black SWAT-type gear pour out of the forest by the dozen.

52

NIKOLAI

I COUNT THIRTY-THREE INVADERS BEFORE I OPEN FIRE, aiming at what I suspect to be the gaps in their full-body armor. I have to give Alexei credit—this is a military-grade operation, complete with a full-blown, well-equipped army.

They came prepared for war, and war is what I intend to give them.

I don't think about Chloe, Alina, and my son hidden in the safe room underneath the house, don't focus on what will happen to them if I fail. I can't, not if I'm to succeed. In front of me is a far bigger than anticipated force; as prepared as we were for an attack, it wasn't for one of this ferocity or scale.

I underestimated how much the Leonovs want Slava back, what Alexei is willing to do to take my son —his nephew—from me. Unless... Slava isn't the only member of my family he's after.

But no. That's madness. That betrothal contract has

always been a sick man's joke, a useless, toothless piece of paper.

There's no way Alexei brought this army to acquire Alina.

My bullets take down five of the invaders before they realize where I am and open fire in my direction. I wait ten seconds, letting their bullets tear pieces of bark off my tree, then fire back, not bothering to aim. The goal now is to buy time for Pavel to get to the roof, and for our reinforcements to arrive—assuming they ever do.

Given the numbers we're up against, it's possible Kirilov and his men have already been taken out.

A hail of bullets ricochets off the nearby trees, missing my shoulder by centimeters. Alexei's men are coming closer and fanning out, I realize grimly. If I stay here, I'll be surrounded in no time, but if I make a run for it, their bullets will mow me down even faster.

Reaching a decision, I drop onto my stomach and smear dirt over my face to hide the light hue of my skin. Then I carefully peer out from behind the tree, using the tall weeds around me as cover.

As I suspected, the attackers have split into two groups—one to surround me, the other to continue on toward the house. Eight of the black-clad figures are on the driveway, approaching the front door, while five others are creeping around the house to the garage, presumably to try to get into the house from there.

My heartbeat thunders in my ears, sweat soaking my back as a fresh hail of bullets kicks up chunks of dirt around me, yet I wait, still and silent, all my attention on the threat to my family, to the woman and child who are my entire life.

If I can save them, I'll die happy.

If I can ensure their safety, nothing else matters.

I wait, and when the moment is right, I set off the driveway bomb, and a second later, the one by the garage entrance. They go off with the force of landmines, ripping apart everyone within a three-meter radius and painting the nighttime landscape red.

They also distract the men hunting me, who spin around to see their teammates being blown apart. Two seconds is all it buys me, but that's all I need to jump to my feet and sprint for the cluster of trees by the side of the garage, looping around the line of heavily armed men in front of me. My goal is simple: protect the garage entrance at all costs, keeping them away from the underground safe room.

A bullet whizzes past my ear as I run. Another kisses my bicep with stinging fire.

They're on to me.

It's over.

A peculiar calm descends on me, the certainty that death is coming. My heartbeat slows fatalistically, yet my body keeps moving, my leg muscles pumping with greater effort. Some sixth sense makes me angle sharply right, then left, but a bullet still grazes my right shoulder, leaving another streak of fire in its wake.

The cluster of trees is closer now, a few long jumps away, but even a meter is too far when you're out in the open with fuck knows how many guns spitting out lethal chunks of lead.

On instinct, I tuck and roll, and several bullets whizz above me, exactly where my torso and head would've been. The next set of bullets won't be fooled, I know, but just as I prepare to feel them tear through my flesh, a violent explosion of sound erupts above—and my pulse speeds back to life as I recognize the rattle of a machine gun.

Pavel got to the roof.

I finally have cover.

Sure enough, he mows down the black-clad figures as they scatter back toward the forest, and I make it to the tree cluster and add my fire to Pavel's efforts. Before long, all of our attackers—the ones who can still move, that is—have pulled back, their answering gunfire dying down as they take cover.

The machine gun ceases firing as well.

I wipe the sweat and dirt off my face and bring up my radio. "Kirilov? You there?"

A crackle, followed by static.

Fuck.

I switch channels. "Pavel?"

"Still here. But I think they got most of our men."

I ignore the sharp pinching in my chest. "I know. It's going to be a long fucking night."

As I speak, I scan the forest, searching for any hint of movement. By my count, only twenty-four of our attackers are on the ground, leaving nine unaccounted for—plus however many of their comrades survived the battle with our guards.

I'm so focused on my task I almost miss the dark figure melting out of the shadows right by the garage entrance—and by the time I swing my gun toward it, it's too late.

As the enemy dives aside to avoid my bullets, the garage door explodes into pieces, the shockwave nearly rupturing my eardrums.

53

NIKOLAI

I SPRING INTO ACTION BEFORE THE SOUND OF THE explosion fades.

"Cover me," I hiss into the radio and sprint for the burning hole in the garage, ignoring the high-pitched ringing in my ears.

I have to get to the garage before the attacker recovers from the blast.

I have to intercept him before he gets inside and finds the safe room.

As I run, bullets strike the ground around me, kicking up chunks of grass and dirt, but Pavel's machine gun keeps the shooters sufficiently far away to interfere with their aim.

The closer I get to the garage, the more the extent of the damage becomes apparent. The fucker must've glued explosives directly to the bottom of the door, as the force of the blast not only tore apart the heavy metal but left a blackened hole in the floor around it too. And—*fuck*. Those are indeed exposed wires.

The explosion must've knocked out power to the safe room too.

It won't stay out; in a few minutes, the second backup generator will kick in, but I can only imagine how scared Chloe and Slava must be right now. As thick as the ceiling and the walls of the safe room are, there's no way they didn't hear this explosion—or, come to think of it, the bomb I set off nearby.

No matter. I'll comfort them as soon as we're all safe.

Speaking of which, where is the bomb-setting fucker? Is it too much to hope the bastard didn't survive his own blast?

My heart pumps pure adrenaline, my nerves thrumming with heightened awareness as I step through the burning opening into the dark garage, holding my breath to avoid inhaling smoke. It's futile; as I advance deeper, I realize the smoke has filled every crevice of the space, so thick in places it dims the red glow of the flames.

Swearing silently, I tear a chunk of material off the bottom of my shirt and press the makeshift handkerchief to my face to avoid coughing as I step around one of our SUVs, scanning the hazy darkness for signs of movement... listening for someone else's cough.

And then I hear it.

A single cough, followed by a full-blown coughing fit—only it's not a man's deep-throated hacking but a small, high-pitched one.

The cough of a young child.

54

CHLOE

"Slava? Slava, where are you?" I grope around me in the darkness, my heart pounding sickeningly fast as I stuff the gun into my bodice. "Alina, Lyudmila, you there? Where is he? I can't find Slava."

"He was right next to you." Alina's tone is as tense as mine. "Slava! Slavochka, *ti gdye?*"

No reply.

I whirl around, arms outstretched. "Slava! This isn't a game. We're not playing hide-and-seek. Lyudmila, do you see him?"

"No." She sounds equally worried. "Maybe he hurt. I search now for light."

Right. There have to be some flashlights around here. I squeeze my eyes shut, then open them, trying to get my vision to adjust to the darkness—and to my surprise, it works.

It's not pitch-black around me now. In fact, there's faint light coming from the other side of the room.

The side where the ladder is.

My heartbeat speeds up further as I head toward it, doing my best not to trip. "Slava? Slava, come here!" My panic is growing by the second. Not only is the child missing, but I'm beginning to smell something sharp and acrid.

Smoke.

"Slava!" My voice rises in pitch and volume as more light reaches my eyeballs, filling my stomach with cold terror.

There's no longer any doubt where Slava has gone.

The ceiling door at the top of the ladder is propped open.

55

NIKOLAI

The terror that seizes me is so absolute that for a moment, I'm certain I misheard, that the child's cough was nothing more than a hallucination brought on by all the smoke.

It can't be my son. He's down in the safe room, where it's fucking safe. Where he's supposed to be with Chloe and my sister.

But no. There's that cough again, followed by an achingly familiar, "Papa? Daddy?"

My stomach is a ball of ice, but I retain enough presence of mind not to yell out that I'm here, in case the enemy is also inside. Instead, I get down and crouch-walk over to where I heard Slava's voice—a move that has the benefit of helping me breathe cleaner air, as there's more smoke higher up.

Still, the urge to cough is growing, the toxic particles filling up my lungs. My chest heaves convulsively, my eyes watering from the effort of suppressing the reflex, and I know I will betray myself before long.

I have to locate Slava ASAP.

"Papa? Where are you?"

Fuck. His voice sounds farther away.

He's heading for the garage door, seeking to escape the smoke.

How the fuck is he by himself? Has something happened to Chloe and Alina?

Staying low to the floor, I hurry after him, my heart thudding heavily as my lungs continue screaming that I need to cough, to expel the contaminated air.

"Daddy?"

Slava's tiny figure is briefly outlined by the glow of the flames, and then he steps through the burning hole, disappearing outside.

Fuck it. Coughing hard, I jerk up to my feet and launch into a sprint.

If I catch a bullet, so be it.

I burst outside, gun at the ready, and I see him.

My son, standing just a few meters away, his small face brightening at the sight of me.

"Daddy!" He waves a knife in the air. "I came to help —like Superman."

My heart thunders with a mix of fear and relief as I start toward him—only to freeze in place as a dark figure melts out of the shadows behind him, gun pointed at me.

"Come here, Slavchik," Alexei Leonov says, pulling off his face mask with one hand to reveal black eyes glowing with the light of the sputtering flames behind me. "You're safe now, kid. Your uncle's come to take you home."

56

CHLOE

FORGETTING EVERYTHING, I HIKE UP THE LONG SKIRT OF my dress and climb up the ladder, my terror growing as I climb through the open ceiling door and thicker smoke envelops me, the acrid smell snaking into my nostrils and making my eyes burn.

"Slava!" I cough, peering through the hazy, red-tinted darkness. "Slava, come back!"

Nothing. No response.

"Chloe, wait!"

Ignoring Alina's cry, I climb out completely and survey the smoky hell that is the inside of the garage. It's like a scene from a disaster movie, complete with plaster-covered cars with shattered windows and flickering flames by the big metal door—a door that sports a giant, burning hole.

My pulse skyrockets and I launch into a run, ignoring the shards of glass and rock-like bits of broken concrete biting into my bare feet. The pain is nothing compared to the dread sawing at my stomach.

That hole is where Slava must've gone.

He must've come up here right after the explosion and run outside, straight into God knows what danger.

At least there's no sound of gunfire now—but that could change at any moment. Coughing, I pull the heavy gun out of my bodice and grip it tightly with both hands, lest it slips from my sweaty fingers.

"Slava!" I run through the hole, ignoring the flames eating at its edges—only to skid to a halt, gripped by horror.

In front of me is a scene straight out of a western: Nikolai and an unknown man, guns pointed at each other in a lethal standoff, with wide-eyed Slava in the middle.

57

CHLOE

Hyperventilating, I bring up my gun, pointing the barrel at the stranger. "Drop your weapon and back away!"

I mean to sound authoritative, but instead, my words come out in a hoarse, trembling croak, my throat raw from smoke.

The man's dark gaze flicks toward me for a millisecond, but he doesn't move an inch. "*Idi syuda*, Slavchik." His deep voice is eerily calm. "*Bystro*."

To my shock, I recognize the first portion of the Russian phrase.

Come here, the stranger said, using another diminutive of the child's name.

Nikolai's gaze doesn't leave his opponent's face, though I know he's aware of my presence. I can feel the lethal tension emanating from him, see his hard jaw flexing.

"My son isn't going anywhere with you," he growls

in English at the stranger. "Slavochka, get behind me. Go now."

Slava looks confused, his gaze shifting back and forth between the two men. "*Dyadya Lyosha? Papa?*"

Dyadya. I strain my brain for a translation, and then it comes to me.

Uncle, that word means. And *Lyosha* is probably diminutive for *Alexei*.

Nikolai was right. It *is* the Leonovs—or at least one of them.

Slava's uncle.

The gun is heavy in my outstretched hands, much heavier than they portray in movies. My shoulders and neck muscles are beginning to ache, my forearms tiring from gripping the weapon so tightly. Ignoring the discomfort, I keep it pointed at the man, my mind spinning frantically, trying to think of a way out of this fucked-up situation.

After everything Nikolai has told me about the Leonovs, I half expected horns and a tail, and there *is* something demonic in Alexei's harsh features—especially his eyes. They're so dark they appear black, making me think of tar pools in the depths of a volcano, complete with a reddish cast from the flickering flames reflecting in them. Yet the man isn't ugly, far from it.

If Nikolai hadn't set an impossibly high bar for male beauty, I might've found Slava's uncle dangerously attractive.

Not that his looks matter when he's holding that

gun pointed at Nikolai—and *his* thickly muscled arms don't show any signs of tiring. Neither do Nikolai's. Both men might as well be made of steel, their faces taut with mutual hatred.

Slava, on the other hand, doesn't seem to partake in that sentiment. If anything, he appears torn between his father and his uncle, his head swiveling back and forth, his posture speaking of bewilderment at the tension between the two adults rather than fear of the invader.

If the child experienced any abuse while living with his mother's family, it wasn't at this man's hands.

Coming to a decision, I cautiously edge forward. As terrified as I am for Nikolai, I have to get Slava out of the direct line of fire.

"Slavochka..." I make my voice as calm and gentle as I can. "Please come to me. Mama Chloe needs you here."

The boy doesn't move. Somehow, he must sense that his presence is the only thing keeping the violence from escalating.

I risk another half-step forward, and Slava finally moves, dashing toward me. As soon as he's near enough, I grab him by the arm and shove him behind me, blocking him with my body as I begin to back away.

The stranger lets out a rough laugh, his dark eyes flashing briefly to the ring on my finger. "Mama Chloe, is it?" Like Nikolai's, his English is as American as they come. "Sweetheart... if you move another muscle, I'll blow your brains out and then your dear husband's. Congratulations on your nuptials by the way," he continues as I freeze in place. "I'm guessing the wedding was very recent?"

Nikolai's eyes are slitted, his voice deadly soft. "None of your fucking business. Now leave before I paint the ground with *your* brains. Since we seem to be family and all, I'll let you walk away before the guards get here."

"What guards?" Alexei's sharp-edged smile is all white teeth and cruelty. "It's just me and my men here now. And you're fucking high if you think I'm leaving without what I came for. Hand over my sister's son and Alina—and maybe, just maybe, I'll let you and your pretty bride live. Seeing as we're about to be even closer family and all."

I blink. Alina? What does she have to do with anything? And what does he mean about closer family?

Nikolai's voice softens further, a lethal threat in every smoothly spoken syllable. "You have exactly thirty seconds to shut up and back away before I open fire."

"With her and the child here? I don't think so." His eyes cut toward me for another millisecond. "Besides, my snipers have you both in their sights."

My stomach drops, but Nikolai just bares his teeth. "Bullshit. They don't have a clear shot."

"No? Want to bet?" Alexei grins savagely. "Either way, all I need to do is wait, and my men will take down the shooter on your roof—at which point you'll be completely surrounded, and I'll take what I came for."

"Not if you're dead by then." Nikolai's expression is dark ice. "You have twenty seconds left. Nineteen. Eighteen..."

My heartbeat surges, my terror doubling with each second counted. He means it, I can see it—and so can Alexei, whose black eyes narrow as well. The smoke-scented air is so thick with incipient violence I can practically taste the warm, coppery spray of blood as bullets rip through flesh and bone.

One or both of these men will die here tonight.

Nikolai won't let his son be taken, and Alexei won't back down.

I have to do something.

If Nikolai is right about the snipers not having a clear shot, it's two of us against Alexei. If I shoot, maybe—

"Stop!" Like a wraith, Alina emerges from the smoky darkness of the garage, the blood-red of her gown contrasting with the ghostly paleness of her skin and the jet-black curtain of her hair.

Like me, she's armed, but unlike me, she's holding her gun loosely at her side, the barrel pointed at the ground.

"Stop, Alexei, please." She steps through the jagged opening, the glow of the dying flames turning her jade eyes a greenish shade of hazel. "Slava isn't going anywhere, you know that. My brother won't give up his son. And he's not—" Her voice cracks. "He's not the one you want anyway."

I suck in a breath, finally comprehending what's happening. This man and Alina—they know each other.

More than that, he thinks he has some type of claim on her.

"Alina, get back." Nikolai's tone takes on a sharper edge as Alexei's entire posture alters, a terrifying sort of hunger kindling in his demonic gaze as it locks on Alina's face.

She raises her gun, aiming it at his face. "You have a choice," she says evenly. "I know you're an excellent shot, but so is my brother—and so am I. And so is Lyudmila in there." She tips her head toward the dark garage. "Maybe you can take down one or two of us before our bullets find you—and maybe your snipers can help—but nobody is going to walk away unscathed. You might have the advantage of the forces surrounding us, but here, we outnumber you. Besides..." Her voice takes on a sardonic inflection. "What good am I to you dead, right?"

"Alina, shut up and get back inside," Nikolai growls. "You don't have to—"

"I will come with you," she continues, ignoring her brother. "I will honor the betrothal contract. And in exchange, you will call off your men and forget all about my nephew. He belongs here, with his father and Chloe—you can see that for yourself."

Alexei's eyes flash toward me for another fraction

of a second, taking in the child I'm shielding with my body, absorbing the way he's clinging to my legs while observing the proceedings with enormous, uncomprehending eyes.

That's why they're all speaking English, I realize with a distant corner of my mind. They're hoping Slava won't understand everything with his still-limited knowledge of the language—and it's at least partially working. He can see the adults pointing guns at each other, but he doesn't fully get why.

Alexei's gaze returns to Alina, the black orbs burning with even darker hunger. "All right. We have a deal. Lay down the gun and walk toward me."

"Do not fucking do it." Nikolai's voice is whip sharp. "I can take him."

"Maybe." She lays her weapon on the ground. "Or maybe you'll both die. Maybe Chloe and Slava will as well. Think about that."

Nikolai's jaw clenches. "I'm not letting you do this."

A bitter smile touches her lips. "It's not your call, brother. Nor is it mine. That whole fate business you believe in? Well, mine was decided when I was fifteen, and it's time I stopped running from it. You and Konstantin have shielded me long enough."

Nikolai is about to argue further, I can see it, but she forestalls any further discussion by swiftly walking over to Alexei—who grabs her elbow and pulls her to his side as soon as she's within reach.

The possessive way he holds her pinned against him leaves no doubt of his intent, his dark figure looming over her making me think of Hades dragging Persephone down into the underworld.

Nikolai must see the same thing because his face twists with fury and he takes a half-step forward—only to halt when Alexei's finger tightens warningly on the trigger.

"Don't, Kolya." Alina's eyes glitter brightly as Alexei begins backing up toward the tree line, dragging her along while keeping his gun trained on Nikolai. "I'll be fine. Just take care of Chloe and Slava, and I'll see you back in Moscow sometime, okay? And tell Konstantin not to look for me. I don't want blood spilled on my behalf!"

The last words reach us as a shout from the distance, and Nikolai's gaze burns with hatred as he watches his enemy disappear into the darkness with his prize, the shadows closing around them like a lover's fierce embrace.

58

CHLOE

I WAKE UP TO A CACOPHONY OF DRILLS AND HAMMERS IN the distance—a familiar soundtrack for the past few days. Ever since the attack last week, both the house and the grounds of the compound have been undergoing major renovations and security upgrades, including a quintupling of our guard force.

Nikolai is determined to ensure that no one, be it the Leonovs or some other enemy of ours, can breach our walls again, no matter how many mercenaries or advanced weapons they have at their disposal.

Opening my eyes, I take in the empty mattress next to me and the faint morning light seeping in through the blinds. It's barely sunrise, so my husband must've gotten up early for the videoconference with his brothers regarding the ongoing search for Alina—if he slept at all last night, that is. Much to my worry, his middle-of-the-night runs have increased in both frequency and duration since the attack, so much so that I don't know when he's getting any rest at all.

The door swings open, and the object of my musings enters the bedroom.

I sit up, my heart squeezing at the bleak expression on his face.

"Nothing?" I ask quietly as he crosses the room toward me.

He shakes his head. "It's like they've disappeared off the face of the fucking planet. Konstantin thinks he's holding her somewhere completely off the grid, but where is anyone's guess at this point."

"I'm so sorry." I reach over to squeeze his hand as he sits on the edge of the bed, but he pulls me onto his lap instead. Wrapping his powerful arms tightly around me, he buries his face in my hair and inhales deeply.

When he pulls back to meet my gaze, some of the tension in his face has eased. Cupping my cheek, he asks softly, "How are you feeling, zaychik? Did you sleep well?"

I turn my face to press a kiss into his palm before bringing his hand down to my chest. "Yes." I smile to dispel the lingering worry in his eyes. "I'm fine, I promise."

To say that Nikolai has been babying me over the past few days would be a major understatement. Though a few shallow cuts and bruises on my bare feet were the extent of my injuries, he's been treating me like I've sustained another gunshot wound—or at the very least, have been severely traumatized. And while it's true that I've been having nightmares again, I'm far from falling apart.

Not that I'm not worried about Alina—I am. Nikolai told me about the betrothal agreement their father made with Boris Leonov when Alina was barely fifteen, and if I still had any doubts that the man deserved his fate at Nikolai's hands, they disappeared in that moment.

No wonder Alexei had acted as if he had a claim on her. By that barbaric—and undoubtedly illegal—contract, he does. I can only hope his feelings for her extend beyond the dark lust I saw on his face that night, and that he isn't as terrible of a man as his reputation suggests.

Nikolai's lips curve in an answering smile as he moves to shift me off his lap, but I wrap my arms around his neck, refusing to let him go. "Lie down with me, please," I murmur into his ear. "I'm not ready to get up yet."

As concerned as I am about Alina, I'm almost as worried about how hard Nikolai is taking what happened. He hasn't had a single decent night of sleep over the past week, and it shows in the darker hollows around his striking eyes, the deeper grooves bracketing his sensuous mouth… his unrelenting obsession with Slava's and my safety.

Not only did Nikolai refuse to remove the cameras from inside the house when I asked, but he's having me and Slava wear tracker bracelets that tell him our exact location and measure our vital signs at all times.

I've opted not to fight him on this for now, as we've had much bigger issues to focus on, including the funerals for the fallen guards—yet another reason for Nikolai's grim mood. More than a dozen of our men were killed in the attack, and several others were severely injured—though, luckily, most of Nikolai's army friends weren't among the former.

Alexei's men pinned them down in a ravine, preventing them from coming to our aid or radioing for help, but everybody except Ivanko survived. Even Arkash, who caught a bullet perilously close to his spine, is expected to make a full recovery.

The other bright spot in all of this is Slava. Once we explained that what he saw was a part of the security drill, and that Alina went on vacation with "Uncle Lyosha," the boy has gone right back to his cheerful self, pestering me, Pavel, and Lyudmila with a million questions about the new guards and the construction going on at the compound.

"Zaychik..." Nikolai's voice takes on a hoarser note as I oh-so-innocently let my lips graze his earlobe. "I wish I could join you, but I have a lot of work this morning."

Of course he does, but it can wait until he gets some sleep. Dropping all pretense of innocence, I wriggle my butt against the growing bulge in his pants and kiss the hard underside of his jaw. "Please... pretty please."

If there's one thing the events of last week haven't affected, it's Nikolai's sex drive—and sure enough, that kiss is all it takes for him to flip me onto my back and fuck me until we're both sweaty, sore, and beyond satisfied. And, as I hoped, exhausted enough to sleep… at least those of us who haven't gotten any shuteye.

I wait until I'm sure Nikolai is deep in the embrace of slumber before I carefully wriggle out from underneath his arm and pad over to the bathroom to shower and get ready for the day.

When I come out, he's still asleep, the stamp of exhaustion heavy upon his beautiful features. Smiling tenderly, I watch him for a while. Then I plop into a lounge chair by the window and open my laptop to check the news, as has been my custom every morning for the past few days.

As we hoped, more of Bransford's victims have come forward since the story about his assault on Masha broke—and not just the two women Nikolai found. Every day has brought fresh, ever-more-horrifying revelations… which is why I've been so addicted to the news.

Every damning headline avenges my mom further.

Opening a browser, I navigate to my favorite news site—only to freeze at the words splashed boldly across the screen:

BRANSFORD COMMITS SUICIDE IN HOTEL ROOM

Stomach churning, I click on the article.

Apparently, some thirty-nine minutes ago, Tom Bransford was found in a Four Seasons penthouse with his wrists slit, the suicide note by his bed leaving little doubt as to what happened.

That is, little doubt for anyone who doesn't know my husband and what he's capable of.

Setting the laptop aside, I get up and walk over to the bed, my heart beating unevenly as I stare at the man sleeping there—the husband I've grown to love more than life itself.

Did he do this?

Did he decide that, even stripped of his political pull and on the verge of being criminally prosecuted, Bransford poses too great of a threat to me?

Did Masha or someone like her slip into that Four Seasons penthouse and set everything up to make it look like Bransford killed himself—same as his assassins had done to my mom?

I should wake up Nikolai and demand the answer to these questions, get him to admit the truth—but I know I won't. Not because I'm still afraid to face the darkness within him, but because I'm realizing that this particular truth doesn't matter to me.

Suicide or assassination, Bransford is gone, and that vengeful part of me—the part I wanted to pretend wasn't there—is happy. No, more than happy. It's downright ecstatic.

Whether at Nikolai's hand or his own, Tom Bransford got exactly what he deserved.

I stand by the bed for a minute longer, absorbing the sheer relief of that knowledge, the lifting of the weight I hadn't realized still sat across my shoulders. I let that sensation filter through as I think about the lethal beauty of my husband's face and the terrible darkness in his soul—a darkness I now realize exists in me as well.

Then, carefully, so as not to interrupt his much-needed rest, I lie down next to him and drape my arm across his chest. His eyes don't open and his breathing doesn't alter, but he turns and gathers me against him, his powerful body curving around me, warming me, shielding me from the world.

My chest expands, my heart so full it feels on the verge of bursting. Just a couple of months ago, I was an orphan on the run from her mother's killers, a woman all alone in the world with a life expectancy measured in days. Now I have my husband and my son, and a future full of possibilities.

Maybe we'll stay here for the next few years, and I'll get a teaching job at a local school—a school that Slava will attend as well. Or maybe we'll go to Moscow, and Nikolai will take up the reins of his family organization again, with all that it entails. Or maybe it'll be something else entirely, a path I can't even imagine at the moment.

Whatever that path is, wherever we go from here, doesn't matter.

As long as I have my dark protector, I fear nothing.

Together, Nikolai and I can take on the whole world.

SNEAK PEAKS

Thank you for following Chloe & Nikolai's epic romance! If you would consider leaving a review, it would be greatly appreciated. While *Angel's Cage* concludes their story, Alina and Alexei's journey continues in *Terrible Beauty*.

To be notified about my future books, sign up for my newsletter at www.annazaires.com.

Are you craving more dark, suspenseful romance? My latest collaboration with Charmaine Pauls, *White Nights,* tells the addictive story of a dangerous Russian oligarch and the American nurse he sets his sights on.

Do you enjoy laugh-out-loud romantic comedy? My hubby and I co-write raunchy, geeky romcoms under the pen name Misha Bell. Grab a copy of *Of Octopuses and Men,* an enemies-to-lovers romcom featuring

Olive, a sun-fearing marine biologist, and Oliver, her sizzling hot (and infuriating) new boss.

Are you an Urban Fantasy fan? Check out *Dream Walker*! Written by my hubby Dima Zales, this is an action-packed tale of a dreamwalker on a mission to save her mom, without falling in love with the dangerous illusionist helping her.

If you like audiobooks, please visit www.annazaires.com to check out this duet and our other books in audio.

Now, please turn the page to read excerpts from *Terrible Beauty* and *White Nights.*

EXCERPT FROM TERRIBLE BEAUTY BY ANNA ZAIRES

A family contract. A dark bargain. No escape.

Eleven years ago, I met him. A year later, I was betrothed to him. Now he's come to claim me, slaughtering anyone standing in his way.

My husband-to-be is a monster from a family as ruthless and powerful as mine, a man who deals in violence and destruction... a man terrifyingly like my father. For over a decade, he's stalked me, shadowing my life.

I fear him. I hate him. Worst of all, I want him.

My name is Alina Molotova, and Alexei Leonov is a fate I can't escape.

Cool lips brush my throbbing forehead, bringing with them a faint aroma of pine, ocean, and leather. "Shh… It's okay. You're okay. I just gave you something to ease your headache and make this easier."

The male voice is deep and dark, strangely familiar. The words are spoken in Russian. My fuzzy mind struggles to focus. Why Russian? I'm in America, aren't I? How do I know this voice? This scent?

I try to pry open my heavy lids, but they refuse to budge. Same goes for my hand when I attempt to lift it. Everything feels impossibly heavy, like my very bones are made of metal, my flesh of concrete. My head lolls to one side, my neck muscles unable to support its weight. It's as if I were a newborn. I try to speak, but an incoherent noise escapes my throat, blending with a distant roar that my ears can now discern.

Maybe I am a newborn. That would explain why I'm so ridiculously helpless and can't make sense of anything.

"Here, lie down." Strong hands guide me onto some soft, flat surface. Well, most of me. My head ends up on something elevated and hard, yet comfortable. Not a pillow, too hard for that, but not a stone either. There isn't much give in the object, but there is some. Also, it's oddly warm.

The object shifts slightly, and from the foggy recesses of my mind, the answer to the mystery emerges. *A lap.* My head is lying on someone's lap. A male someone, judging by the steely, thickly muscled thighs underneath my aching skull.

My pulse accelerates. Even with my thoughts sluggish and tangled, I know this isn't normal for me. I don't do laps or men. At least I haven't thus far in all of my twenty-five years.

Twenty-five. I latch on to that sliver of knowledge. I'm twenty-five, not a newborn. Encouraged, I sift through more of the tangled threads, seeking an answer as to what's happening, but it eludes me, the recollections coming slowly, if at all.

Darkness. Fire. A nightmare demon coming to claim me.

Is that a memory or something I saw in a movie?

A needle biting deep into my neck. Unwelcome lassitude spreading through my body.

That part feels real. My mind might not be functioning, but my body knows the truth. It senses the threat. My heart rate intensifies as adrenaline saturates my veins. Yes. Yes, that's it. I can do it. With strength born of growing terror, I force open my leaden lids and look up into a pair of eyes darker than the night surrounding us. Eyes set in a cruelly handsome face that haunts my dreams… and my nightmares.

"Don't fight it, Alinyonok," Alexei Leonov murmurs. His dark voice holds both a promise and a threat as he gently threads his fingers through my hair, massaging away the throbbing tension in my skull. "You'll only make it harder on yourself."

The edges of his calluses catch on the tangles in my long hair, and he pulls his fingers out, only to curve his palm around my jaw. He has big hands, dangerous hands. Hands that have killed dozens today alone. The recollection roils my stomach even as some knot of tension deep inside me unravels. For ten long years, I've dreaded this moment, and finally, it's here.

He's here.

He's come for me.

"Don't cry," my husband-to-be says softly, brushing away the wetness on my face with the rough edge of his thumb. "It won't help. You know that."

Yes, I do. Nothing and no one can help me now. I recognize that distant roar. It's the sound of a plane engine. We're in the air.

I close my eyes and let the hazy darkness take me.

EXCERPT FROM WHITE NIGHTS BY ANNA ZAIRES AND CHARMAINE PAULS

Power. That's what I think of when I spot him across the ER. Power and danger.

One of the wealthiest Russian oligarchs, Alex Volkov is as ruthless as he is magnetic. He always gets what he wants, and what he wants is me, in his bed.

He's the kind of trouble every woman should run from. The bullet his bodyguard took for him proves that.

I should stay far away, but for one night, I give in to temptation. Before I know it, he's pulling me deeper into his world of excess and violence, invading not only my life but my heart.

How much trust can I place in a man so dangerous? How much do I dare risk for his love?

Turning away from the sink, I look back at the wounded man, making sure everything is okay with him before I go check on my other patients.

At that moment, I catch a pair of steely blue eyes looking at me.

It's one of the men standing near the victim, likely one of his relatives. Visitors are generally not allowed in the hospital at night, but the ER is an exception.

Instead of looking away, as most people will when caught staring, the man continues to study me.

Both intrigued and slightly annoyed, I study him back.

He's tall, well over six feet in height, and broad-shouldered. He's not handsome in the traditional sense. That's too weak of a word to describe him. Instead, he's magnetic.

Power. That's what comes to mind when I look at him. It's there in the arrogant tilt of his head, in the way he looks at me so calmly, utterly sure of himself and his ability to control all around him. I don't know who he is or what he does, but I doubt he's a pencil pusher in some office. This is a man used to issuing orders and having them obeyed.

His clothes fit him well and look expensive. Maybe even custom made. He's wearing a gray trench coat, dark gray pants with a subtle pinstripe, and a pair of black Italian leather shoes. His brown hair is cut short, almost military style. The simple haircut suits his face, revealing hard, symmetric features. He has high cheekbones and a blade of a nose with a slight bump, as though it had been broken once.

I have no idea how old he is. His face is unlined, but there's no boyishness to it. No softness whatsoever, not even in the curve of his mouth. I guess his age to be early thirties, but he can just as easily be twenty-five or forty.

He doesn't fidget or look uncomfortable as our staring contest continues. He simply stands there quietly, completely still, his blue gaze trained on me.

To my shock, my heart rate picks up as a tingle of heat runs down my spine. It's as though the temperature in the room has jumped ten degrees. All of a sudden, the atmosphere becomes intensely sexual, making me aware of myself as a woman in a way I've never experienced. I can feel the silky material of my matching underwear set brushing between my legs and against my breasts. My entire body seems flushed and sensitized, my nipples pebbling underneath my layers of clothing.

Holy shit.

So that's what it feels like to be attracted to someone. It's not rational and logical. There's no meeting of minds and hearts involved. No, the urge is basic and primitive. My body has sensed his on some animal level, and it wants to mate.

He feels it too. It shows in the way his blue eyes darken, lids partially lowering, and in the way his nostrils flare as though trying to catch my scent. His fingers twitch, curl into fists, and I somehow know he's trying to control himself, to avoid reaching for me right then and there.

If we were alone, I have no doubt he'd be on me already.

Still staring at the stranger, I back away. The strength of my response to him is frightening, unsettling. We're in the middle of the ER, surrounded by people, and all I can think about is hot, sheet-twisting sex. I have no idea who he is, whether he's married or single. For all I know, he's a criminal or an asshole. *Or a cheating scumbag like Tony.* If anyone has taught me to think twice before trusting a man, it's my ex-boyfriend. I don't want to get involved with anyone so soon after my last, disastrous relationship. I don't want that kind of complication in my life again.

The tall stranger clearly has other ideas.

At my cautious retreat, he narrows his eyes, his gaze becoming sharper, more focused. Then he comes toward me, his stride graceful for such a large man. There's something panther-like in his leisurely movements, and for a second, I feel like a mouse getting stalked by a big cat. Instinctively, I take another step back, and his hard mouth tightens with displeasure.

Dammit, I'm acting like a coward.

I stop backing away and stand my ground instead, straightening to my full five-foot-seven height. I'm always the calm and capable one, handling high-stress situations with ease, yet I'm behaving like a schoolgirl confronted with her first crush. Yes, the man makes me uncomfortable, but there's nothing to be afraid of. What's the worst he can do? Ask me out on a date?

Nevertheless, my hands shake slightly as he approaches, stopping less than two feet away. This close, he's even taller than I thought, a few inches over six feet. I'm not a short woman, but I feel tiny standing in front of him. It's not a feeling I enjoy.

"You're very good at your job." His voice is deep and a little rough, tinged with some Eastern European accent. Just hearing it makes my insides shiver in a strangely pleasurable way.

"Thank you," I say, a bit uncertainly. I *am* good at my job, but I didn't expect a compliment from this stranger.

"You took care of Igor well. Thank you for that."

Igor must be the gunshot patient. It's a foreign-sounding name. Russian, perhaps? That would explain the stranger's accent. Although he speaks English fluently, he's not a native speaker.

"Of course." I'm proud of the steadiness of my tone. Hopefully, the man won't realize how he affects me. "I hope he recovers quickly. Is he a relative?"

"My bodyguard."

Wow. I was right. This man is a big fish. Does that mean—

"Was he shot in the course of duty?" I ask, holding my breath.

"He took a bullet meant for me, yes." His tone is

matter-of-fact, but I get a sense of suppressed rage underneath those words.

I swallow hard. "Did you already speak to the police?"

"I gave them a brief statement. I will talk to them in more detail once Igor is stabilized and regains consciousness."

I nod, not knowing what to say to that. The man standing in front of me was nearly assassinated today. What is he? Some mafia boss? A political figure?

If I had any doubts about the wisdom of exploring this strange attraction between us, they're gone. This stranger is bad news, and I need to stay as far away from him as possible.

"I wish your bodyguard a speedy recovery," I say in a falsely cheerful tone. "Barring any complications, he should be fine."

"Thanks to you."

I give him a half-smile and take a step to the side, hoping to walk around the man and go to my next patient.

He shifts his stance, blocking my way. "I'm Alex Volkov," he says quietly. "And you are?"

My pulse picks up. The male intent in his question makes me nervous. Hoping he'll get the hint, I say, "Just a nurse working here."

He doesn't catch on, or he pretends not to. "What's your name?"

He's certainly persistent. I take a deep breath. "I'm Katherine Morrell. If you'll excuse me—"

"Katherine," he repeats, his accent lending the familiar syllables an exotic edge. His hard mouth softens a bit. "Katerina. It's a beautiful name."

"Thank you. I really have to go."

I'm increasingly anxious to get away. He's too large, too potently male. I need space and some room to breathe. His nearness is overpowering, making me edgy and restless, leaving me craving something that I know will be bad for me.

"You have your job to do. I understand," he says, looking vaguely amused.

Still, he doesn't move out of my way. Instead, as I watch in shock, he raises one large hand and brushes his knuckles over my cheek.

I freeze as a wave of heat zaps through my body. His touch is light, but I feel branded by it, shaken to the core.

"I would like to see you again, Katerina," he says softly, dropping his hand. "When does your shift end tonight?"

I stare at him, feeling like I'm losing control of the situation. "I don't think that's a good idea."

"Why not?" His blue eyes narrow. "Are you married?"

I'm tempted to lie, but honesty wins out. "No, but I'm not interested in dating right now."

"Who said anything about dating?"

I blink. I assumed—

He lifts his hand again, stopping me mid-thought.

This time, he picks up a strand of my hair, rubbing it between his fingers.

"I don't date, Katerina," he murmurs, his accented voice oddly mesmerizing. "But I would like to take you to bed. And I think you'd like that too."

Order your copy of *White Nights* today at www.annazaires.com!

ABOUT THE AUTHOR

Anna Zaires is a *New York Times, USA Today,* and #1 international bestselling author of sci-fi romance and contemporary dark erotic romance. She fell in love with books at the age of five, when her grandmother taught her to read. Since then, she has always lived partially in a fantasy world where the only limits were those of her imagination. Currently residing in Florida, Anna is happily married to Dima Zales (a science fiction and fantasy author) and closely collaborates with him on all their works.

To learn more, please visit www.annazaires.com.